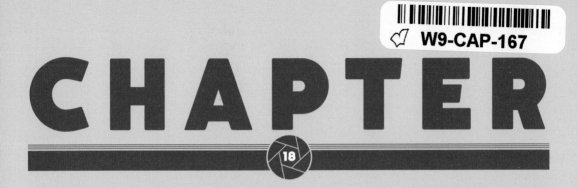

CHAPTER 18

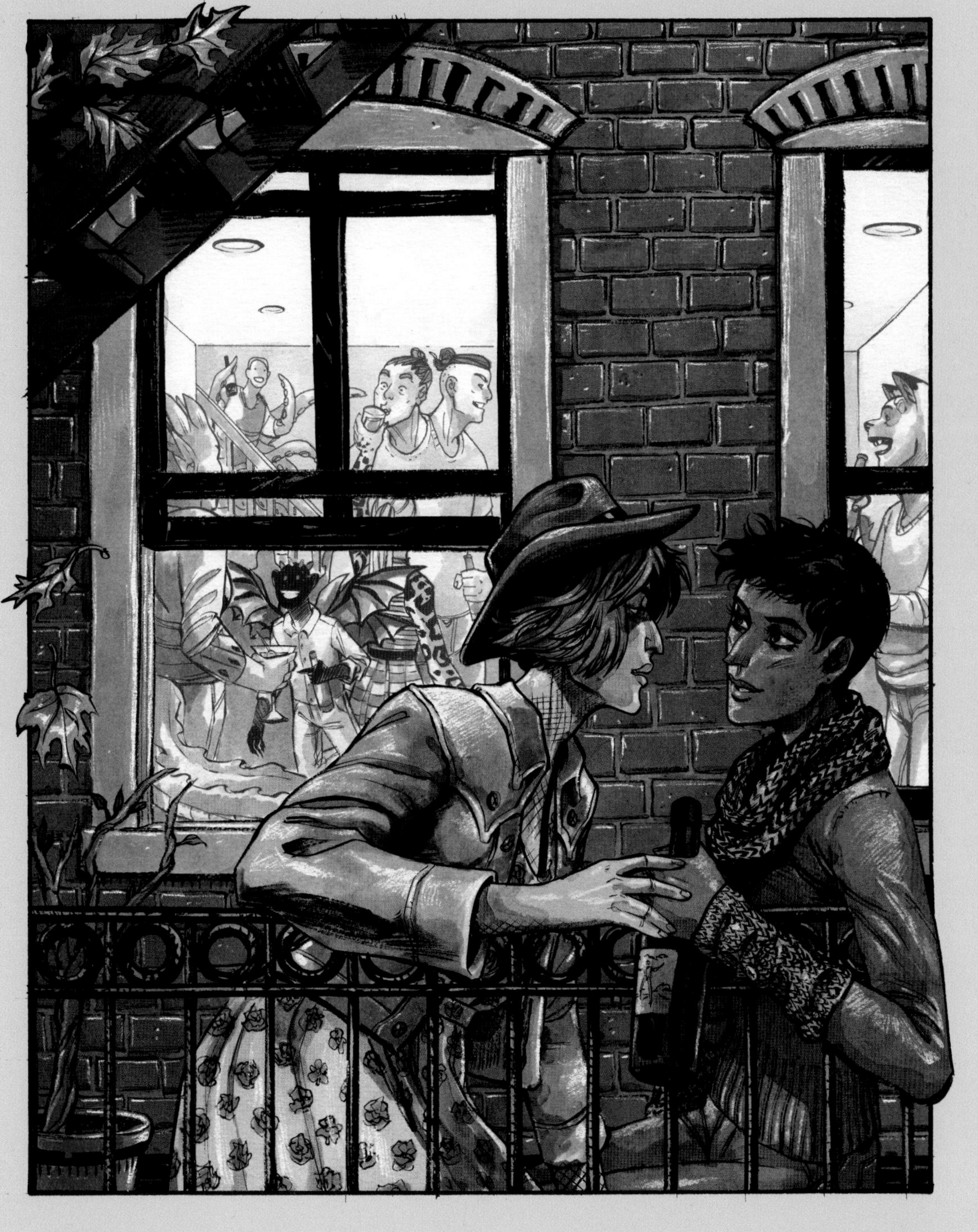

1. THERE WAS YOU

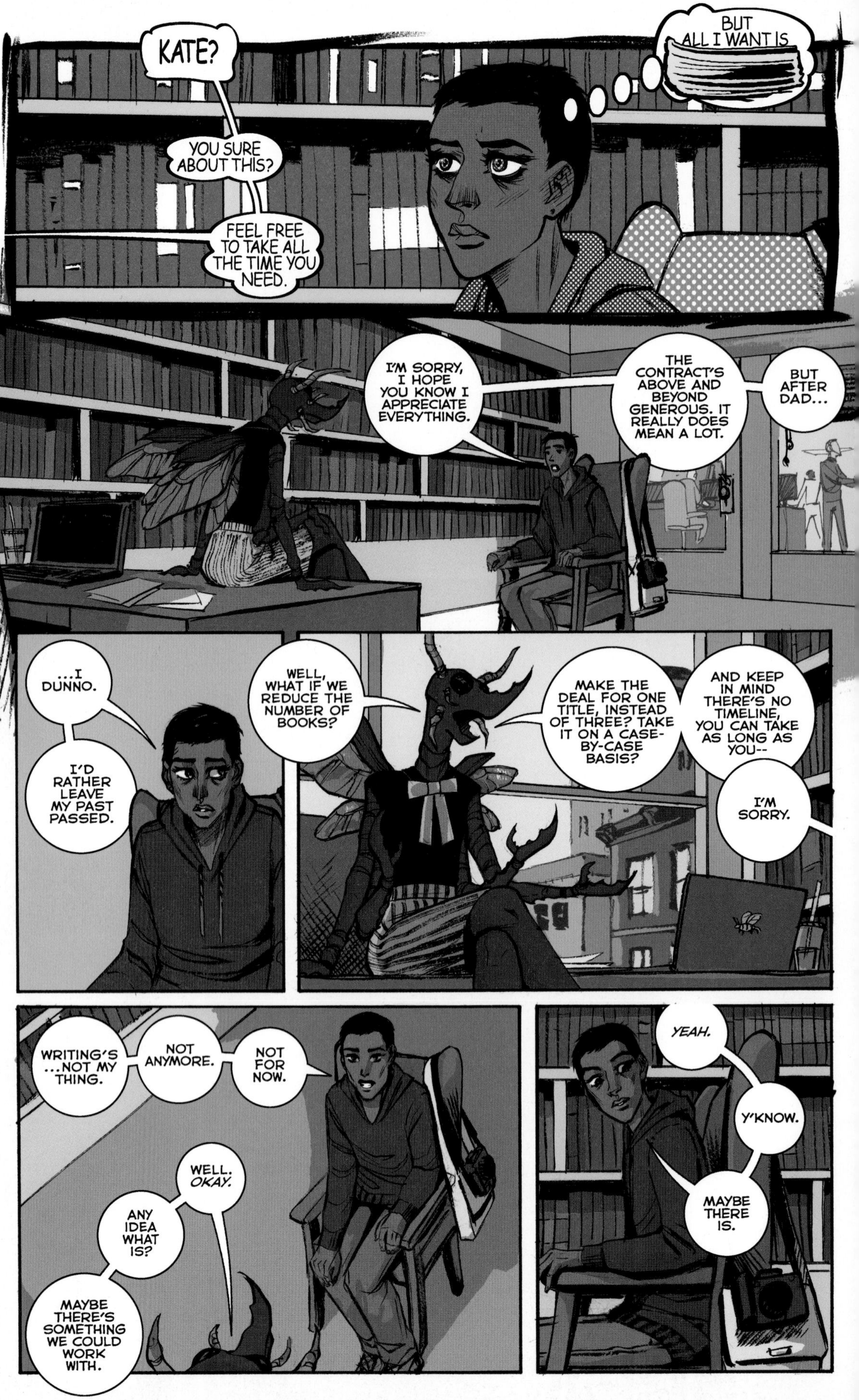
KATE?
YOU SURE ABOUT THIS?
FEEL FREE TO TAKE ALL THE TIME YOU NEED.
BUT ALL I WANT IS
I'M SORRY, I HOPE YOU KNOW I APPRECIATE EVERYTHING.
THE CONTRACT'S ABOVE AND BEYOND GENEROUS. IT REALLY DOES MEAN A LOT.
BUT AFTER DAD...
...I DUNNO.
I'D RATHER LEAVE MY PAST PASSED.
WELL, WHAT IF WE REDUCE THE NUMBER OF BOOKS?
MAKE THE DEAL FOR ONE TITLE, INSTEAD OF THREE? TAKE IT ON A CASE-BY-CASE BASIS?
AND KEEP IN MIND THERE'S NO TIMELINE, YOU CAN TAKE AS LONG AS YOU--
I'M SORRY.
WRITING'S ...NOT MY THING.
NOT ANYMORE.
NOT FOR NOW.
WELL. *OKAY.*
ANY IDEA WHAT IS?
MAYBE THERE'S SOMETHING WE COULD WORK WITH.
YEAH.
Y'KNOW.
MAYBE THERE IS.

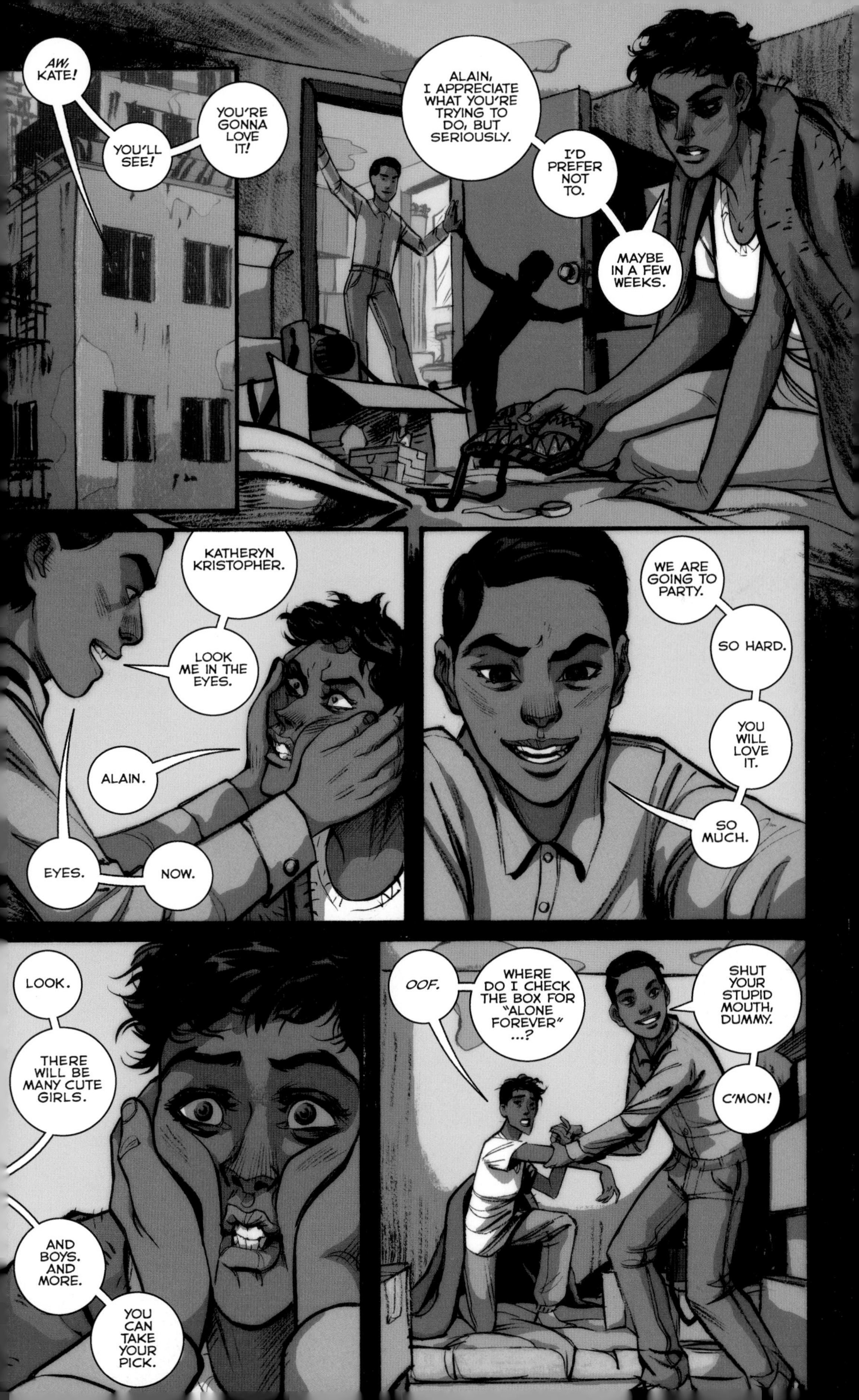
AW, KATE!
YOU'LL SEE!
YOU'RE GONNA LOVE IT!
ALAIN, I APPRECIATE WHAT YOU'RE TRYING TO DO, BUT SERIOUSLY.
I'D PREFER NOT TO.
MAYBE IN A FEW WEEKS.
KATHERYN KRISTOPHER.
LOOK ME IN THE EYES.
ALAIN.
EYES.
NOW.
WE ARE GOING TO PARTY.
SO HARD.
YOU WILL LOVE IT.
SO MUCH.
LOOK.
THERE WILL BE MANY CUTE GIRLS.
AND BOYS. AND MORE.
YOU CAN TAKE YOUR PICK.
OOF.
WHERE DO I CHECK THE BOX FOR "ALONE FOREVER" ...?
SHUT YOUR STUPID MOUTH, DUMMY.
C'MON!

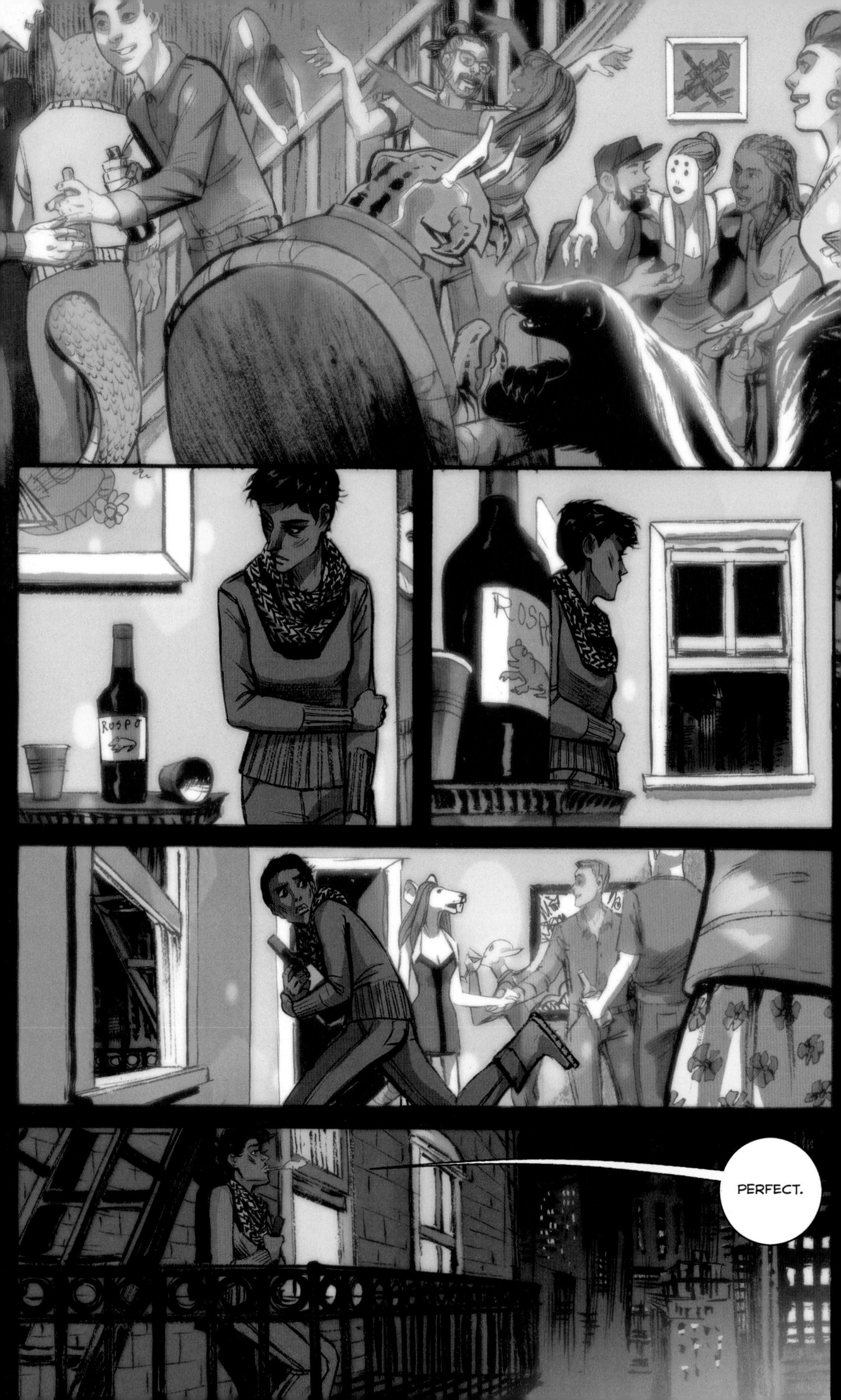
ROSPO
ROSPO
PERFECT.

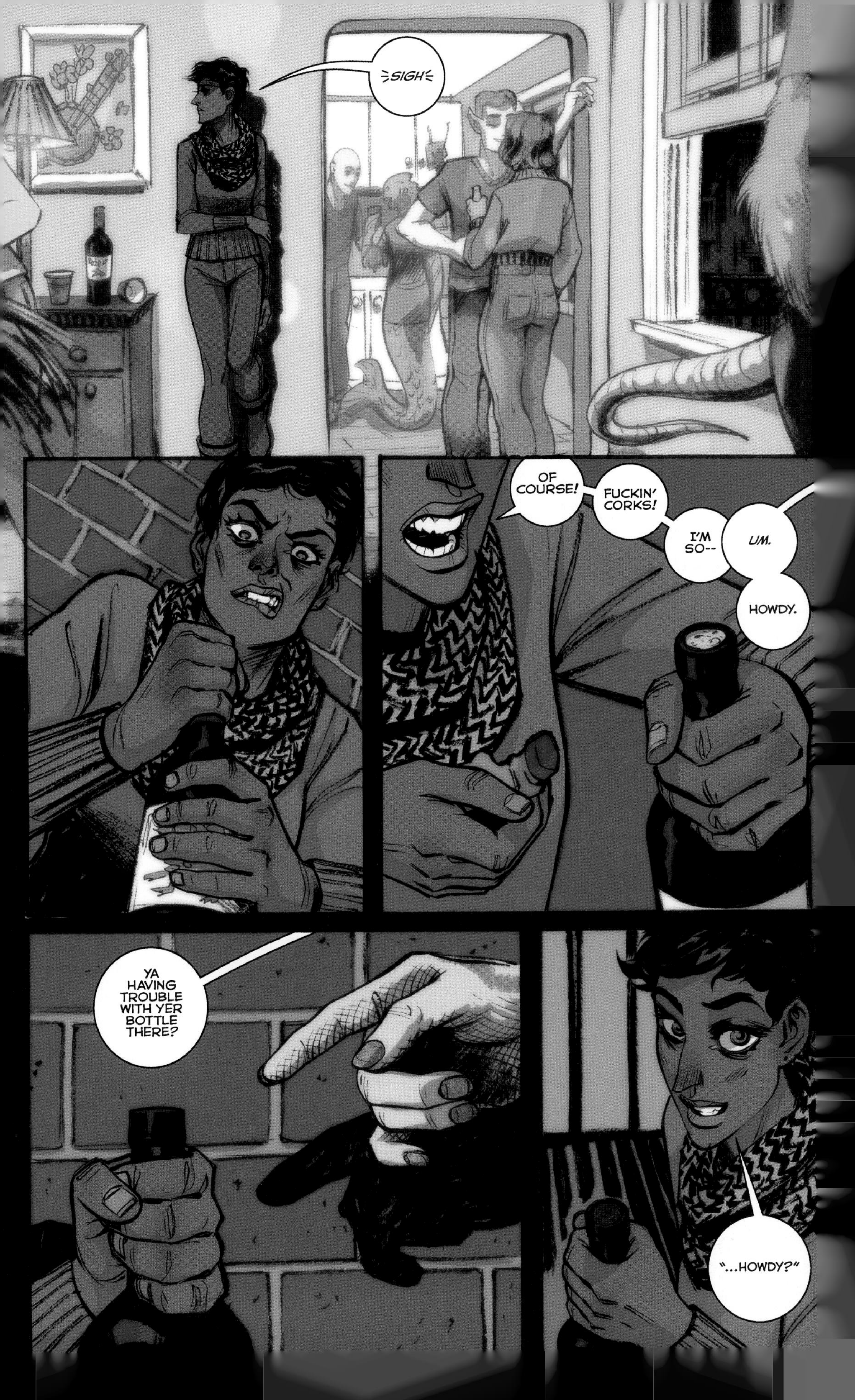
⁼SIGH⁼
OF COURSE!
FUCKIN' CORKS!
I'M SO--
UM.
HOWDY.
YA HAVING TROUBLE WITH YER BOTTLE THERE?
"...HOWDY?"

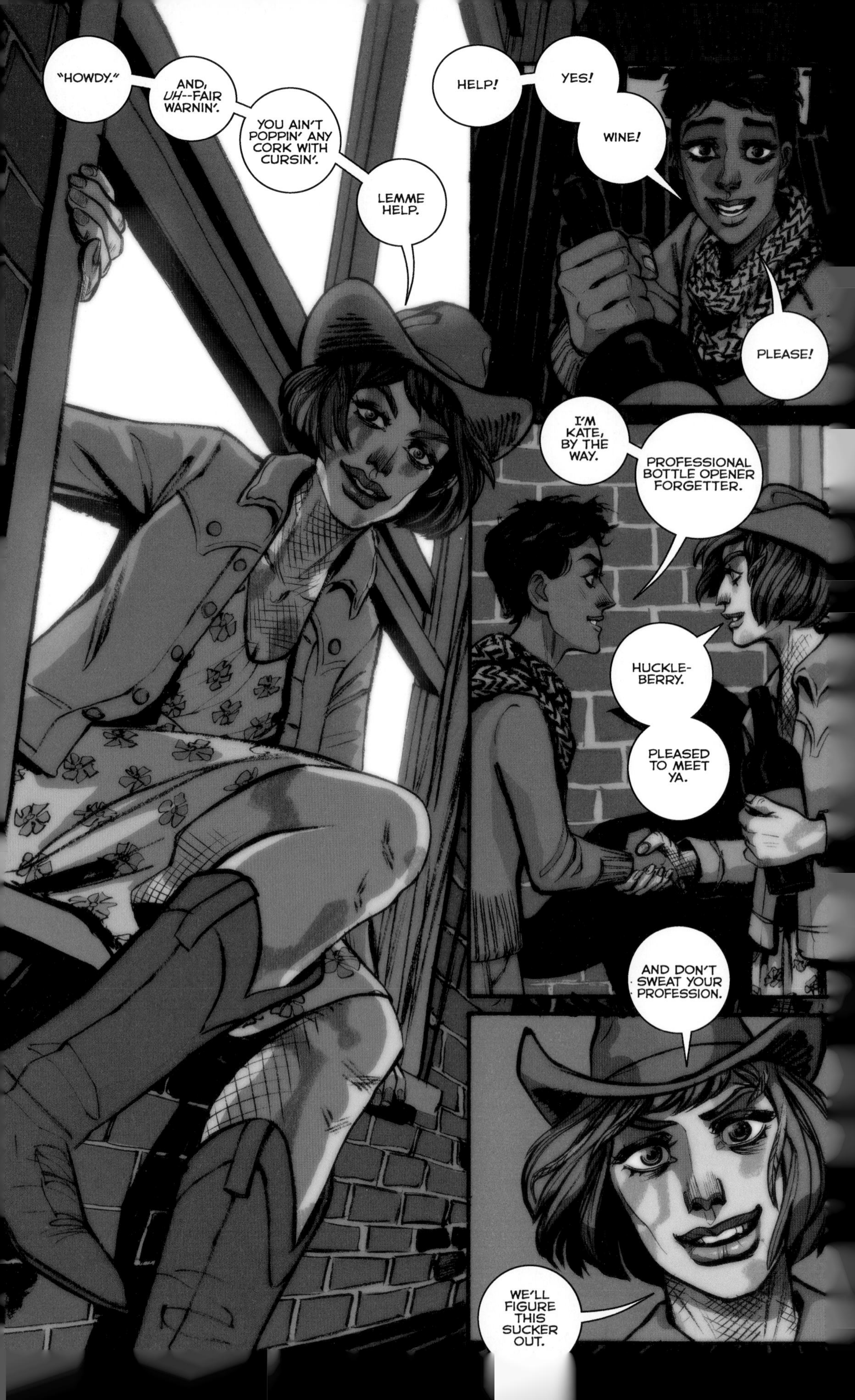
"HOWDY."
AND, UH--FAIR WARNIN'.
YOU AIN'T POPPIN' ANY CORK WITH CURSIN'.
LEMME HELP.
HELP!
YES!
WINE!
PLEASE!
I'M KATE, BY THE WAY.
PROFESSIONAL BOTTLE OPENER FORGETTER.
HUCKLE-BERRY.
PLEASED TO MEET YA.
AND DON'T SWEAT YOUR PROFESSION.
WE'LL FIGURE THIS SUCKER OUT.

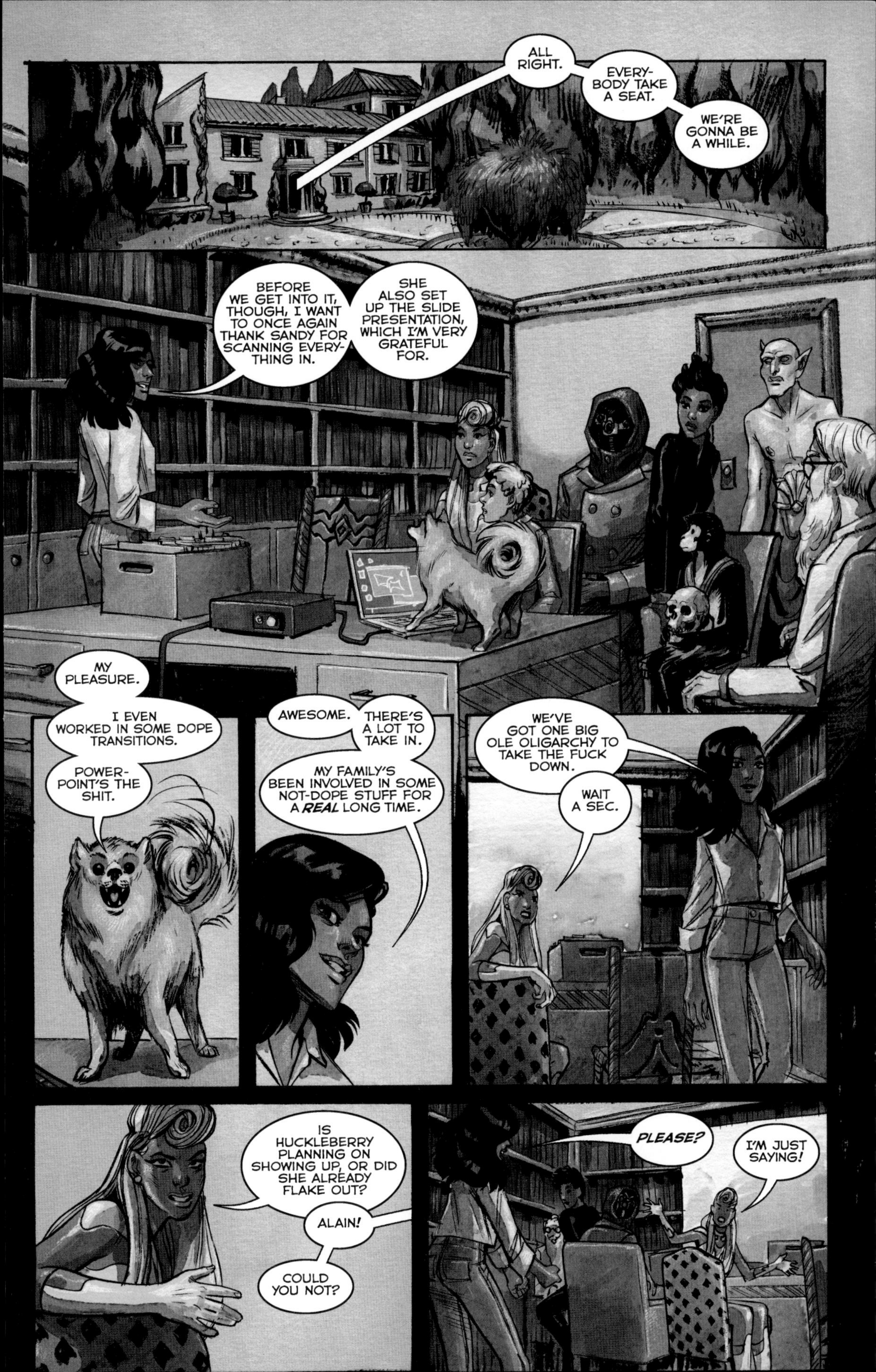
ALL RIGHT.
EVERY-BODY TAKE A SEAT.
WE'RE GONNA BE A WHILE.
BEFORE WE GET INTO IT, THOUGH, I WANT TO ONCE AGAIN THANK SANDY FOR SCANNING EVERY-THING IN.
SHE ALSO SET UP THE SLIDE PRESENTATION, WHICH I'M VERY GRATEFUL FOR.
MY PLEASURE.
I EVEN WORKED IN SOME DOPE TRANSITIONS.
POWER-POINT'S THE SHIT.
AWESOME.
THERE'S A LOT TO TAKE IN.
MY FAMILY'S BEEN INVOLVED IN SOME NOT-DOPE STUFF FOR A *REAL* LONG TIME.
WE'VE GOT ONE BIG OLE OLIGARCHY TO TAKE THE FUCK DOWN.
WAIT A SEC.
IS HUCKLEBERRY PLANNING ON SHOWING UP, OR DID SHE ALREADY FLAKE OUT?
ALAIN!
COULD YOU NOT?
PLEASE?
I'M JUST SAYING!

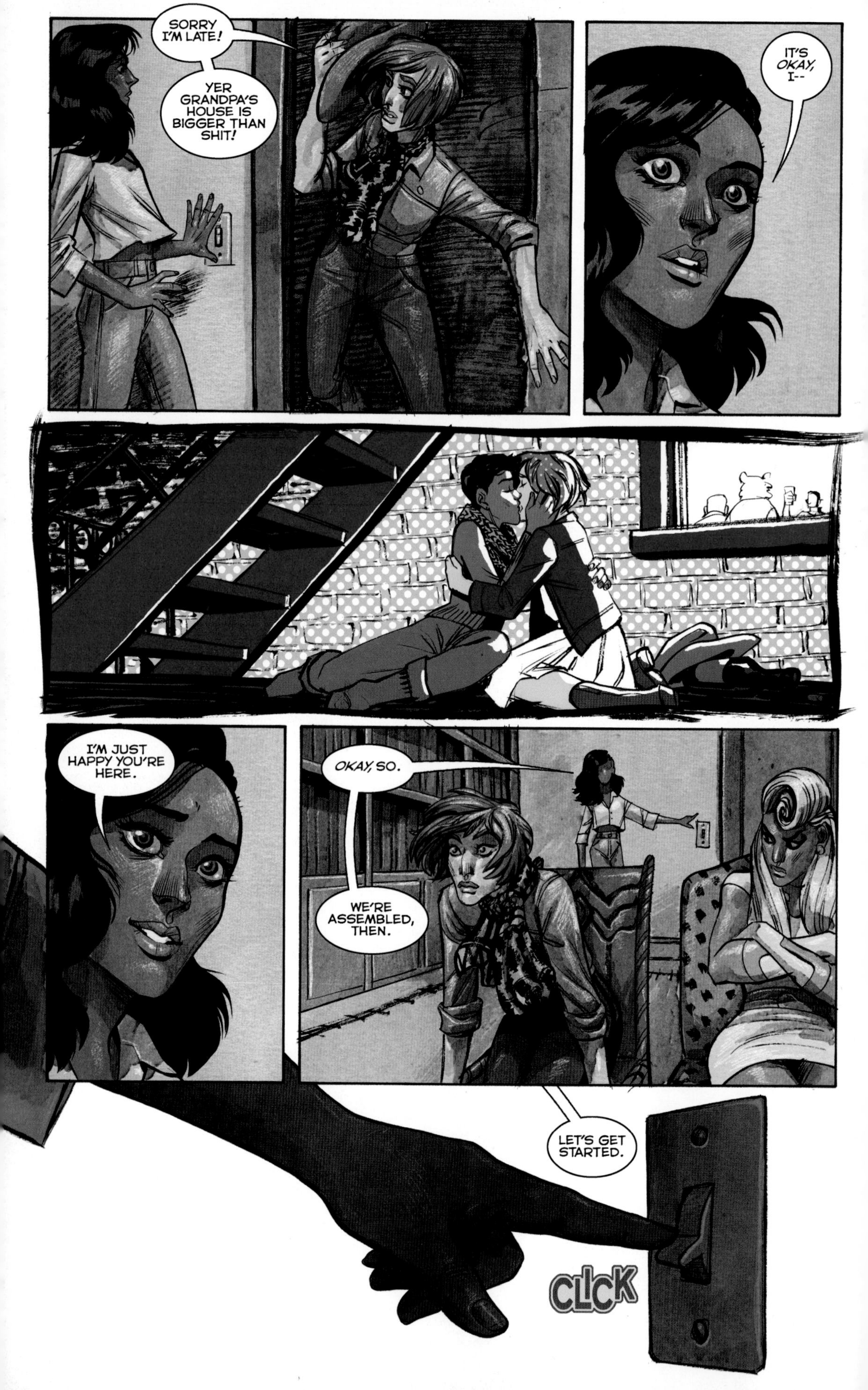
SORRY I'M LATE!
YER GRANDPA'S HOUSE IS BIGGER THAN SHIT!
IT'S OKAY, I--
I'M JUST HAPPY YOU'RE HERE.
OKAY, SO.
WE'RE ASSEMBLED, THEN.
LET'S GET STARTED.
CLICK

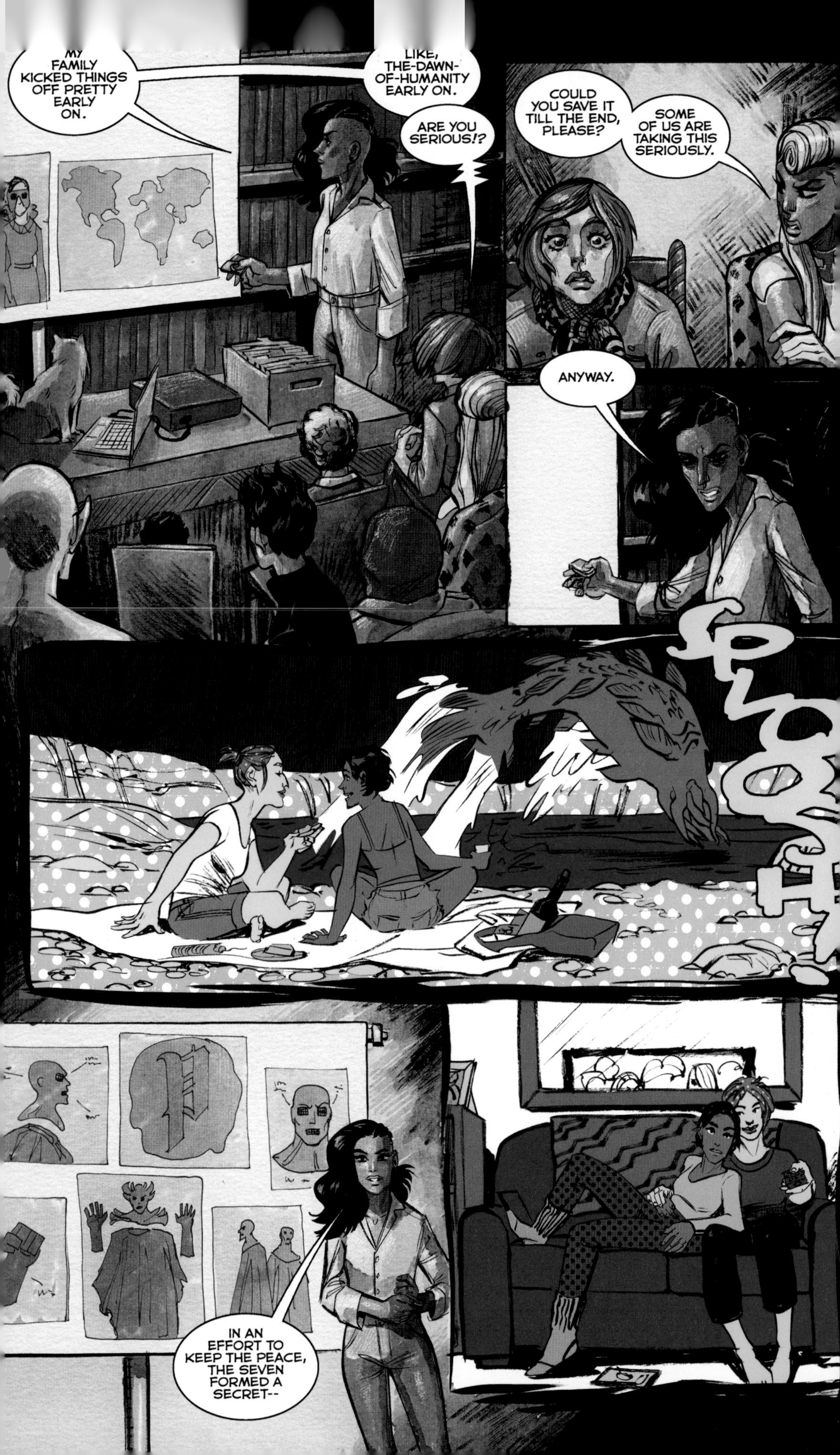
MY FAMILY KICKED THINGS OFF PRETTY EARLY ON.
LIKE, THE-DAWN-OF-HUMANITY EARLY ON.
ARE YOU SERIOUS!?
COULD YOU SAVE IT TILL THE END, PLEASE?
SOME OF US ARE TAKING THIS SERIOUSLY.
ANYWAY.
SPLOOSH
IN AN EFFORT TO KEEP THE PEACE, THE SEVEN FORMED A SECRET--

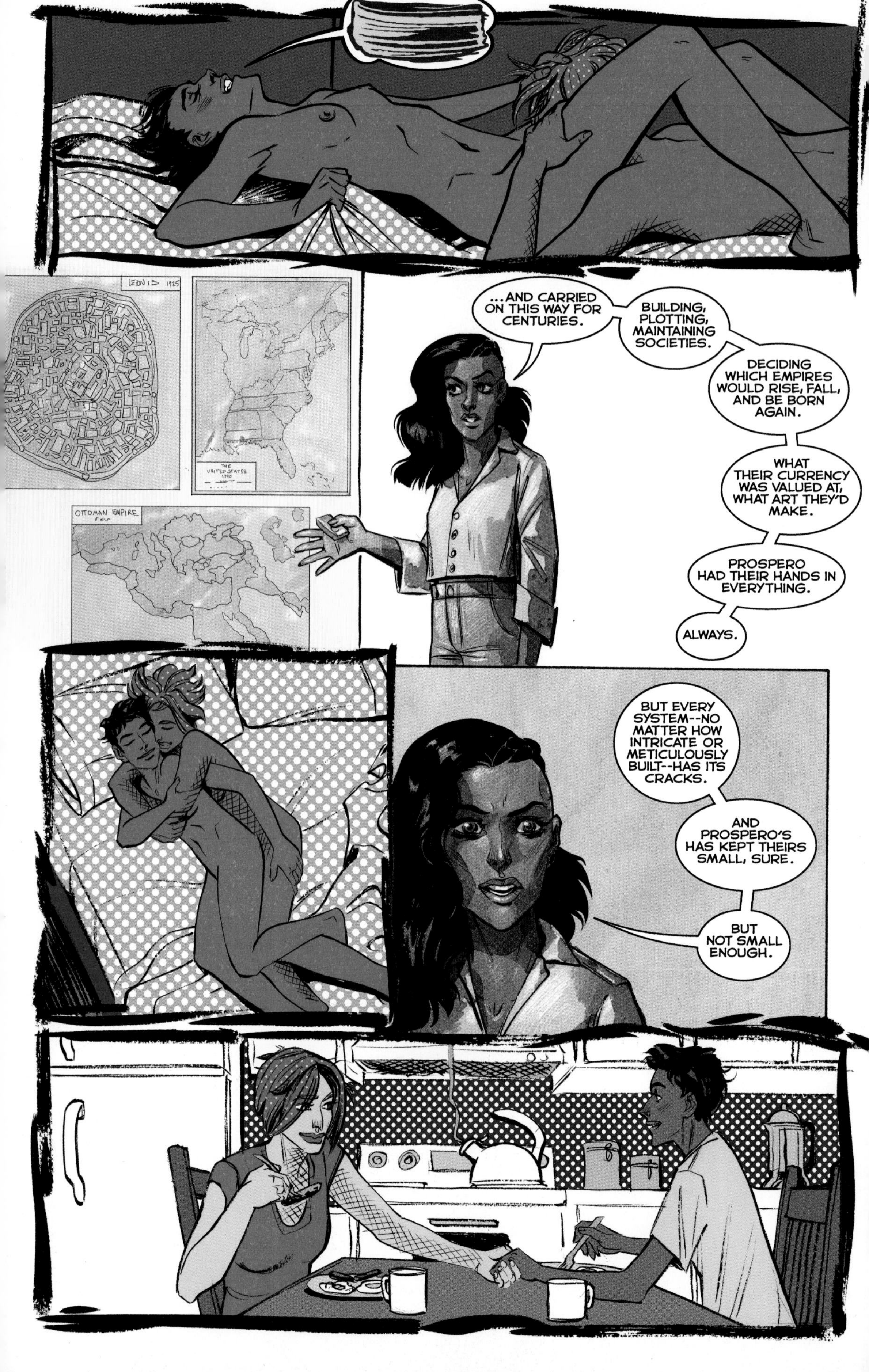
THE UNITED STATES 1790
OTTOMAN EMPIRE
...AND CARRIED ON THIS WAY FOR CENTURIES.
BUILDING, PLOTTING, MAINTAINING SOCIETIES.
DECIDING WHICH EMPIRES WOULD RISE, FALL, AND BE BORN AGAIN.
WHAT THEIR CURRENCY WAS VALUED AT, WHAT ART THEY'D MAKE.
PROSPERO HAD THEIR HANDS IN EVERYTHING.
ALWAYS.
BUT EVERY SYSTEM--NO MATTER HOW INTRICATE OR METICULOUSLY BUILT--HAS ITS CRACKS.
AND PROSPERO'S HAS KEPT THEIRS SMALL, SURE.
BUT NOT SMALL ENOUGH.

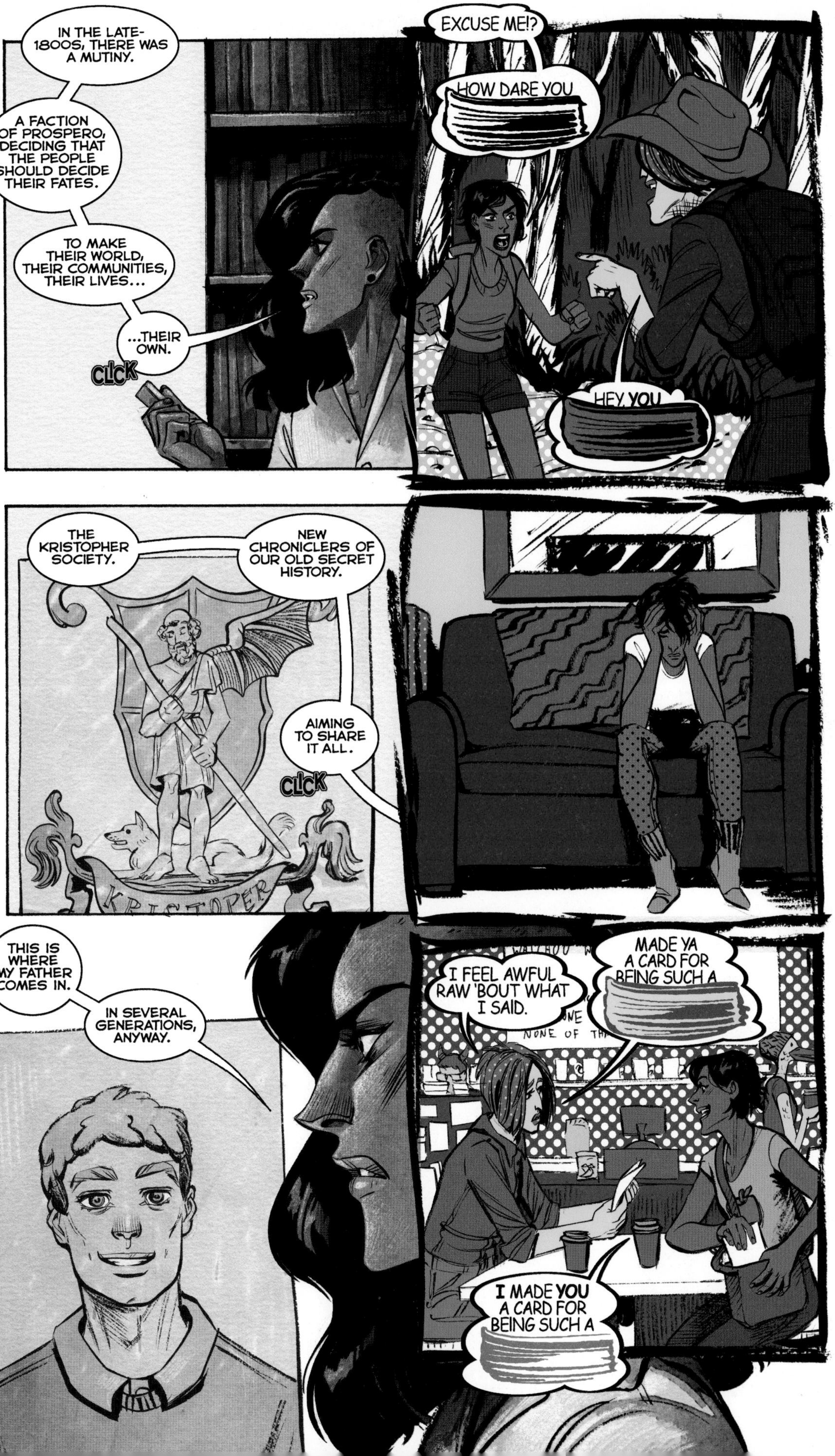

IN THE LATE-1800S, THERE WAS A MUTINY.
A FACTION OF PROSPERO, DECIDING THAT THE PEOPLE SHOULD DECIDE THEIR FATES.
TO MAKE THEIR WORLD, THEIR COMMUNITIES, THEIR LIVES...
...THEIR OWN.
CLICK
EXCUSE ME!?
HOW DARE YOU [redacted]
HEY, YOU [redacted]
THE KRISTOPHER SOCIETY.
NEW CHRONICLERS OF OUR OLD SECRET HISTORY.
AIMING TO SHARE IT ALL.
CLICK
KRISTOPER
THIS IS WHERE MY FATHER COMES IN.
IN SEVERAL GENERATIONS, ANYWAY.
I FEEL AWFUL RAW 'BOUT WHAT I SAID.
MADE YA A CARD FOR BEING SUCH A [redacted]
I MADE YOU A CARD FOR BEING SUCH A [redacted]

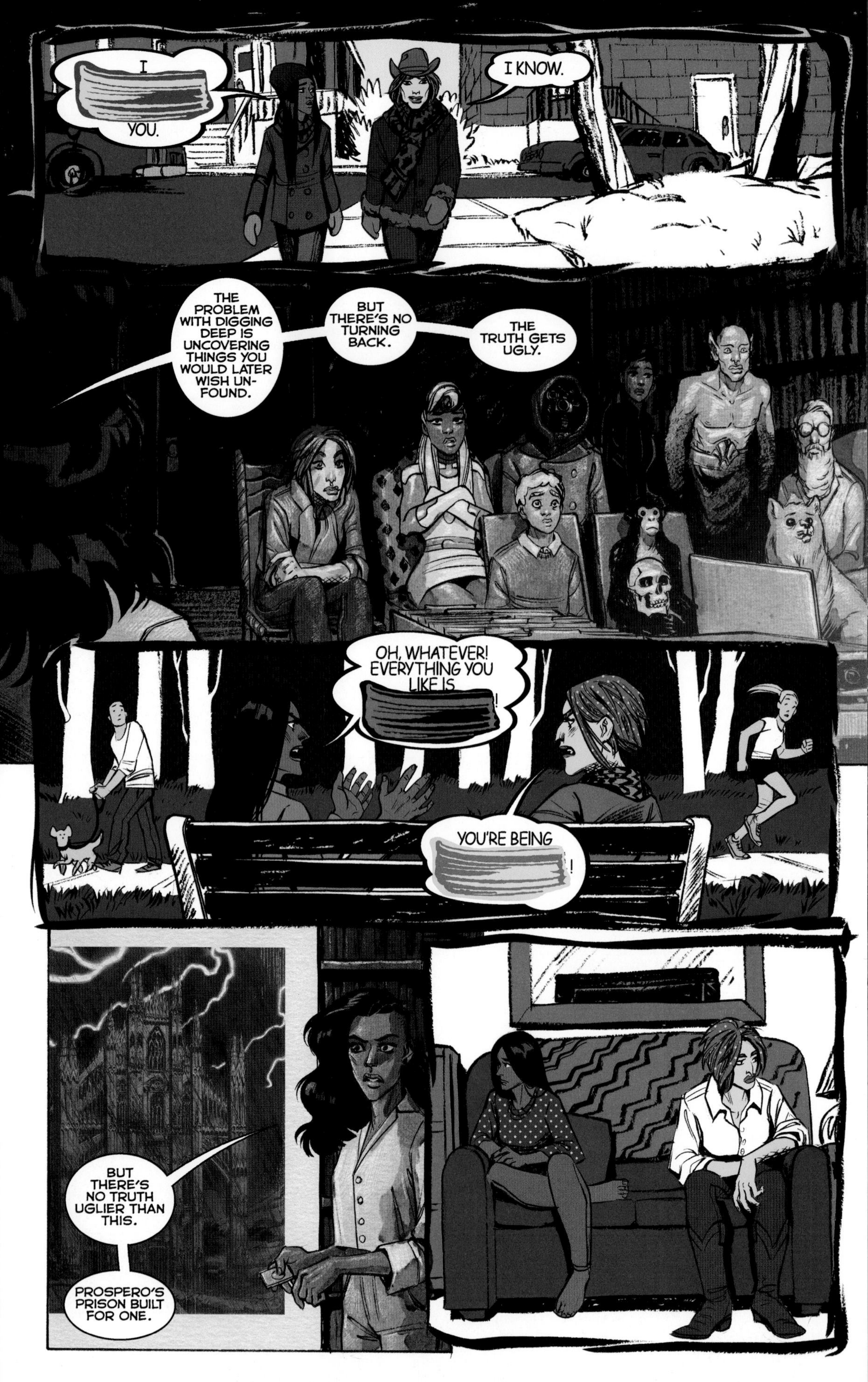
I [redacted] YOU.
I KNOW.
THE PROBLEM WITH DIGGING DEEP IS UNCOVERING THINGS YOU WOULD LATER WISH UN-FOUND.
BUT THERE'S NO TURNING BACK.
THE TRUTH GETS UGLY.
OH, WHATEVER! EVERYTHING YOU LIKE IS [redacted]!
YOU'RE BEING [redacted]!
BUT THERE'S NO TRUTH UGLIER THAN THIS.
PROSPERO'S PRISON BUILT FOR ONE.

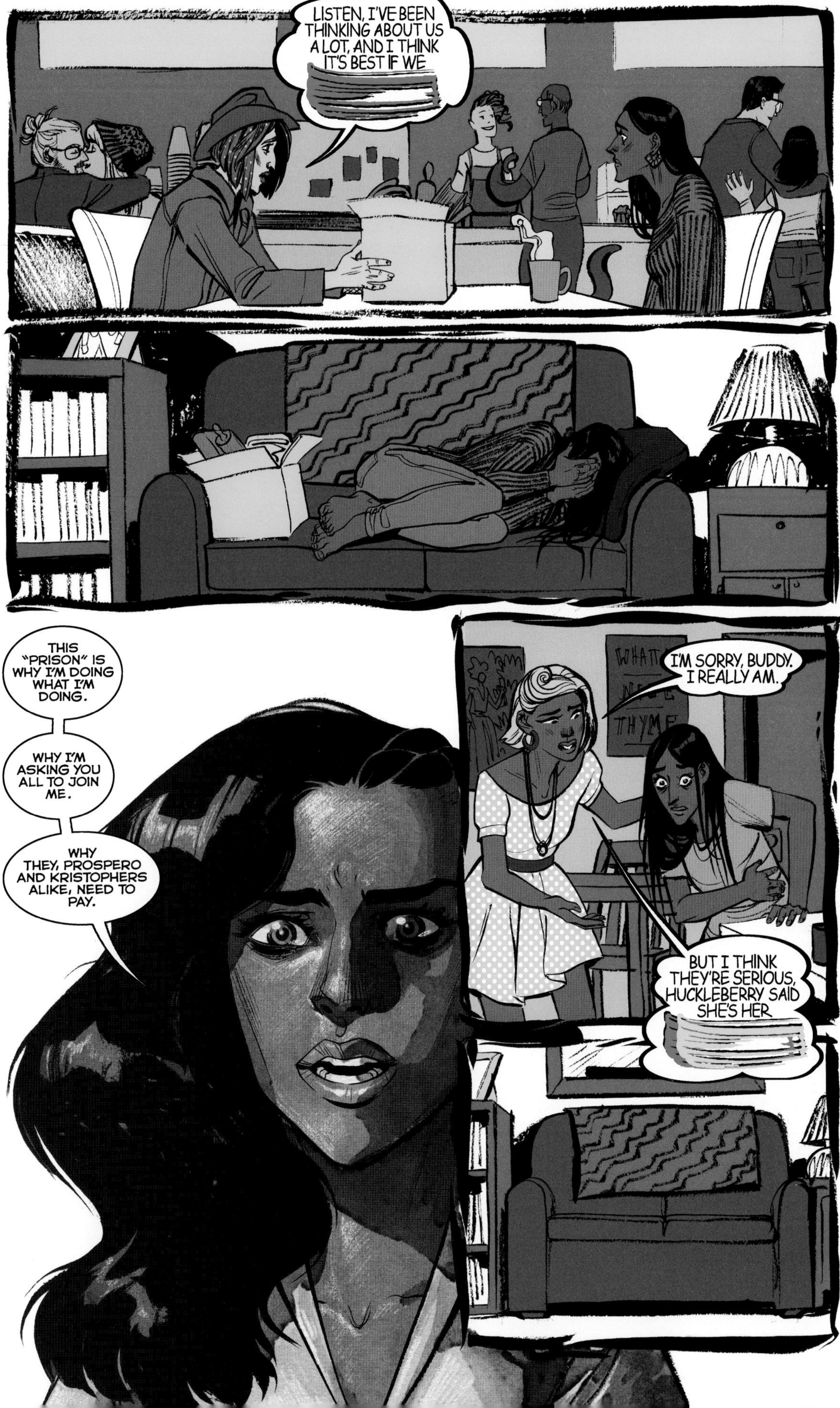
LISTEN, I'VE BEEN THINKING ABOUT US A LOT, AND I THINK IT'S BEST IF WE
THIS "PRISON" IS WHY I'M DOING WHAT I'M DOING.
WHY I'M ASKING YOU ALL TO JOIN ME.
WHY THEY, PROSPERO AND KRISTOPHERS ALIKE, NEED TO PAY.
I'M SORRY, BUDDY. I REALLY AM.
BUT I THINK THEY'RE SERIOUS, HUCKLEBERRY SAID SHE'S HER

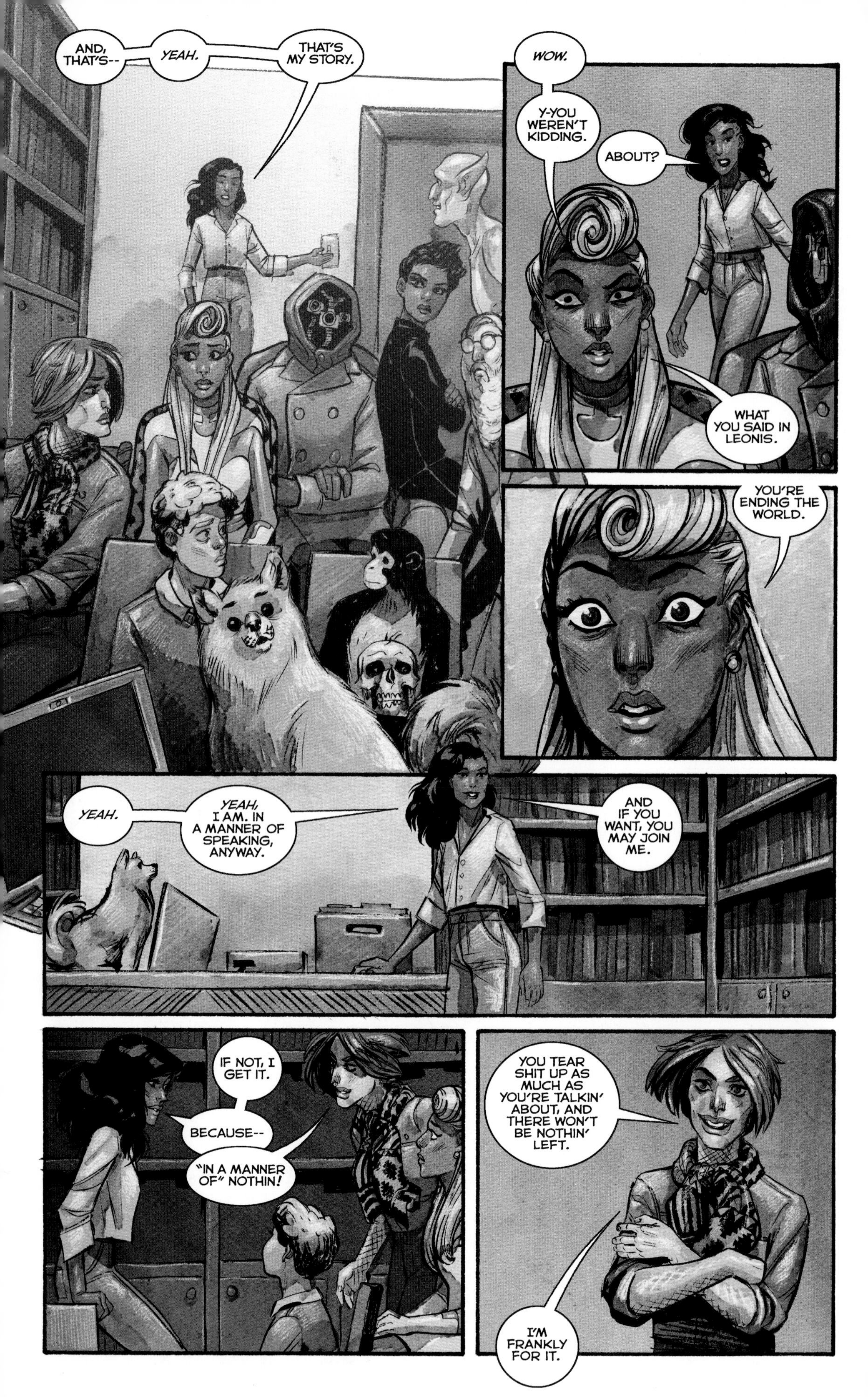
AND, THAT'S--
YEAH.
THAT'S MY STORY.
WOW.
Y-YOU WEREN'T KIDDING.
ABOUT?
WHAT YOU SAID IN LEONIS.
YOU'RE ENDING THE WORLD.
YEAH.
YEAH, I AM. IN A MANNER OF SPEAKING, ANYWAY.
AND IF YOU WANT, YOU MAY JOIN ME.
IF NOT, I GET IT.
BECAUSE--
"IN A MANNER OF" NOTHIN!
YOU TEAR SHIT UP AS MUCH AS YOU'RE TALKIN' ABOUT, AND THERE WON'T BE NOTHIN' LEFT.
I'M FRANKLY FOR IT.

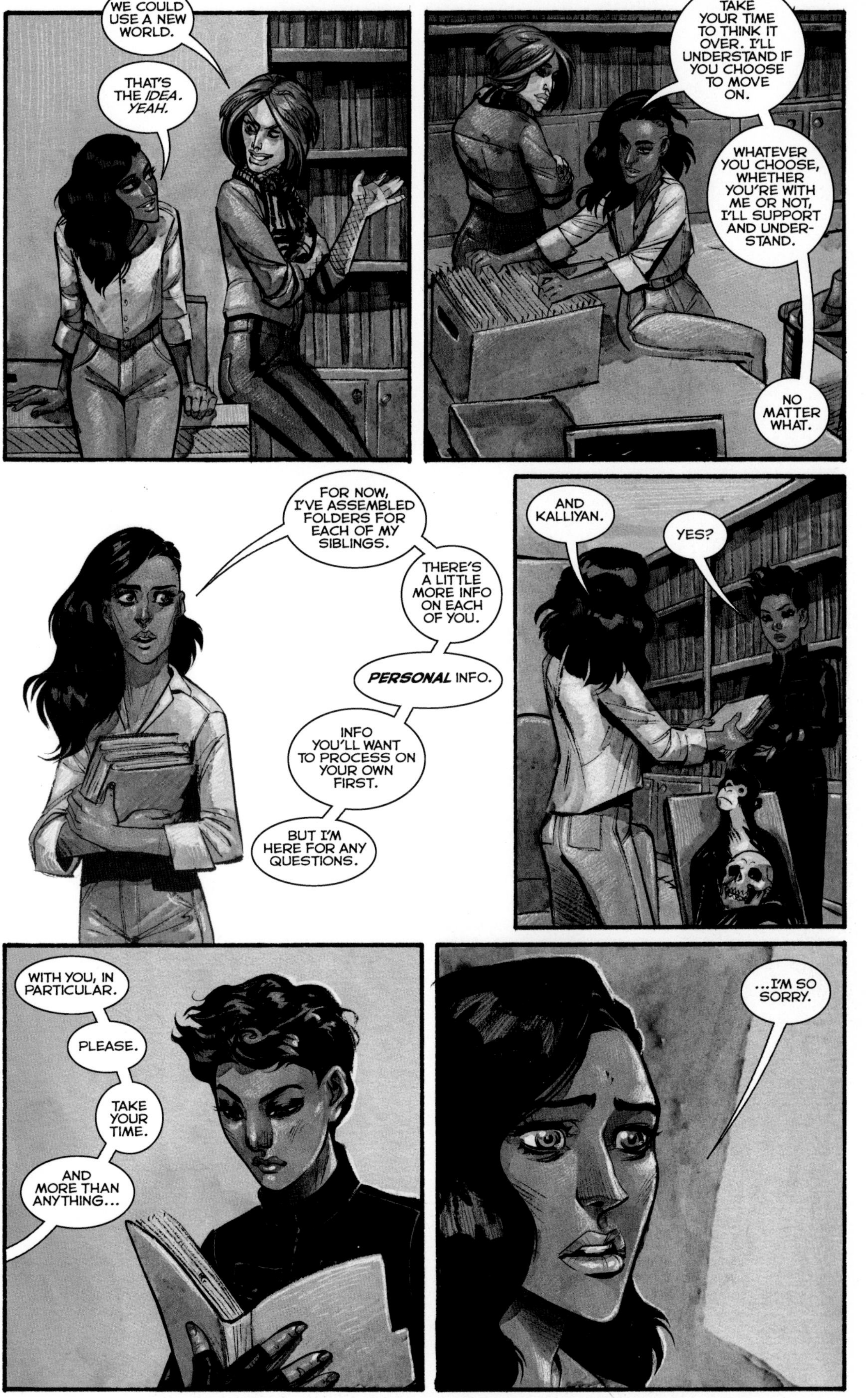
WE COULD USE A NEW WORLD.
THAT'S THE *IDEA.* *YEAH.*
TAKE YOUR TIME TO THINK IT OVER. I'LL UNDERSTAND IF YOU CHOOSE TO MOVE ON.
WHATEVER YOU CHOOSE, WHETHER YOU'RE WITH ME OR NOT, I'LL SUPPORT AND UNDER-STAND.
NO MATTER WHAT.
FOR NOW, I'VE ASSEMBLED FOLDERS FOR EACH OF MY SIBLINGS.
THERE'S A LITTLE MORE INFO ON EACH OF YOU.
PERSONAL INFO.
INFO YOU'LL WANT TO PROCESS ON YOUR OWN FIRST.
BUT I'M HERE FOR ANY QUESTIONS.
AND KALLIYAN.
YES?
WITH YOU, IN PARTICULAR.
PLEASE.
TAKE YOUR TIME.
AND MORE THAN ANYTHING...
...I'M SO SORRY.

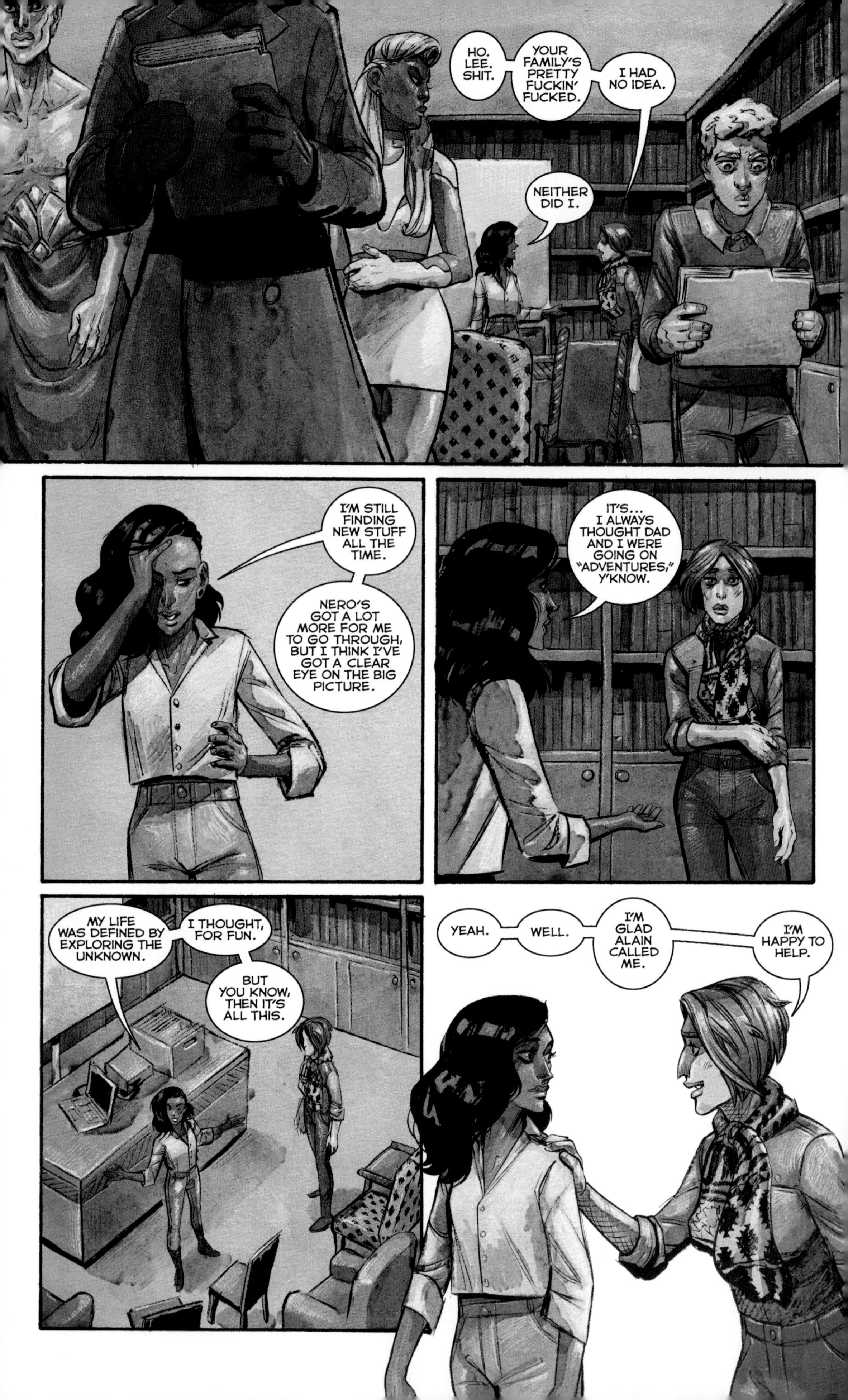
HO. LEE. SHIT.
YOUR FAMILY'S PRETTY FUCKIN' FUCKED.
I HAD NO IDEA.
NEITHER DID I.
I'M STILL FINDING NEW STUFF ALL THE TIME.
NERO'S GOT A LOT MORE FOR ME TO GO THROUGH, BUT I THINK I'VE GOT A CLEAR EYE ON THE BIG PICTURE.
IT'S... I ALWAYS THOUGHT DAD AND I WERE GOING ON "ADVENTURES," Y'KNOW.
MY LIFE WAS DEFINED BY EXPLORING THE UNKNOWN.
I THOUGHT, FOR FUN.
BUT YOU KNOW, THEN IT'S ALL THIS.
YEAH.
WELL.
I'M GLAD ALAIN CALLED ME.
I'M HAPPY TO HELP.

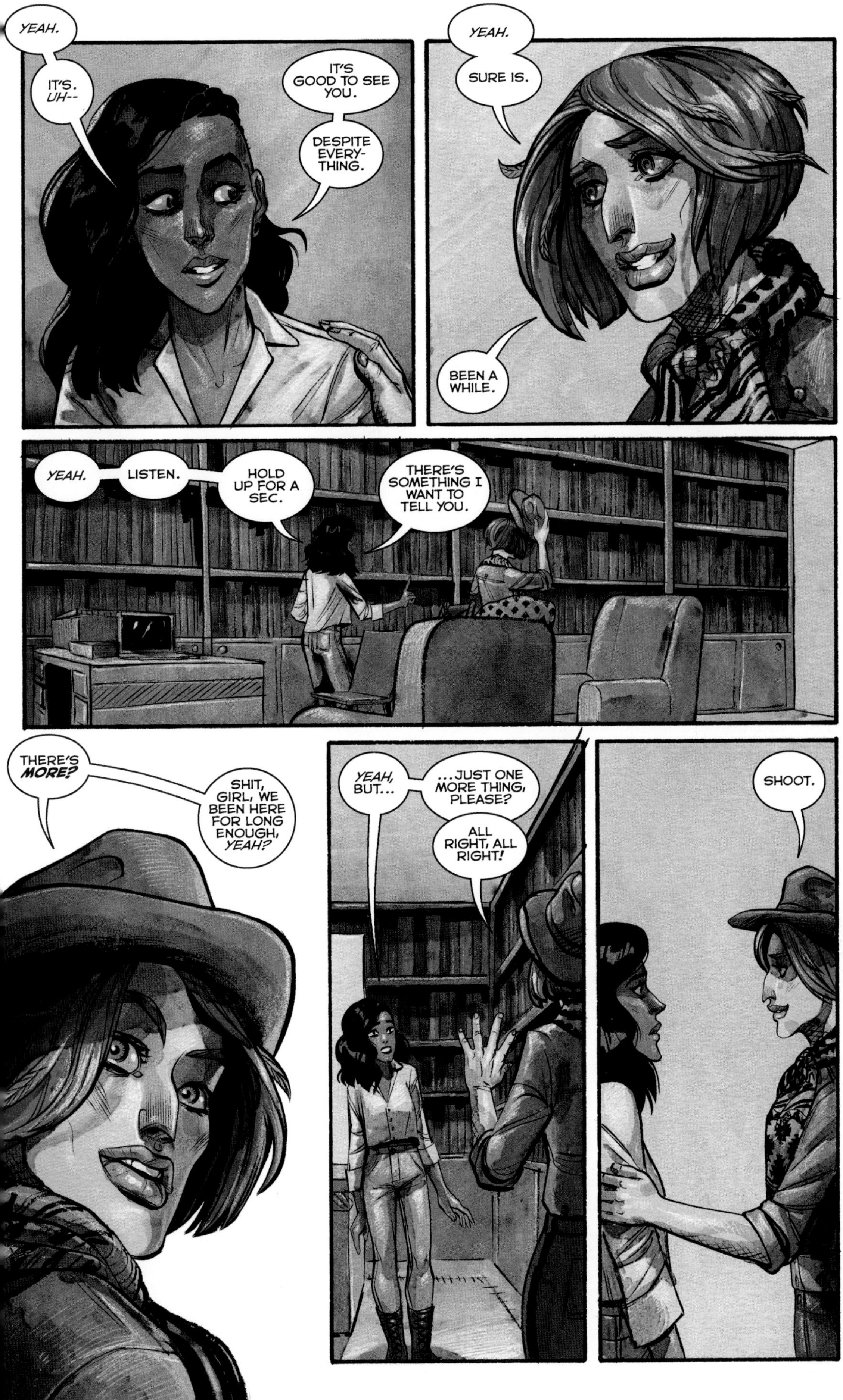
YEAH.
IT'S. UH--
IT'S GOOD TO SEE YOU.
DESPITE EVERY-THING.
YEAH.
SURE IS.
BEEN A WHILE.
YEAH.
LISTEN.
HOLD UP FOR A SEC.
THERE'S SOMETHING I WANT TO TELL YOU.
THERE'S MORE?
SHIT, GIRL, WE BEEN HERE FOR LONG ENOUGH, YEAH?
YEAH, BUT...
...JUST ONE MORE THING, PLEASE?
ALL RIGHT, ALL RIGHT!
SHOOT.

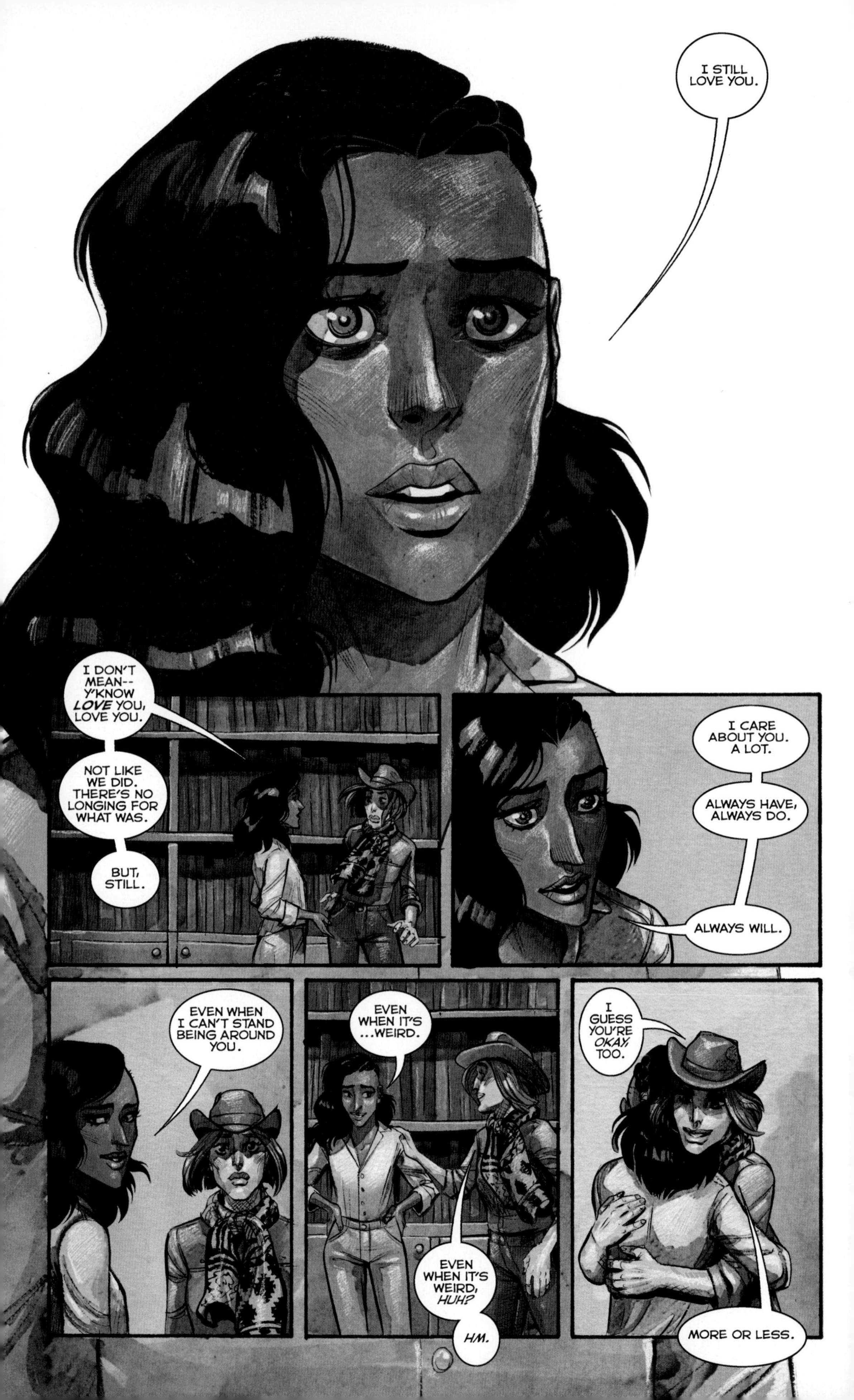
I STILL LOVE YOU.
I DON'T MEAN-- Y'KNOW *LOVE* YOU, LOVE YOU.
NOT LIKE WE DID. THERE'S NO LONGING FOR WHAT WAS.
BUT, STILL.
I CARE ABOUT YOU. A LOT.
ALWAYS HAVE, ALWAYS DO.
ALWAYS WILL.
EVEN WHEN I CAN'T STAND BEING AROUND YOU.
EVEN WHEN IT'S ...WEIRD.
EVEN WHEN IT'S WEIRD, *HUH?*
HM.
I GUESS YOU'RE *OKAY,* TOO.
MORE OR LESS.

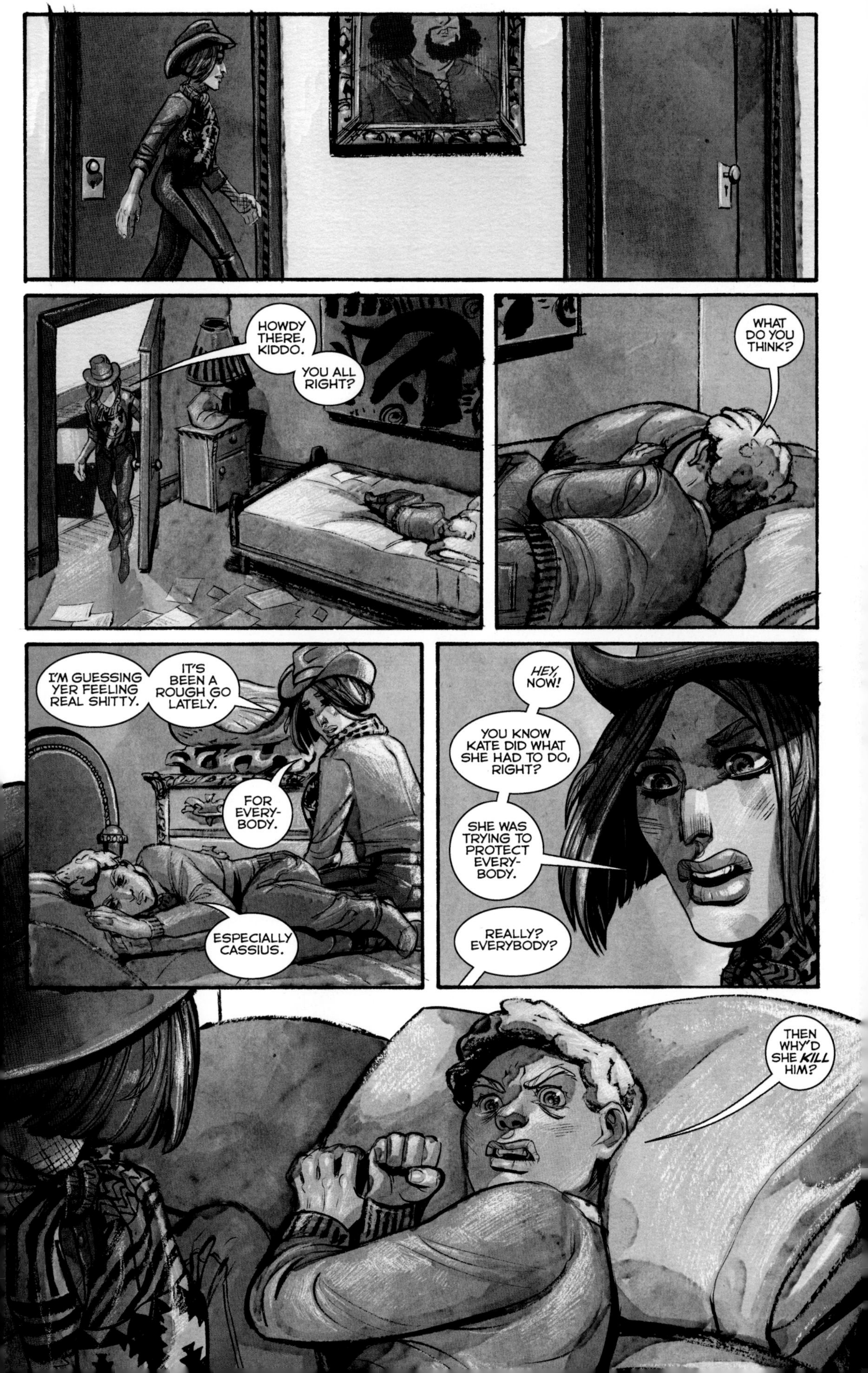
HOWDY THERE, KIDDO.
YOU ALL RIGHT?
WHAT DO YOU THINK?
I'M GUESSING YER FEELING REAL SHITTY.
IT'S BEEN A ROUGH GO LATELY.
FOR EVERY-BODY.
ESPECIALLY CASSIUS.
HEY, NOW!
YOU KNOW KATE DID WHAT SHE HAD TO DO, RIGHT?
SHE WAS TRYING TO PROTECT EVERY-BODY.
REALLY? EVERYBODY?
THEN WHY'D SHE KILL HIM?

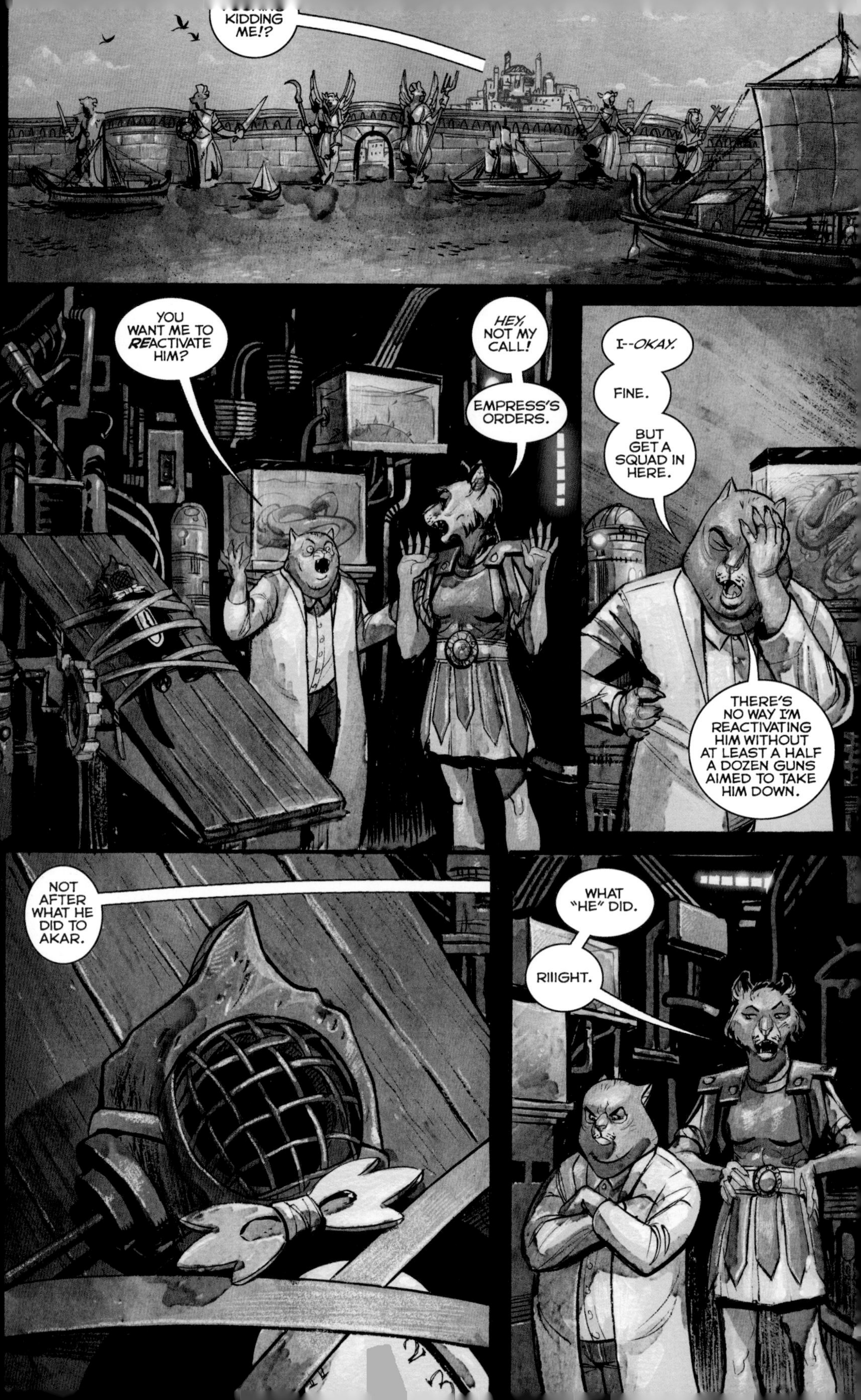
KIDDING ME!?
YOU WANT ME TO *RE*ACTIVATE HIM?
HEY, NOT MY CALL!
EMPRESS'S ORDERS.
I--*OKAY.*
FINE.
BUT GET A SQUAD IN HERE.
THERE'S NO WAY I'M REACTIVATING HIM WITHOUT AT LEAST A HALF A DOZEN GUNS AIMED TO TAKE HIM DOWN.
NOT AFTER WHAT HE DID TO AKAR.
WHAT "HE" DID.
RIIIGHT.

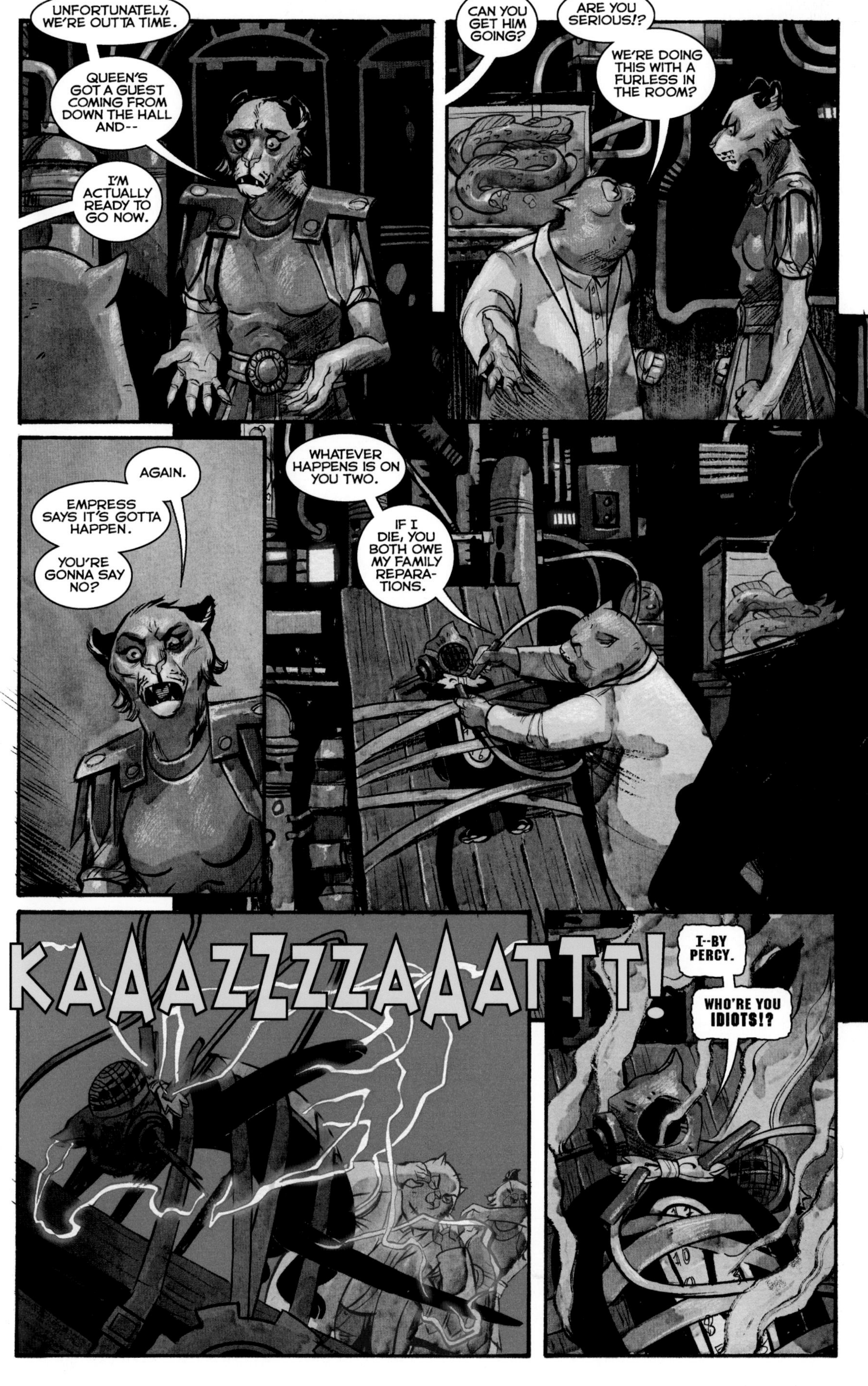
UNFORTUNATELY, WE'RE OUTTA TIME.
QUEEN'S GOT A GUEST COMING FROM DOWN THE HALL AND--
I'M ACTUALLY READY TO GO NOW.
CAN YOU GET HIM GOING?
ARE YOU SERIOUS!?
WE'RE DOING THIS WITH A FURLESS IN THE ROOM?
AGAIN.
EMPRESS SAYS IT'S GOTTA HAPPEN.
YOU'RE GONNA SAY NO?
WHATEVER HAPPENS IS ON YOU TWO.
IF I DIE, YOU BOTH OWE MY FAMILY REPARATIONS.
KAAAZZZZAAATTT!
I--BY PERCY.
WHO'RE YOU IDIOTS!?

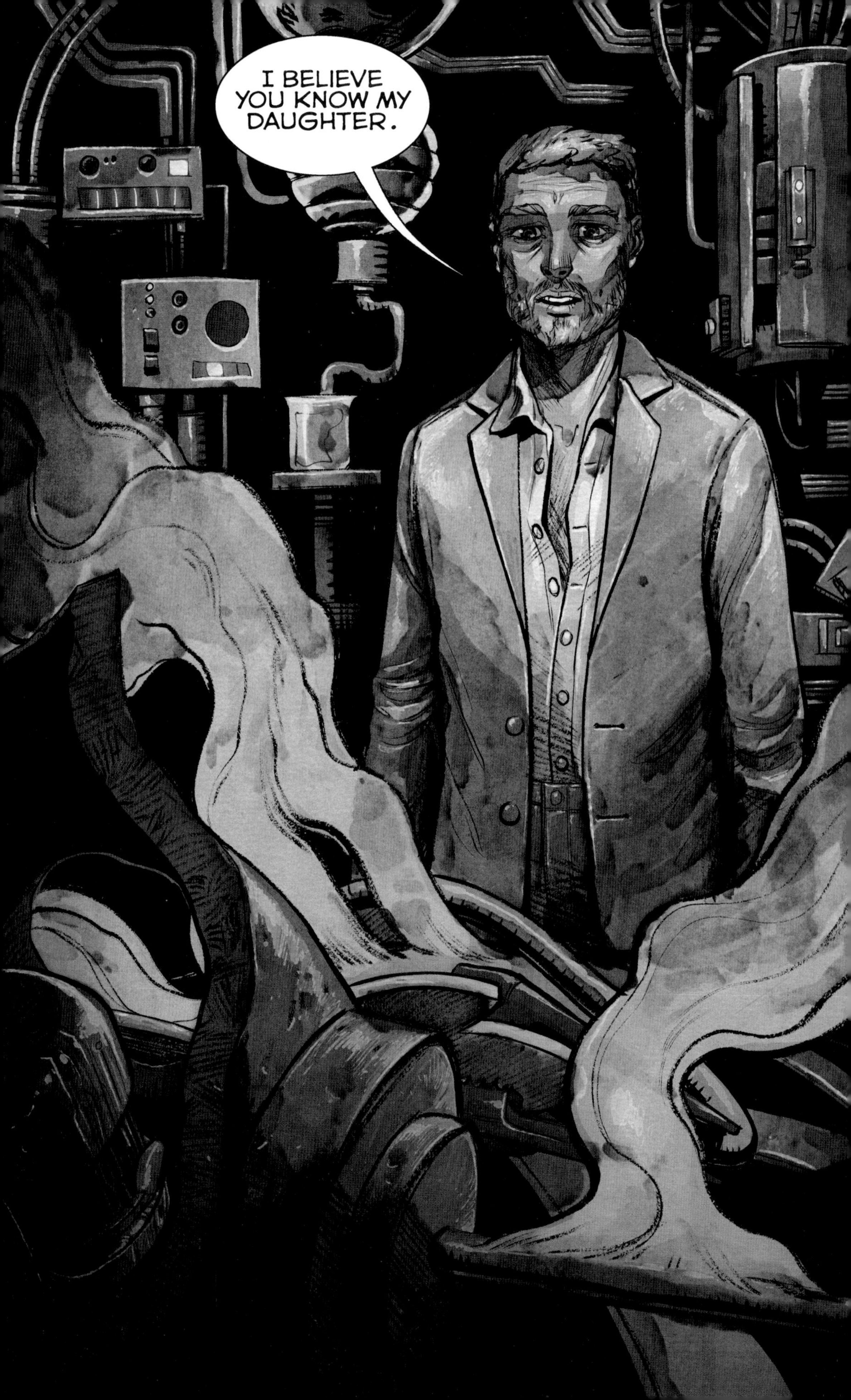
I BELIEVE YOU KNOW MY DAUGHTER.

CHAPTER 19

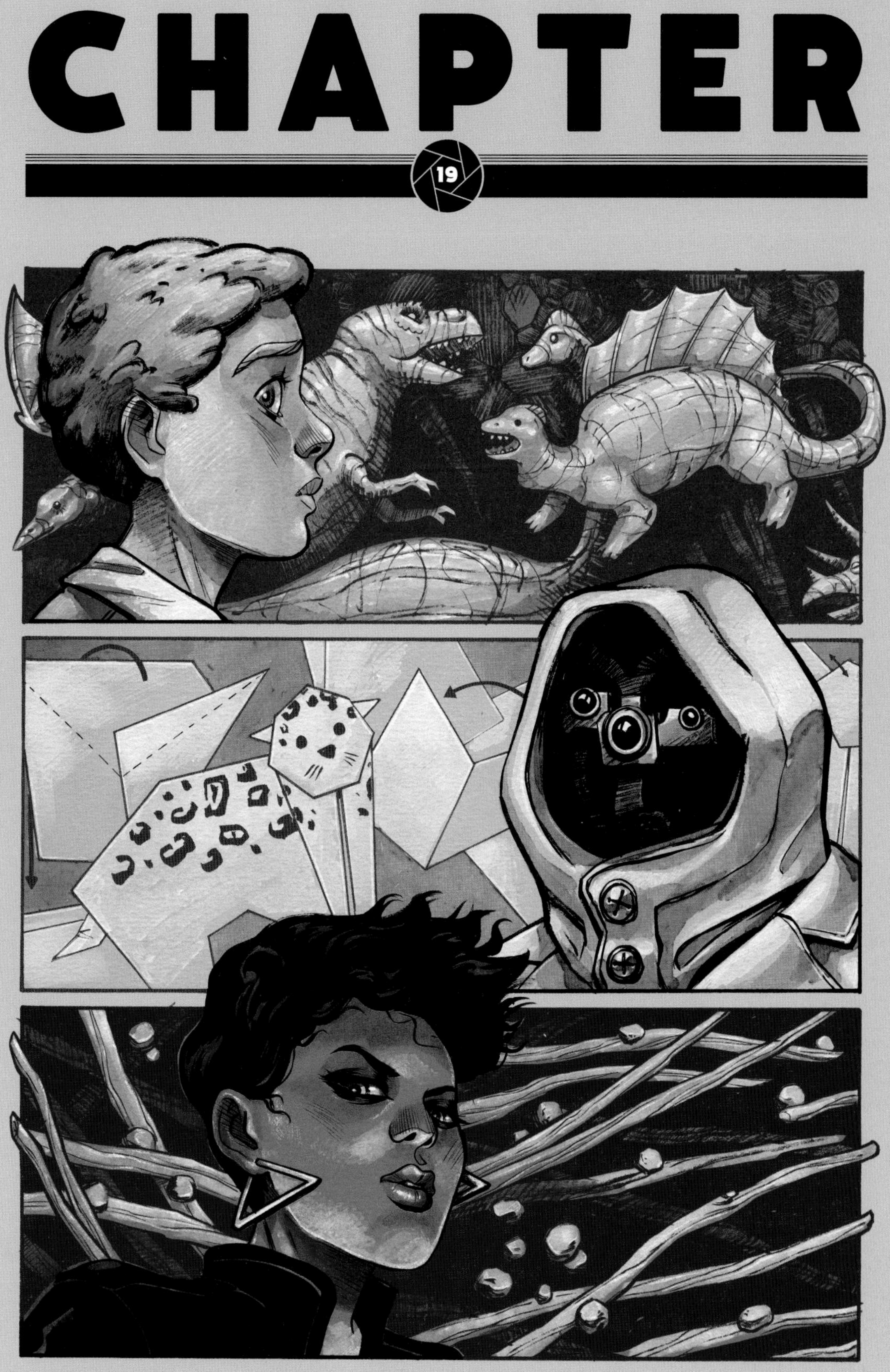

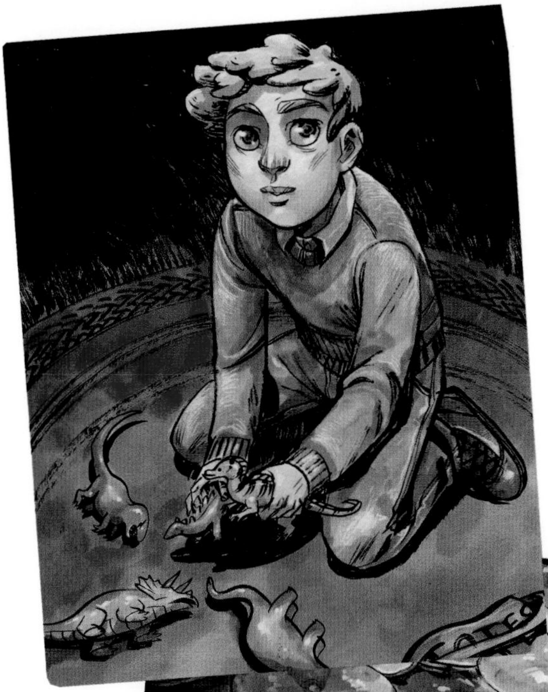

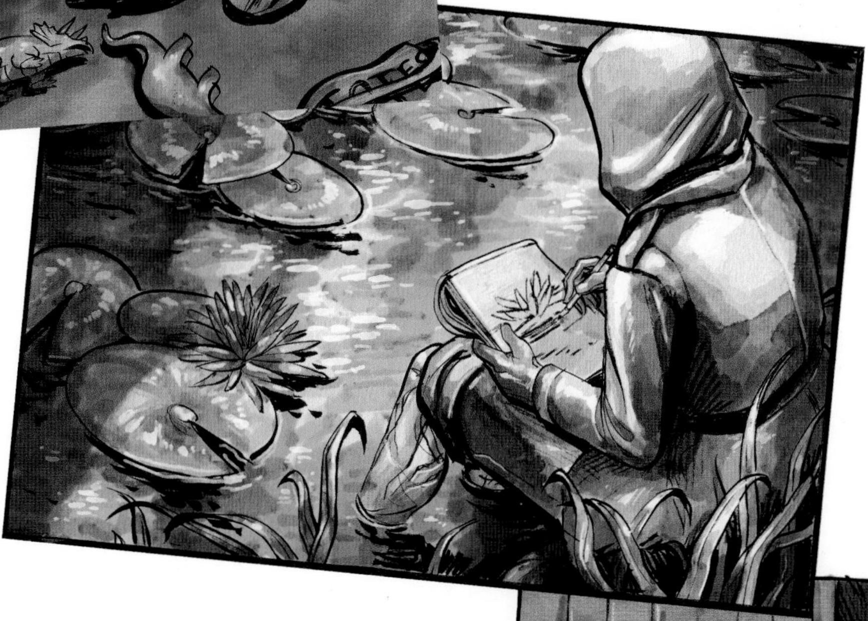

2. TOY SOLDIERS

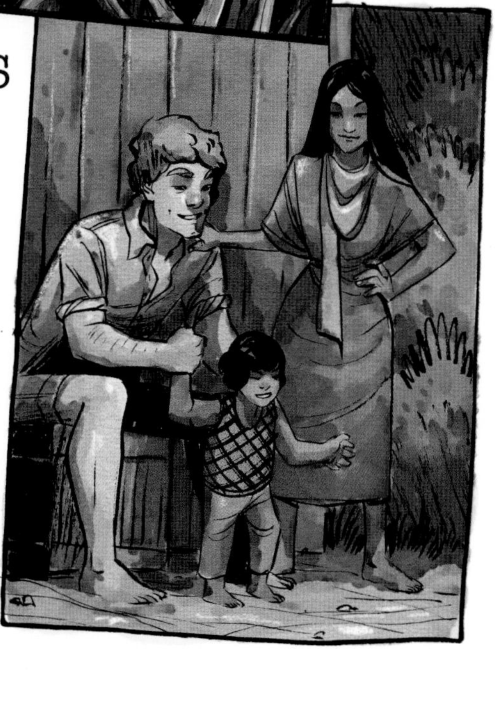

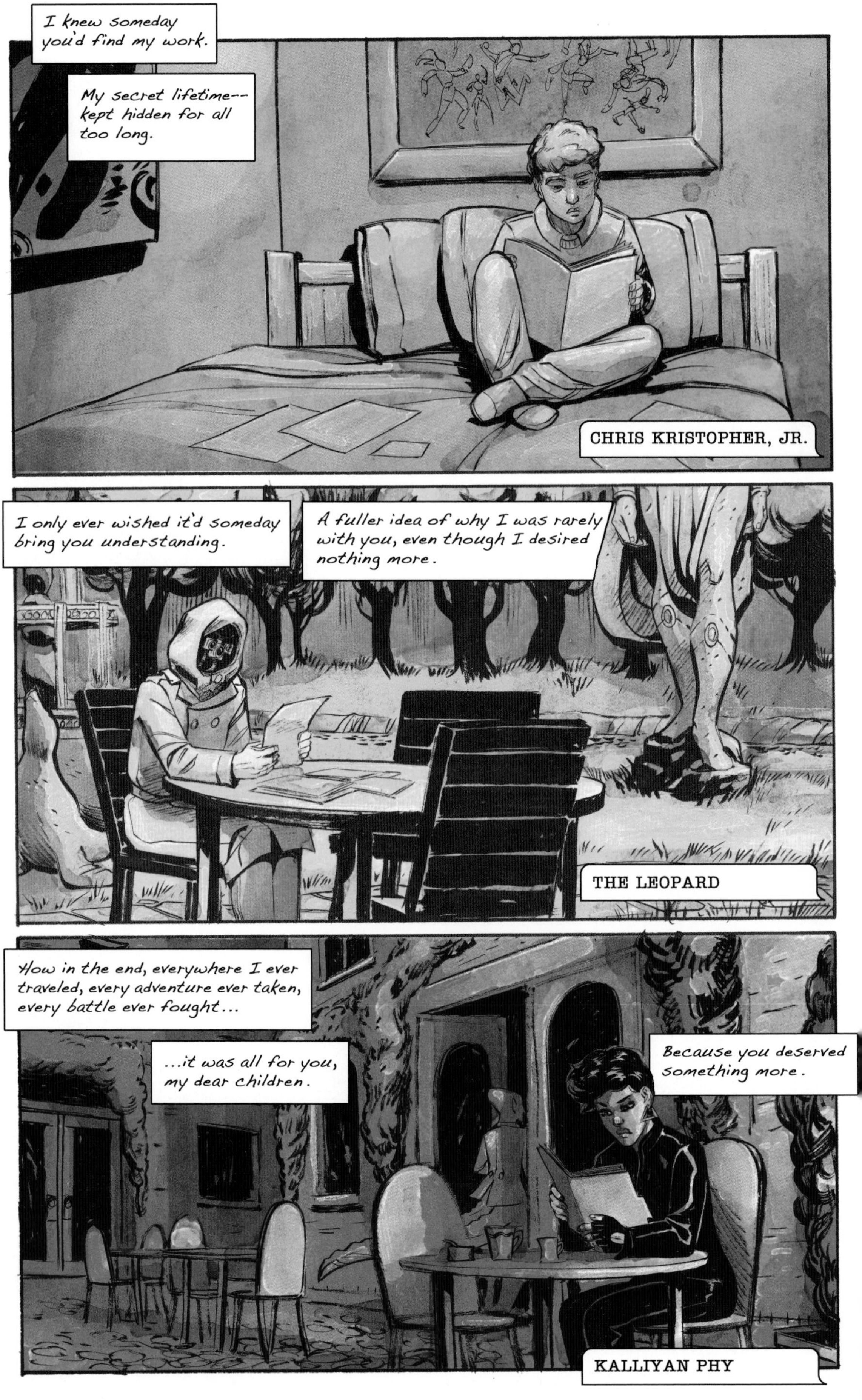
I knew someday you'd find my work.
My secret lifetime-- kept hidden for all too long.
CHRIS KRISTOPHER, JR.
I only ever wished it'd someday bring you understanding.
A fuller idea of why I was rarely with you, even though I desired nothing more.
THE LEOPARD
How in the end, everywhere I ever traveled, every adventure ever taken, every battle ever fought...
...it was all for you, my dear children.
Because you deserved something more.
KALLIYAN PHY

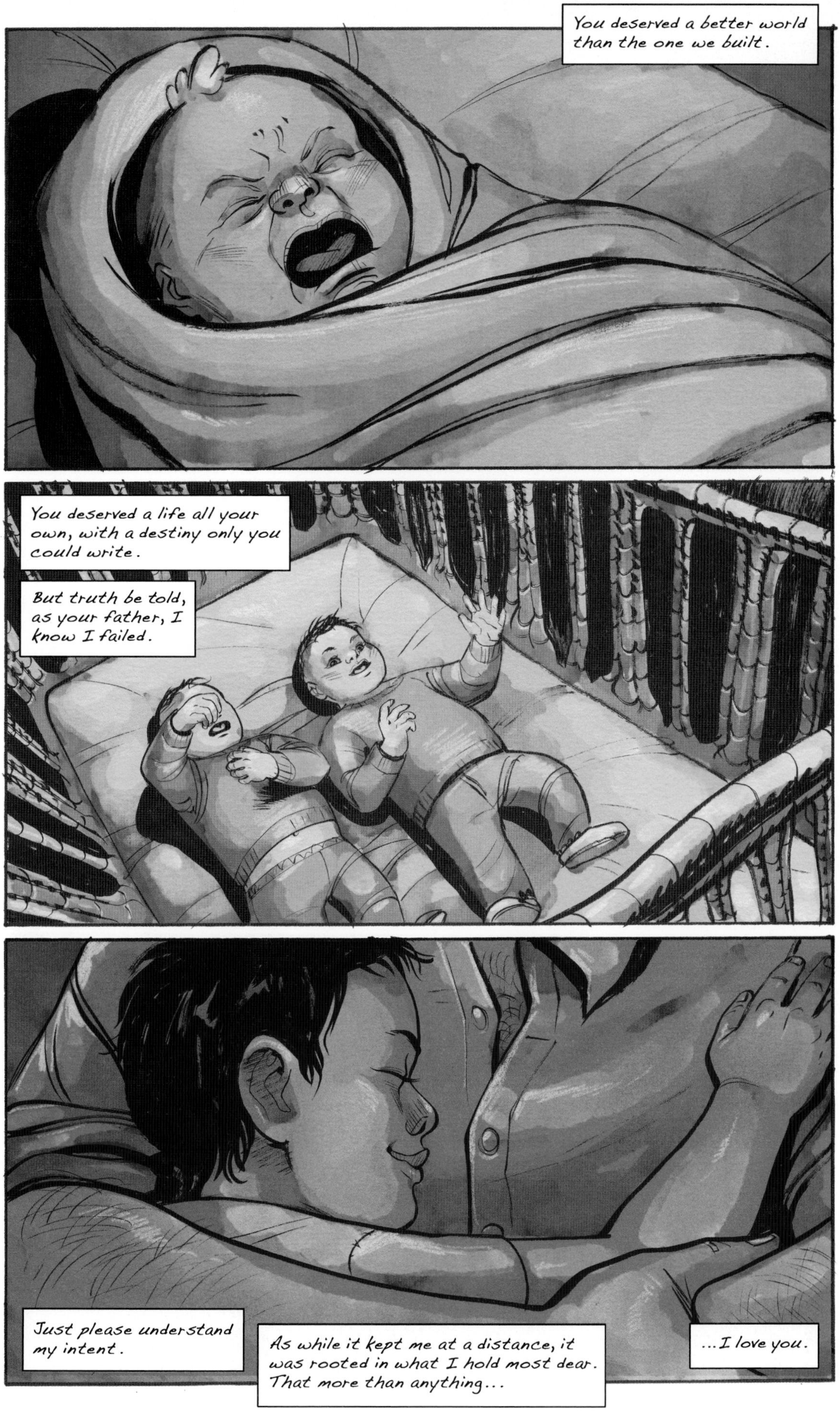
You deserved a better world than the one we built.
You deserved a life all your own, with a destiny only you could write.
But truth be told, as your father, I know I failed.
Just please understand my intent.
As while it kept me at a distance, it was rooted in what I hold most dear. That more than anything...
...I love you.

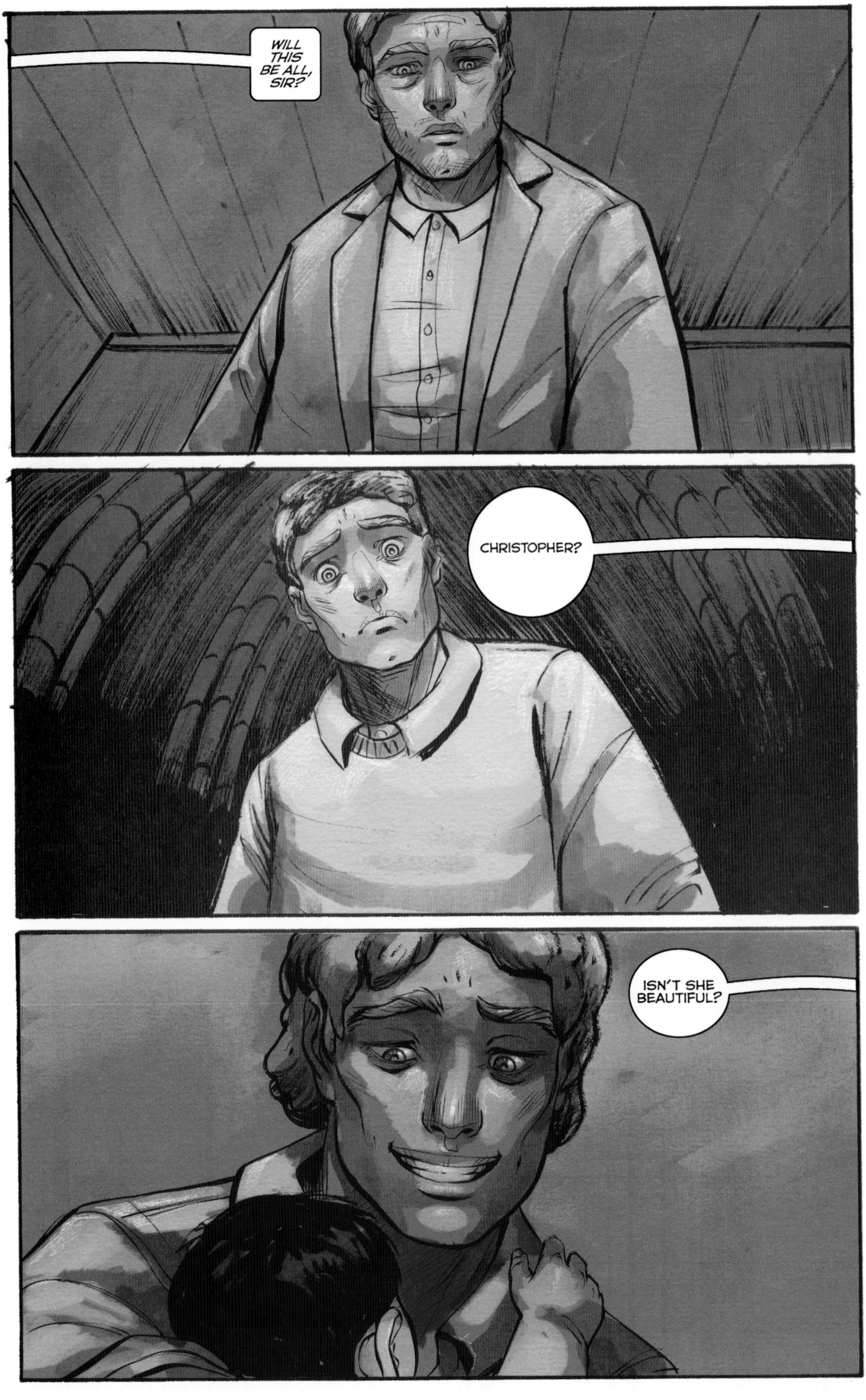
WILL THIS BE ALL, SIR?
CHRISTOPHER?
ISN'T SHE BEAUTIFUL?

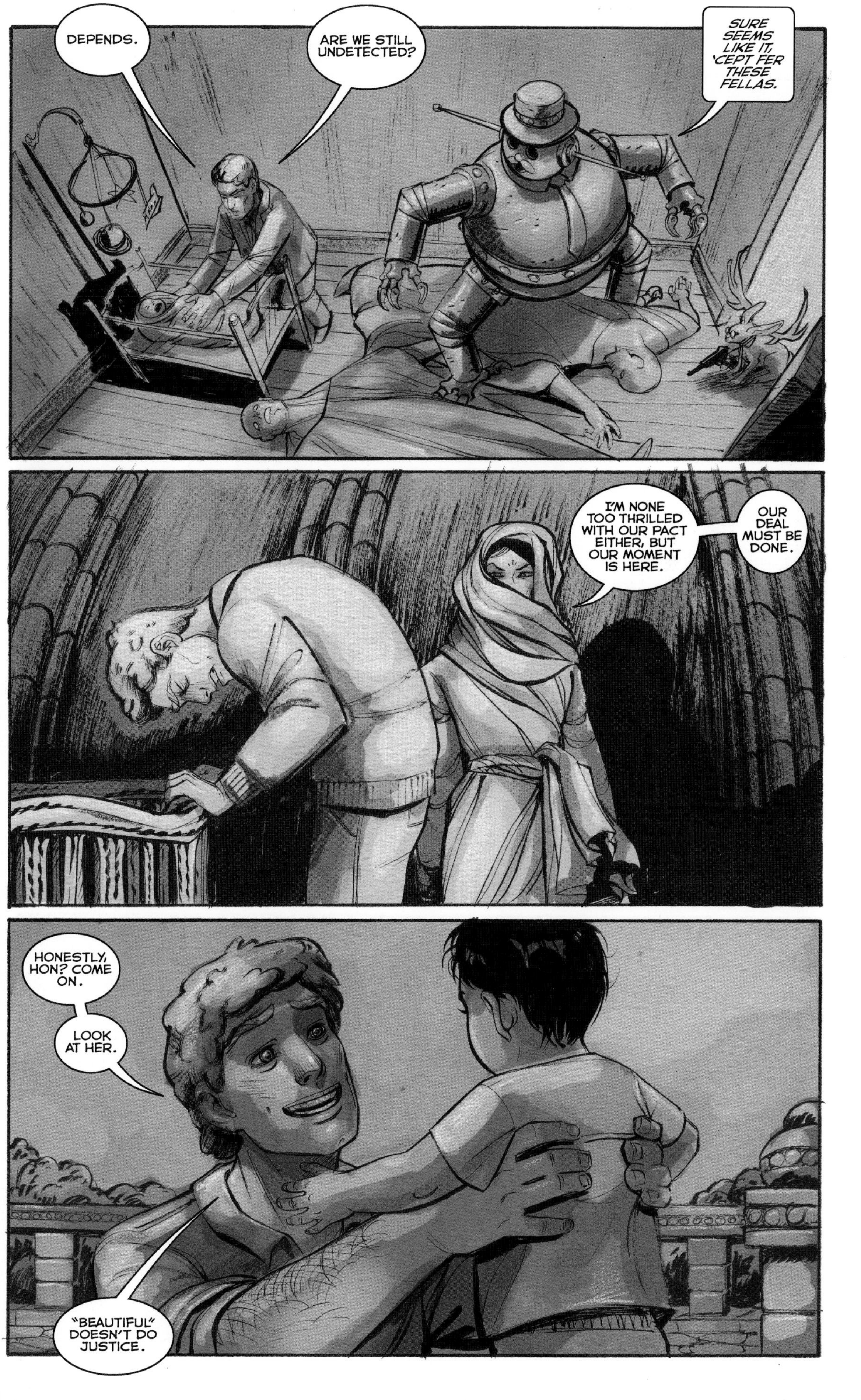
DEPENDS.
ARE WE STILL UNDETECTED?
SURE SEEMS LIKE IT, 'CEPT FER THESE FELLAS.
I'M NONE TOO THRILLED WITH OUR PACT EITHER, BUT OUR MOMENT IS HERE.
OUR DEAL MUST BE DONE.
HONESTLY, HON? COME ON.
LOOK AT HER.
"BEAUTIFUL" DOESN'T DO JUSTICE.

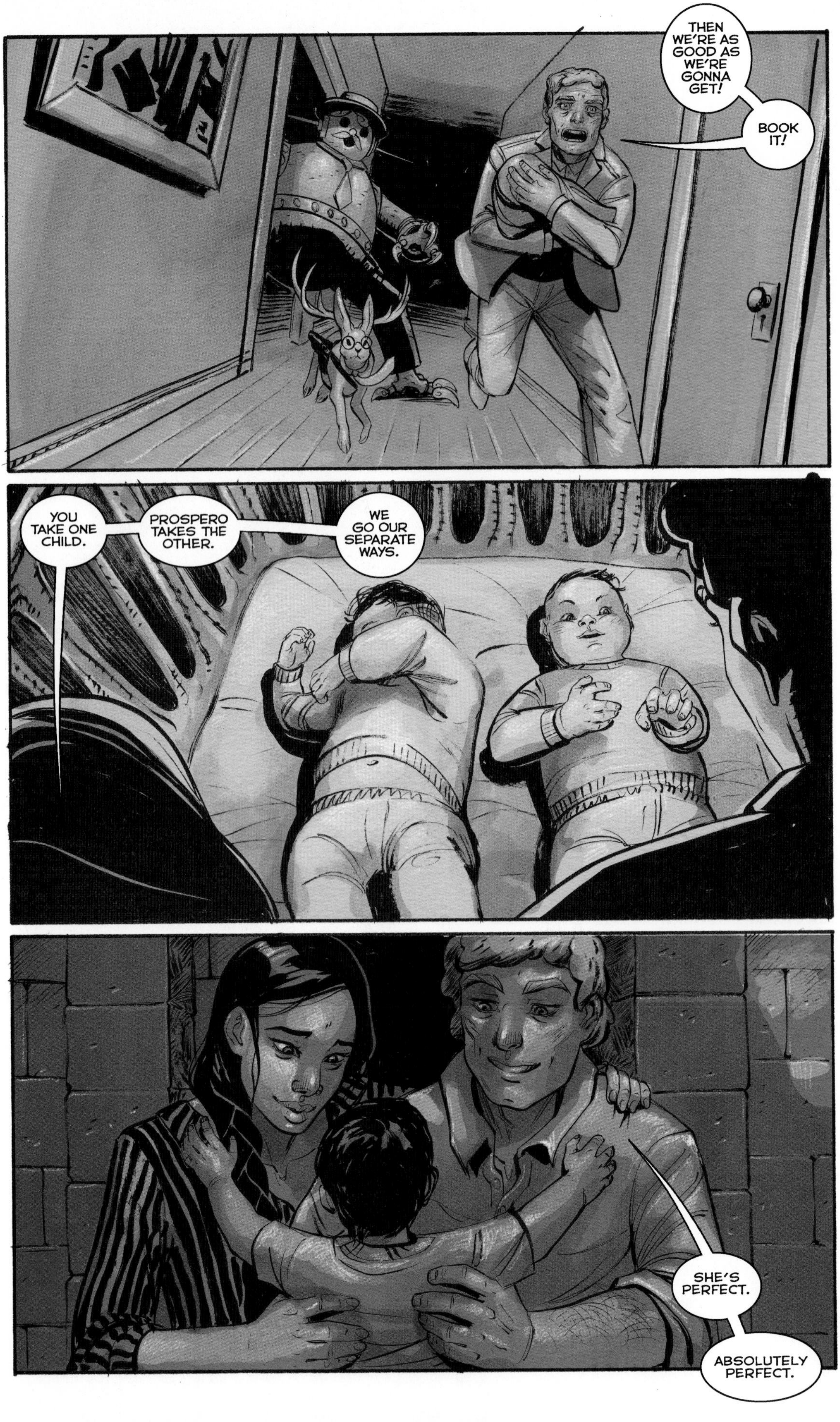
THEN WE'RE AS GOOD AS WE'RE GONNA GET!
BOOK IT!
YOU TAKE ONE CHILD.
PROSPERO TAKES THE OTHER.
WE GO OUR SEPARATE WAYS.
SHE'S PERFECT.
ABSOLUTELY PERFECT.

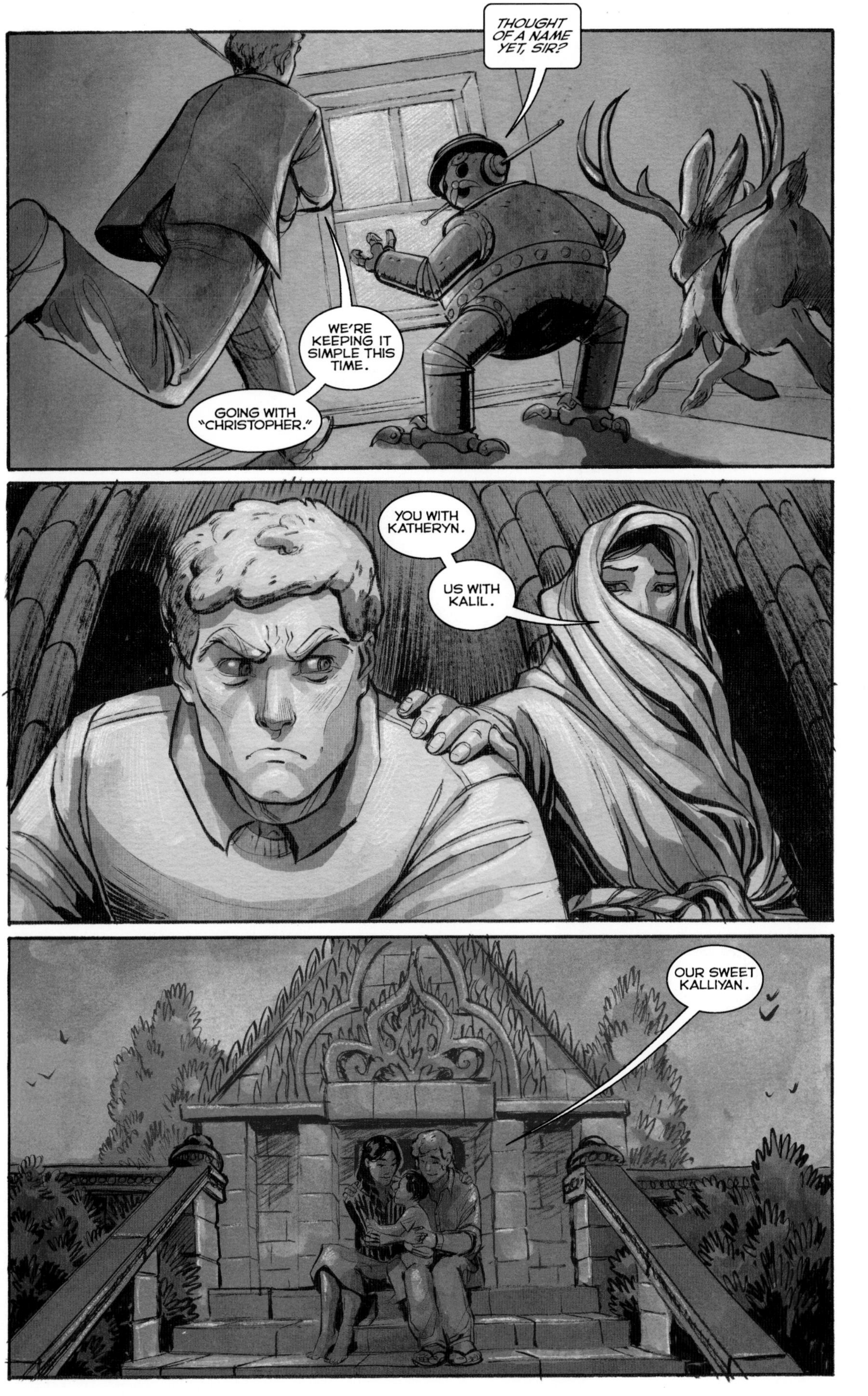
THOUGHT OF A NAME YET, SIR?
WE'RE KEEPING IT SIMPLE THIS TIME.
GOING WITH "CHRISTOPHER."
YOU WITH KATHERYN.
US WITH KALIL.
OUR SWEET KALLIYAN.

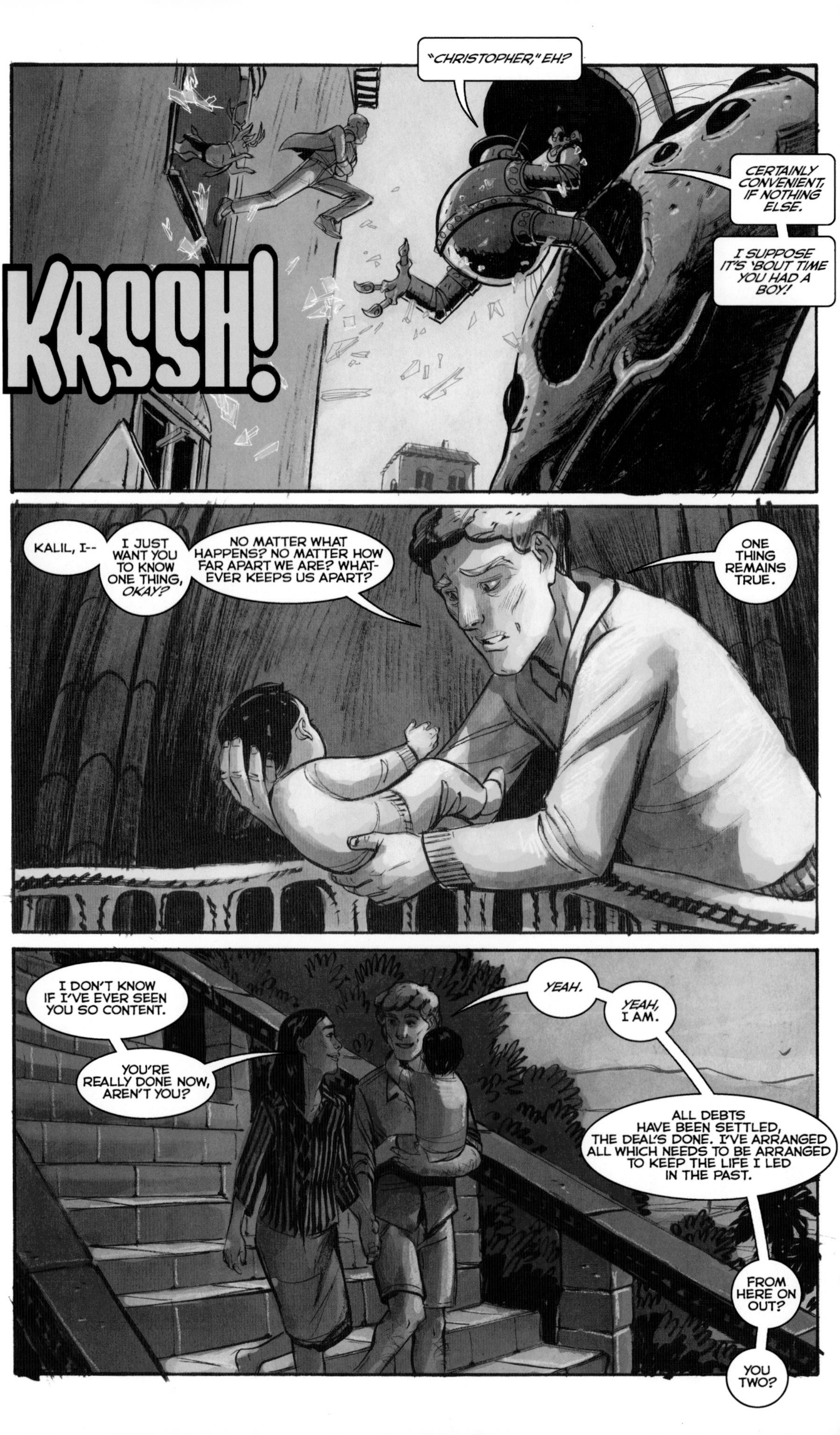
"CHRISTOPHER," EH?
CERTAINLY CONVENIENT, IF NOTHING ELSE.
I SUPPOSE IT'S 'BOUT TIME YOU HAD A BOY!
KRSSH!
KALIL, I--
I JUST WANT YOU TO KNOW ONE THING, OKAY?
NO MATTER WHAT HAPPENS? NO MATTER HOW FAR APART WE ARE? WHAT-EVER KEEPS US APART?
ONE THING REMAINS TRUE.
I DON'T KNOW IF I'VE EVER SEEN YOU SO CONTENT.
YOU'RE REALLY DONE NOW, AREN'T YOU?
YEAH.
YEAH, I AM.
ALL DEBTS HAVE BEEN SETTLED, THE DEAL'S DONE. I'VE ARRANGED ALL WHICH NEEDS TO BE ARRANGED TO KEEP THE LIFE I LED IN THE PAST.
FROM HERE ON OUT?
YOU TWO?

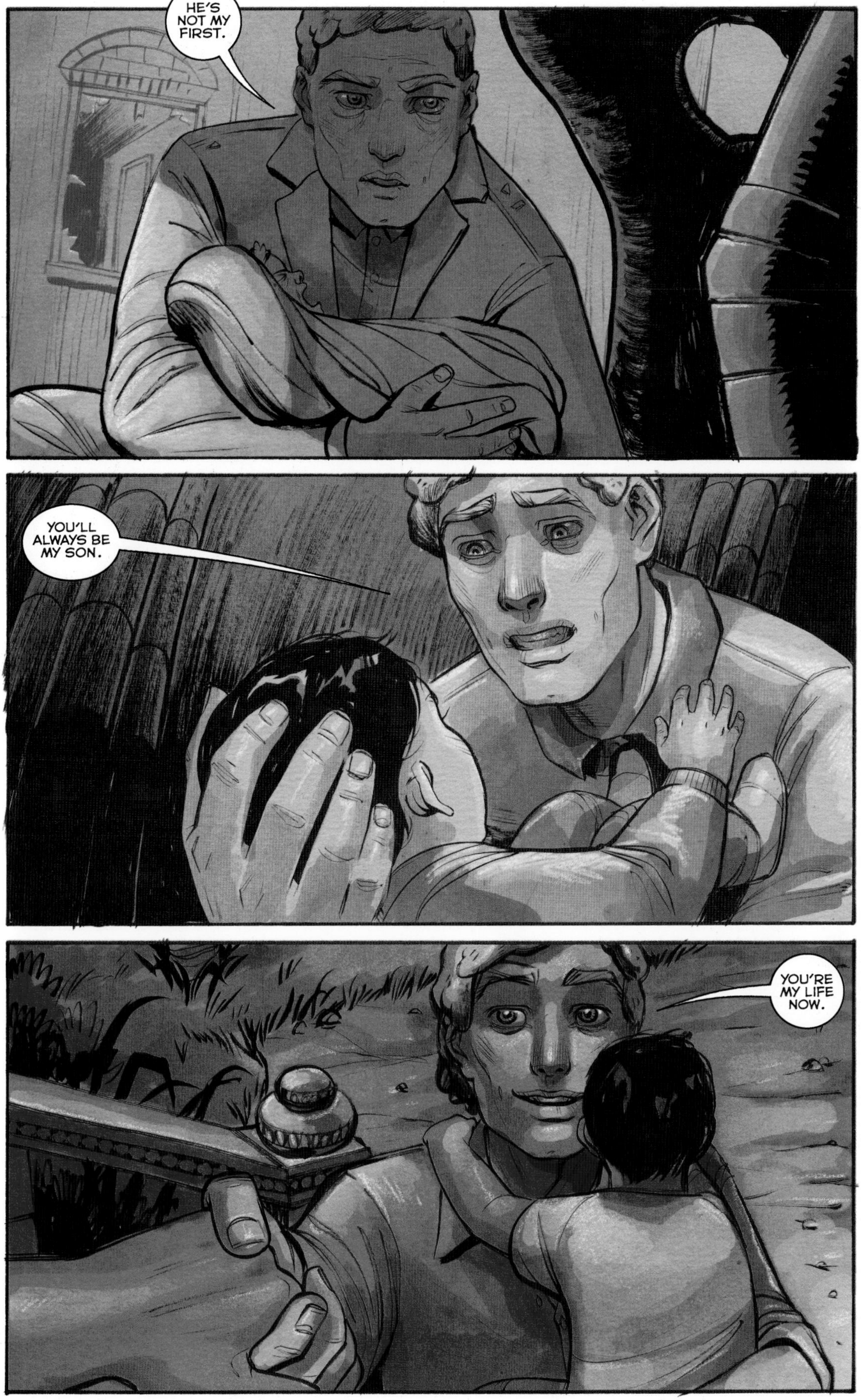
HE'S NOT MY FIRST.
YOU'LL ALWAYS BE MY SON.
YOU'RE MY LIFE NOW.

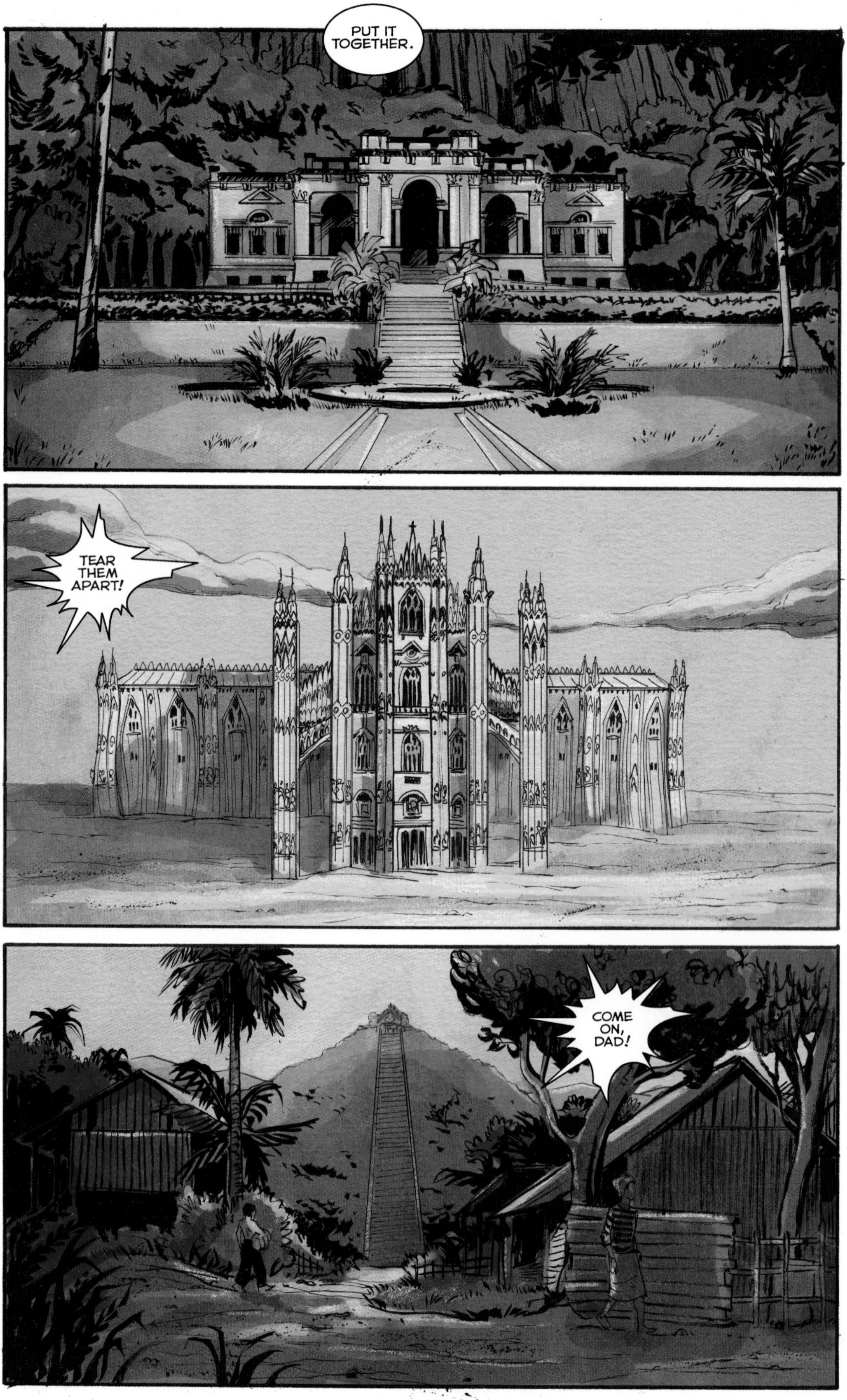
PUT IT TOGETHER.
TEAR THEM APART!
COME ON, DAD!

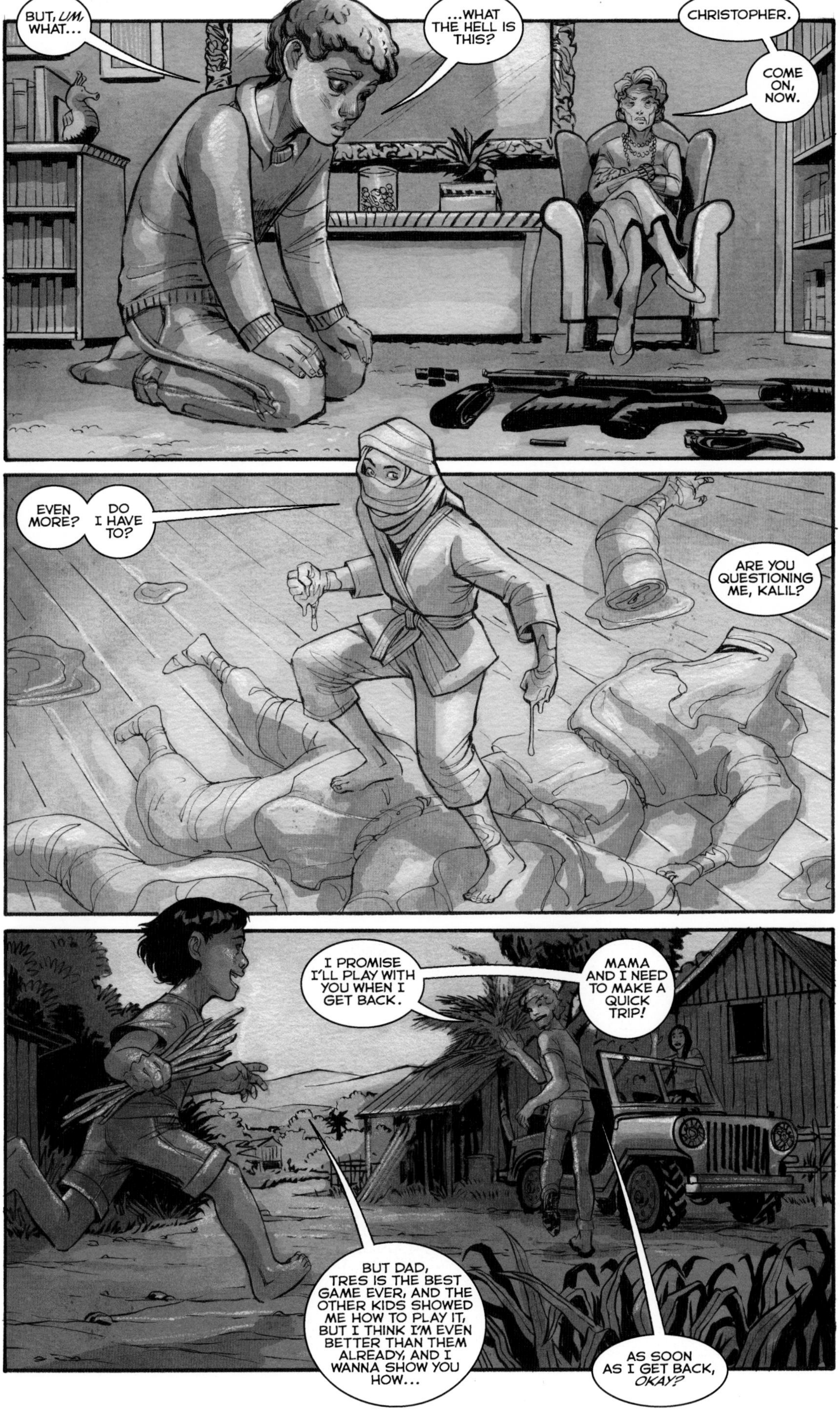
BUT, UM, WHAT...
...WHAT THE HELL IS THIS?
CHRISTOPHER.
COME ON, NOW.
EVEN MORE?
DO I HAVE TO?
ARE YOU QUESTIONING ME, KALIL?
I PROMISE I'LL PLAY WITH YOU WHEN I GET BACK.
MAMA AND I NEED TO MAKE A QUICK TRIP!
BUT DAD, TRES IS THE BEST GAME EVER, AND THE OTHER KIDS SHOWED ME HOW TO PLAY IT, BUT I THINK I'M EVEN BETTER THAN THEM ALREADY, AND I WANNA SHOW YOU HOW...
AS SOON AS I GET BACK, OKAY?

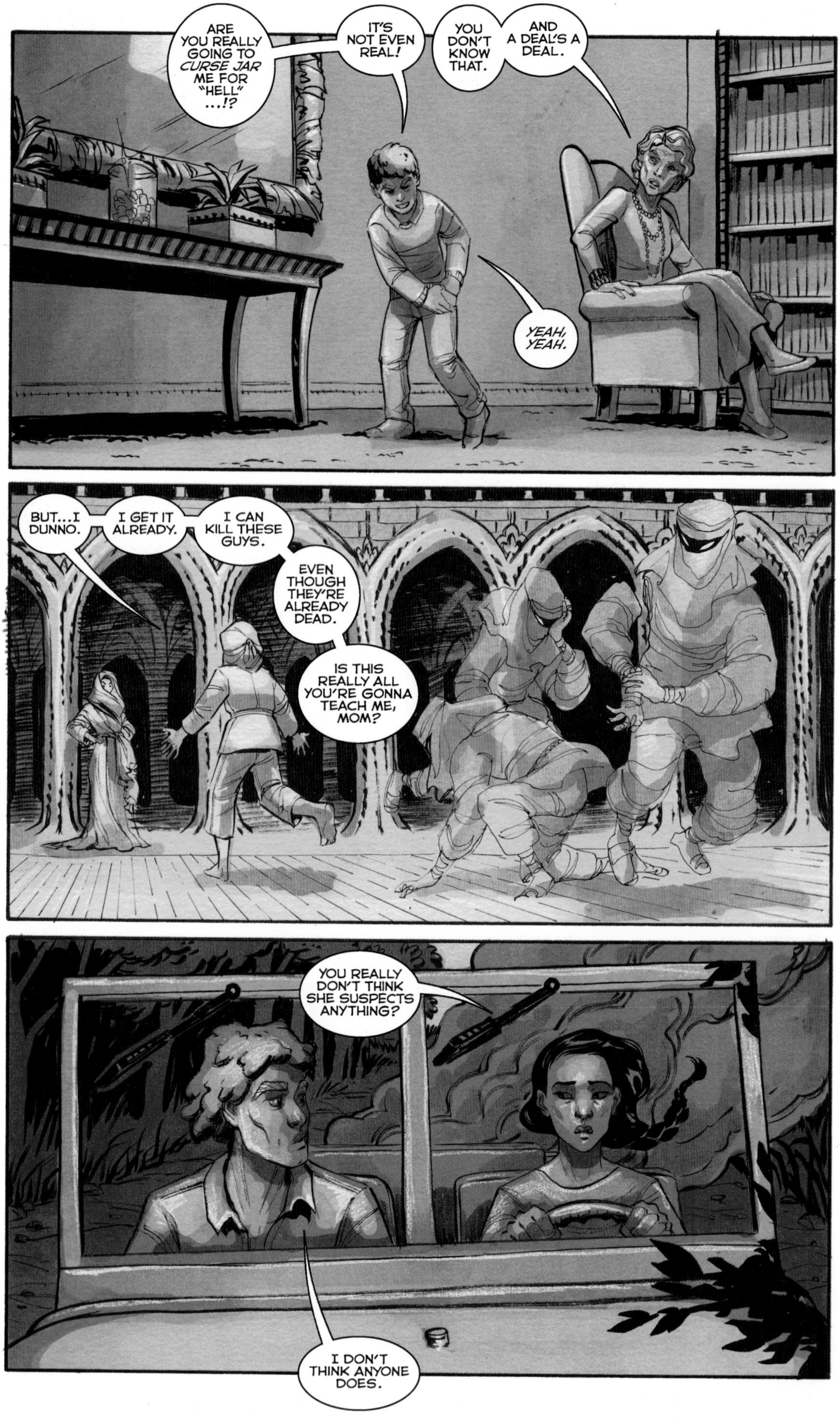
ARE YOU REALLY GOING TO *CURSE JAR* ME FOR "HELL" ...!?
IT'S NOT EVEN REAL!
YOU DON'T KNOW THAT.
AND A DEAL'S A DEAL.
YEAH, YEAH.
BUT...I DUNNO.
I GET IT ALREADY.
I CAN KILL THESE GUYS.
EVEN THOUGH THEY'RE ALREADY DEAD.
IS THIS REALLY ALL YOU'RE GONNA TEACH ME, MOM?
YOU REALLY DON'T THINK SHE SUSPECTS ANYTHING?
I DON'T THINK ANYONE DOES.

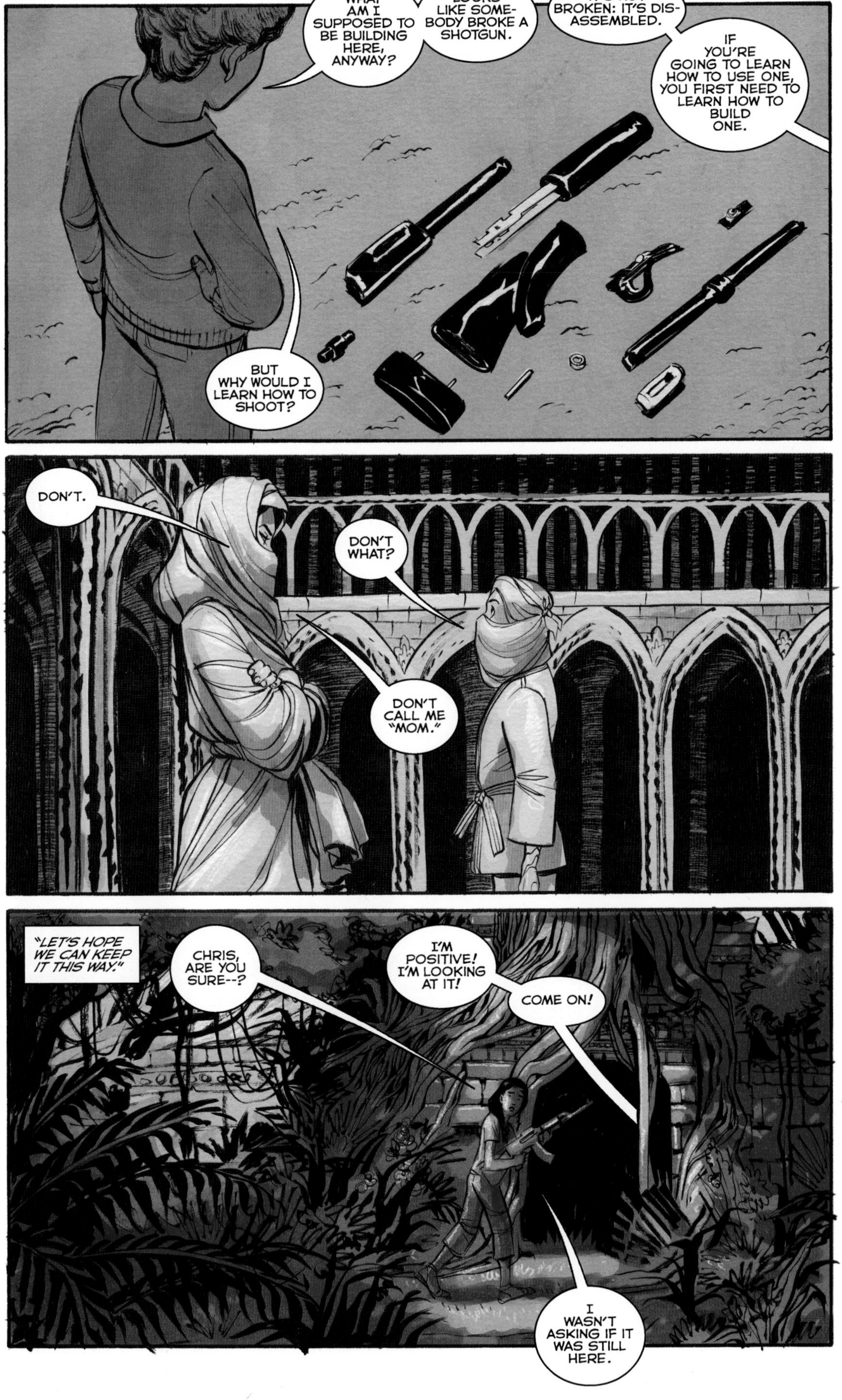
WHAT AM I SUPPOSED TO BE BUILDING HERE, ANYWAY?
LOOKS LIKE SOMEBODY BROKE A SHOTGUN.
IT'S NOT BROKEN: IT'S DISASSEMBLED.
IF YOU'RE GOING TO LEARN HOW TO USE ONE, YOU FIRST NEED TO LEARN HOW TO BUILD ONE.
BUT WHY WOULD I LEARN HOW TO SHOOT?
DON'T.
DON'T WHAT?
DON'T CALL ME "MOM."
"LET'S HOPE WE CAN KEEP IT THIS WAY."
CHRIS, ARE YOU SURE--?
I'M POSITIVE! I'M LOOKING AT IT!
COME ON!
I WASN'T ASKING IF IT WAS STILL HERE.

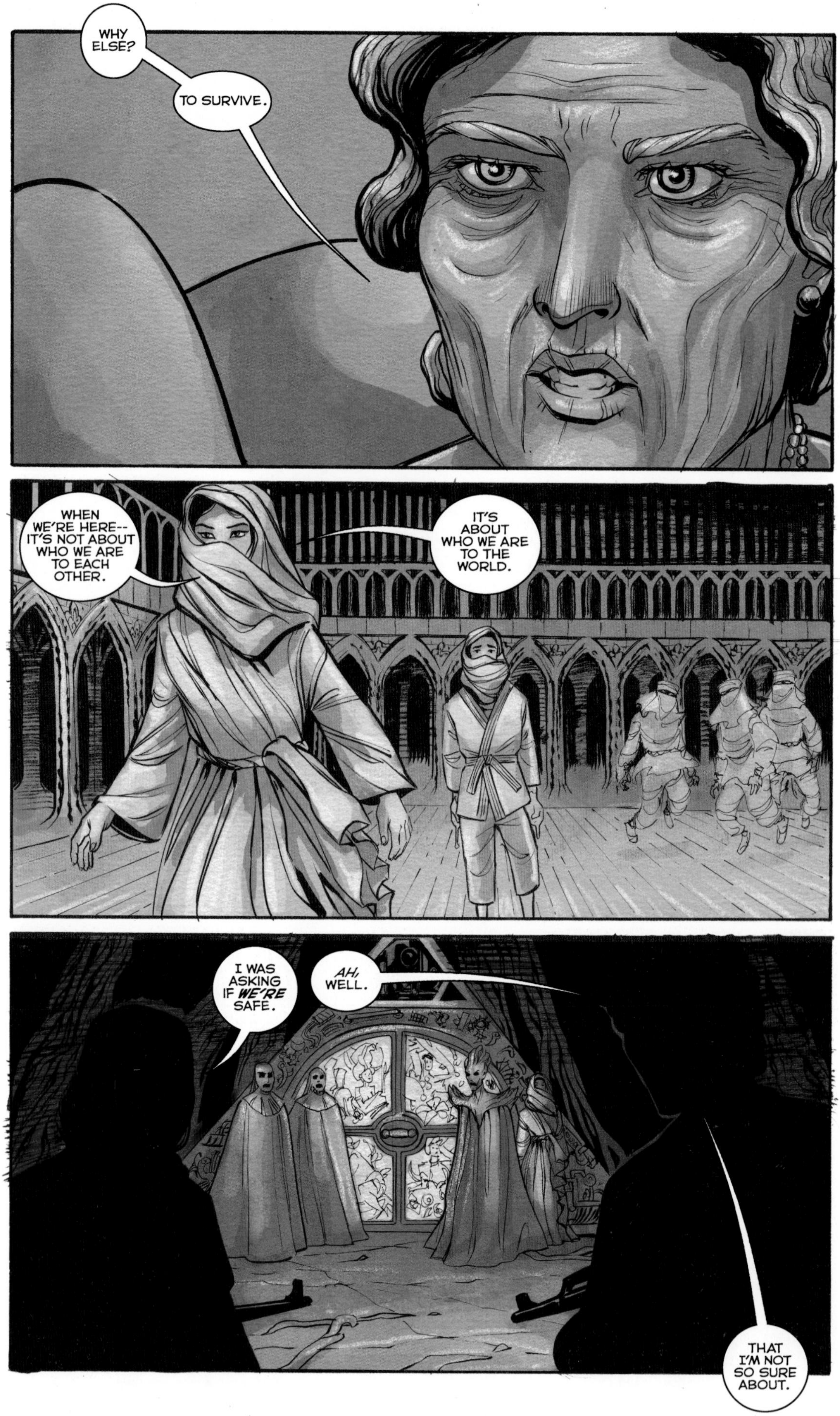
WHY ELSE?
TO SURVIVE.
WHEN WE'RE HERE-- IT'S NOT ABOUT WHO WE ARE TO EACH OTHER.
IT'S ABOUT WHO WE ARE TO THE WORLD.
I WAS ASKING IF *WE'RE* SAFE.
AH, WELL.
THAT I'M NOT SO SURE ABOUT.

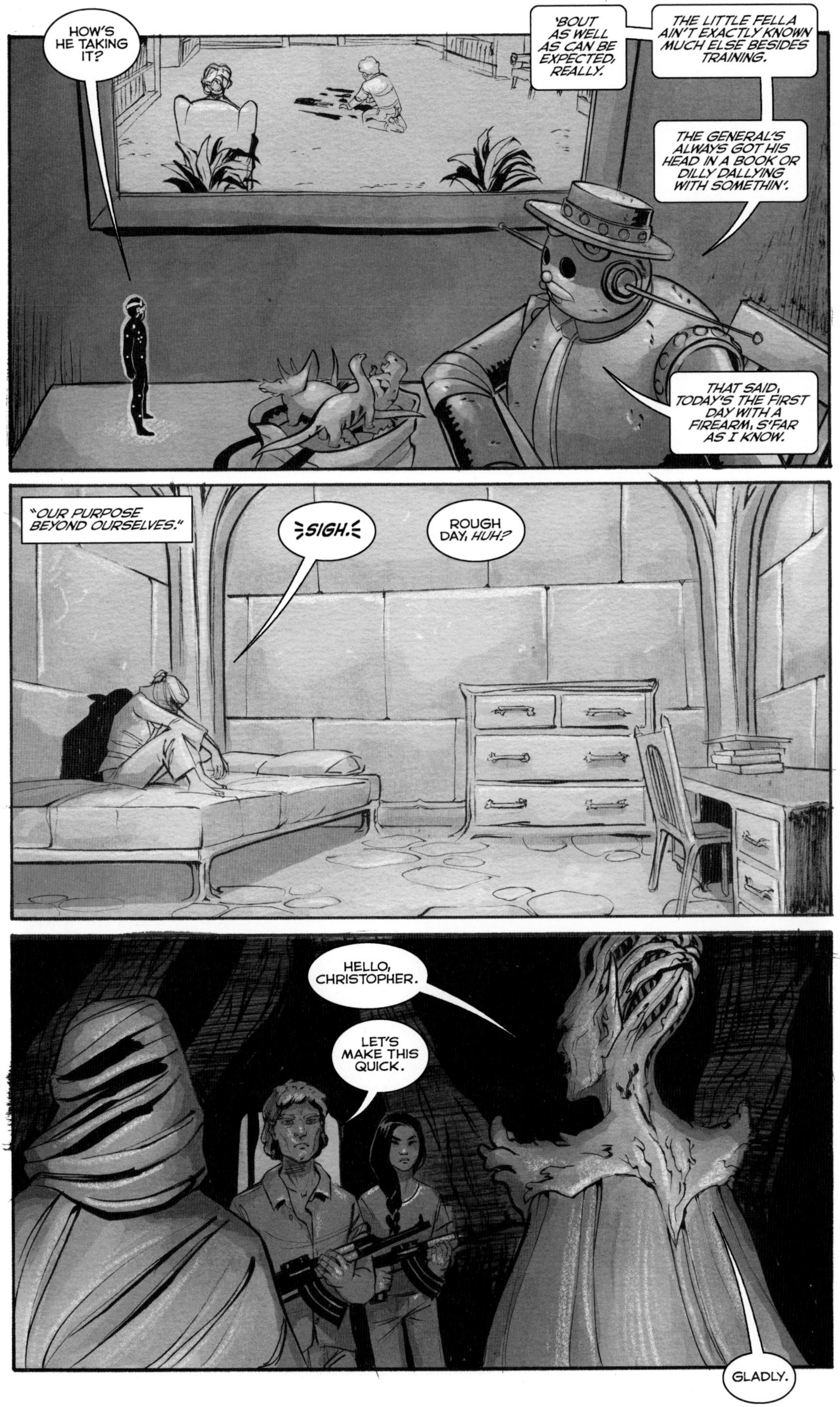
HOW'S HE TAKING IT?
'BOUT AS WELL AS CAN BE EXPECTED, REALLY.
THE LITTLE FELLA AIN'T EXACTLY KNOWN MUCH ELSE BESIDES TRAINING.
THE GENERAL'S ALWAYS GOT HIS HEAD IN A BOOK OR DILLY DALLYING WITH SOMETHIN'.
THAT SAID, TODAY'S THE FIRST DAY WITH A FIREARM, S'FAR AS I KNOW.
"OUR PURPOSE BEYOND OURSELVES."
SIGH.
ROUGH DAY, HUH?
HELLO, CHRISTOPHER.
LET'S MAKE THIS QUICK.
GLADLY.

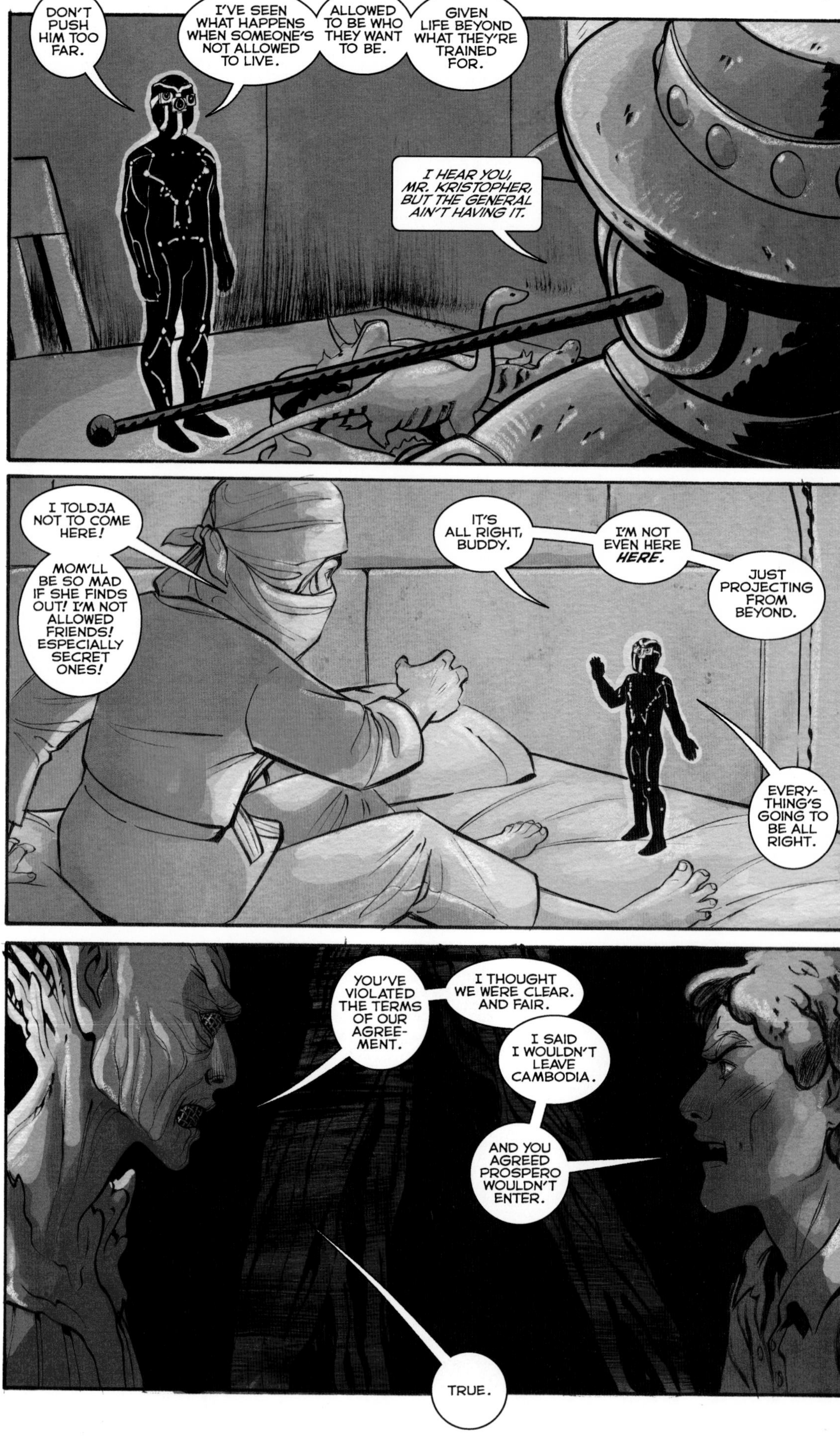
DON'T PUSH HIM TOO FAR.
I'VE SEEN WHAT HAPPENS WHEN SOMEONE'S NOT ALLOWED TO LIVE.
ALLOWED TO BE WHO THEY WANT TO BE.
GIVEN LIFE BEYOND WHAT THEY'RE TRAINED FOR.
I HEAR YOU, MR. KRISTOPHER, BUT THE GENERAL AIN'T HAVING IT.
I TOLDJA NOT TO COME HERE!
MOM'LL BE SO MAD IF SHE FINDS OUT! I'M NOT ALLOWED FRIENDS! ESPECIALLY SECRET ONES!
IT'S ALL RIGHT, BUDDY.
I'M NOT EVEN HERE ***HERE.***
JUST PROJECTING FROM BEYOND.
EVERY-THING'S GOING TO BE ALL RIGHT.
YOU'VE VIOLATED THE TERMS OF OUR AGREE-MENT.
I THOUGHT WE WERE CLEAR. AND FAIR.
I SAID I WOULDN'T LEAVE CAMBODIA.
AND YOU AGREED PROSPERO WOULDN'T ENTER.
TRUE.

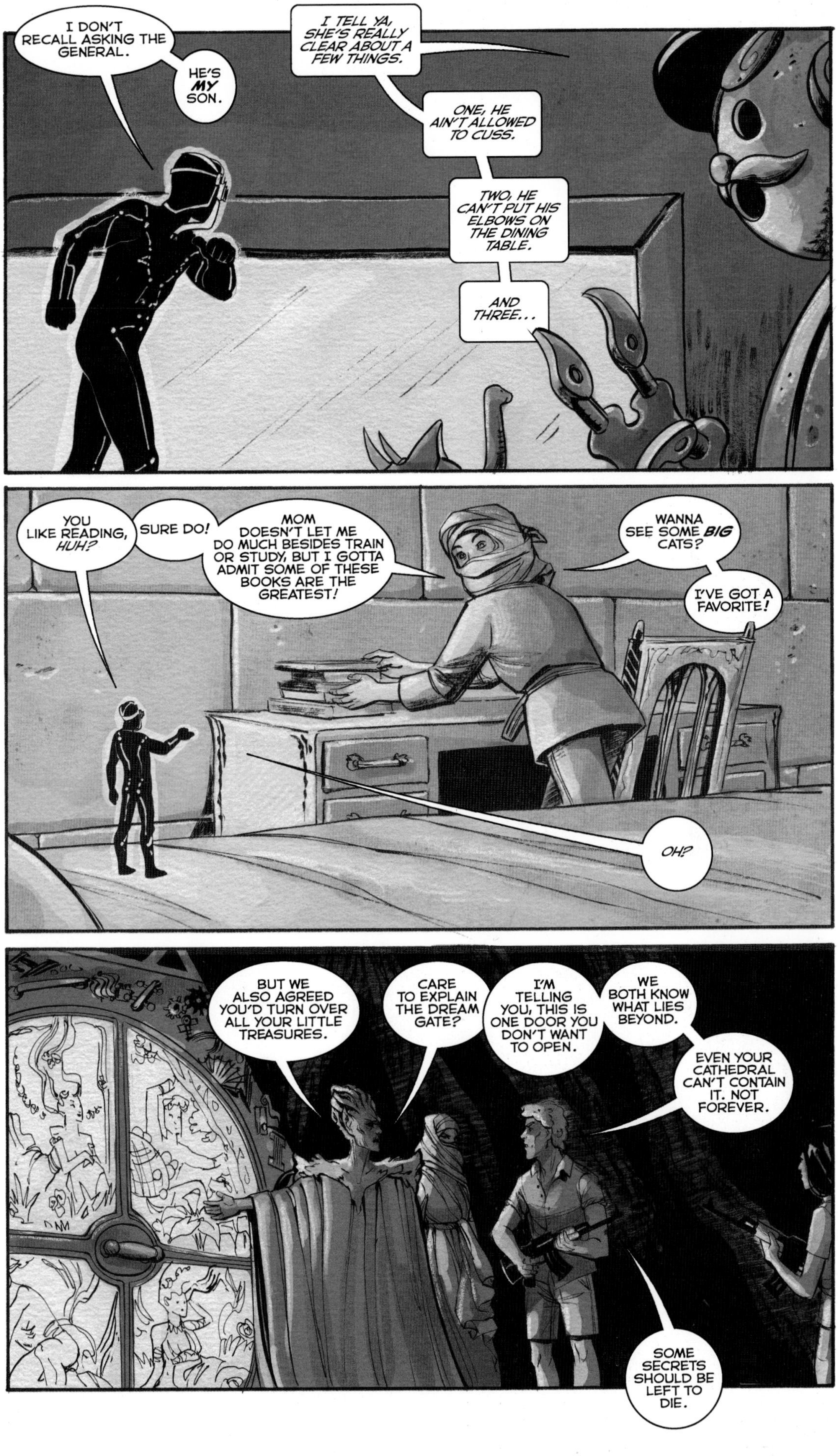
I DON'T RECALL ASKING THE GENERAL.
HE'S MY SON.
I TELL YA, SHE'S REALLY CLEAR ABOUT A FEW THINGS.
ONE, HE AIN'T ALLOWED TO CUSS.
TWO, HE CAN'T PUT HIS ELBOWS ON THE DINING TABLE.
AND THREE...
YOU LIKE READING, HUH?
SURE DO!
MOM DOESN'T LET ME DO MUCH BESIDES TRAIN OR STUDY, BUT I GOTTA ADMIT SOME OF THESE BOOKS ARE THE GREATEST!
WANNA SEE SOME BIG CATS?
I'VE GOT A FAVORITE!
OH?
BUT WE ALSO AGREED YOU'D TURN OVER ALL YOUR LITTLE TREASURES.
CARE TO EXPLAIN THE DREAM GATE?
I'M TELLING YOU, THIS IS ONE DOOR YOU DON'T WANT TO OPEN.
WE BOTH KNOW WHAT LIES BEYOND.
EVEN YOUR CATHEDRAL CAN'T CONTAIN IT. NOT FOREVER.
SOME SECRETS SHOULD BE LEFT TO DIE.

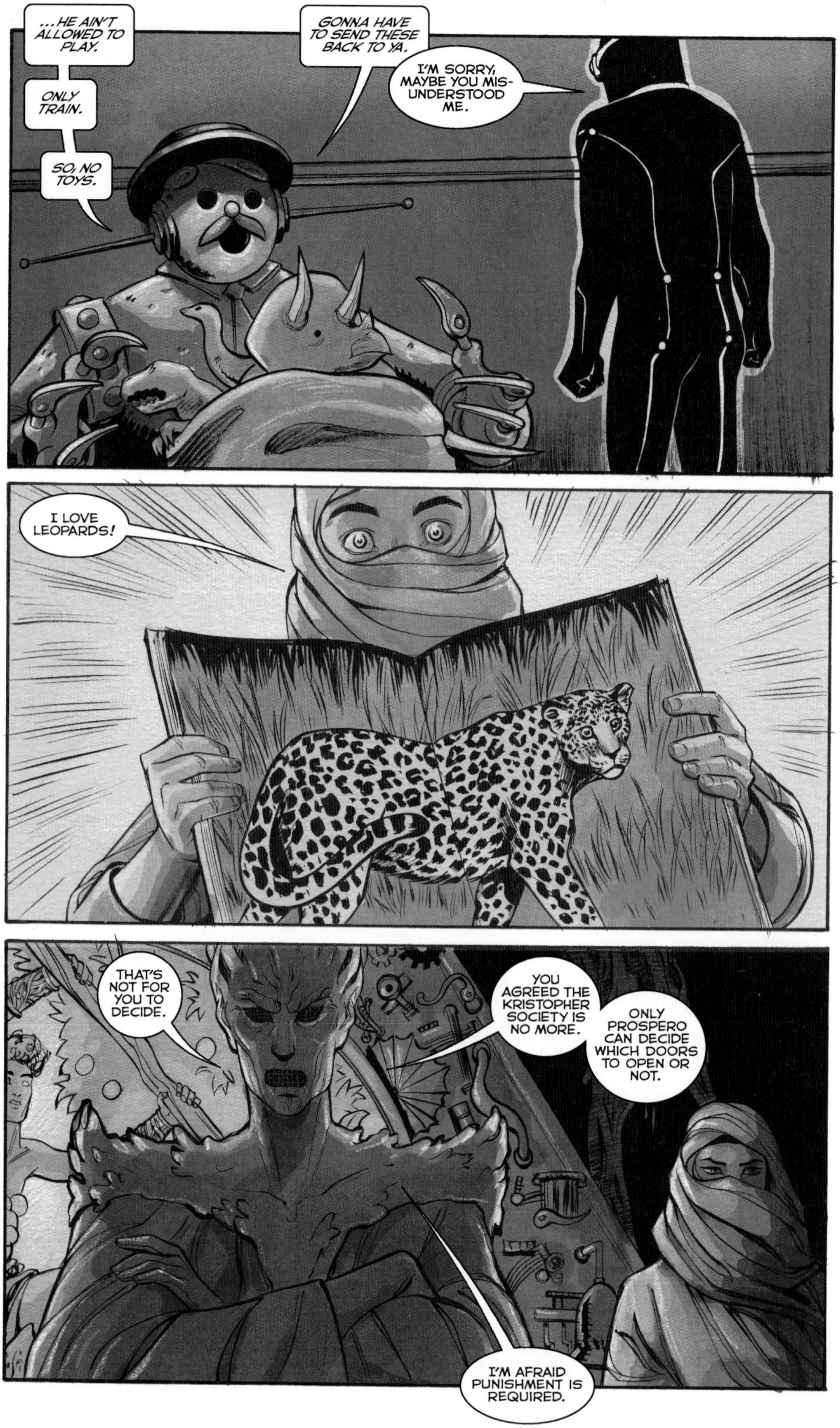
...HE AIN'T ALLOWED TO PLAY.
ONLY TRAIN.
SO, NO TOYS.
GONNA HAVE TO SEND THESE BACK TO YA.
I'M SORRY, MAYBE YOU MIS-UNDERSTOOD ME.
I LOVE LEOPARDS!
THAT'S NOT FOR YOU TO DECIDE.
YOU AGREED THE KRISTOPHER SOCIETY IS NO MORE.
ONLY PROSPERO CAN DECIDE WHICH DOORS TO OPEN OR NOT.
I'M AFRAID PUNISHMENT IS REQUIRED.

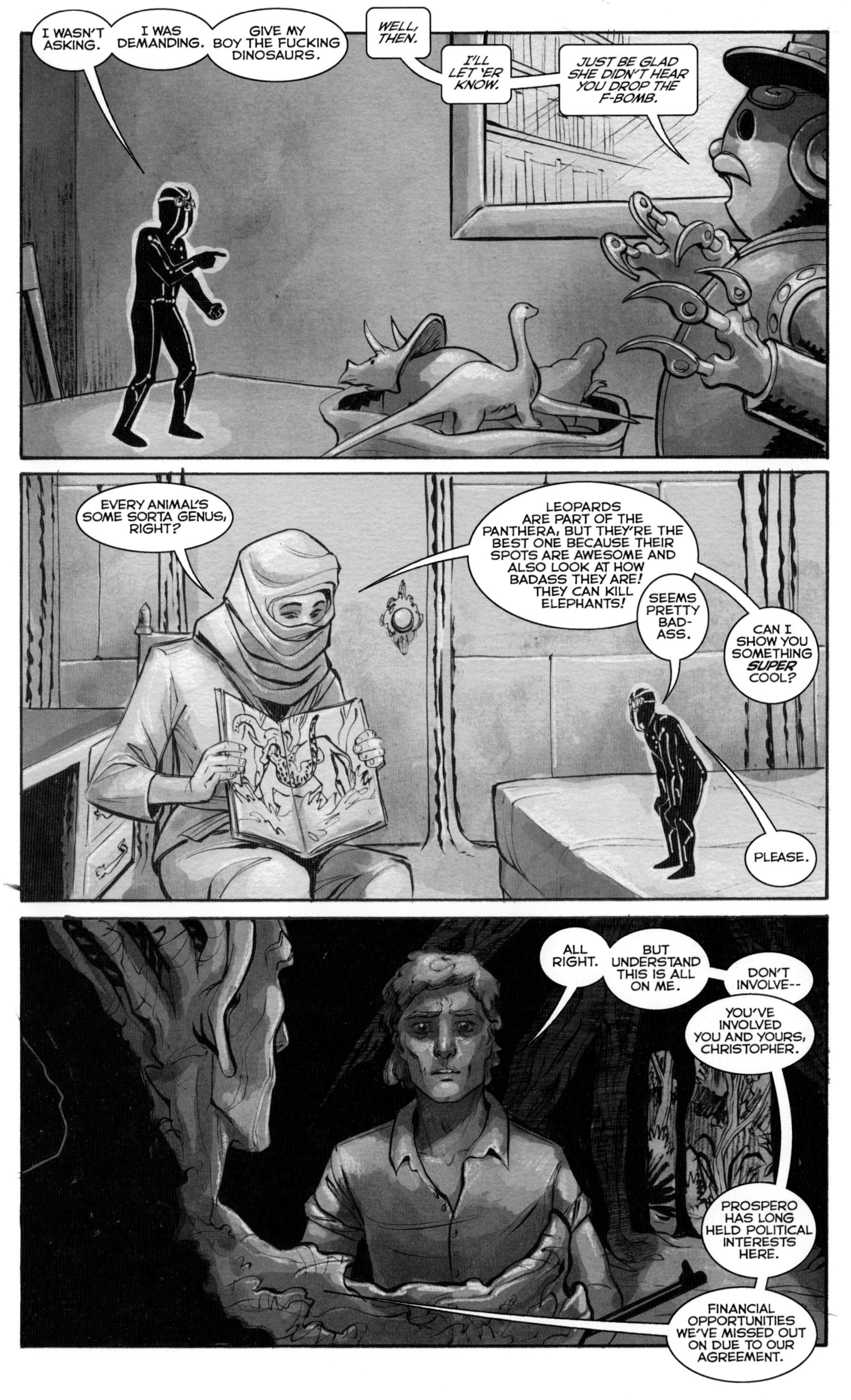
I WASN'T ASKING.
I WAS DEMANDING.
GIVE MY BOY THE FUCKING DINOSAURS.
WELL, THEN.
I'LL LET 'ER KNOW.
JUST BE GLAD SHE DIDN'T HEAR YOU DROP THE F-BOMB.
EVERY ANIMAL'S SOME SORTA GENUS, RIGHT?
LEOPARDS ARE PART OF THE PANTHERA, BUT THEY'RE THE BEST ONE BECAUSE THEIR SPOTS ARE AWESOME AND ALSO LOOK AT HOW BADASS THEY ARE! THEY CAN KILL ELEPHANTS!
SEEMS PRETTY BAD-ASS.
CAN I SHOW YOU SOMETHING SUPER COOL?
PLEASE.
ALL RIGHT.
BUT UNDERSTAND THIS IS ALL ON ME.
DON'T INVOLVE--
YOU'VE INVOLVED YOU AND YOURS, CHRISTOPHER.
PROSPERO HAS LONG HELD POLITICAL INTERESTS HERE.
FINANCIAL OPPORTUNITIES WE'VE MISSED OUT ON DUE TO OUR AGREEMENT.

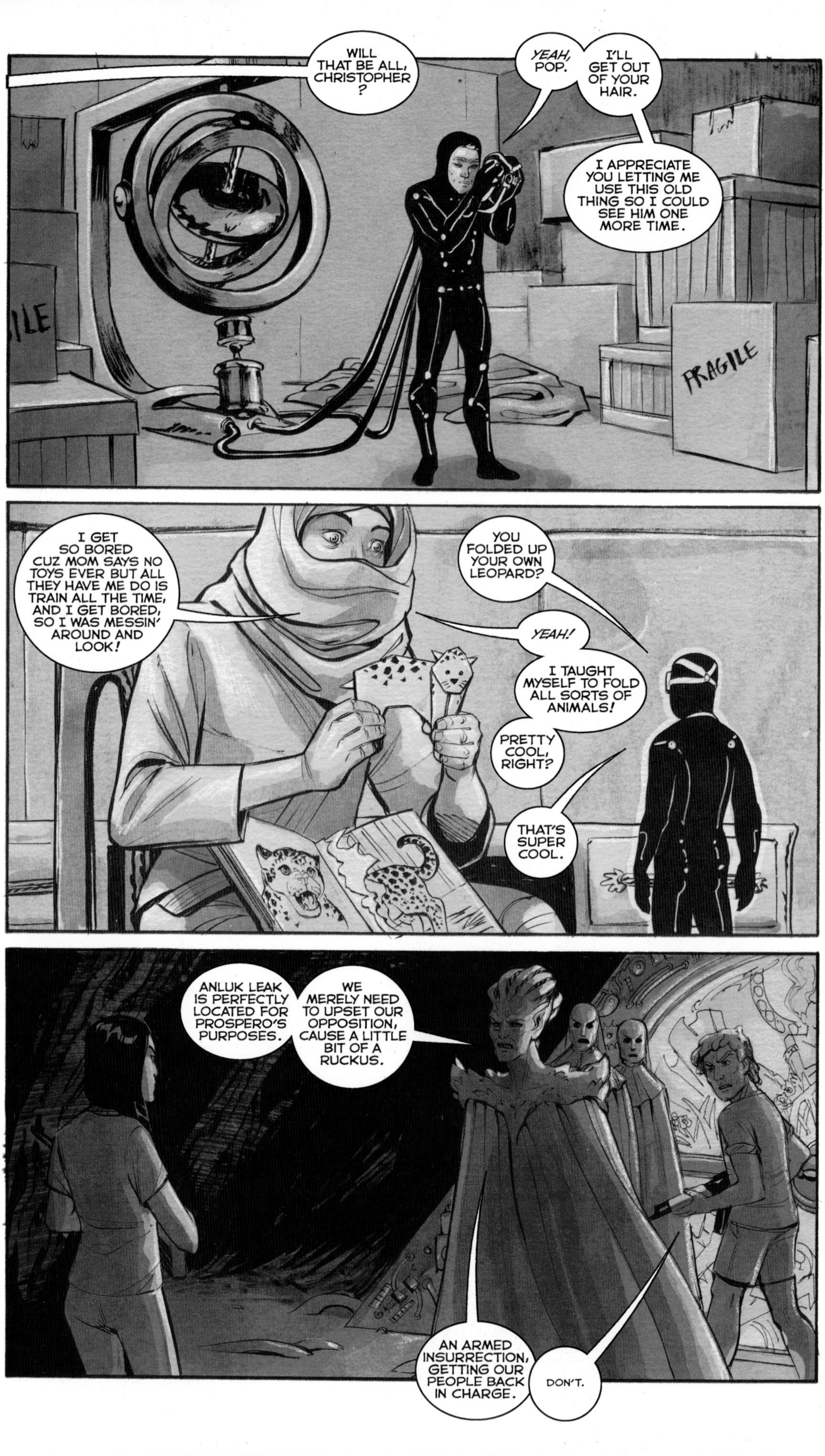
WILL THAT BE ALL, CHRISTOPHER?
YEAH, POP.
I'LL GET OUT OF YOUR HAIR.
I APPRECIATE YOU LETTING ME USE THIS OLD THING SO I COULD SEE HIM ONE MORE TIME.
FRAGILE
I GET SO BORED CUZ MOM SAYS NO TOYS EVER BUT ALL THEY HAVE ME DO IS TRAIN ALL THE TIME, AND I GET BORED, SO I WAS MESSIN' AROUND AND LOOK!
YOU FOLDED UP YOUR OWN LEOPARD?
YEAH!
I TAUGHT MYSELF TO FOLD ALL SORTS OF ANIMALS!
PRETTY COOL, RIGHT?
THAT'S SUPER COOL.
ANLUK LEAK IS PERFECTLY LOCATED FOR PROSPERO'S PURPOSES.
WE MERELY NEED TO UPSET OUR OPPOSITION, CAUSE A LITTLE BIT OF A RUCKUS.
AN ARMED INSURRECTION, GETTING OUR PEOPLE BACK IN CHARGE.
DON'T.

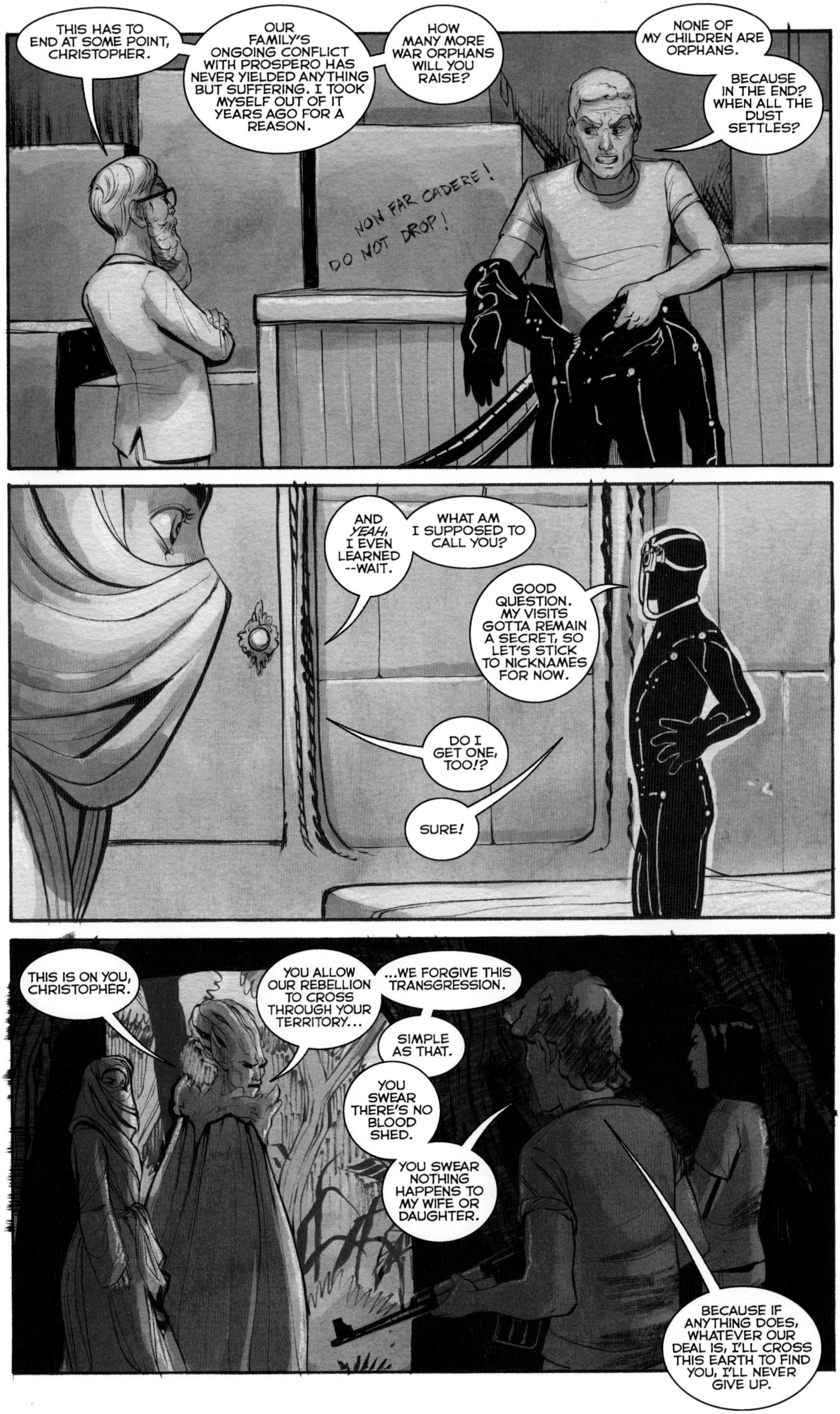
THIS HAS TO END AT SOME POINT, CHRISTOPHER.
OUR FAMILY'S ONGOING CONFLICT WITH PROSPERO HAS NEVER YIELDED ANYTHING BUT SUFFERING. I TOOK MYSELF OUT OF IT YEARS AGO FOR A REASON.
HOW MANY MORE WAR ORPHANS WILL YOU RAISE?
NONE OF MY CHILDREN ARE ORPHANS.
BECAUSE IN THE END? WHEN ALL THE DUST SETTLES?
NON FAR CADERE!
DO NOT DROP!
AND *YEAH*, I EVEN LEARNED --WAIT.
WHAT AM I SUPPOSED TO CALL YOU?
GOOD QUESTION. MY VISITS GOTTA REMAIN A SECRET, SO LET'S STICK TO NICKNAMES FOR NOW.
DO I GET ONE, TOO!?
SURE!
THIS IS ON YOU, CHRISTOPHER.
YOU ALLOW OUR REBELLION TO CROSS THROUGH YOUR TERRITORY...
...WE FORGIVE THIS TRANSGRESSION.
SIMPLE AS THAT.
YOU SWEAR THERE'S NO BLOOD SHED.
YOU SWEAR NOTHING HAPPENS TO MY WIFE OR DAUGHTER.
BECAUSE IF ANYTHING DOES, WHATEVER OUR DEAL IS, I'LL CROSS THIS EARTH TO FIND YOU, I'LL NEVER GIVE UP.

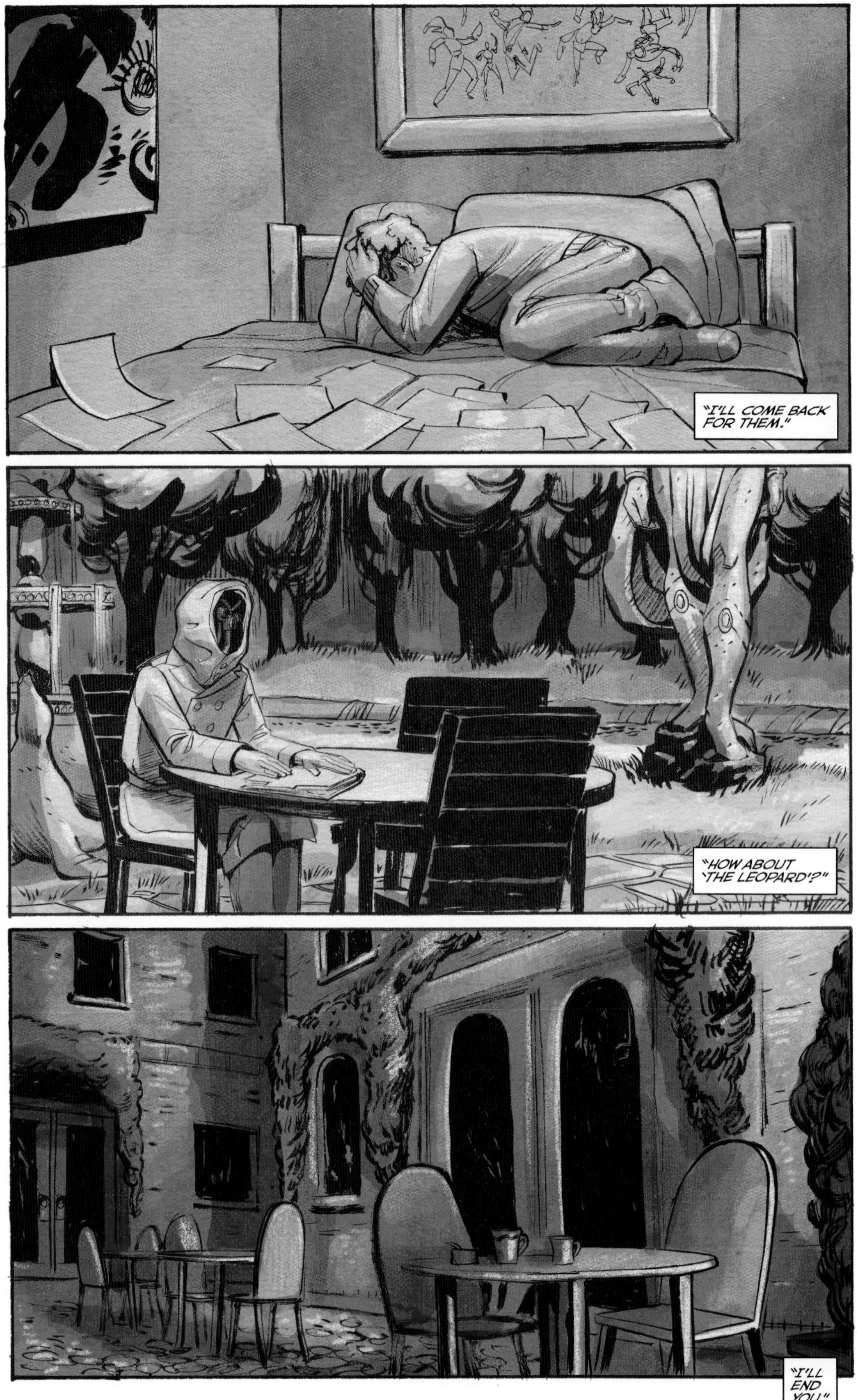
"I'LL COME BACK FOR THEM."
"HOW ABOUT 'THE LEOPARD'?"
"I'LL END YOU."

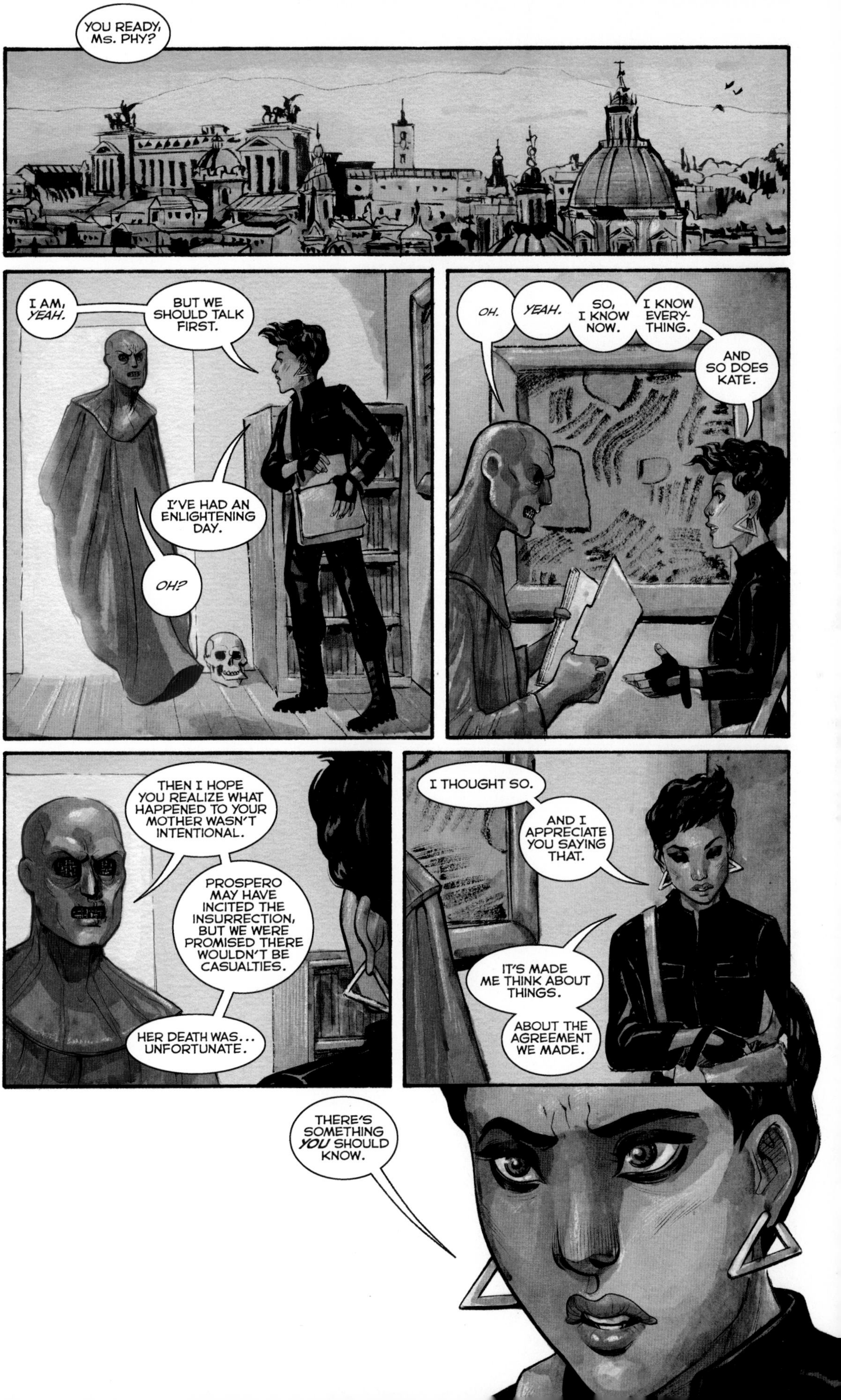

YOU READY, Ms. PHY?
I AM, *YEAH.*
BUT WE SHOULD TALK FIRST.
I'VE HAD AN ENLIGHTENING DAY.
OH?
OH.
YEAH.
SO, I KNOW NOW.
I KNOW EVERY- THING.
AND SO DOES KATE.
THEN I HOPE YOU REALIZE WHAT HAPPENED TO YOUR MOTHER WASN'T INTENTIONAL.
PROSPERO MAY HAVE INCITED THE INSURRECTION, BUT WE WERE PROMISED THERE WOULDN'T BE CASUALTIES.
HER DEATH WAS... UNFORTUNATE.
I THOUGHT SO.
AND I APPRECIATE YOU SAYING THAT.
IT'S MADE ME THINK ABOUT THINGS.
ABOUT THE AGREEMENT WE MADE.
THERE'S SOMETHING *YOU* SHOULD KNOW.

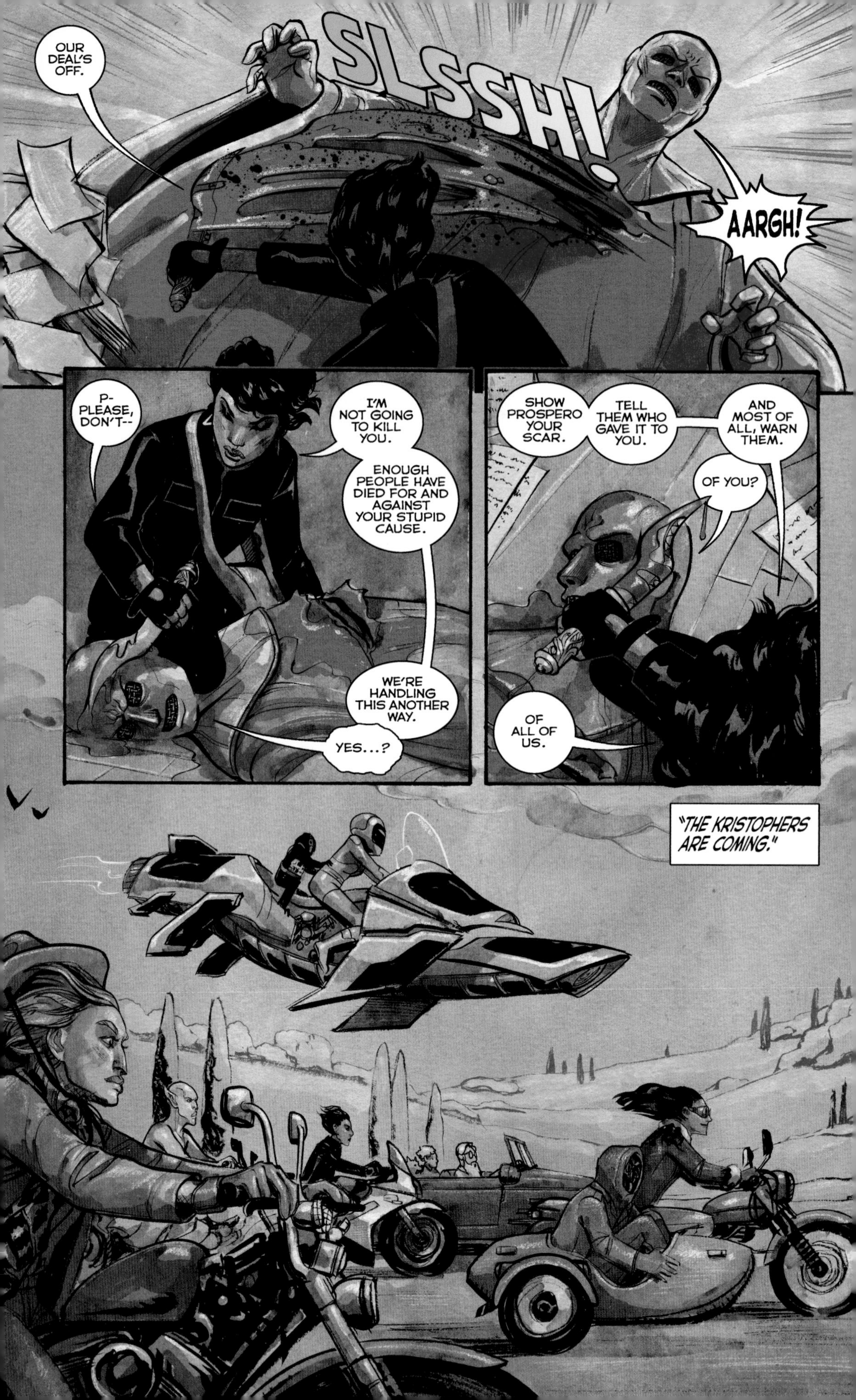
OUR DEAL'S OFF.
SLSSH!
AARGH!
P-PLEASE, DON'T--
I'M NOT GOING TO KILL YOU.
ENOUGH PEOPLE HAVE DIED FOR AND AGAINST YOUR STUPID CAUSE.
WE'RE HANDLING THIS ANOTHER WAY.
YES...?
SHOW PROSPERO YOUR SCAR.
TELL THEM WHO GAVE IT TO YOU.
AND MOST OF ALL, WARN THEM.
OF YOU?
OF ALL OF US.
"THE KRISTOPHERS ARE COMING."

CHAPTER

20

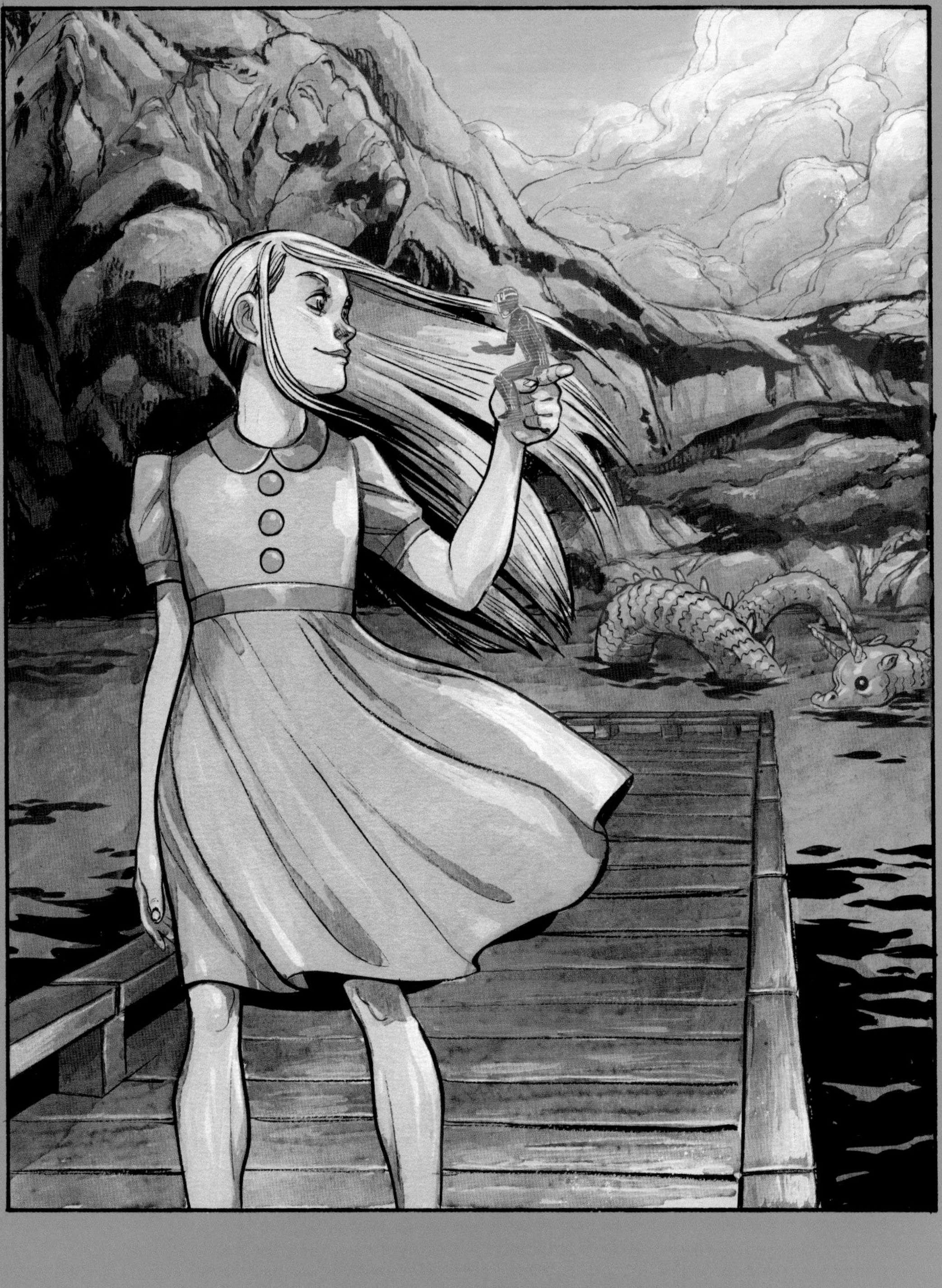

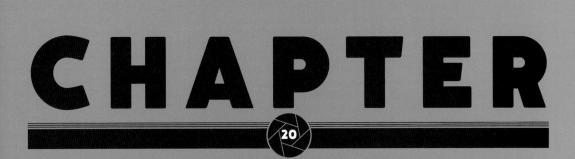

3. ACROSS

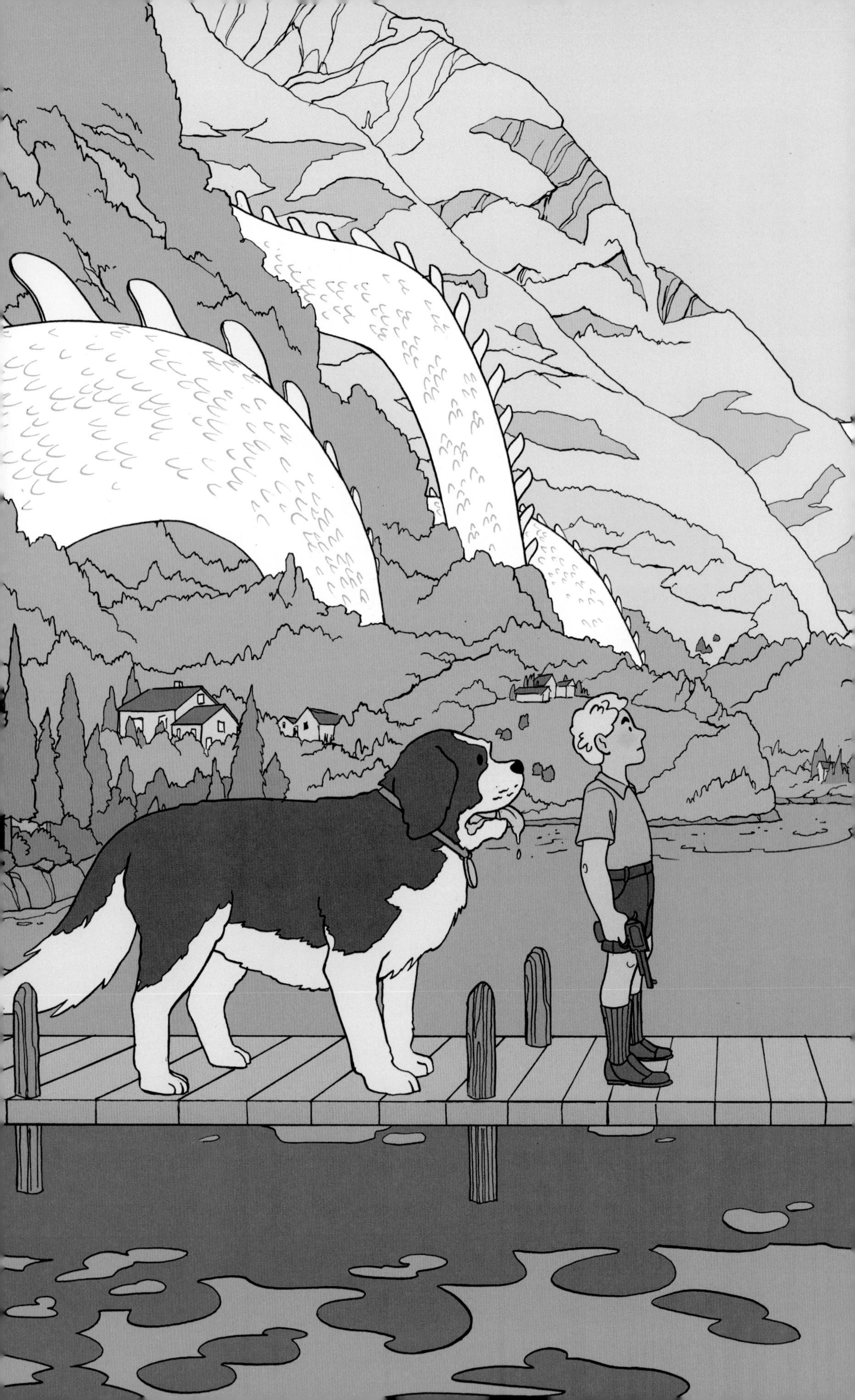

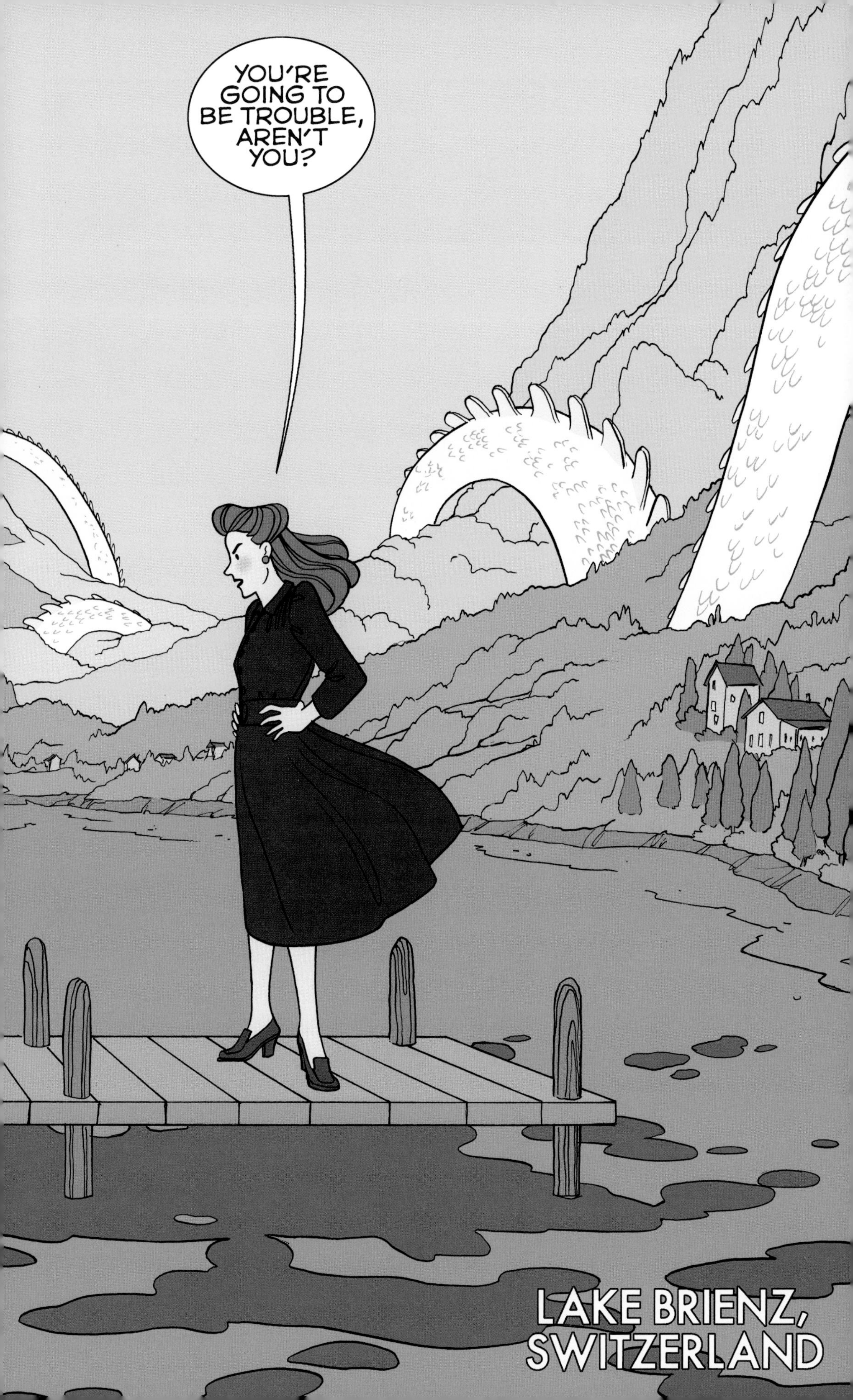
YOU'RE GOING TO BE TROUBLE, AREN'T YOU?
LAKE BRIENZ, SWITZERLAND

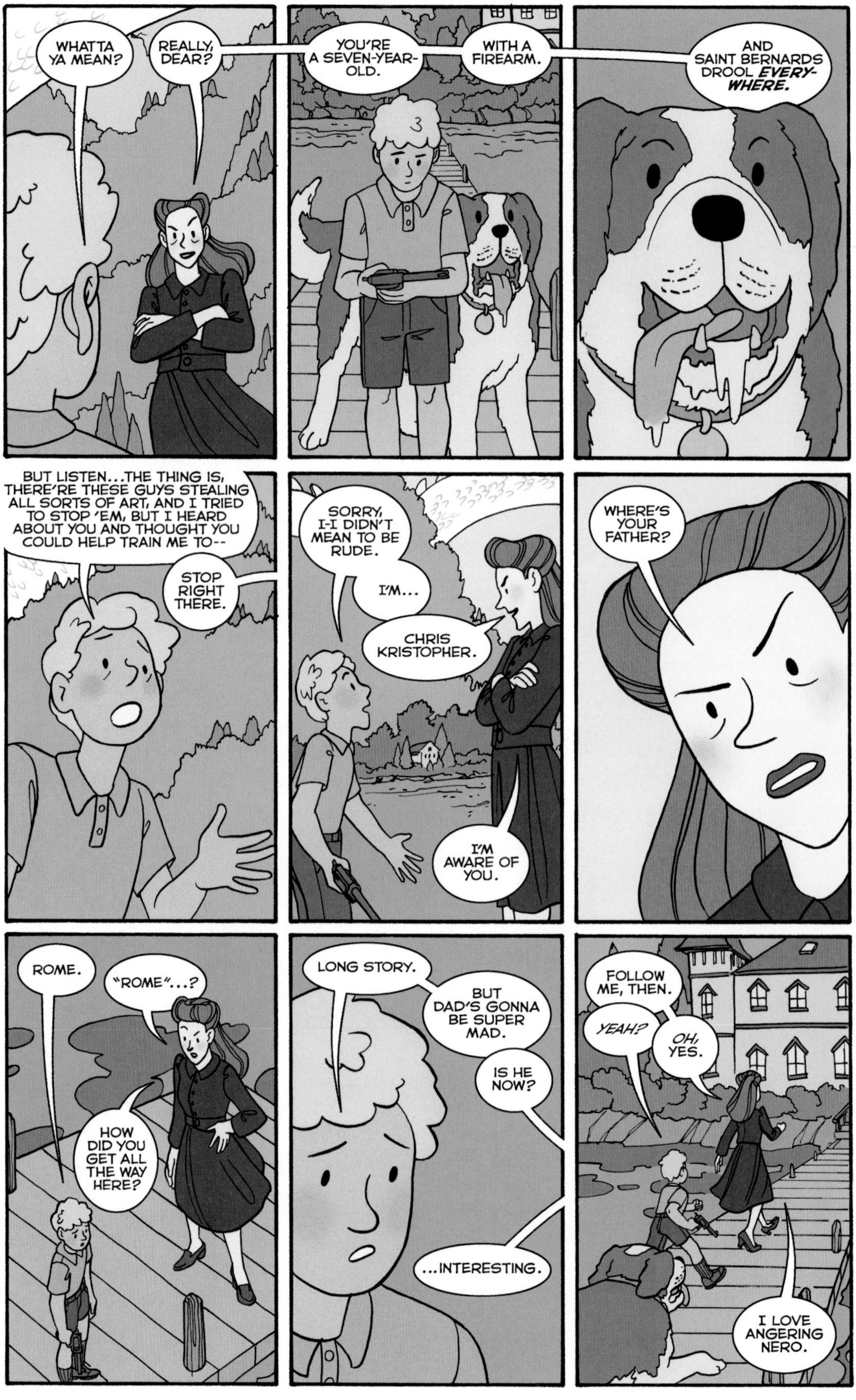
WHATTA YA MEAN?
REALLY, DEAR?
YOU'RE A SEVEN-YEAR-OLD.
WITH A FIREARM.
AND SAINT BERNARDS DROOL *EVERY-WHERE.*
BUT LISTEN...THE THING IS, THERE'RE THESE GUYS STEALING ALL SORTS OF ART, AND I TRIED TO STOP 'EM, BUT I HEARD ABOUT YOU AND THOUGHT YOU COULD HELP TRAIN ME TO--
STOP RIGHT THERE.
SORRY, I-I DIDN'T MEAN TO BE RUDE.
I'M...
CHRIS KRISTOPHER.
I'M AWARE OF YOU.
WHERE'S YOUR FATHER?
ROME.
"ROME"...?
HOW DID YOU GET ALL THE WAY HERE?
LONG STORY.
BUT DAD'S GONNA BE SUPER MAD.
IS HE NOW?
...INTERESTING.
FOLLOW ME, THEN.
YEAH?
OH, YES.
I LOVE ANGERING NERO.

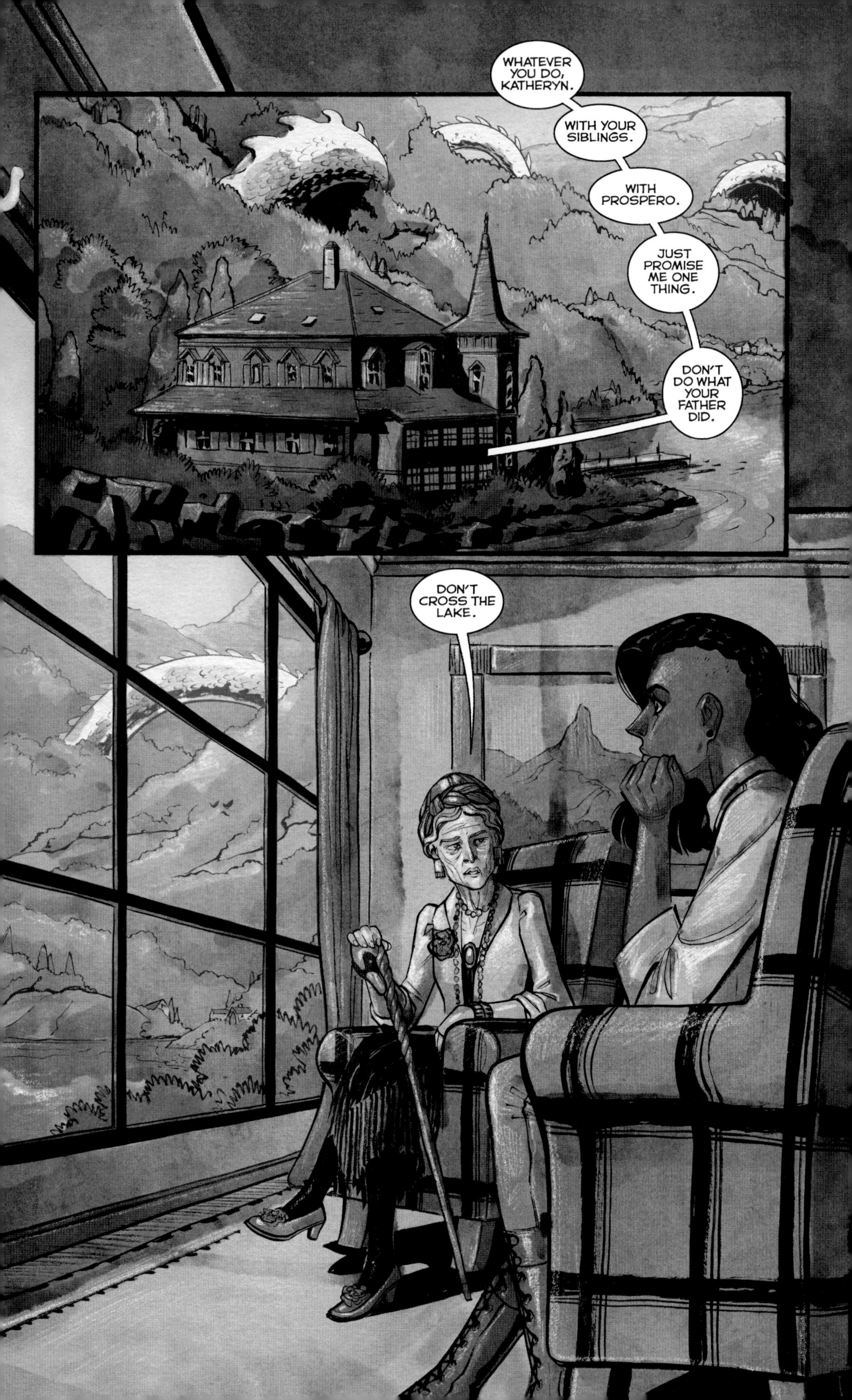
WHATEVER YOU DO, KATHERYN.
WITH YOUR SIBLINGS.
WITH PROSPERO.
JUST PROMISE ME ONE THING.
DON'T DO WHAT YOUR FATHER DID.
DON'T CROSS THE LAKE.

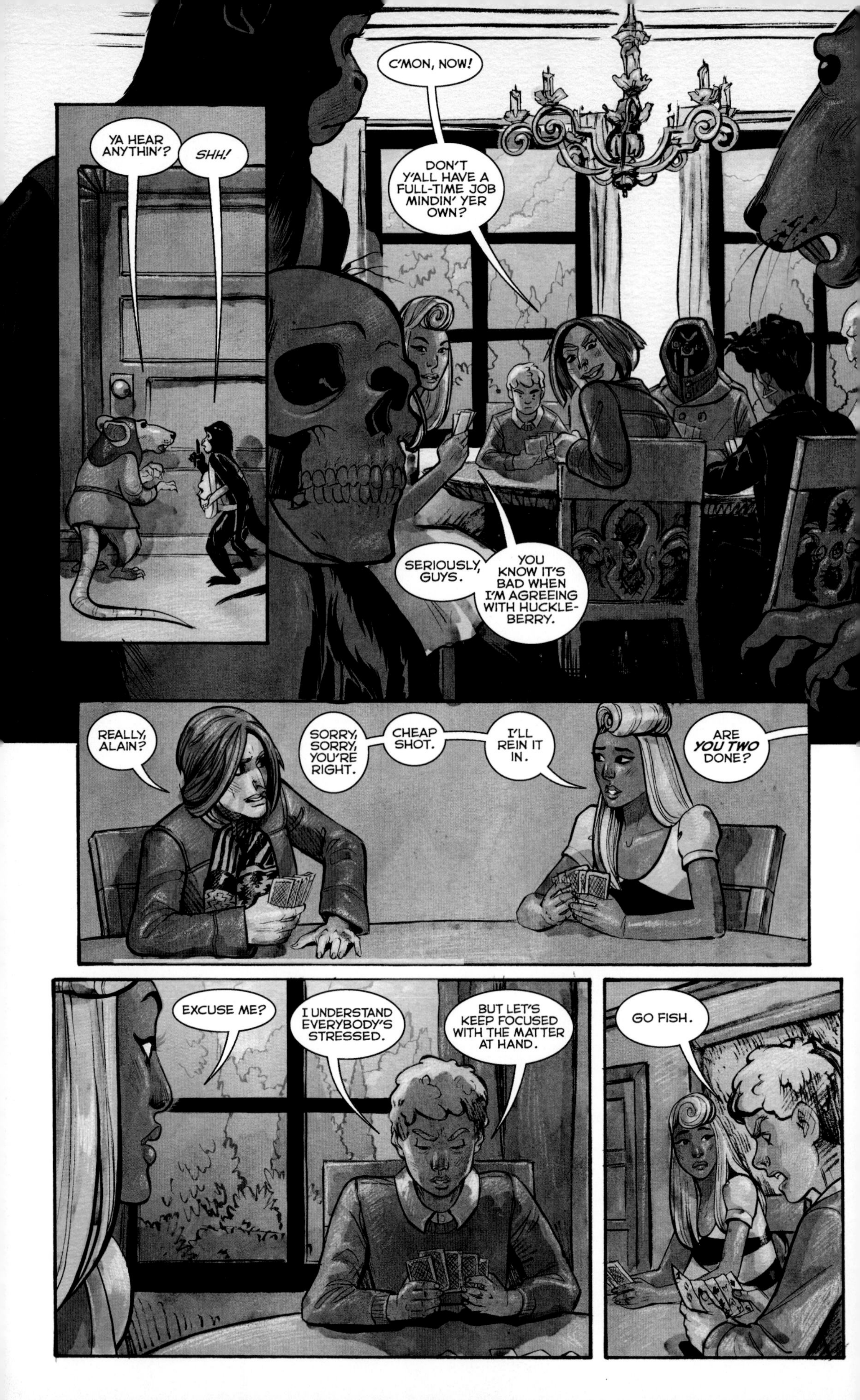
C'MON, NOW!
DON'T Y'ALL HAVE A FULL-TIME JOB MINDIN' YER OWN?
YA HEAR ANYTHIN'?
SHH!
SERIOUSLY, GUYS.
YOU KNOW IT'S BAD WHEN I'M AGREEING WITH HUCKLEBERRY.
REALLY, ALAIN?
SORRY, SORRY, YOU'RE RIGHT.
CHEAP SHOT.
I'LL REIN IT IN.
ARE YOU TWO DONE?
EXCUSE ME?
I UNDERSTAND EVERYBODY'S STRESSED.
BUT LET'S KEEP FOCUSED WITH THE MATTER AT HAND.
GO FISH.

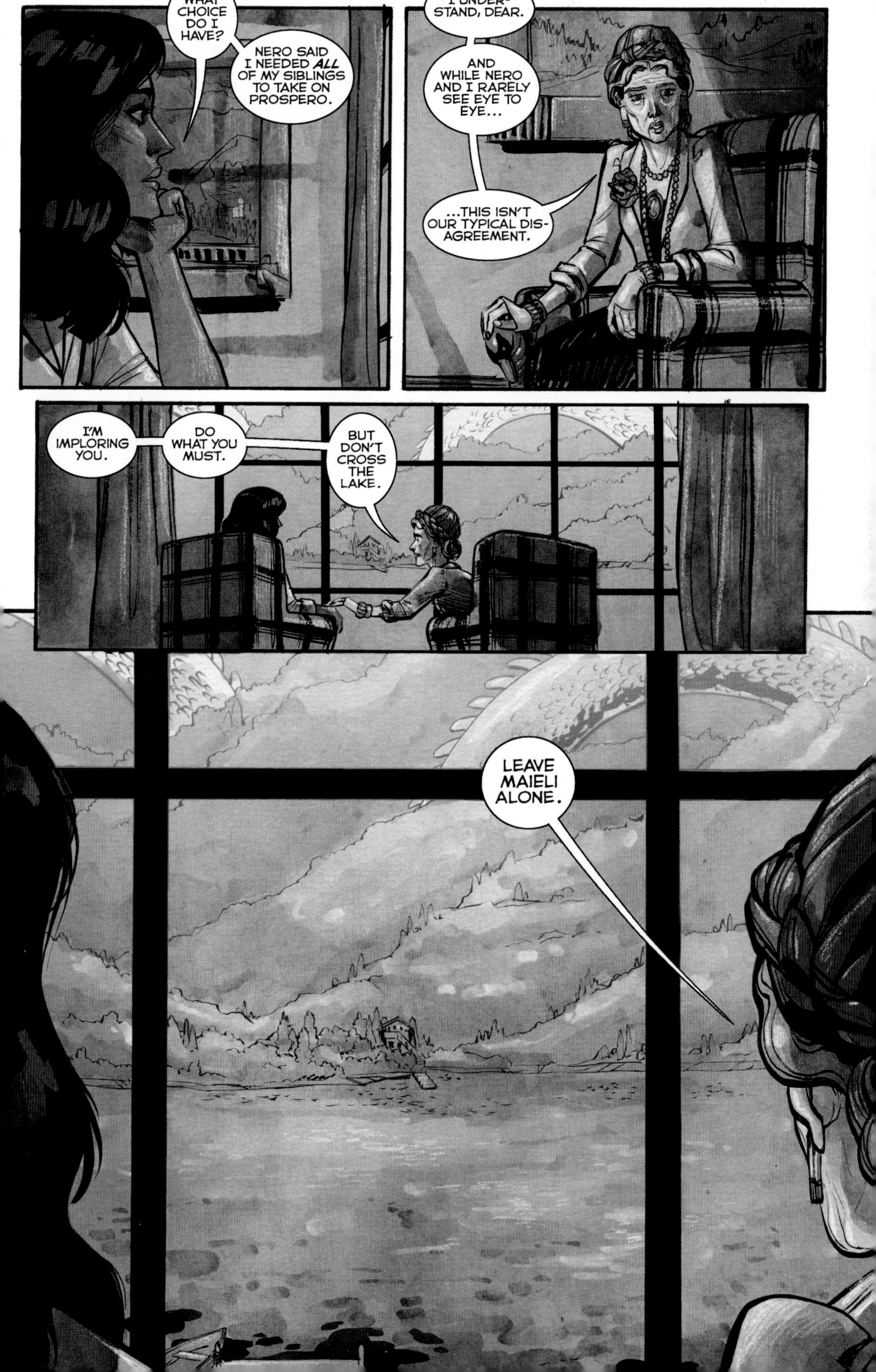
WHAT CHOICE DO I HAVE?
NERO SAID I NEEDED ALL OF MY SIBLINGS TO TAKE ON PROSPERO.
I UNDER-STAND, DEAR.
AND WHILE NERO AND I RARELY SEE EYE TO EYE...
...THIS ISN'T OUR TYPICAL DIS-AGREEMENT.
I'M IMPLORING YOU.
DO WHAT YOU MUST.
BUT DON'T CROSS THE LAKE.
LEAVE MAIELI ALONE.

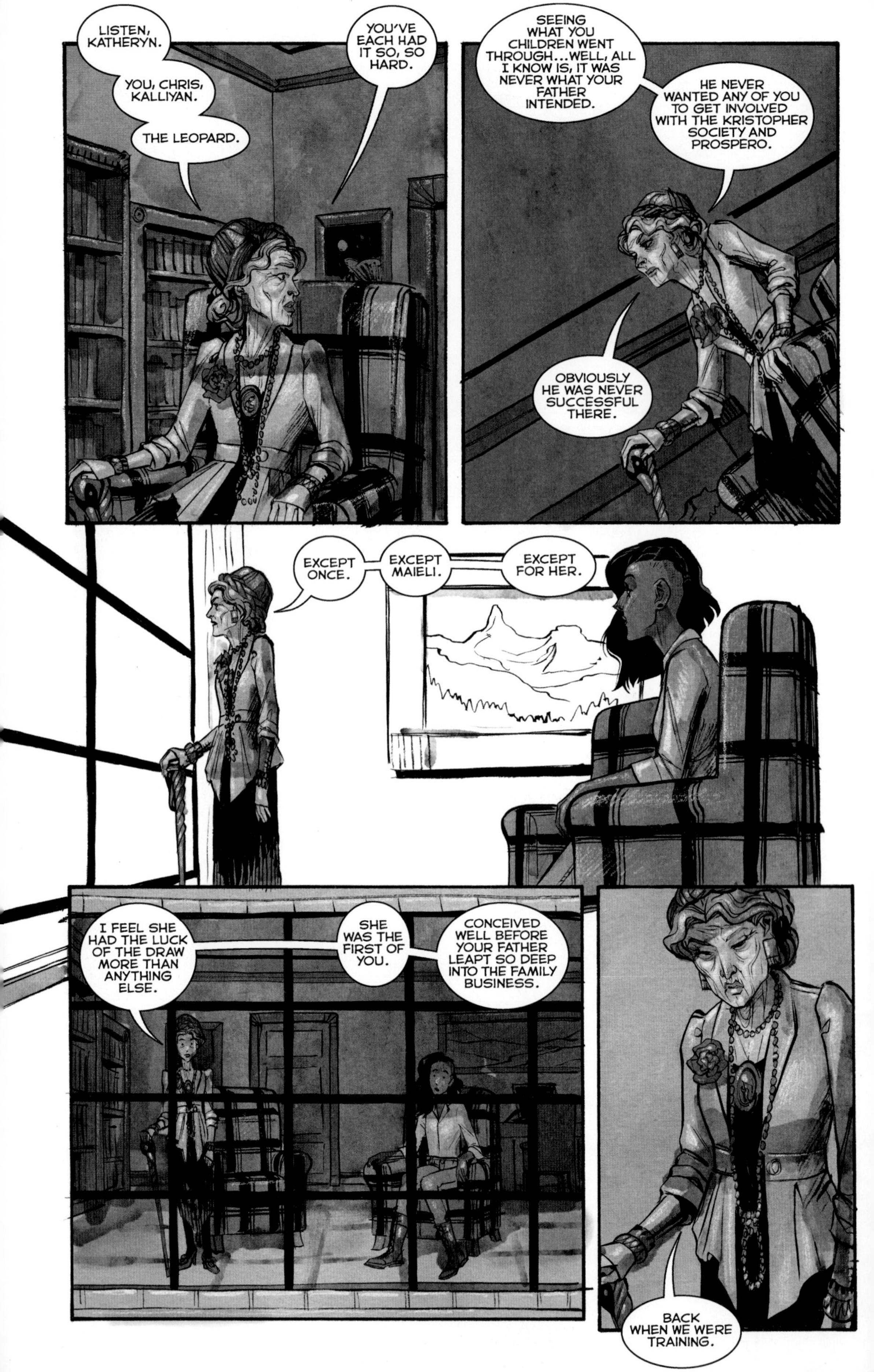
LISTEN, KATHERYN.
YOU, CHRIS, KALLIYAN.
THE LEOPARD.
YOU'VE EACH HAD IT SO, SO HARD.
SEEING WHAT YOU CHILDREN WENT THROUGH...WELL, ALL I KNOW IS, IT WAS NEVER WHAT YOUR FATHER INTENDED.
HE NEVER WANTED ANY OF YOU TO GET INVOLVED WITH THE KRISTOPHER SOCIETY AND PROSPERO.
OBVIOUSLY HE WAS NEVER SUCCESSFUL THERE.
EXCEPT ONCE.
EXCEPT MAIELI.
EXCEPT FOR HER.
I FEEL SHE HAD THE LUCK OF THE DRAW MORE THAN ANYTHING ELSE.
SHE WAS THE FIRST OF YOU.
CONCEIVED WELL BEFORE YOUR FATHER LEAPT SO DEEP INTO THE FAMILY BUSINESS.
BACK WHEN WE WERE TRAINING.

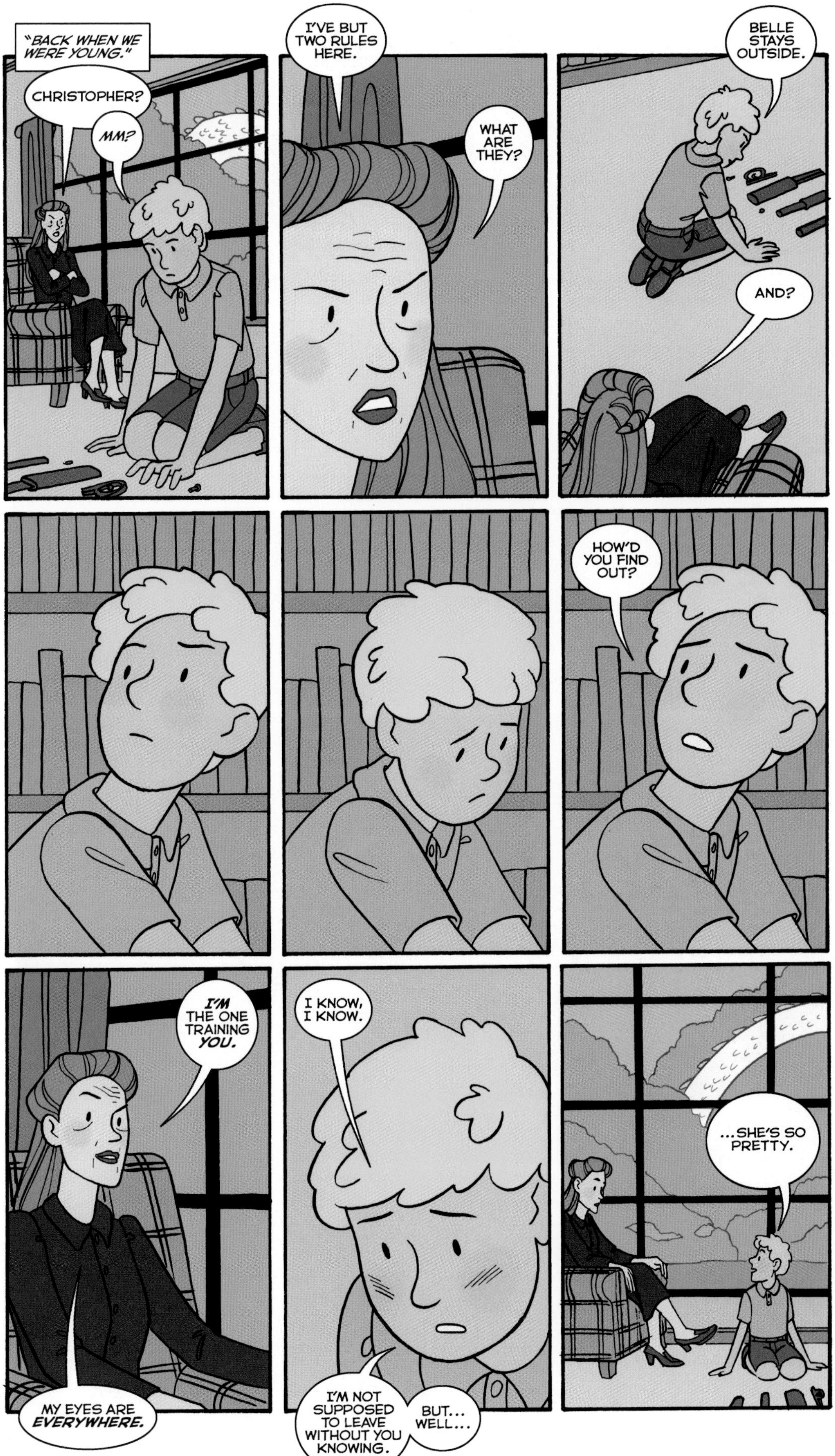
"BACK WHEN WE WERE YOUNG."
CHRISTOPHER?
MM?
I'VE BUT TWO RULES HERE.
WHAT ARE THEY?
BELLE STAYS OUTSIDE.
AND?
HOW'D YOU FIND OUT?
I'M THE ONE TRAINING YOU.
MY EYES ARE EVERYWHERE.
I KNOW, I KNOW.
I'M NOT SUPPOSED TO LEAVE WITHOUT YOU KNOWING.
BUT... WELL...
...SHE'S SO PRETTY.

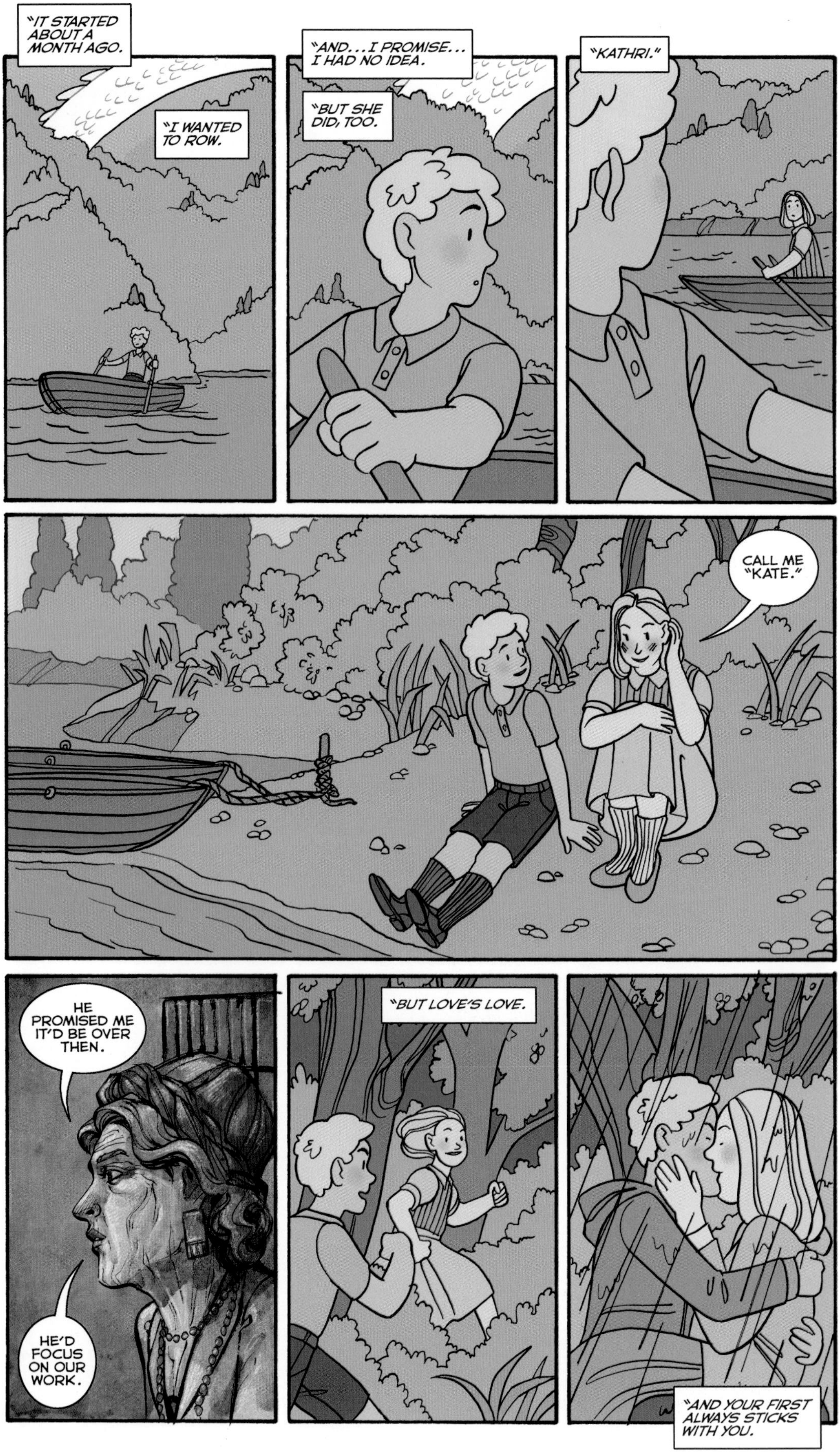
"IT STARTED ABOUT A MONTH AGO.
"I WANTED TO ROW.
"AND... I PROMISE... I HAD NO IDEA.
"BUT SHE DID, TOO.
"KATHRI."
CALL ME "KATE."
HE PROMISED ME IT'D BE OVER THEN.
HE'D FOCUS ON OUR WORK.
"BUT LOVE'S LOVE.
"AND YOUR FIRST ALWAYS STICKS WITH YOU.

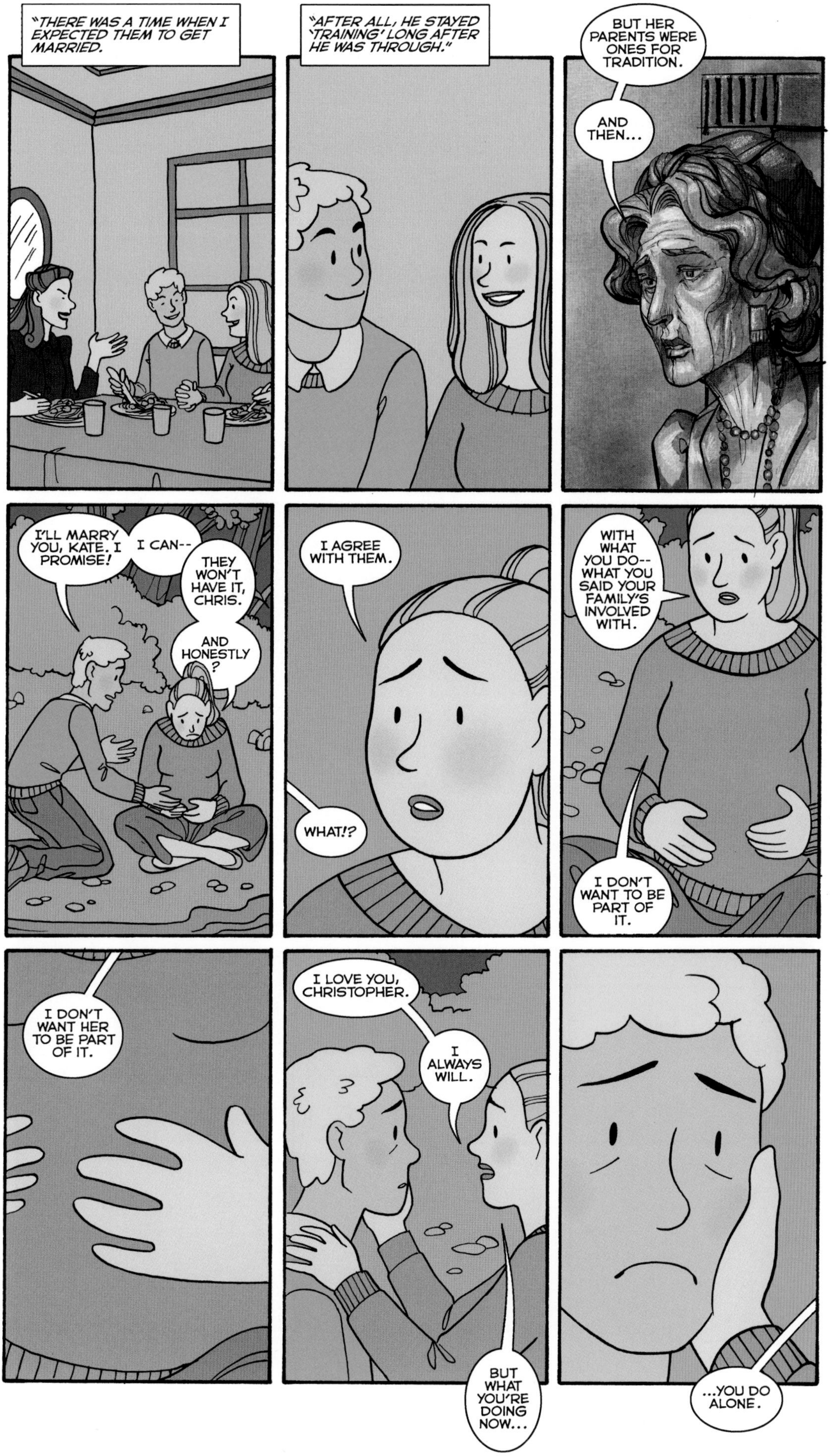
"THERE WAS A TIME WHEN I EXPECTED THEM TO GET MARRIED.
"AFTER ALL, HE STAYED 'TRAINING' LONG AFTER HE WAS THROUGH."
BUT HER PARENTS WERE ONES FOR TRADITION.
AND THEN...
I'LL MARRY YOU, KATE. I PROMISE!
I CAN--
THEY WON'T HAVE IT, CHRIS.
AND HONESTLY?
I AGREE WITH THEM.
WHAT!?
WITH WHAT YOU DO-- WHAT YOU SAID YOUR FAMILY'S INVOLVED WITH.
I DON'T WANT TO BE PART OF IT.
I DON'T WANT HER TO BE PART OF IT.
I LOVE YOU, CHRISTOPHER.
I ALWAYS WILL.
BUT WHAT YOU'RE DOING NOW...
...YOU DO ALONE.

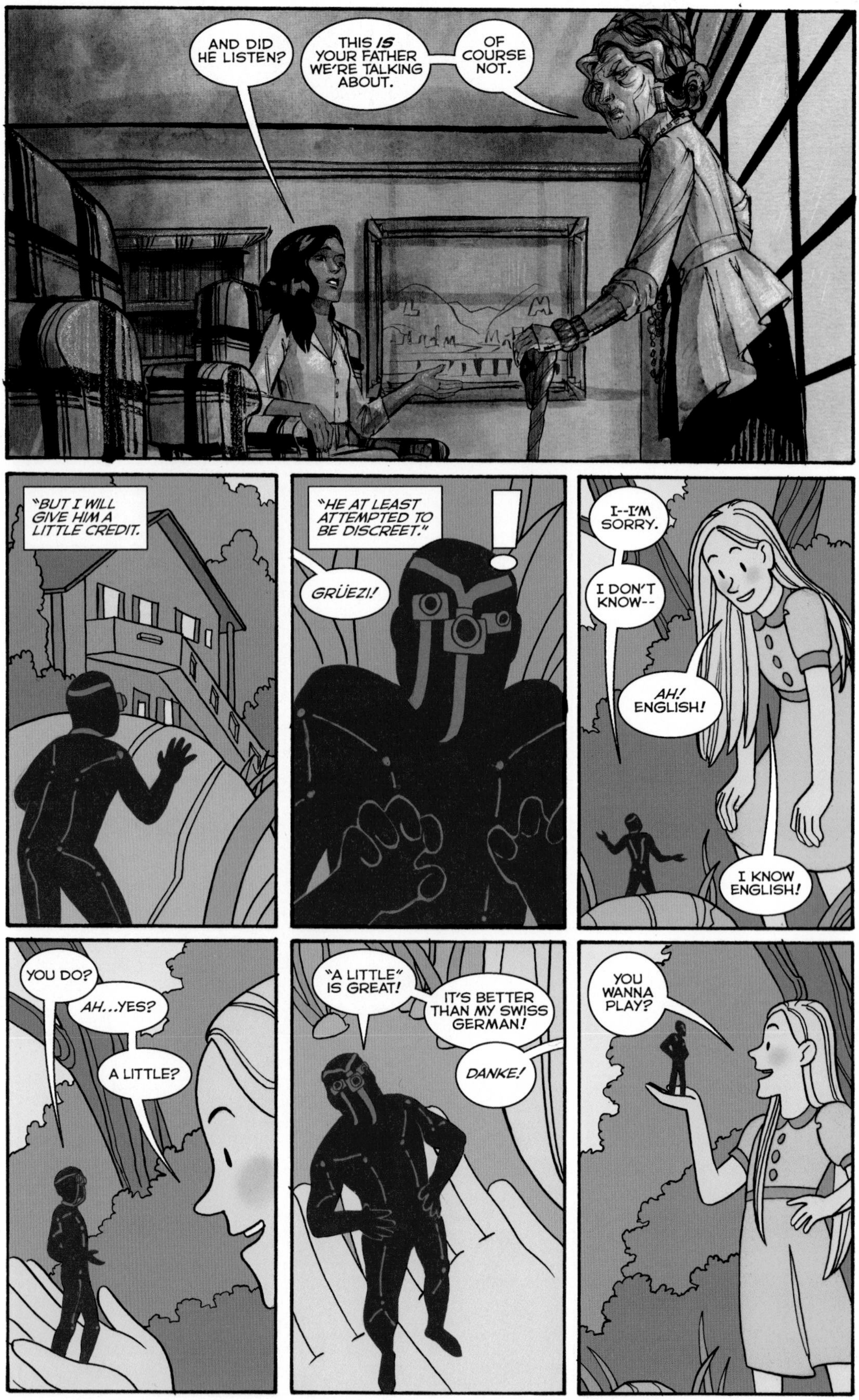
AND DID HE LISTEN?
THIS *IS* YOUR FATHER WE'RE TALKING ABOUT.
OF COURSE NOT.
"BUT I WILL GIVE HIM A LITTLE CREDIT.
"HE AT LEAST ATTEMPTED TO BE DISCREET."
GRÜEZI!
!
I--I'M SORRY.
I DON'T KNOW--
AH! ENGLISH!
I KNOW ENGLISH!
YOU DO?
AH...YES?
A LITTLE?
"A LITTLE" IS GREAT!
IT'S BETTER THAN MY SWISS GERMAN!
DANKE!
YOU WANNA PLAY?

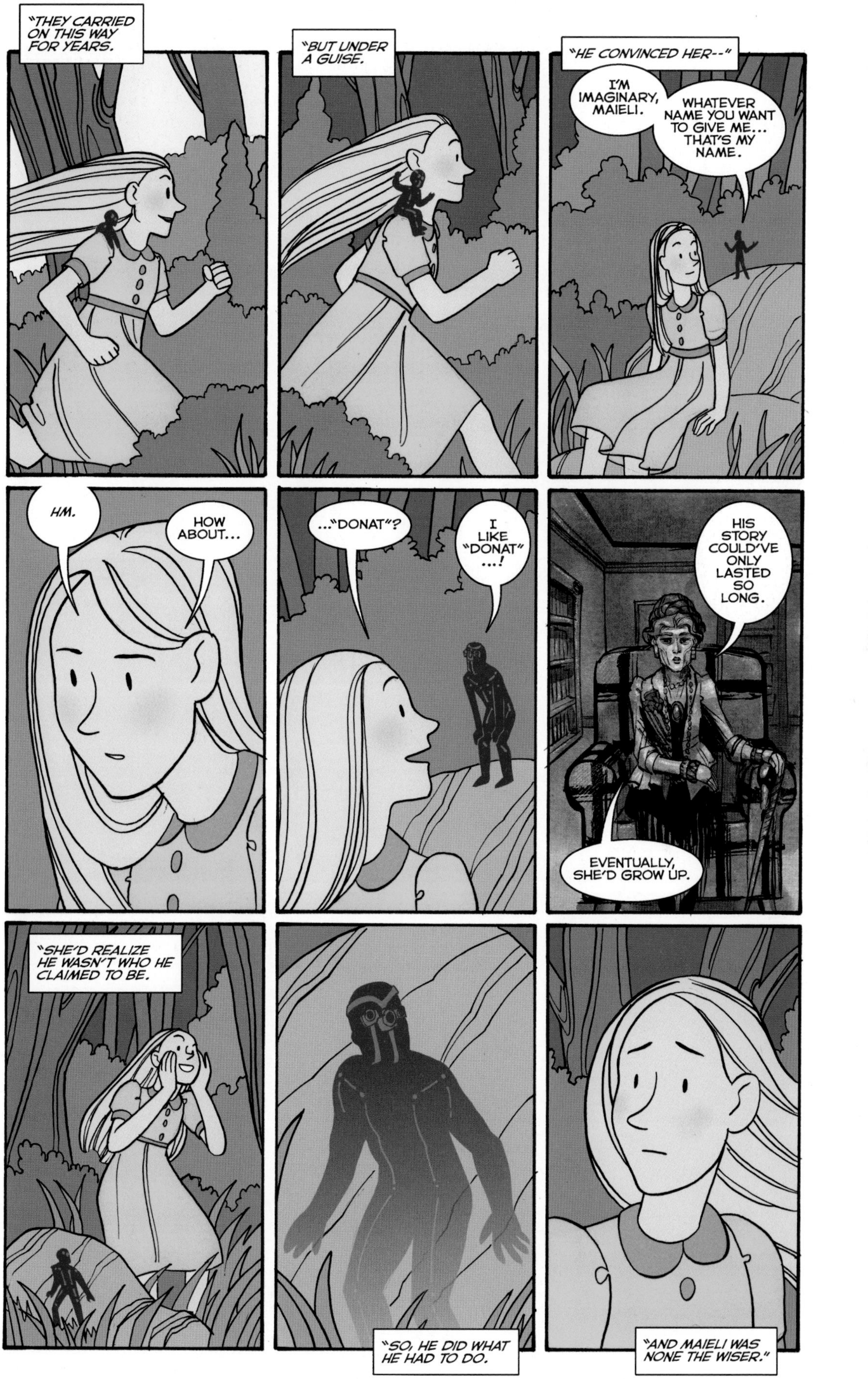
"THEY CARRIED ON THIS WAY FOR YEARS.
"BUT UNDER A GUISE.
"HE CONVINCED HER--"
I'M IMAGINARY, MAIELI.
WHATEVER NAME YOU WANT TO GIVE ME... THAT'S MY NAME.
HM.
HOW ABOUT...
..."DONAT"?
I LIKE "DONAT" ...!
HIS STORY COULD'VE ONLY LASTED SO LONG.
EVENTUALLY, SHE'D GROW UP.
"SHE'D REALIZE HE WASN'T WHO HE CLAIMED TO BE.
"SO, HE DID WHAT HE HAD TO DO.
"AND MAIELI WAS NONE THE WISER."

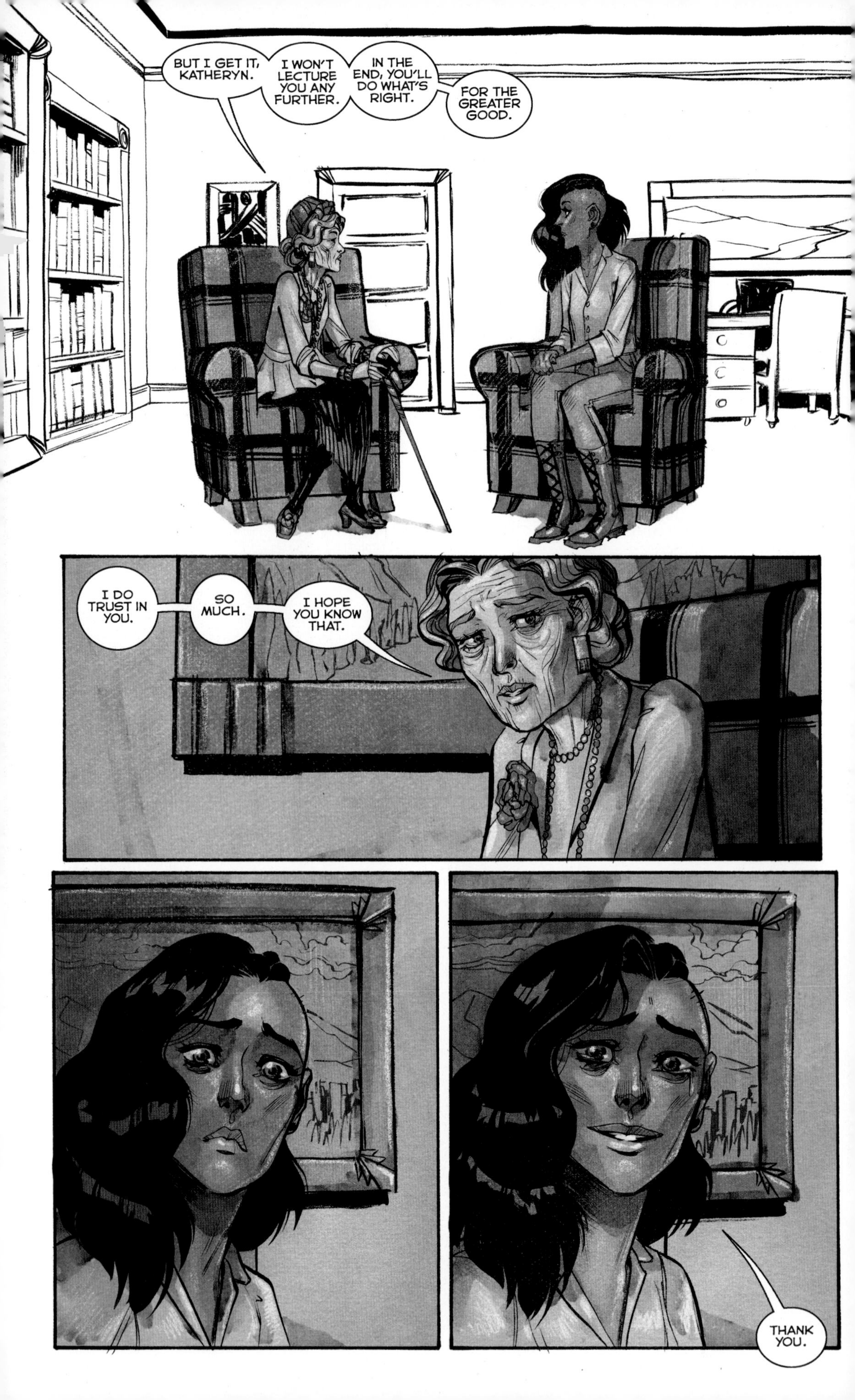

BUT I GET IT, KATHERYN.
I WON'T LECTURE YOU ANY FURTHER.
IN THE END, YOU'LL DO WHAT'S RIGHT.
FOR THE GREATER GOOD.
I DO TRUST IN YOU.
SO MUCH.
I HOPE YOU KNOW THAT.
THANK YOU.

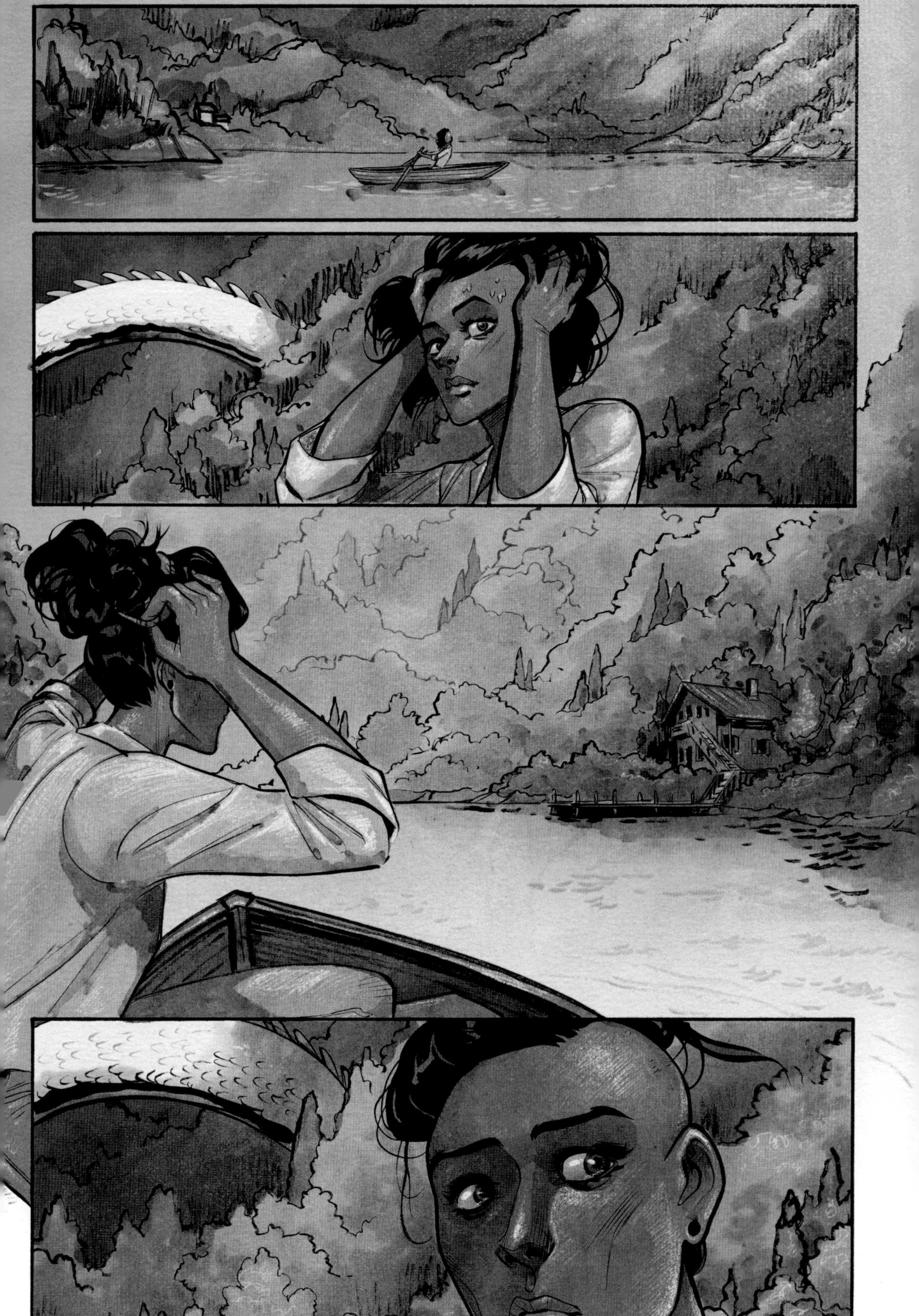

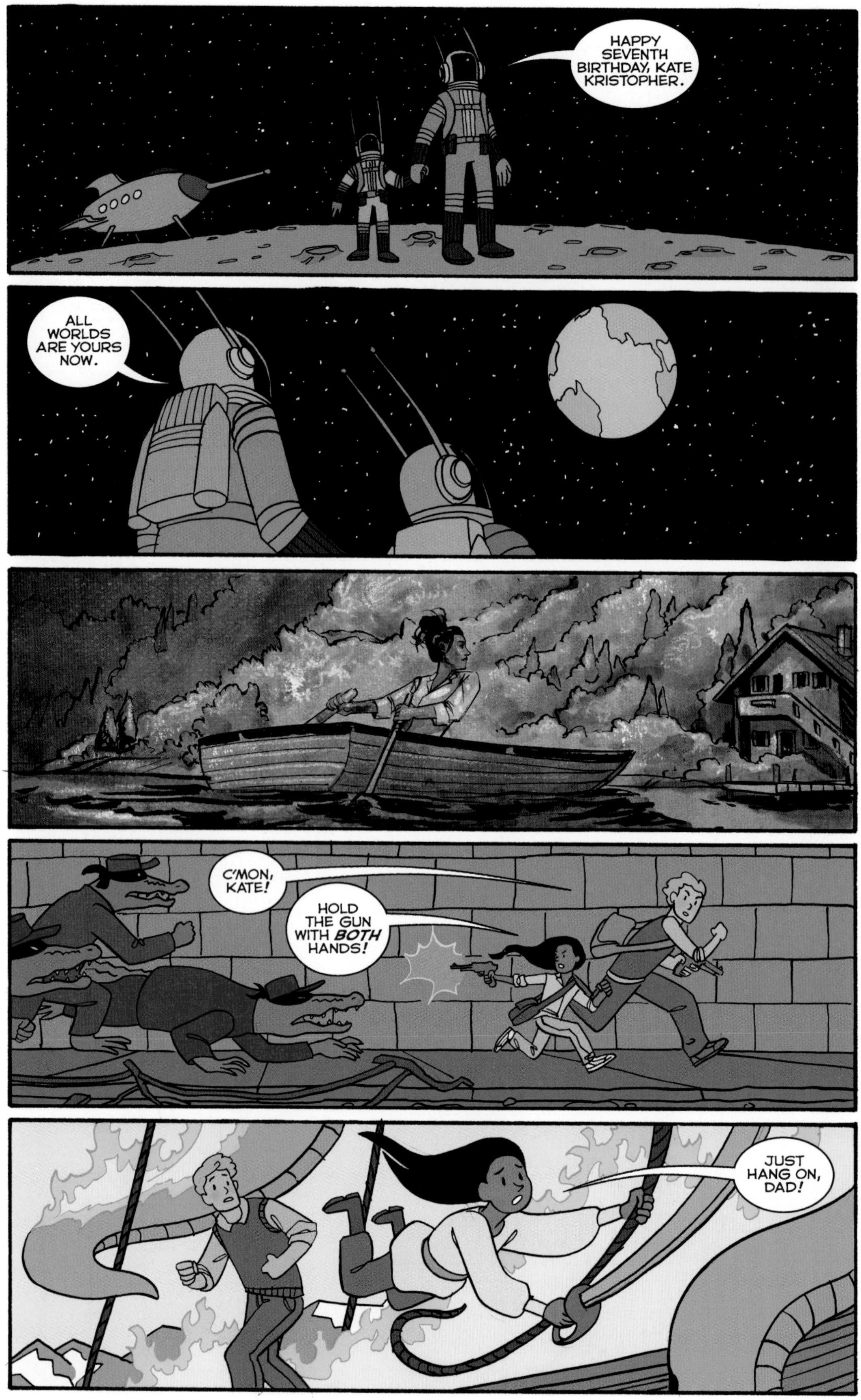
HAPPY SEVENTH BIRTHDAY, KATE KRISTOPHER.
ALL WORLDS ARE YOURS NOW.
C'MON, KATE!
HOLD THE GUN WITH BOTH HANDS!
JUST HANG ON, DAD!

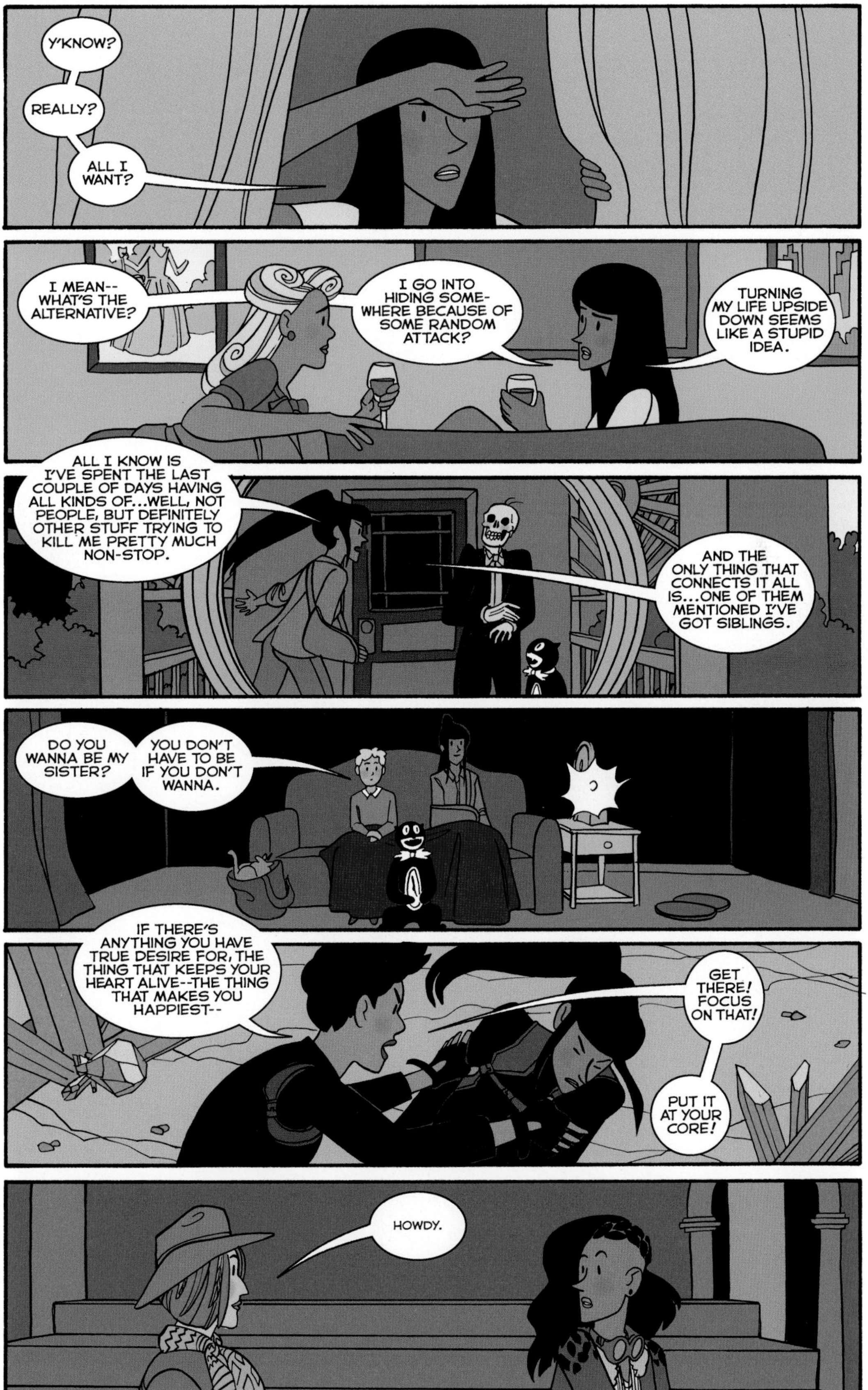
Y'KNOW?
REALLY?
ALL I WANT?
I MEAN--WHAT'S THE ALTERNATIVE?
I GO INTO HIDING SOME-WHERE BECAUSE OF SOME RANDOM ATTACK?
TURNING MY LIFE UPSIDE DOWN SEEMS LIKE A STUPID IDEA.
ALL I KNOW IS I'VE SPENT THE LAST COUPLE OF DAYS HAVING ALL KINDS OF...WELL, NOT PEOPLE, BUT DEFINITELY OTHER STUFF TRYING TO KILL ME PRETTY MUCH NON-STOP.
AND THE ONLY THING THAT CONNECTS IT ALL IS...ONE OF THEM MENTIONED I'VE GOT SIBLINGS.
DO YOU WANNA BE MY SISTER?
YOU DON'T HAVE TO BE IF YOU DON'T WANNA.
IF THERE'S ANYTHING YOU HAVE TRUE DESIRE FOR, THE THING THAT KEEPS YOUR HEART ALIVE--THE THING THAT MAKES YOU HAPPIEST--
GET THERE! FOCUS ON THAT!
PUT IT AT YOUR CORE!
HOWDY.

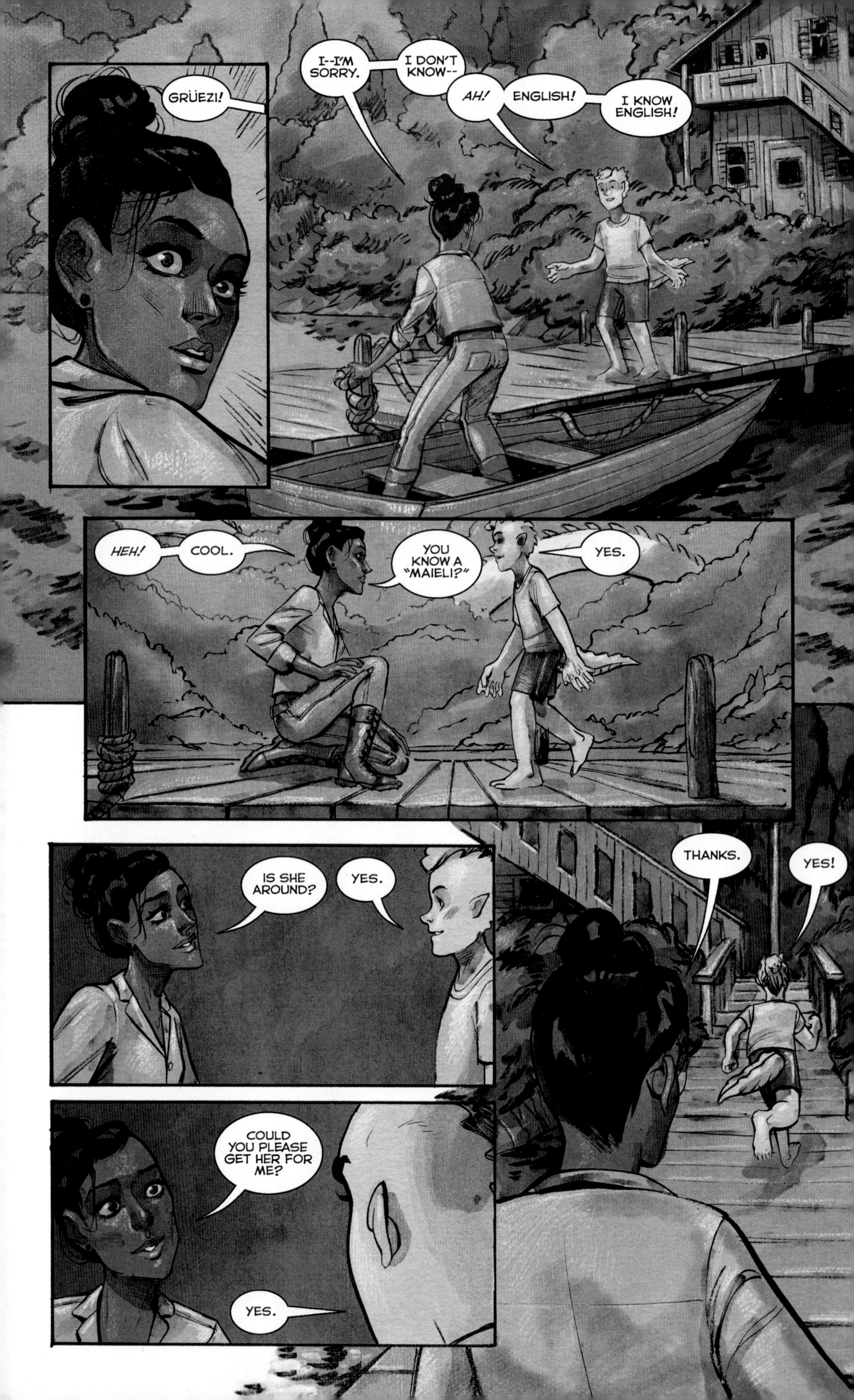
GRÜEZI!
I--I'M SORRY.
I DON'T KNOW--
AH!
ENGLISH!
I KNOW ENGLISH!
HEH!
COOL.
YOU KNOW A "MAIELI?"
YES.
IS SHE AROUND?
YES.
COULD YOU PLEASE GET HER FOR ME?
YES.
THANKS.
YES!

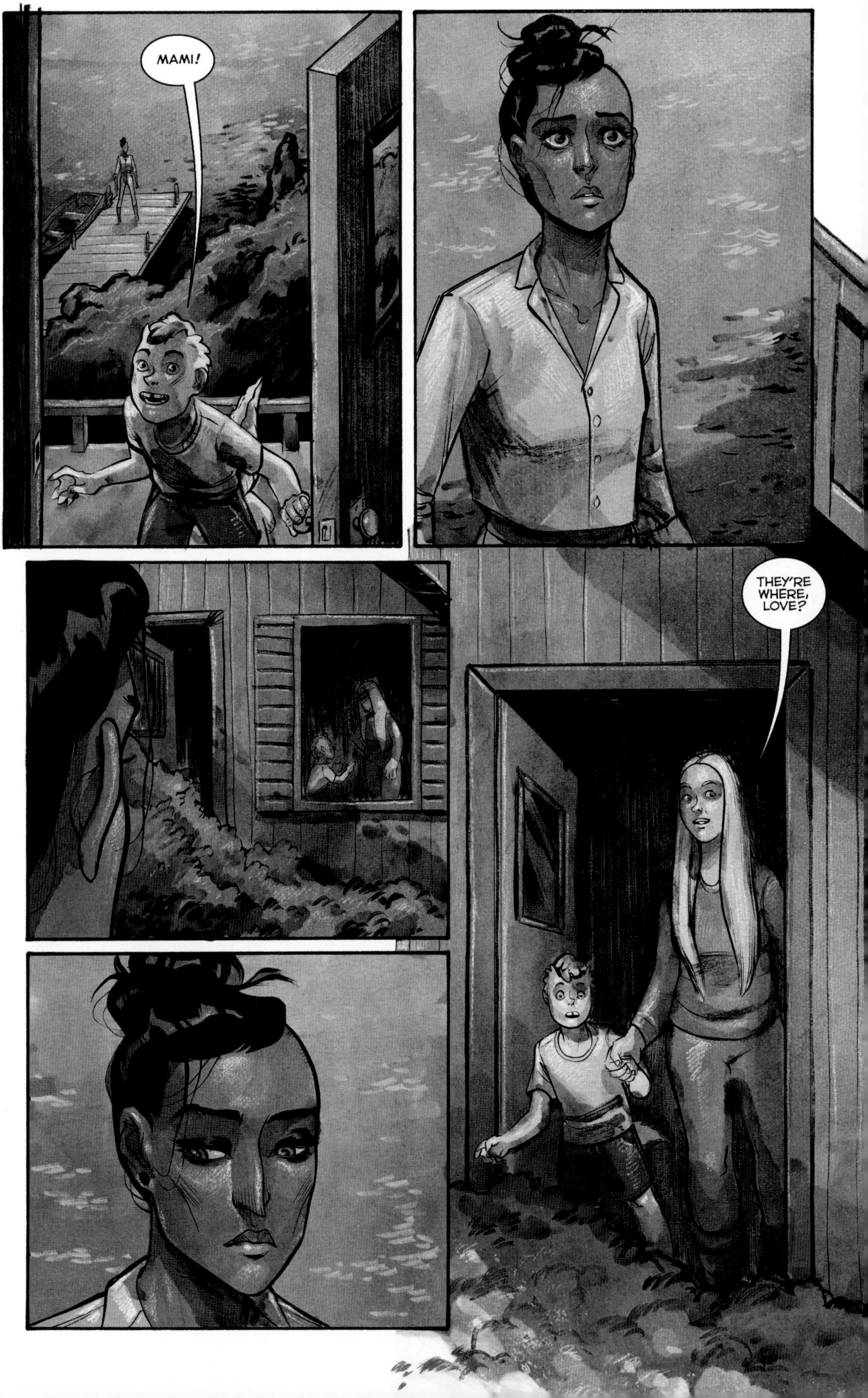
MAMI!
THEY'RE WHERE, LOVE?

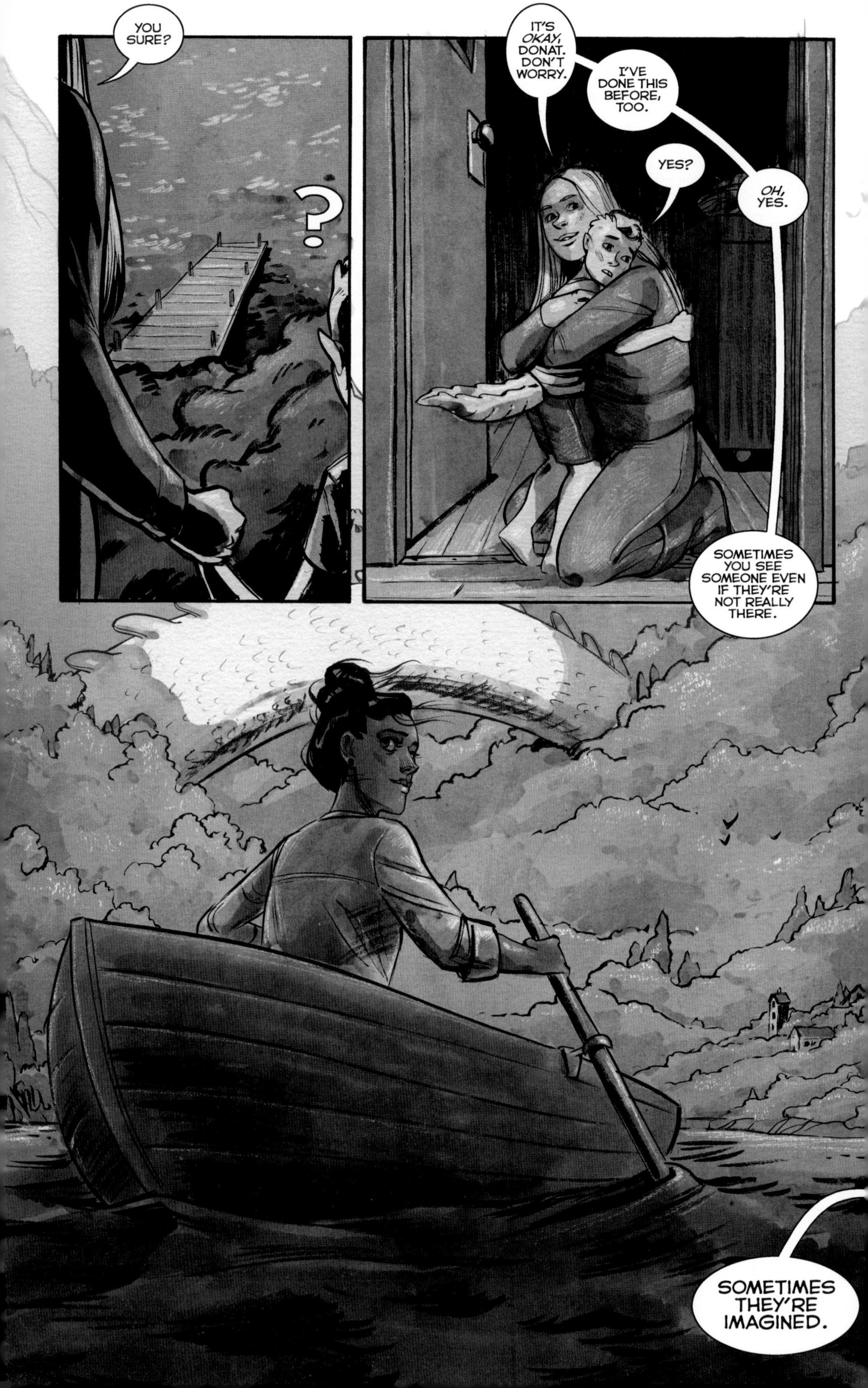
YOU SURE?
?
IT'S *OKAY*, DONAT. DON'T WORRY.
I'VE DONE THIS BEFORE, TOO.
YES?
OH, YES.
SOMETIMES YOU SEE SOMEONE EVEN IF THEY'RE NOT REALLY THERE.
SOMETIMES THEY'RE IMAGINED.

CHAPTER 21

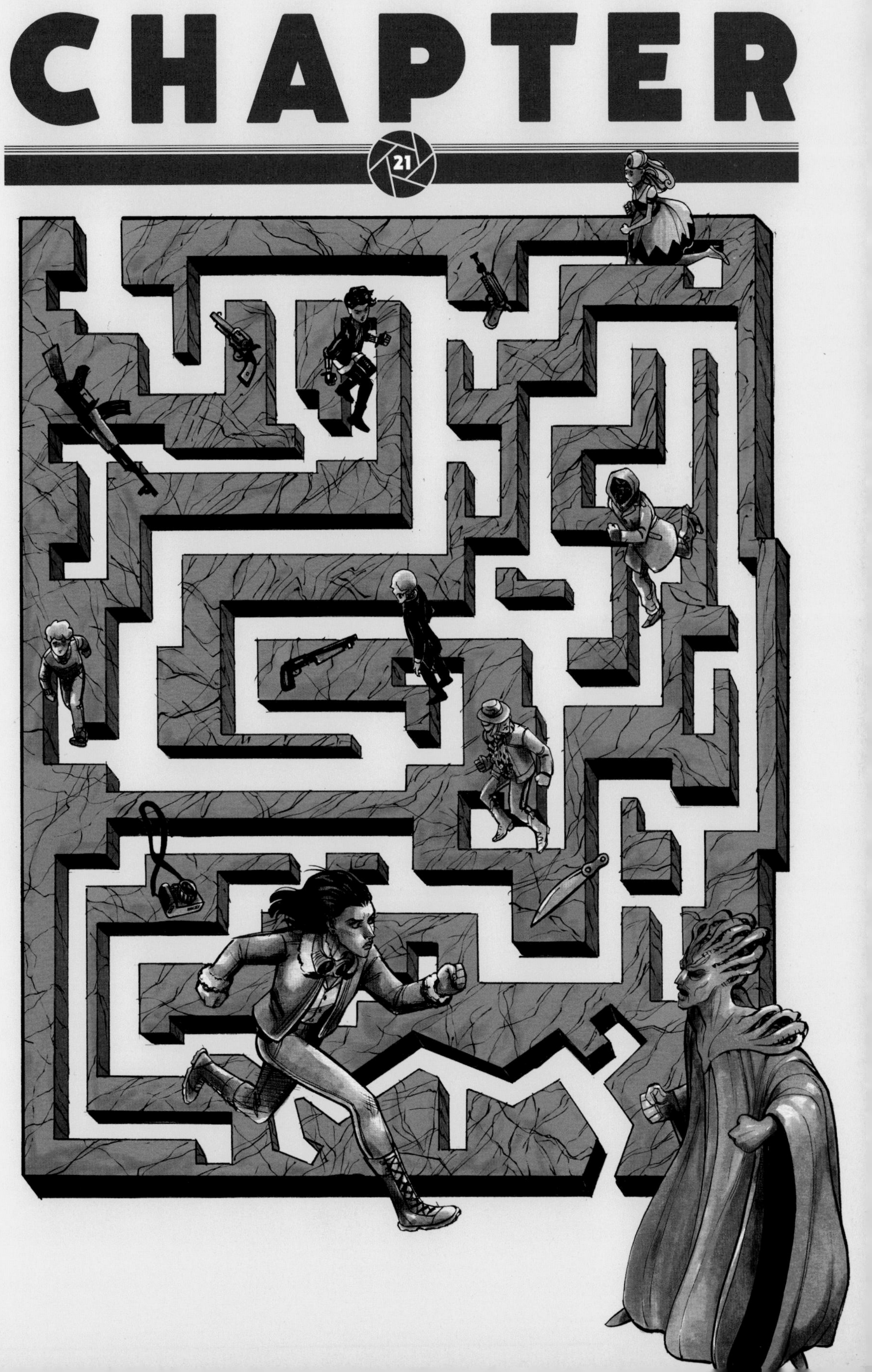

4. PAST IS PRESENT

WARNING
NAME
KRISTOPHER, CHRISTOPHER J.
BIRTH DATE
8 MAY 19[redacted]
HEIGHT
FEET
INCHES
WIFE
X X X
MINORS
X X X
BIRTHPLACE
NEW YORK, U.S.A
HAIR
BLOND
EYES
BLUE
ISSUE DATE
17 JANU[redacted]
EXPIRATION DATE
IMPORTANT: THIS PASSPORT IS NOT VALID UNTIL SIGNED BY THE BEARER
UNITED STATES OF AMERICA
PASSPORT

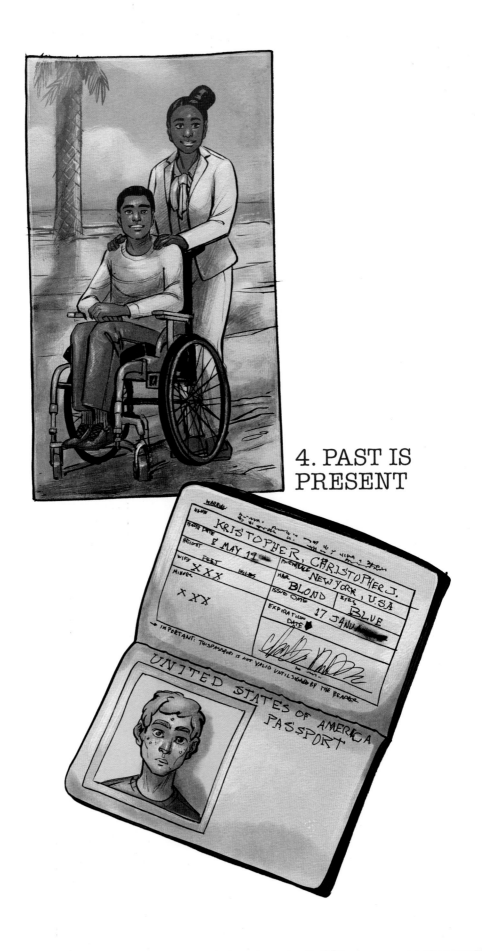

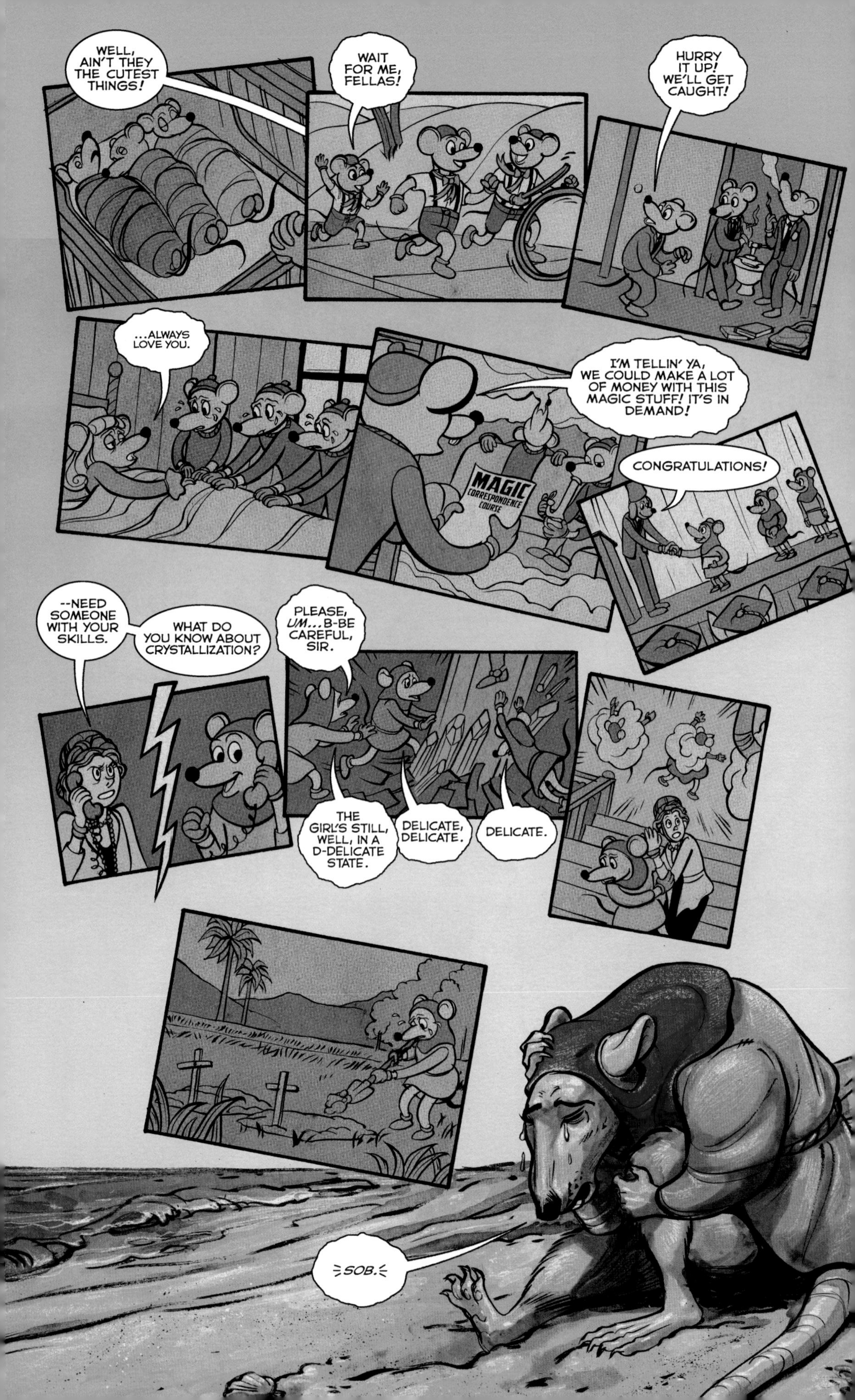
WELL, AIN'T THEY THE CUTEST THINGS!
WAIT FOR ME, FELLAS!
HURRY IT UP! WE'LL GET CAUGHT!
...ALWAYS LOVE YOU.
I'M TELLIN' YA, WE COULD MAKE A LOT OF MONEY WITH THIS MAGIC STUFF! IT'S IN DEMAND!
MAGIC CORRESPONDENCE COURSE
CONGRATULATIONS!
--NEED SOMEONE WITH YOUR SKILLS.
WHAT DO YOU KNOW ABOUT CRYSTALLIZATION?
PLEASE, UM... B-BE CAREFUL, SIR.
THE GIRL'S STILL, WELL, IN A D-DELICATE STATE.
DELICATE, DELICATE.
DELICATE.
SOB.

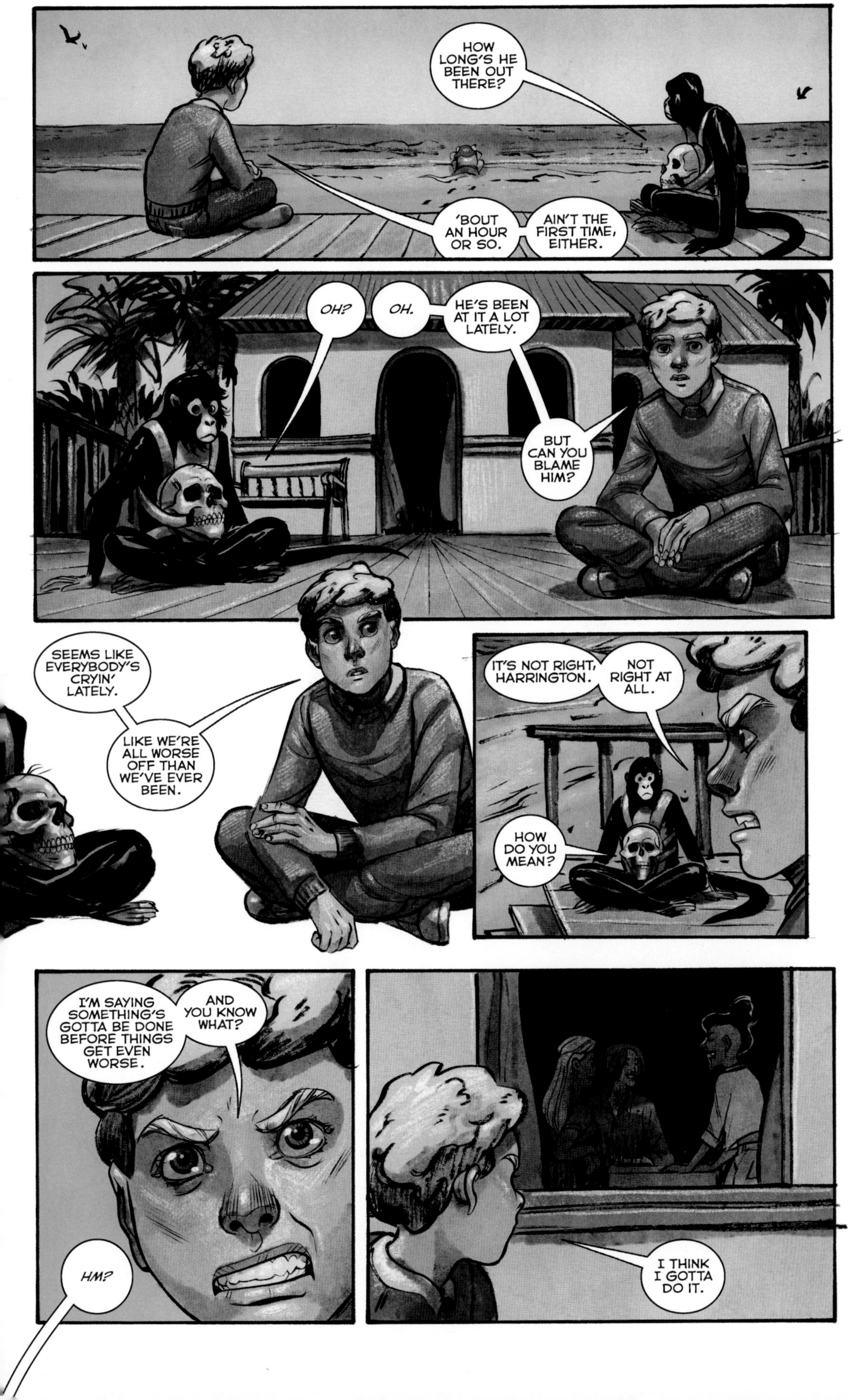
HOW LONG'S HE BEEN OUT THERE?
'BOUT AN HOUR OR SO.
AIN'T THE FIRST TIME, EITHER.
OH?
OH.
HE'S BEEN AT IT A LOT LATELY.
BUT CAN YOU BLAME HIM?
SEEMS LIKE EVERYBODY'S CRYIN' LATELY.
LIKE WE'RE ALL WORSE OFF THAN WE'VE EVER BEEN.
IT'S NOT RIGHT, HARRINGTON.
NOT RIGHT AT ALL.
HOW DO YOU MEAN?
I'M SAYING SOMETHING'S GOTTA BE DONE BEFORE THINGS GET EVEN WORSE.
AND YOU KNOW WHAT?
HM?
I THINK I GOTTA DO IT.

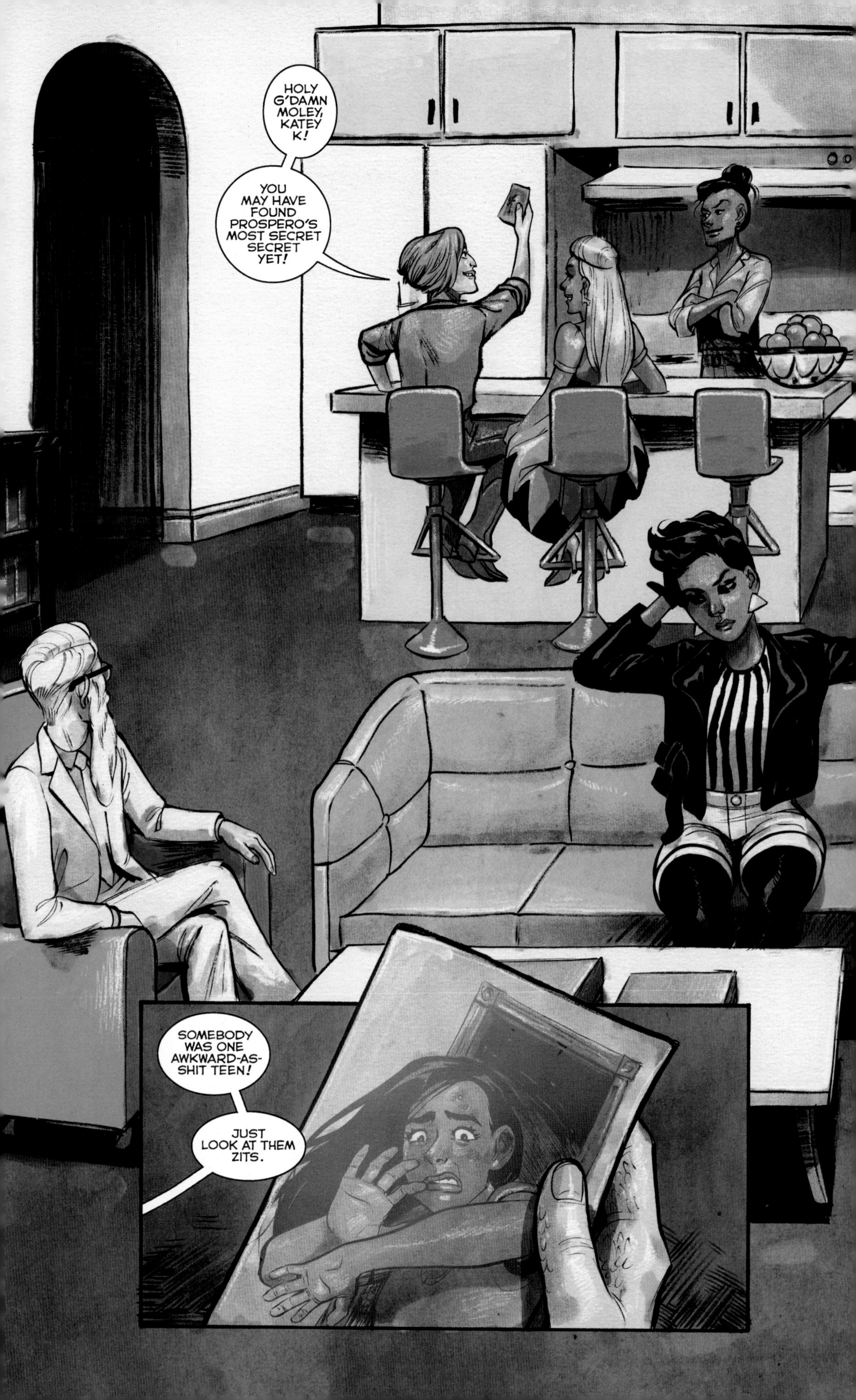
HOLY G'DAMN MOLEY, KATEY K!
YOU MAY HAVE FOUND PROSPERO'S MOST SECRET SECRET YET!
SOMEBODY WAS ONE AWKWARD-AS-SHIT TEEN!
JUST LOOK AT THEM ZITS.

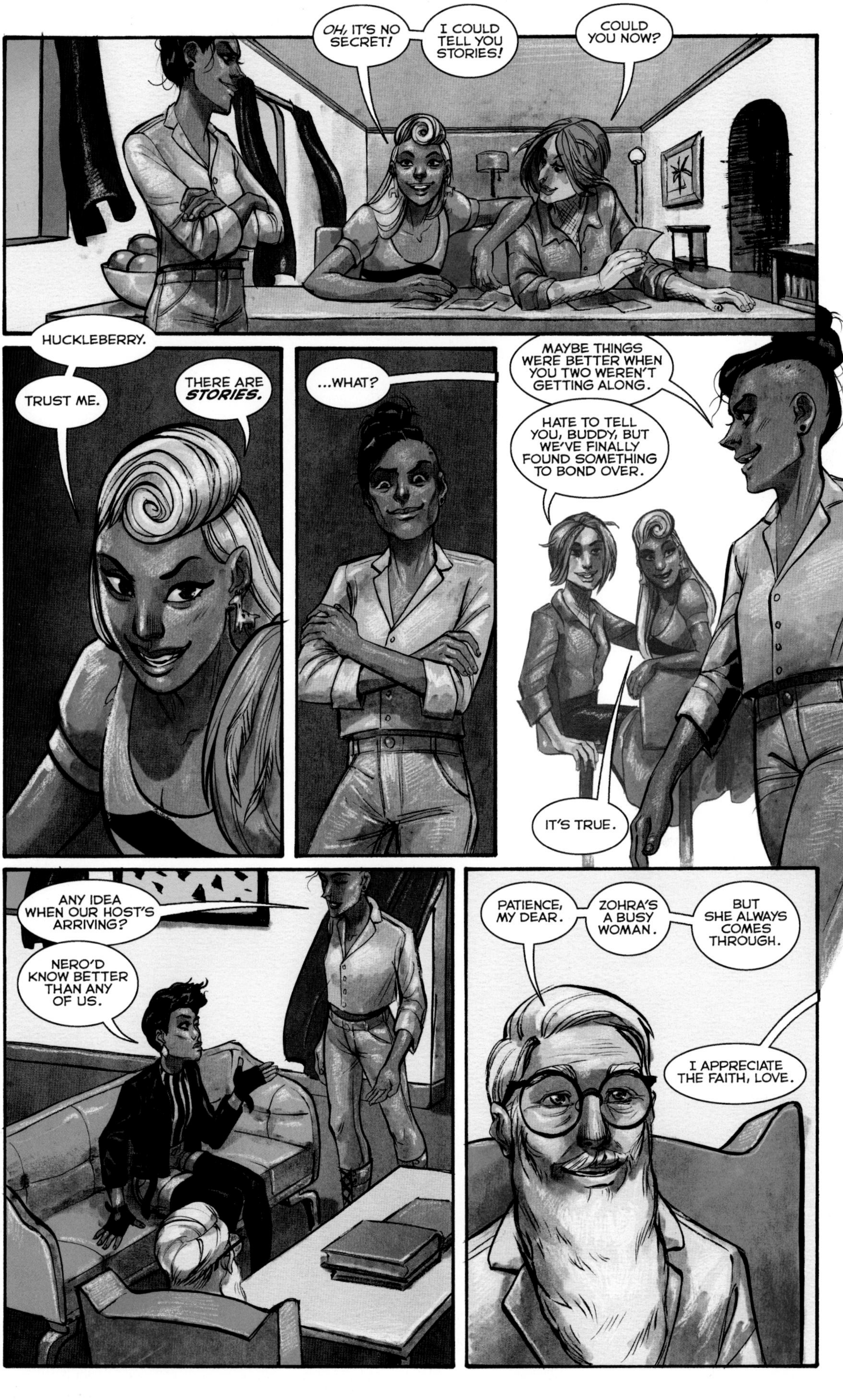
OH, IT'S NO SECRET!
I COULD TELL YOU STORIES!
COULD YOU NOW?
HUCKLEBERRY.
TRUST ME.
THERE ARE STORIES.
...WHAT?
MAYBE THINGS WERE BETTER WHEN YOU TWO WEREN'T GETTING ALONG.
HATE TO TELL YOU, BUDDY, BUT WE'VE FINALLY FOUND SOMETHING TO BOND OVER.
IT'S TRUE.
ANY IDEA WHEN OUR HOST'S ARRIVING?
NERO'D KNOW BETTER THAN ANY OF US.
PATIENCE, MY DEAR.
ZOHRA'S A BUSY WOMAN.
BUT SHE ALWAYS COMES THROUGH.
I APPRECIATE THE FAITH, LOVE.

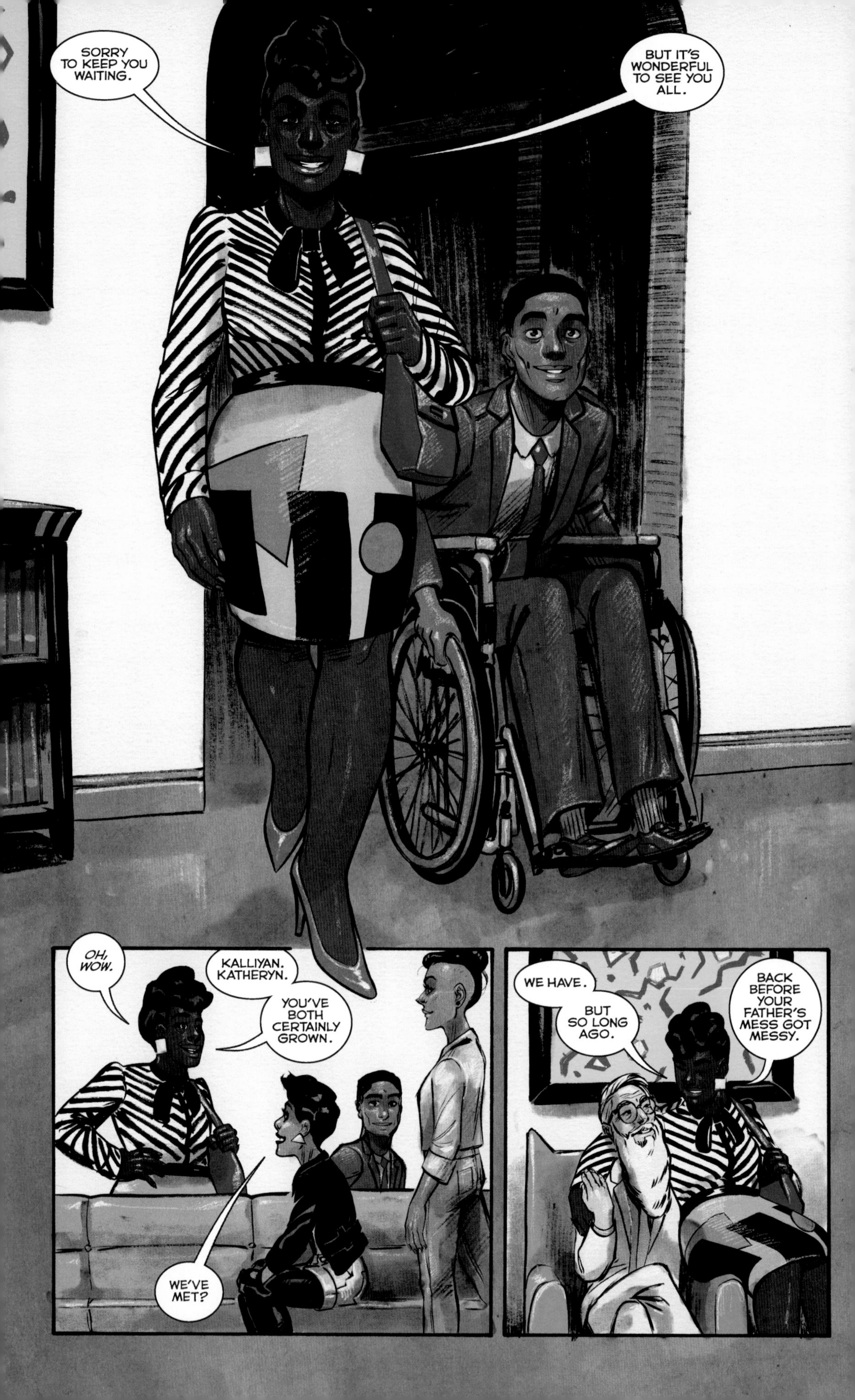
SORRY TO KEEP YOU WAITING.
BUT IT'S WONDERFUL TO SEE YOU ALL.
OH, WOW.
KALLIYAN. KATHERYN.
YOU'VE BOTH CERTAINLY GROWN.
WE'VE MET?
WE HAVE.
BUT SO LONG AGO.
BACK BEFORE YOUR FATHER'S MESS GOT MESSY.

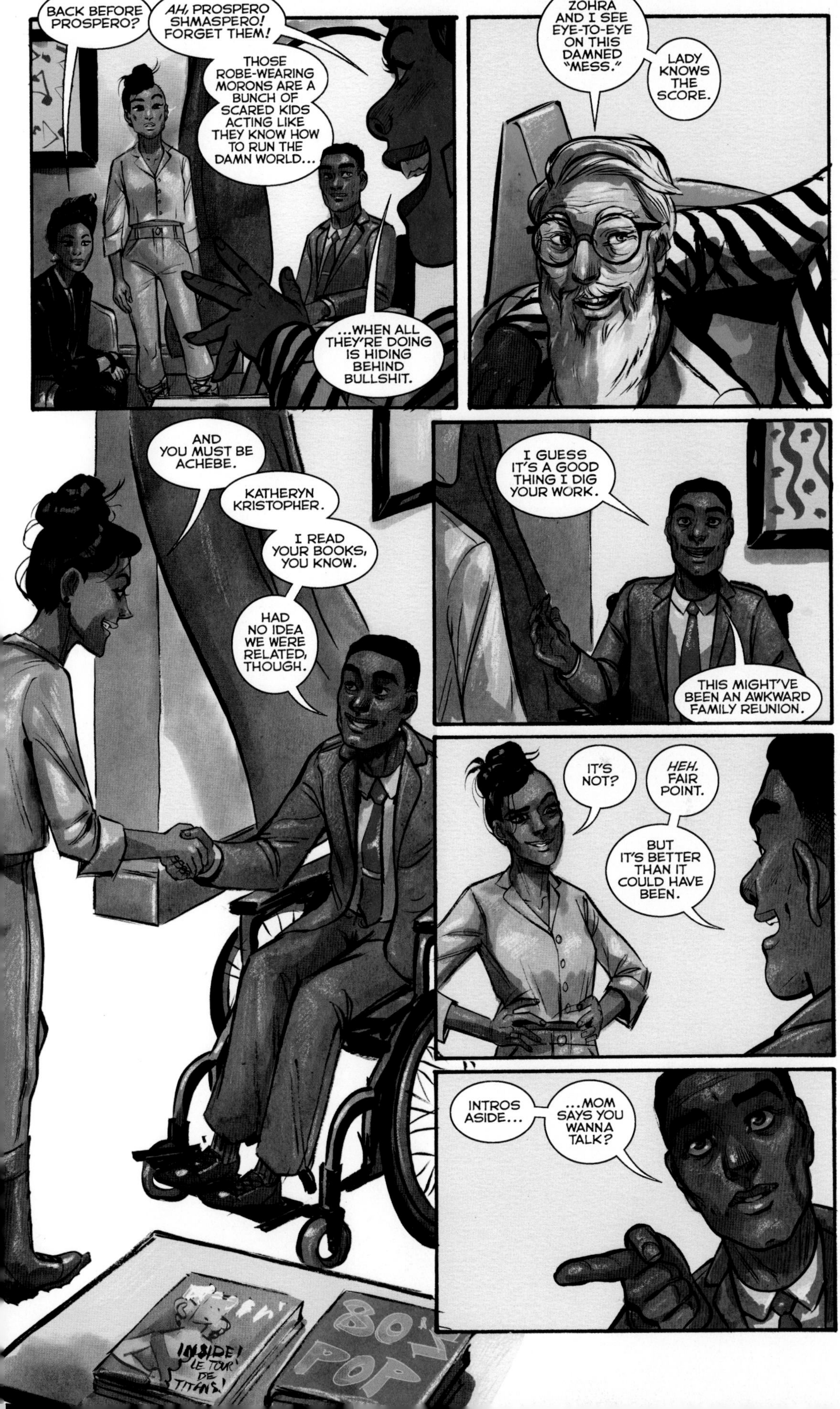
BACK BEFORE PROSPERO?
AH, PROSPERO SHMASPERO! FORGET THEM!
THOSE ROBE-WEARING MORONS ARE A BUNCH OF SCARED KIDS ACTING LIKE THEY KNOW HOW TO RUN THE DAMN WORLD...
...WHEN ALL THEY'RE DOING IS HIDING BEHIND BULLSHIT.
ZOHRA AND I SEE EYE-TO-EYE ON THIS DAMNED "MESS."
LADY KNOWS THE SCORE.
AND YOU MUST BE ACHEBE.
KATHERYN KRISTOPHER.
I READ YOUR BOOKS, YOU KNOW.
HAD NO IDEA WE WERE RELATED, THOUGH.
I GUESS IT'S A GOOD THING I DIG YOUR WORK.
THIS MIGHT'VE BEEN AN AWKWARD FAMILY REUNION.
IT'S NOT?
HEH. FAIR POINT.
BUT IT'S BETTER THAN IT COULD HAVE BEEN.
INTROS ASIDE...
...MOM SAYS YOU WANNA TALK?
INSIDE! LE TOUR DE TITANS!
80's POP

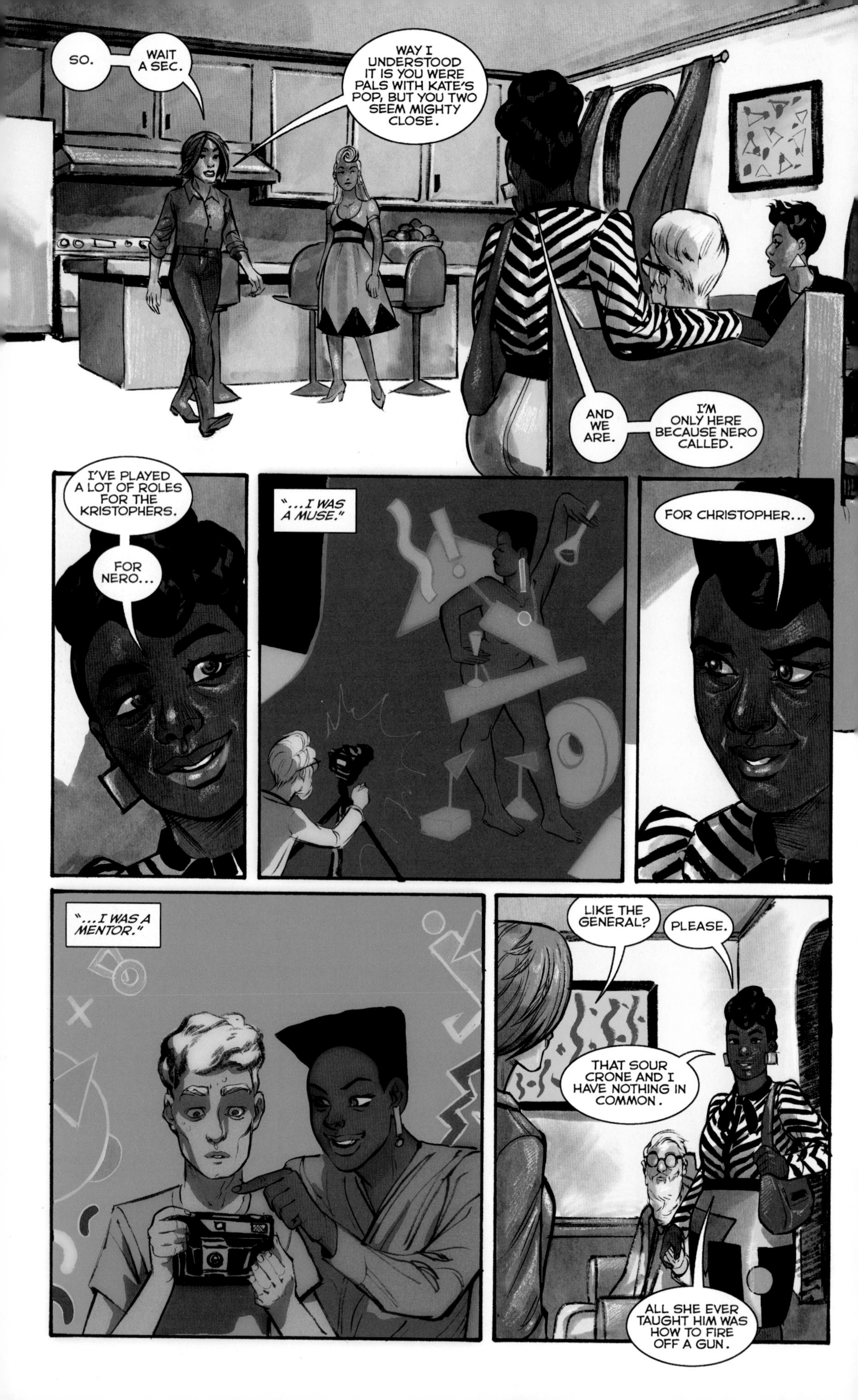
SO.
WAIT A SEC.
WAY I UNDERSTOOD IT IS YOU WERE PALS WITH KATE'S POP, BUT YOU TWO SEEM MIGHTY CLOSE.
AND WE ARE.
I'M ONLY HERE BECAUSE NERO CALLED.
I'VE PLAYED A LOT OF ROLES FOR THE KRISTOPHERS.
FOR NERO...
"...I WAS A MUSE."
FOR CHRISTOPHER...
"...I WAS A MENTOR."
LIKE THE GENERAL?
PLEASE.
THAT SOUR CRONE AND I HAVE NOTHING IN COMMON.
ALL SHE EVER TAUGHT HIM WAS HOW TO FIRE OFF A GUN.

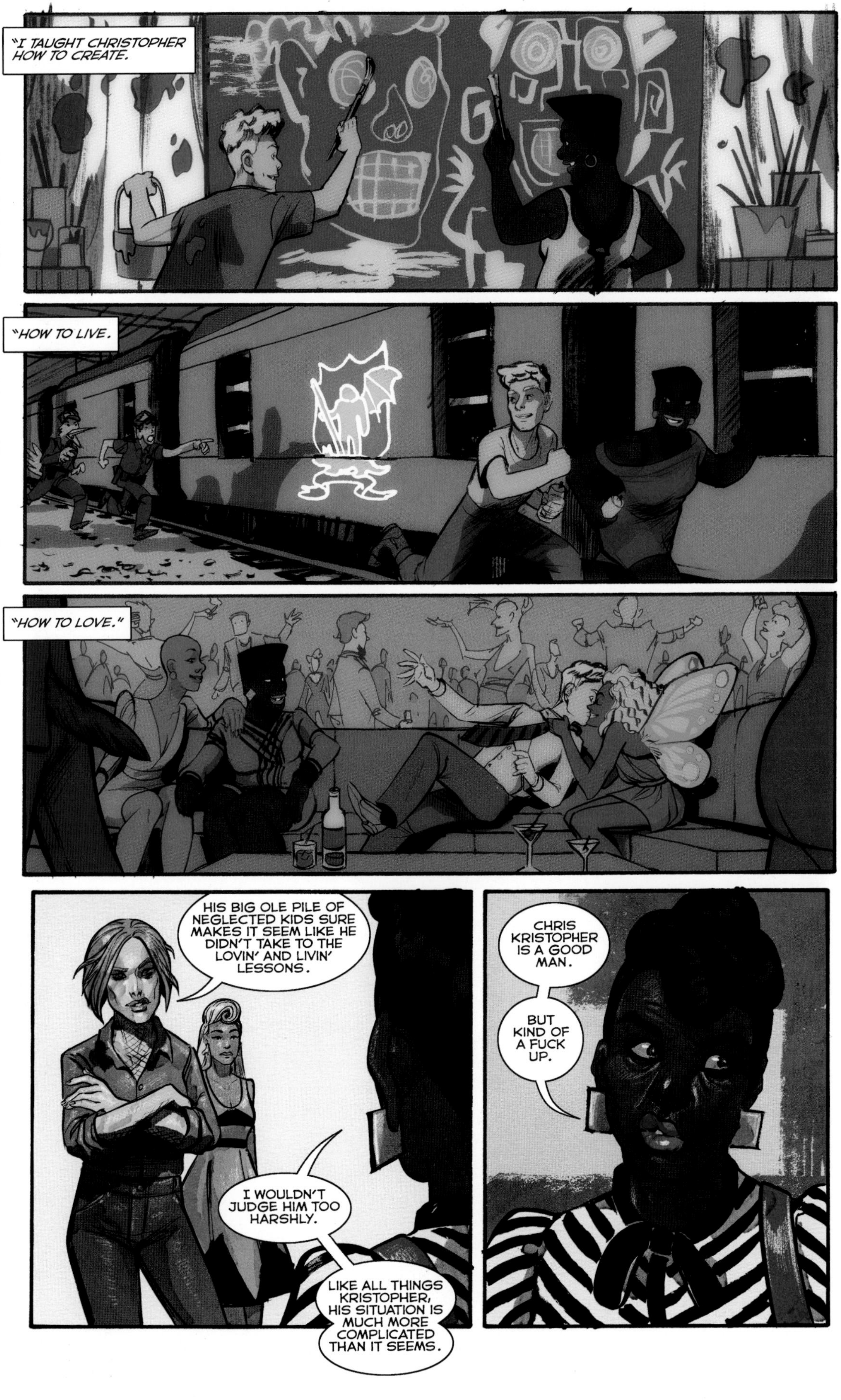
"I TAUGHT CHRISTOPHER HOW TO CREATE.
"HOW TO LIVE.
"HOW TO LOVE."
HIS BIG OLE PILE OF NEGLECTED KIDS SURE MAKES IT SEEM LIKE HE DIDN'T TAKE TO THE LOVIN' AND LIVIN' LESSONS.
I WOULDN'T JUDGE HIM TOO HARSHLY.
LIKE ALL THINGS KRISTOPHER, HIS SITUATION IS MUCH MORE COMPLICATED THAN IT SEEMS.
CHRIS KRISTOPHER IS A GOOD MAN.
BUT KIND OF A FUCK UP.

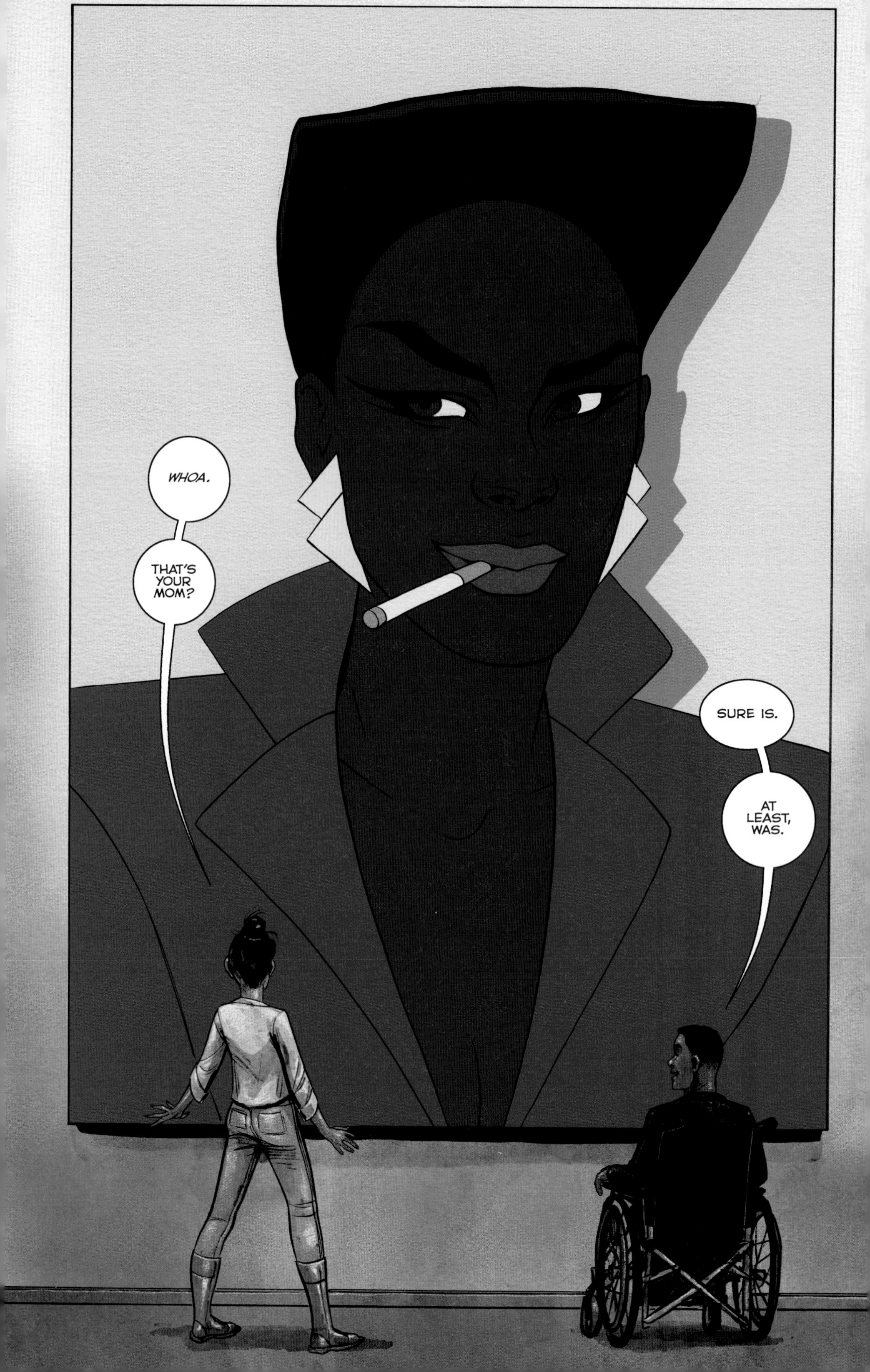
WHOA.
THAT'S YOUR MOM?
SURE IS.
AT LEAST, WAS.

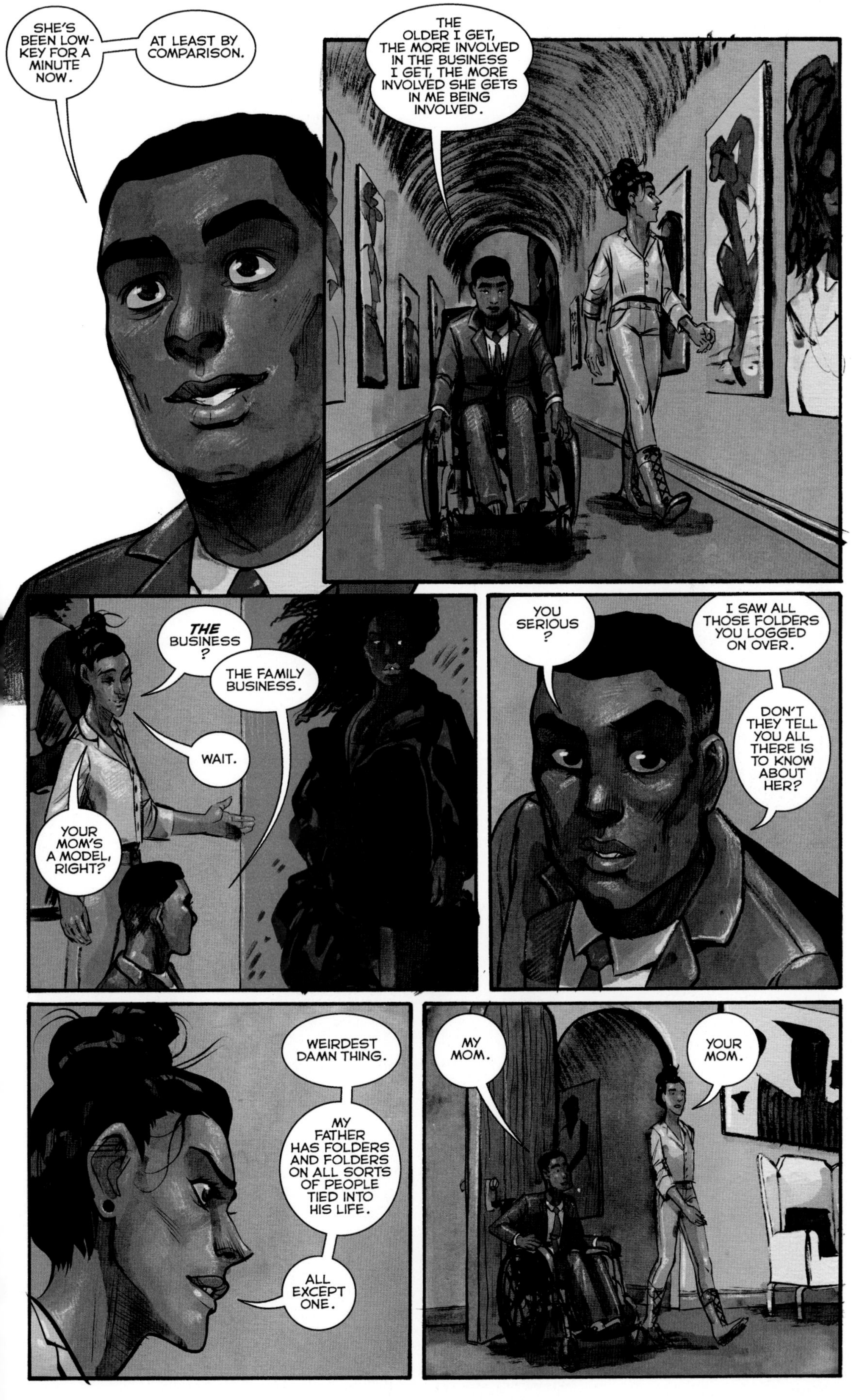
SHE'S BEEN LOW-KEY FOR A MINUTE NOW.
AT LEAST BY COMPARISON.
THE OLDER I GET, THE MORE INVOLVED IN THE BUSINESS I GET, THE MORE INVOLVED SHE GETS IN ME BEING INVOLVED.
THE BUSINESS?
THE FAMILY BUSINESS.
WAIT.
YOUR MOM'S A MODEL, RIGHT?
YOU SERIOUS?
I SAW ALL THOSE FOLDERS YOU LOGGED ON OVER.
DON'T THEY TELL YOU ALL THERE IS TO KNOW ABOUT HER?
WEIRDEST DAMN THING.
MY FATHER HAS FOLDERS AND FOLDERS ON ALL SORTS OF PEOPLE TIED INTO HIS LIFE.
ALL EXCEPT ONE.
MY MOM.
YOUR MOM.

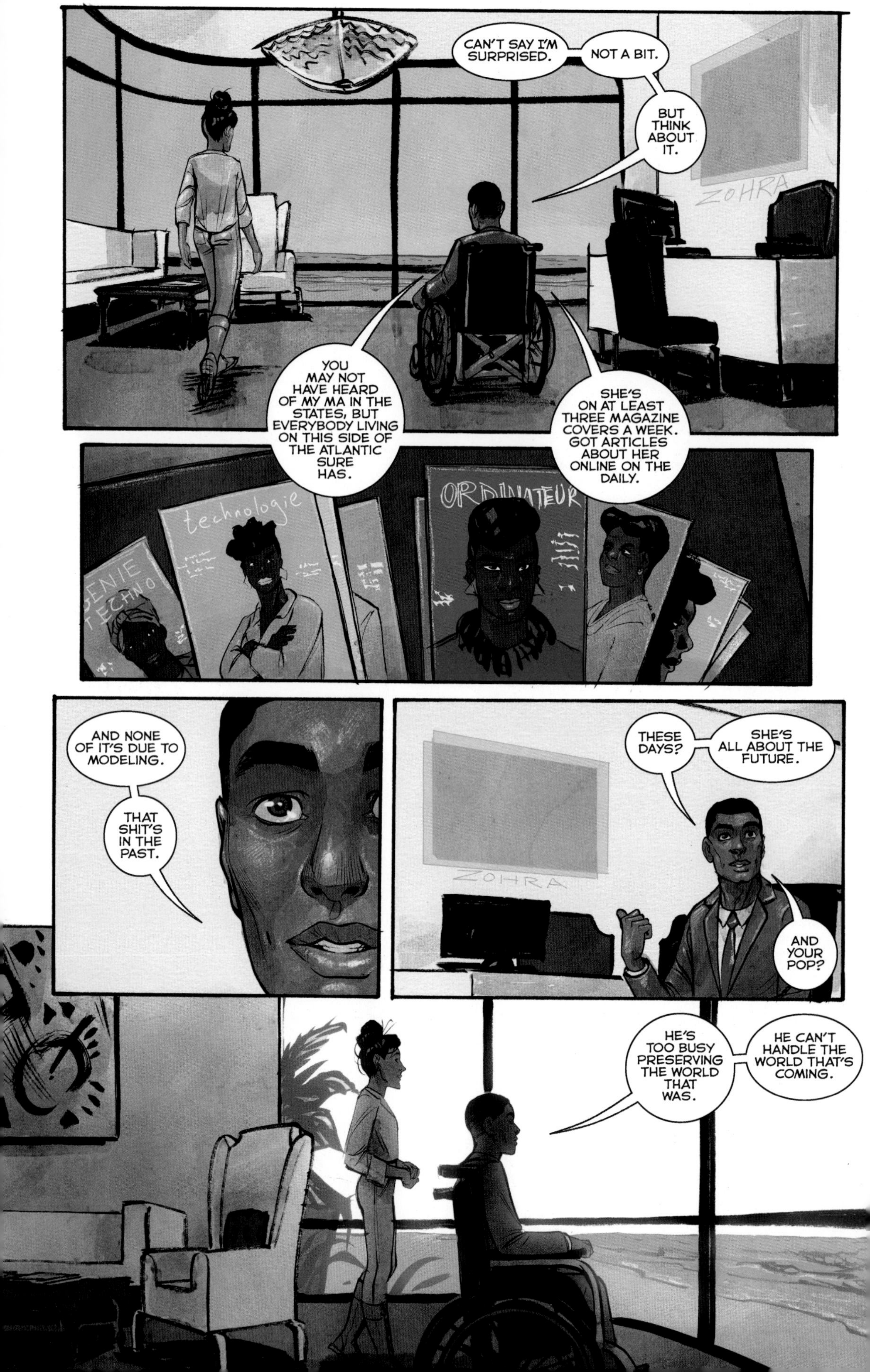
CAN'T SAY I'M SURPRISED.
NOT A BIT.
BUT THINK ABOUT IT.
ZOHRA
YOU MAY NOT HAVE HEARD OF MY MA IN THE STATES, BUT EVERYBODY LIVING ON THIS SIDE OF THE ATLANTIC SURE HAS.
SHE'S ON AT LEAST THREE MAGAZINE COVERS A WEEK. GOT ARTICLES ABOUT HER ONLINE ON THE DAILY.
GENIE TECHNO
technologie
ORDINATEUR
AND NONE OF IT'S DUE TO MODELING.
THAT SHIT'S IN THE PAST.
THESE DAYS?
SHE'S ALL ABOUT THE FUTURE.
ZOHRA
AND YOUR POP?
HE'S TOO BUSY PRESERVING THE WORLD THAT WAS.
HE CAN'T HANDLE THE WORLD THAT'S COMING.

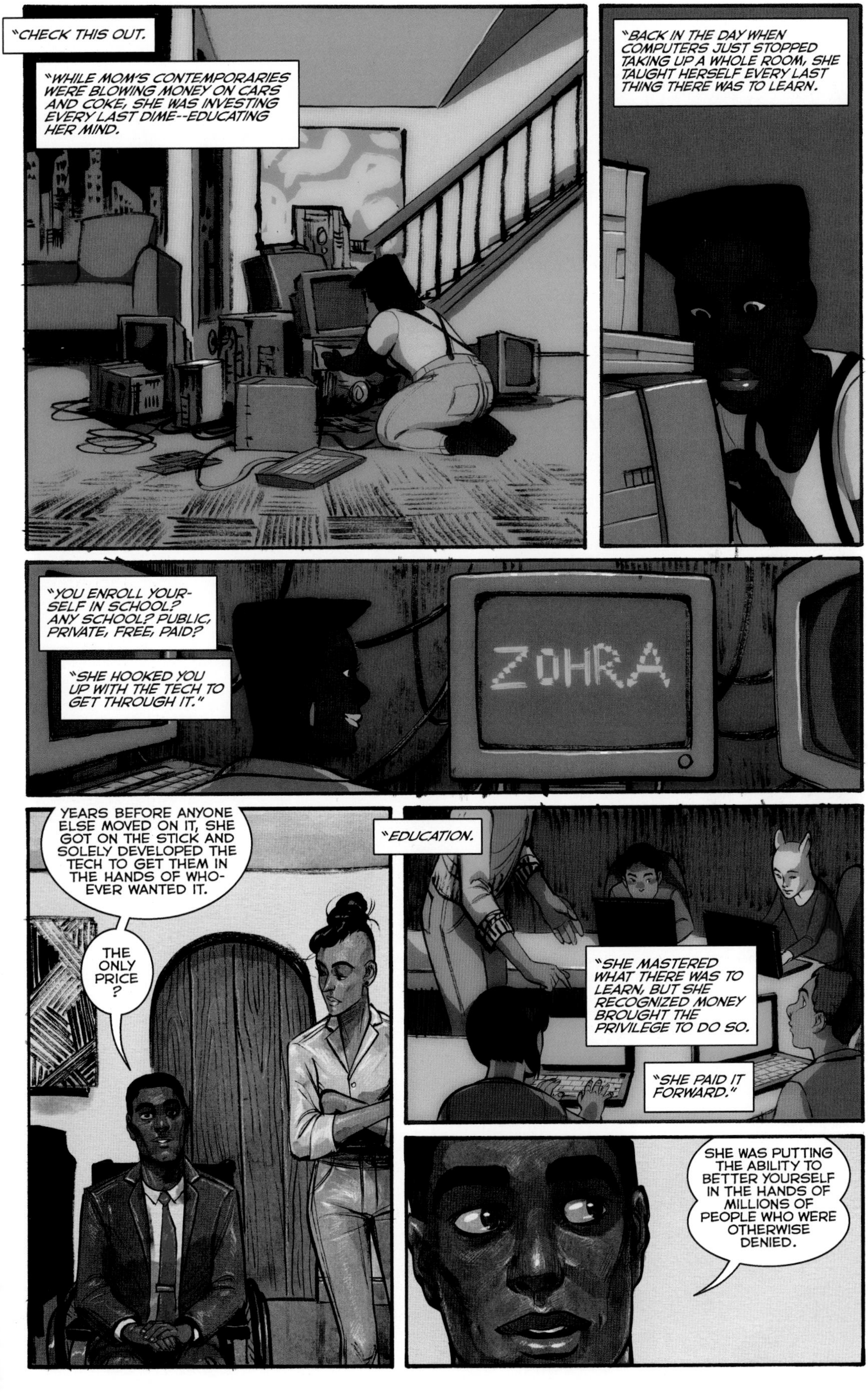
"CHECK THIS OUT.
"WHILE MOM'S CONTEMPORARIES WERE BLOWING MONEY ON CARS AND COKE, SHE WAS INVESTING EVERY LAST DIME--EDUCATING HER MIND.
"BACK IN THE DAY WHEN COMPUTERS JUST STOPPED TAKING UP A WHOLE ROOM, SHE TAUGHT HERSELF EVERY LAST THING THERE WAS TO LEARN.
"YOU ENROLL YOURSELF IN SCHOOL? ANY SCHOOL? PUBLIC, PRIVATE, FREE, PAID?
"SHE HOOKED YOU UP WITH THE TECH TO GET THROUGH IT."
ZOHRA
YEARS BEFORE ANYONE ELSE MOVED ON IT, SHE GOT ON THE STICK AND SOLELY DEVELOPED THE TECH TO GET THEM IN THE HANDS OF WHOEVER WANTED IT.
THE ONLY PRICE?
"EDUCATION.
"SHE MASTERED WHAT THERE WAS TO LEARN, BUT SHE RECOGNIZED MONEY BROUGHT THE PRIVILEGE TO DO SO.
"SHE PAID IT FORWARD."
SHE WAS PUTTING THE ABILITY TO BETTER YOURSELF IN THE HANDS OF MILLIONS OF PEOPLE WHO WERE OTHERWISE DENIED.

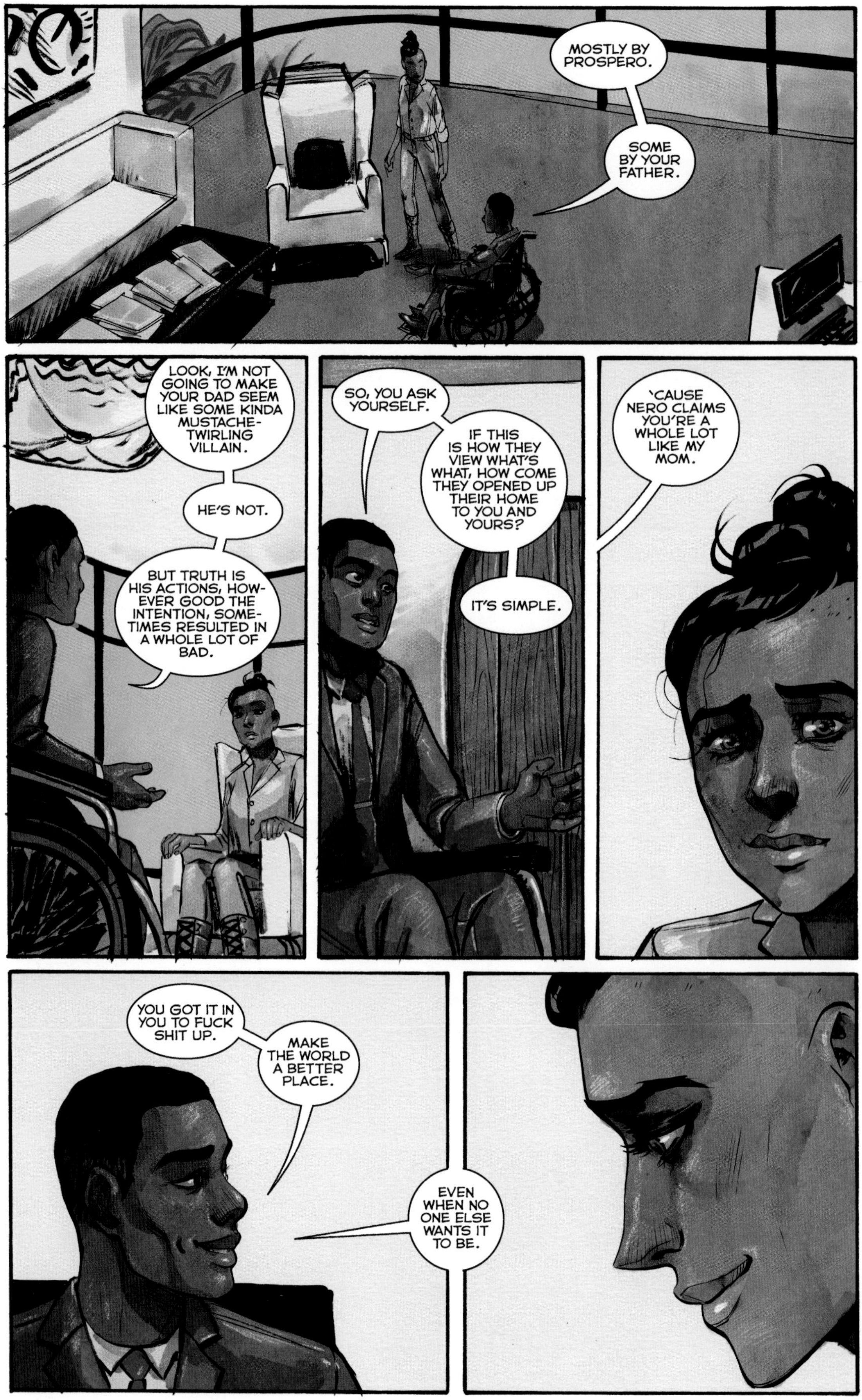
MOSTLY BY PROSPERO.
SOME BY YOUR FATHER.
LOOK, I'M NOT GOING TO MAKE YOUR DAD SEEM LIKE SOME KINDA MUSTACHE-TWIRLING VILLAIN.
HE'S NOT.
BUT TRUTH IS HIS ACTIONS, HOWEVER GOOD THE INTENTION, SOMETIMES RESULTED IN A WHOLE LOT OF BAD.
SO, YOU ASK YOURSELF.
IF THIS IS HOW THEY VIEW WHAT'S WHAT, HOW COME THEY OPENED UP THEIR HOME TO YOU AND YOURS?
IT'S SIMPLE.
'CAUSE NERO CLAIMS YOU'RE A WHOLE LOT LIKE MY MOM.
YOU GOT IT IN YOU TO FUCK SHIT UP.
MAKE THE WORLD A BETTER PLACE.
EVEN WHEN NO ONE ELSE WANTS IT TO BE.

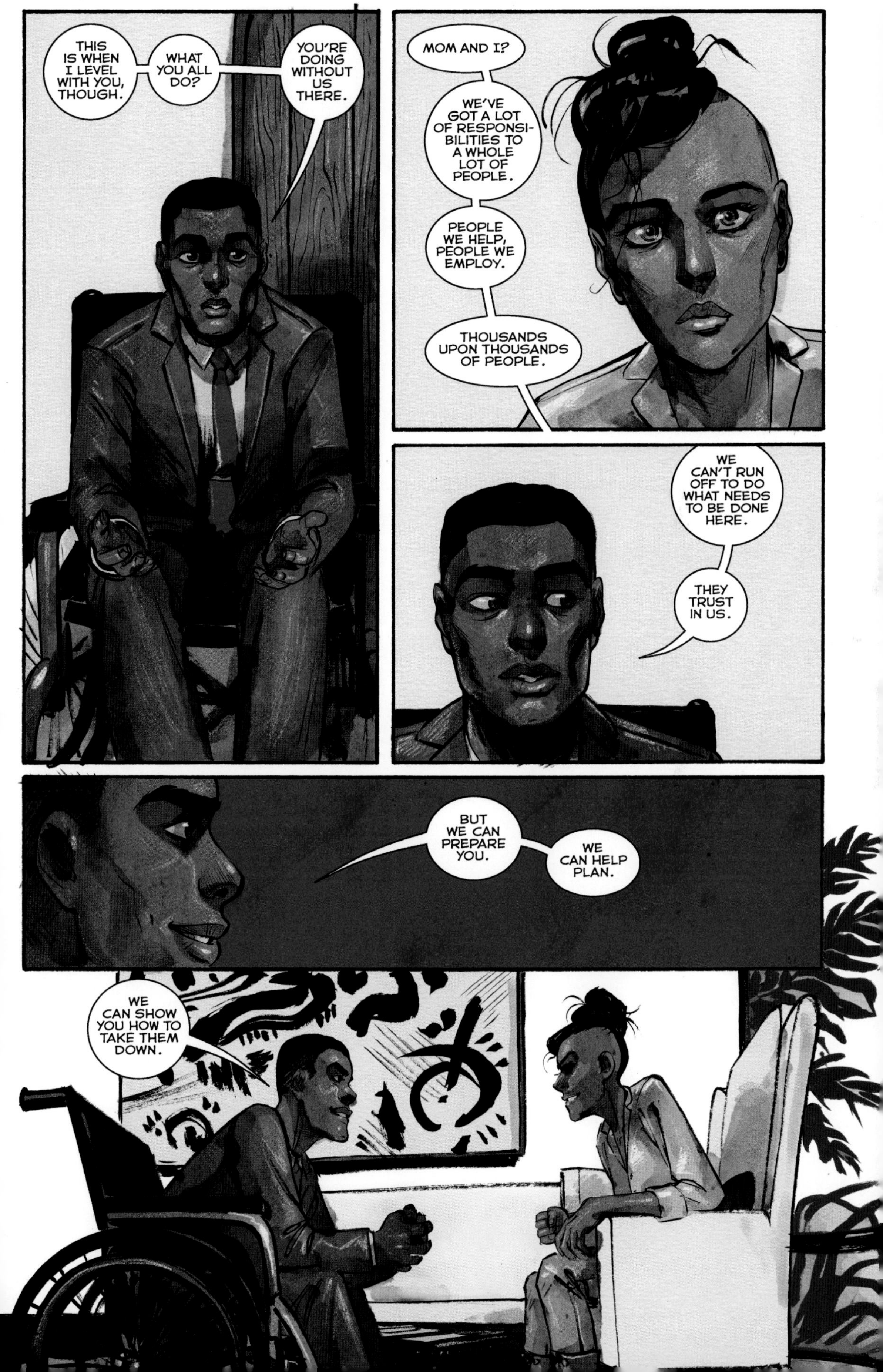
THIS IS WHEN I LEVEL WITH YOU, THOUGH.
WHAT YOU ALL DO?
YOU'RE DOING WITHOUT US THERE.
MOM AND I?
WE'VE GOT A LOT OF RESPONSI-BILITIES TO A WHOLE LOT OF PEOPLE.
PEOPLE WE HELP, PEOPLE WE EMPLOY.
THOUSANDS UPON THOUSANDS OF PEOPLE.
WE CAN'T RUN OFF TO DO WHAT NEEDS TO BE DONE HERE.
THEY TRUST IN US.
BUT WE CAN PREPARE YOU.
WE CAN HELP PLAN.
WE CAN SHOW YOU HOW TO TAKE THEM DOWN.

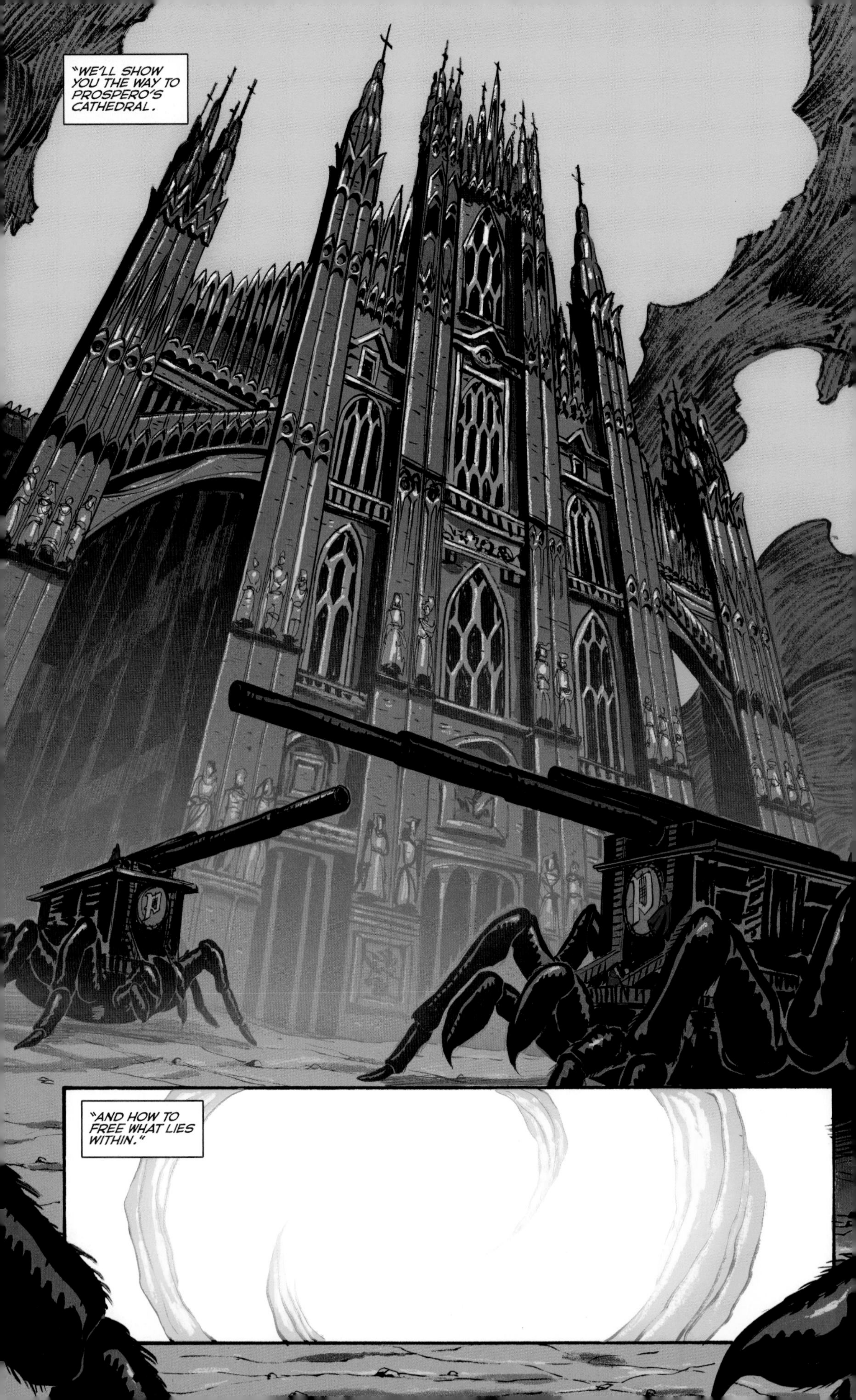
"WE'LL SHOW YOU THE WAY TO PROSPERO'S CATHEDRAL.
"AND HOW TO FREE WHAT LIES WITHIN."

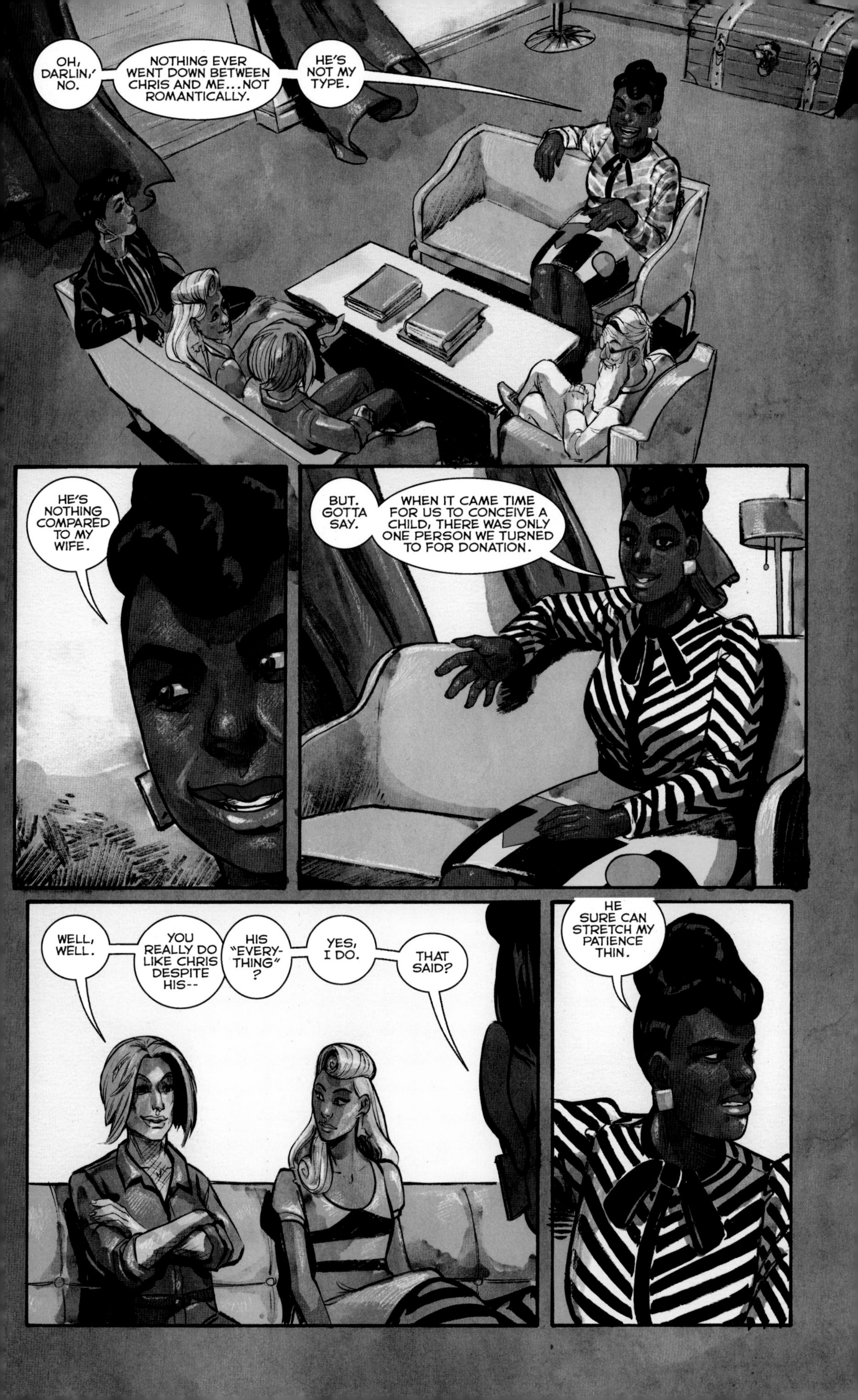
OH, DARLIN,' NO.
NOTHING EVER WENT DOWN BETWEEN CHRIS AND ME...NOT ROMANTICALLY.
HE'S NOT MY TYPE.
HE'S NOTHING COMPARED TO MY WIFE.
BUT. GOTTA SAY.
WHEN IT CAME TIME FOR US TO CONCEIVE A CHILD, THERE WAS ONLY ONE PERSON WE TURNED TO FOR DONATION.
WELL, WELL.
YOU REALLY DO LIKE CHRIS DESPITE HIS--
HIS "EVERY-THING"?
YES, I DO.
THAT SAID?
HE SURE CAN STRETCH MY PATIENCE THIN.

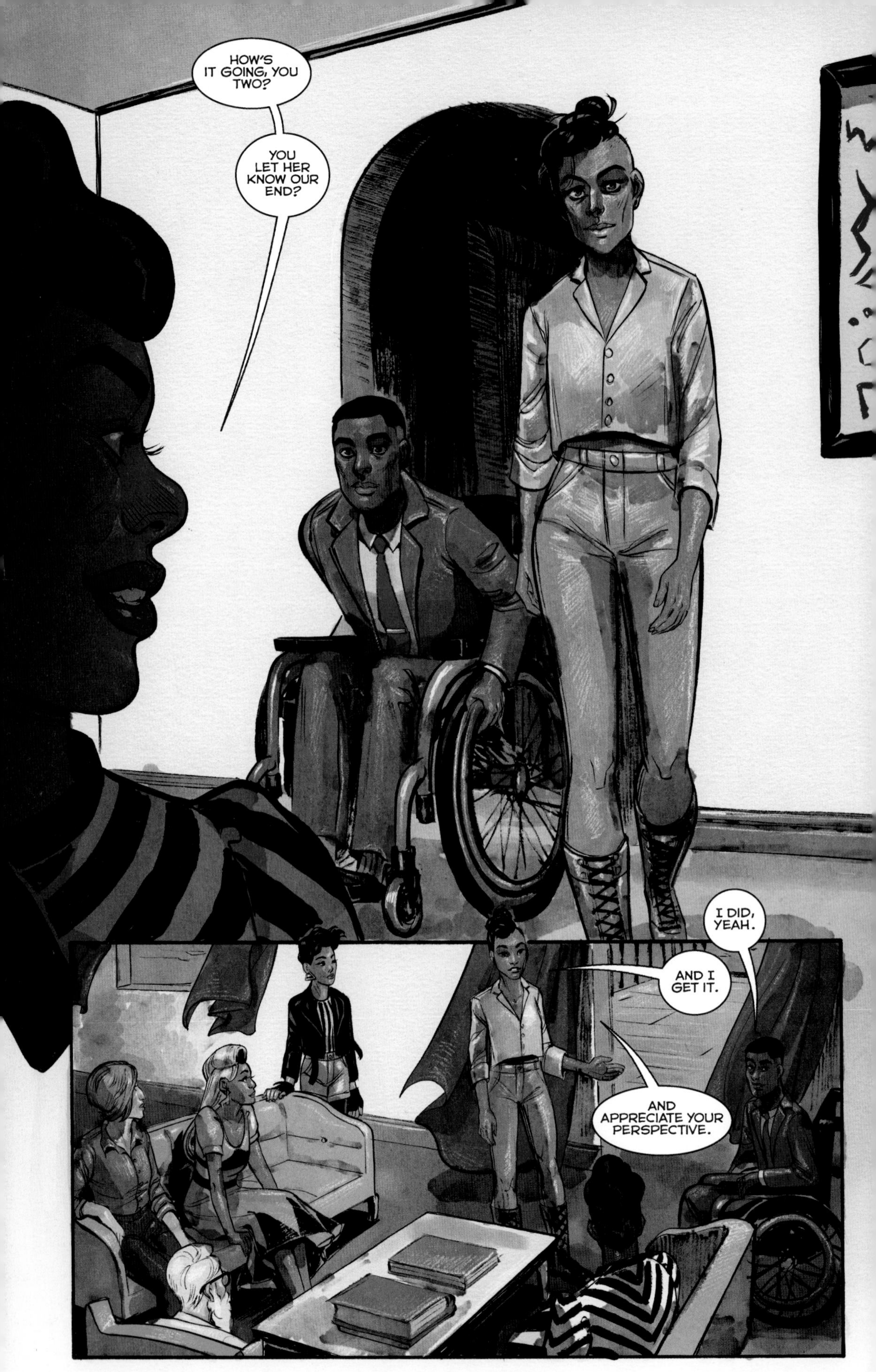
HOW'S IT GOING, YOU TWO?
YOU LET HER KNOW OUR END?
I DID, YEAH.
AND I GET IT.
AND APPRECIATE YOUR PERSPECTIVE.

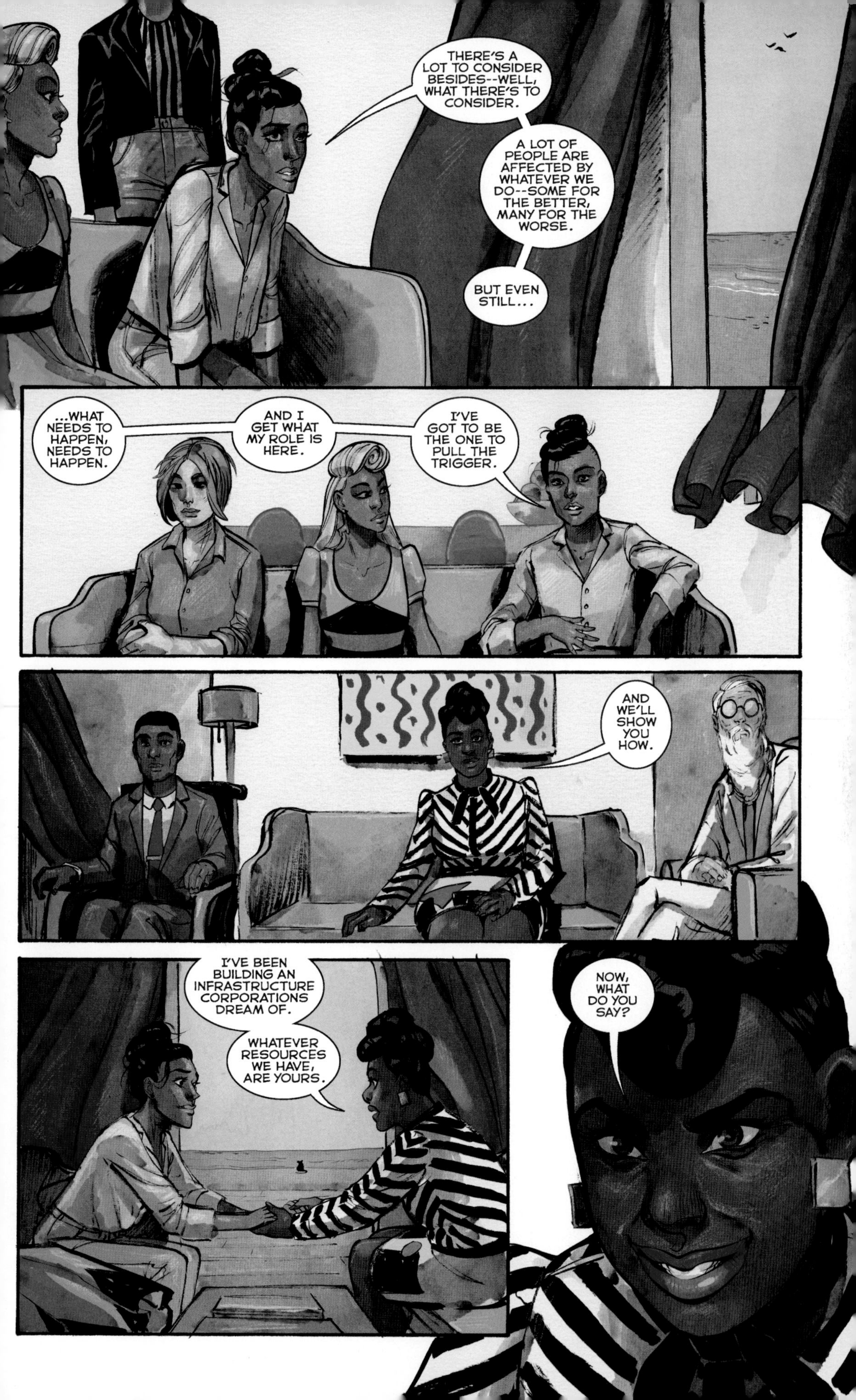
THERE'S A LOT TO CONSIDER BESIDES--WELL, WHAT THERE'S TO CONSIDER.
A LOT OF PEOPLE ARE AFFECTED BY WHATEVER WE DO--SOME FOR THE BETTER, MANY FOR THE WORSE.
BUT EVEN STILL...
...WHAT NEEDS TO HAPPEN, NEEDS TO HAPPEN.
AND I GET WHAT MY ROLE IS HERE.
I'VE GOT TO BE THE ONE TO PULL THE TRIGGER.
AND WE'LL SHOW YOU HOW.
I'VE BEEN BUILDING AN INFRASTRUCTURE CORPORATIONS DREAM OF.
WHATEVER RESOURCES WE HAVE, ARE YOURS.
NOW, WHAT DO YOU SAY?

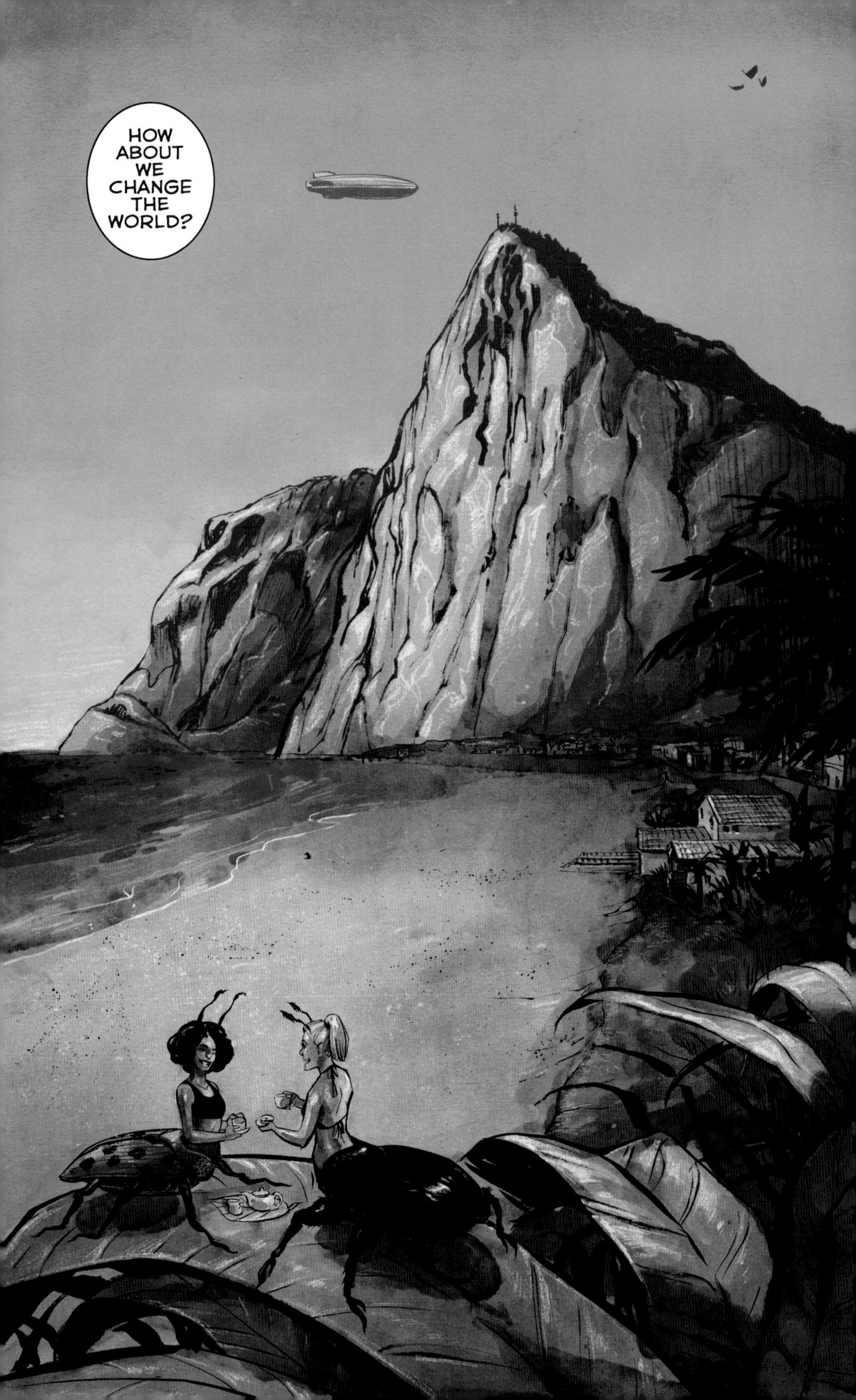
HOW ABOUT WE CHANGE THE WORLD?

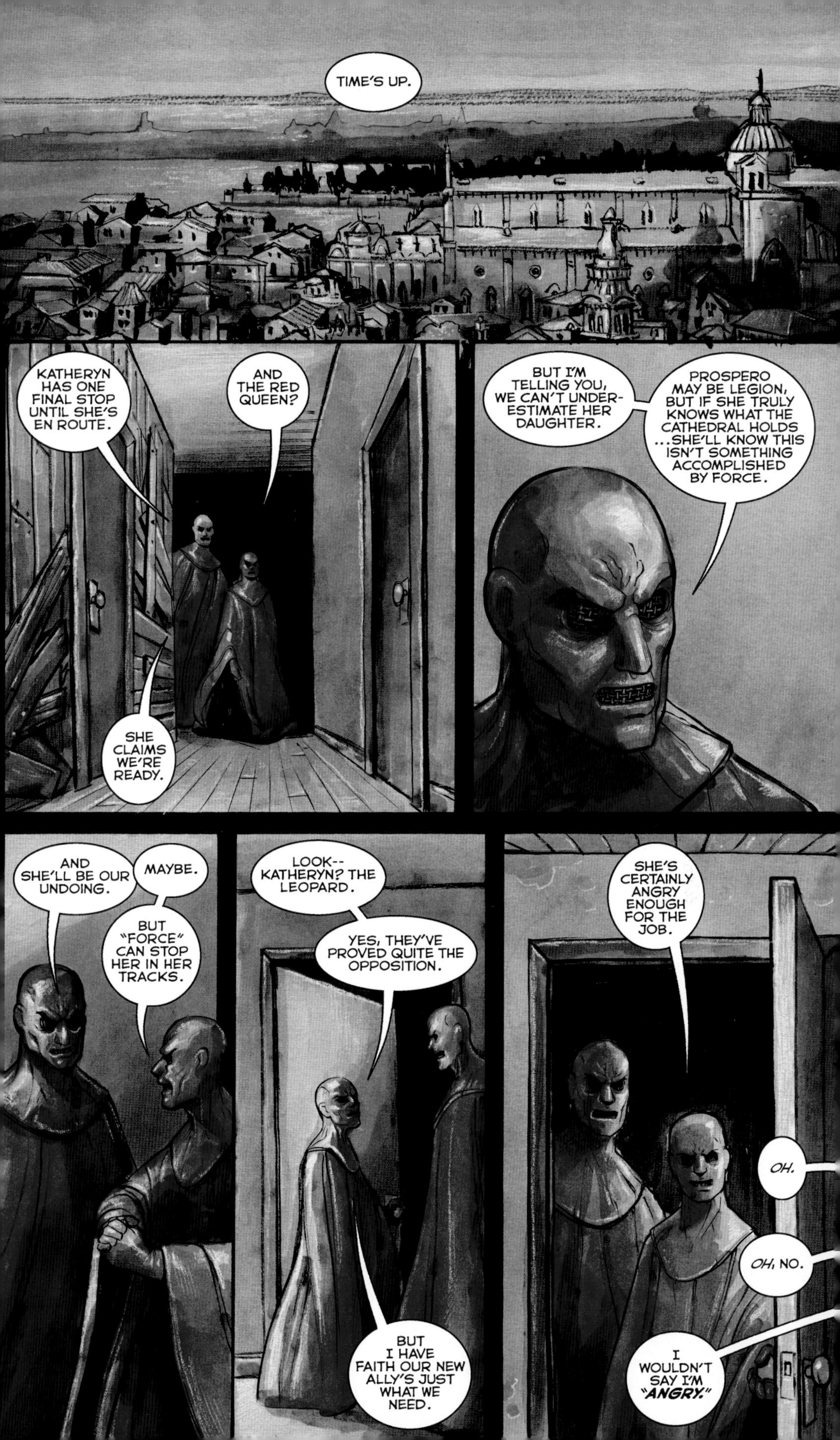
TIME'S UP.
KATHERYN HAS ONE FINAL STOP UNTIL SHE'S EN ROUTE.
AND THE RED QUEEN?
SHE CLAIMS WE'RE READY.
BUT I'M TELLING YOU, WE CAN'T UNDER-ESTIMATE HER DAUGHTER.
PROSPERO MAY BE LEGION, BUT IF SHE TRULY KNOWS WHAT THE CATHEDRAL HOLDS ...SHE'LL KNOW THIS ISN'T SOMETHING ACCOMPLISHED BY FORCE.
AND SHE'LL BE OUR UNDOING.
MAYBE.
BUT "FORCE" CAN STOP HER IN HER TRACKS.
LOOK-- KATHERYN? THE LEOPARD.
YES, THEY'VE PROVED QUITE THE OPPOSITION.
BUT I HAVE FAITH OUR NEW ALLY'S JUST WHAT WE NEED.
SHE'S CERTAINLY ANGRY ENOUGH FOR THE JOB.
OH.
OH, NO.
I WOULDN'T SAY I'M "ANGRY."

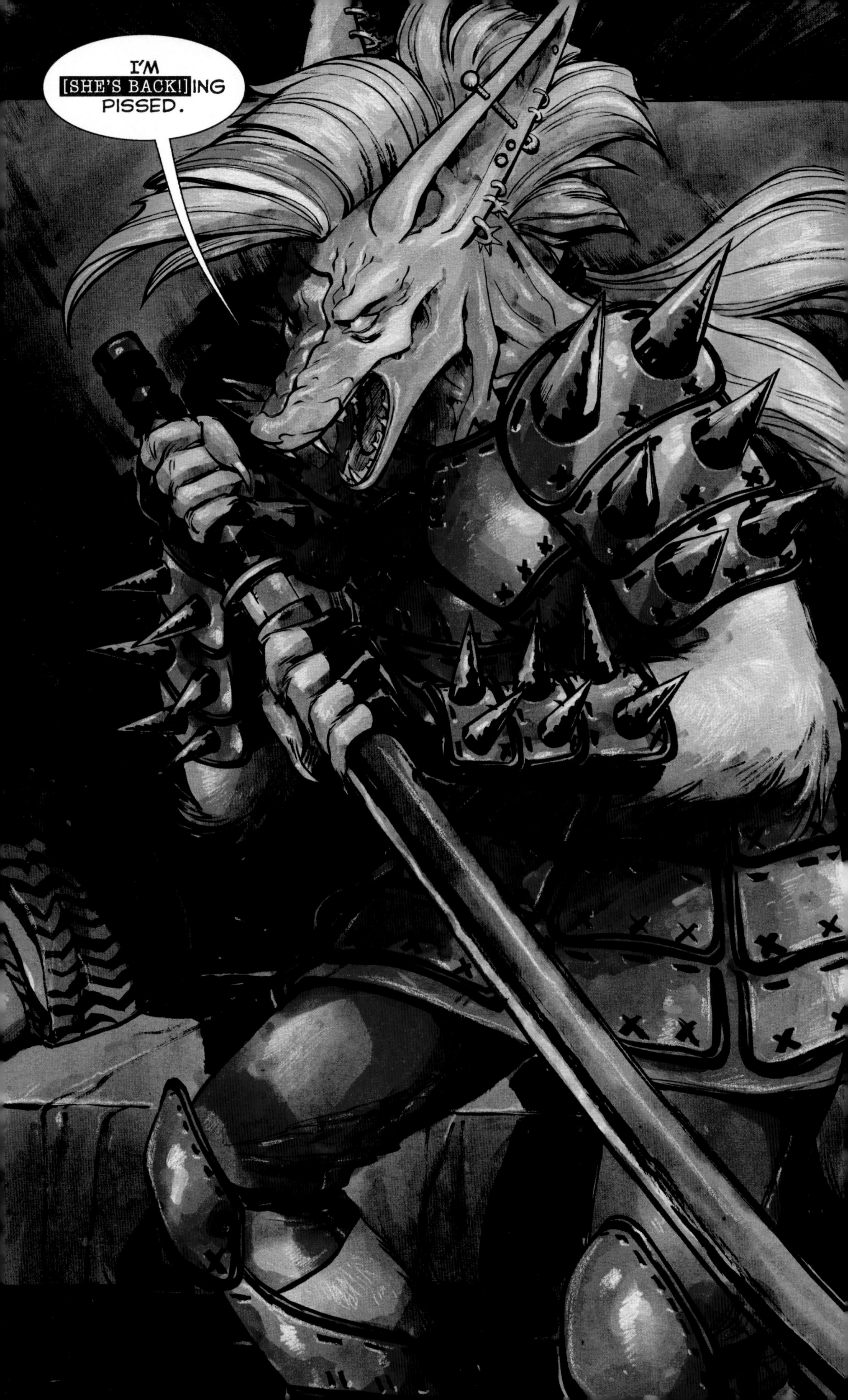
I'M [SHE'S BACK!]ING PISSED.

CHAPTER

22

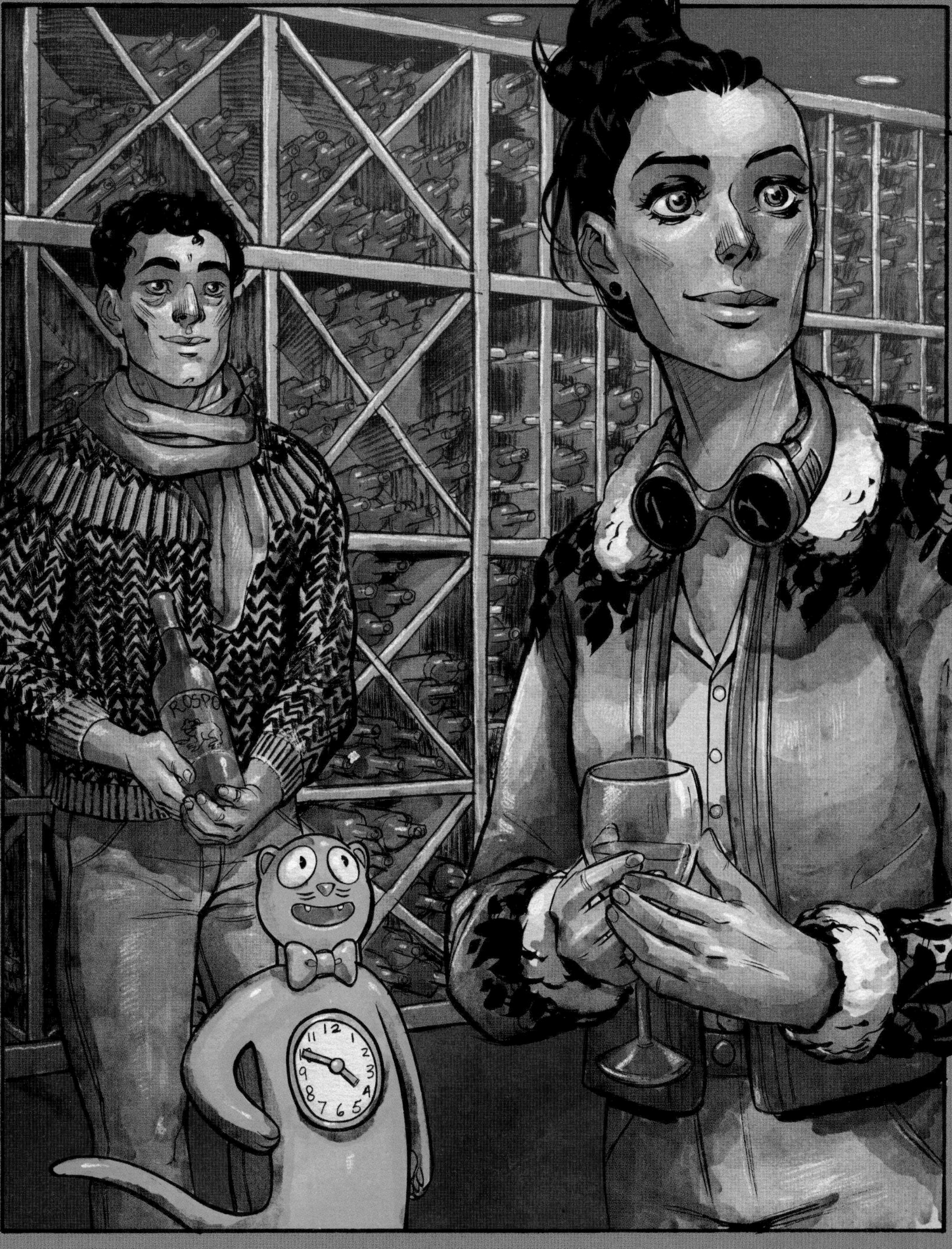
ROSPO

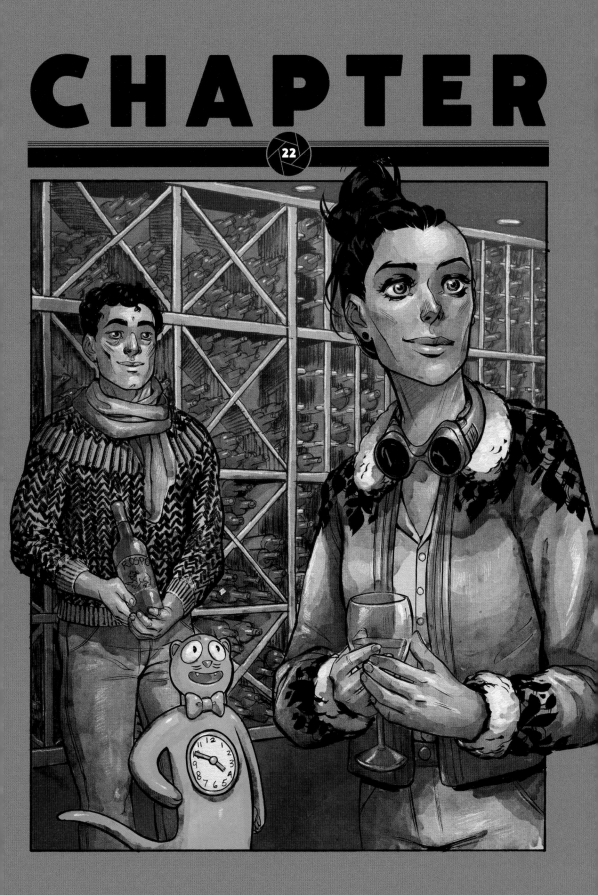

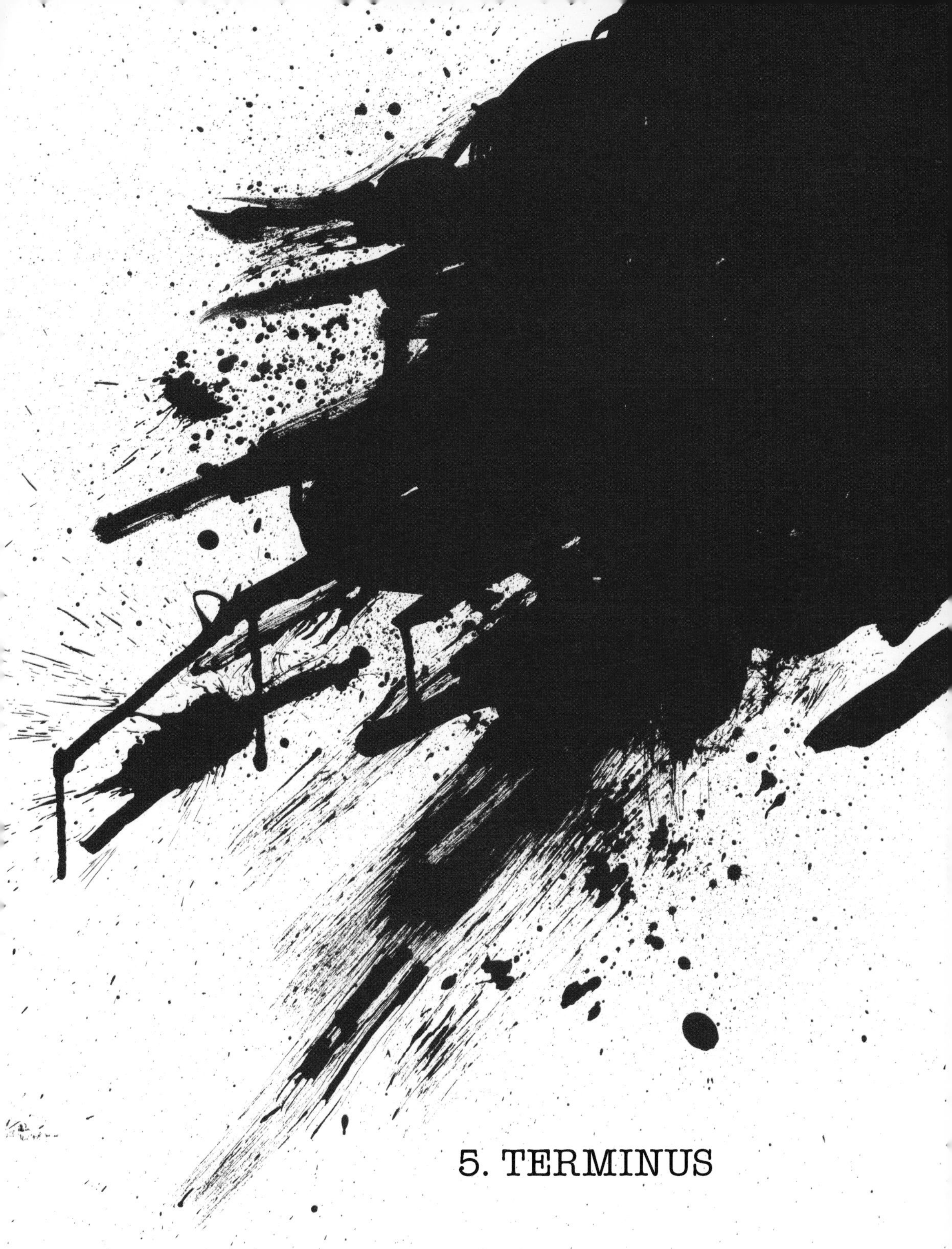

5. TERMINUS

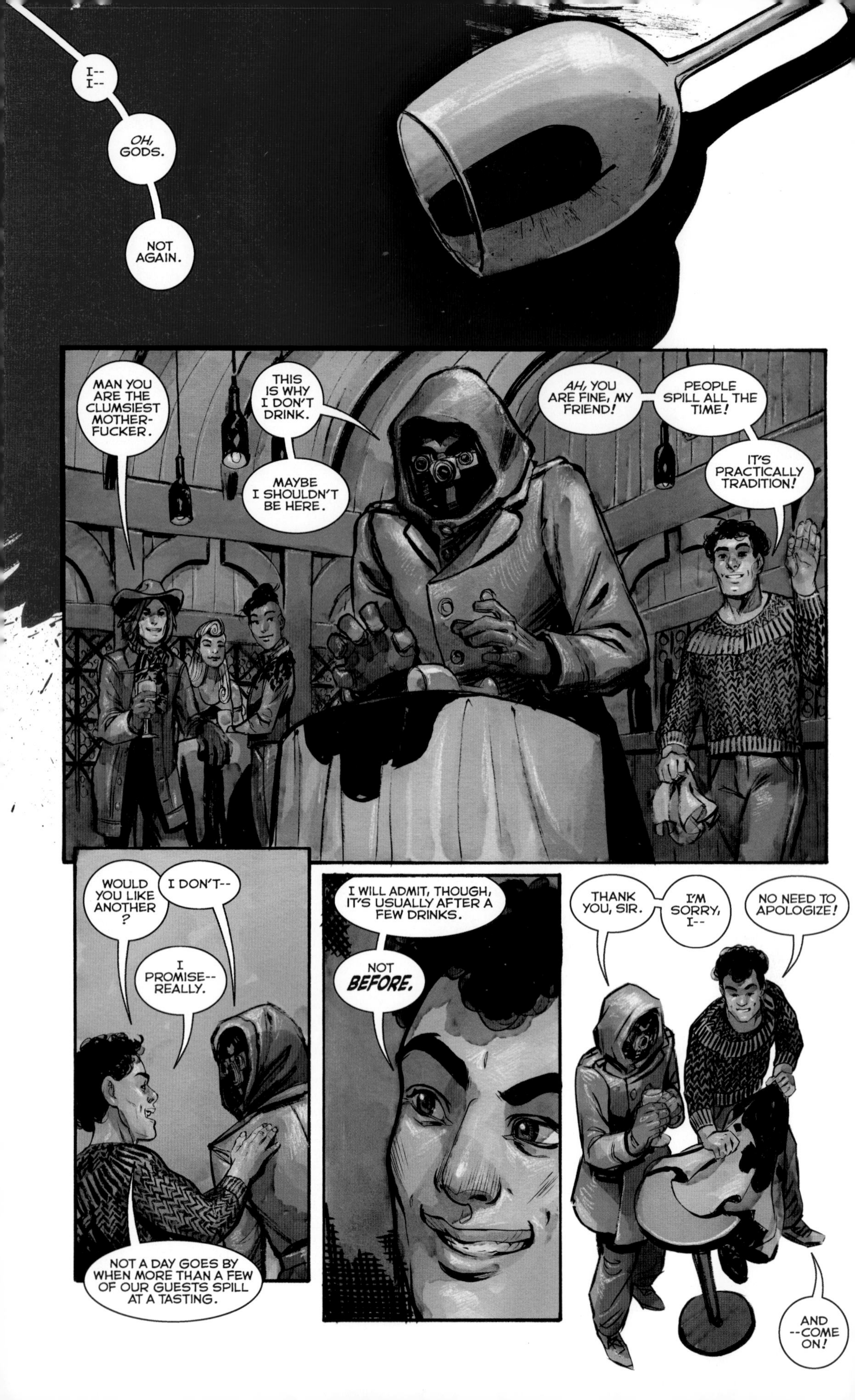
I--
I--
OH, GODS.
NOT AGAIN.
MAN YOU ARE THE CLUMSIEST MOTHER-FUCKER.
THIS IS WHY I DON'T DRINK.
MAYBE I SHOULDN'T BE HERE.
AH, YOU ARE FINE, MY FRIEND!
PEOPLE SPILL ALL THE TIME!
IT'S PRACTICALLY TRADITION!
WOULD YOU LIKE ANOTHER?
I DON'T--
I PROMISE-- REALLY.
NOT A DAY GOES BY WHEN MORE THAN A FEW OF OUR GUESTS SPILL AT A TASTING.
I WILL ADMIT, THOUGH, IT'S USUALLY AFTER A FEW DRINKS.
NOT BEFORE.
THANK YOU, SIR.
I'M SORRY, I--
NO NEED TO APOLOGIZE!
AND --COME ON!

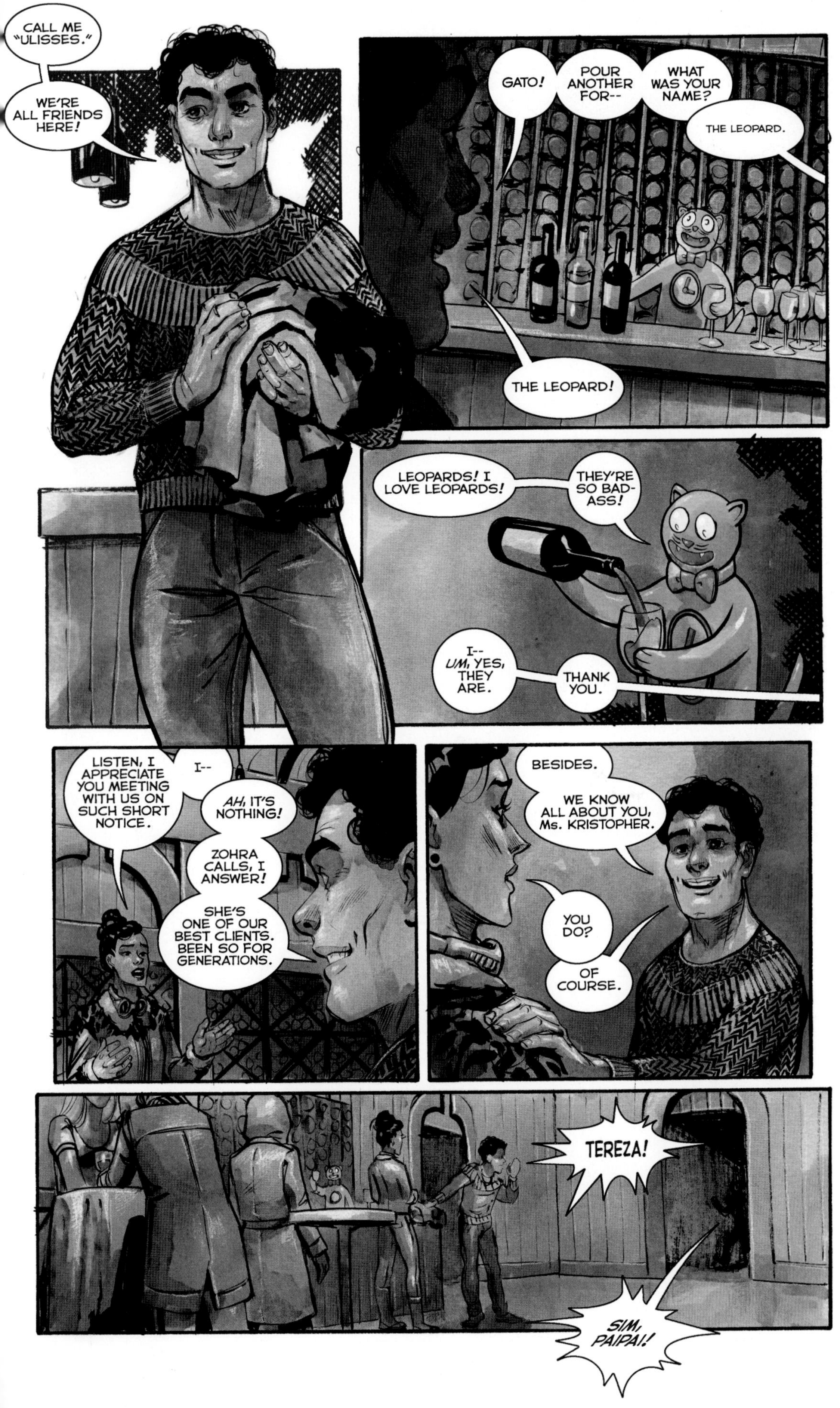
CALL ME "ULISSES."
WE'RE ALL FRIENDS HERE!
GATO!
POUR ANOTHER FOR--
WHAT WAS YOUR NAME?
THE LEOPARD.
THE LEOPARD!
LEOPARDS! I LOVE LEOPARDS!
THEY'RE SO BAD-ASS!
I-- UM, YES, THEY ARE.
THANK YOU.
LISTEN, I APPRECIATE YOU MEETING WITH US ON SUCH SHORT NOTICE.
I--
AH, IT'S NOTHING!
ZOHRA CALLS, I ANSWER!
SHE'S ONE OF OUR BEST CLIENTS. BEEN SO FOR GENERATIONS.
BESIDES.
WE KNOW ALL ABOUT YOU, Ms. KRISTOPHER.
YOU DO?
OF COURSE.
TEREZA!
SIM, PAIPAI!

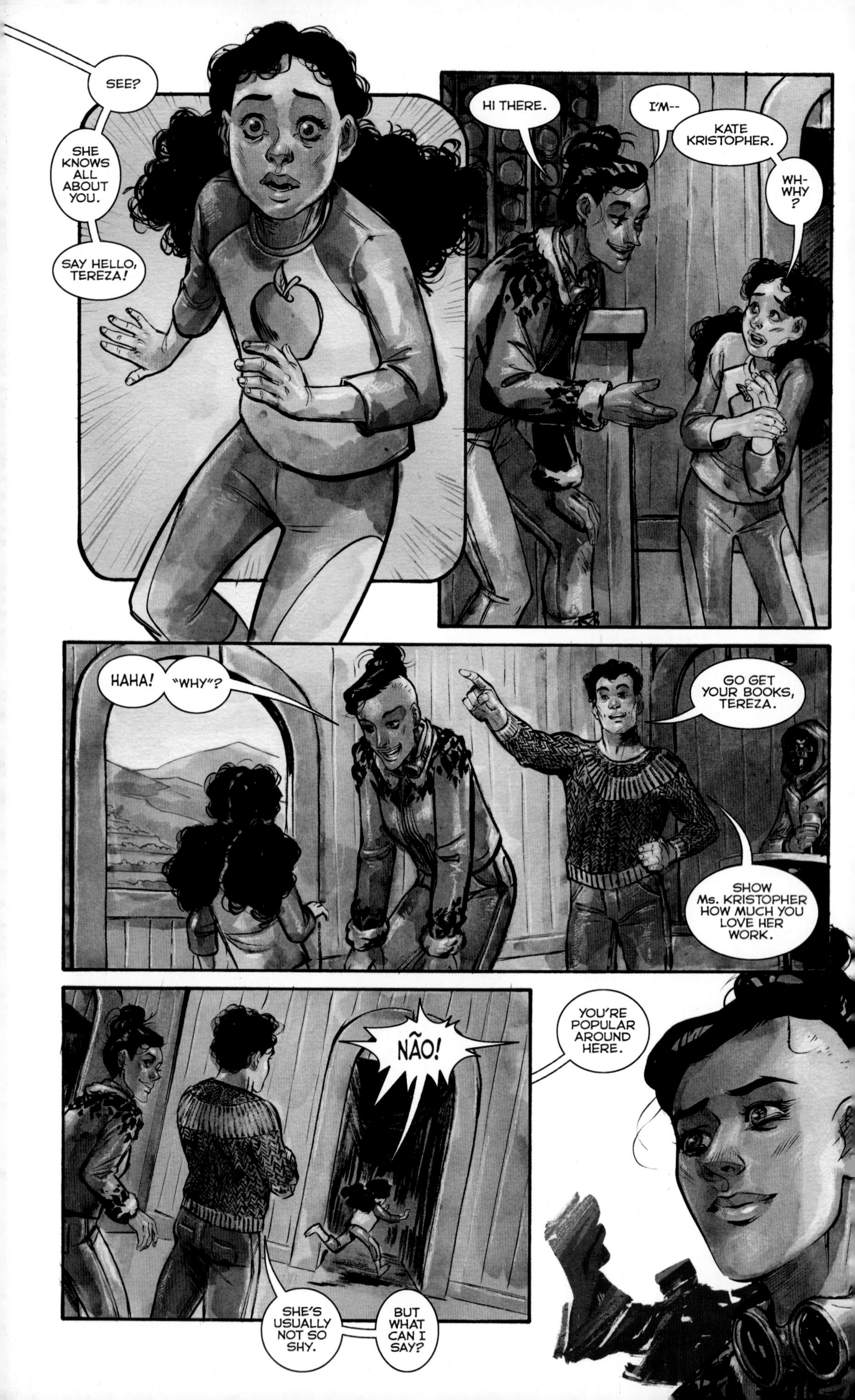
SEE?
SHE KNOWS ALL ABOUT YOU.
SAY HELLO, TEREZA!
HI THERE.
I'M--
KATE KRISTOPHER.
WH-WHY?
HAHA!
"WHY"?
GO GET YOUR BOOKS, TEREZA.
SHOW Ms. KRISTOPHER HOW MUCH YOU LOVE HER WORK.
NÃO!
SHE'S USUALLY NOT SO SHY.
BUT WHAT CAN I SAY?
YOU'RE POPULAR AROUND HERE.

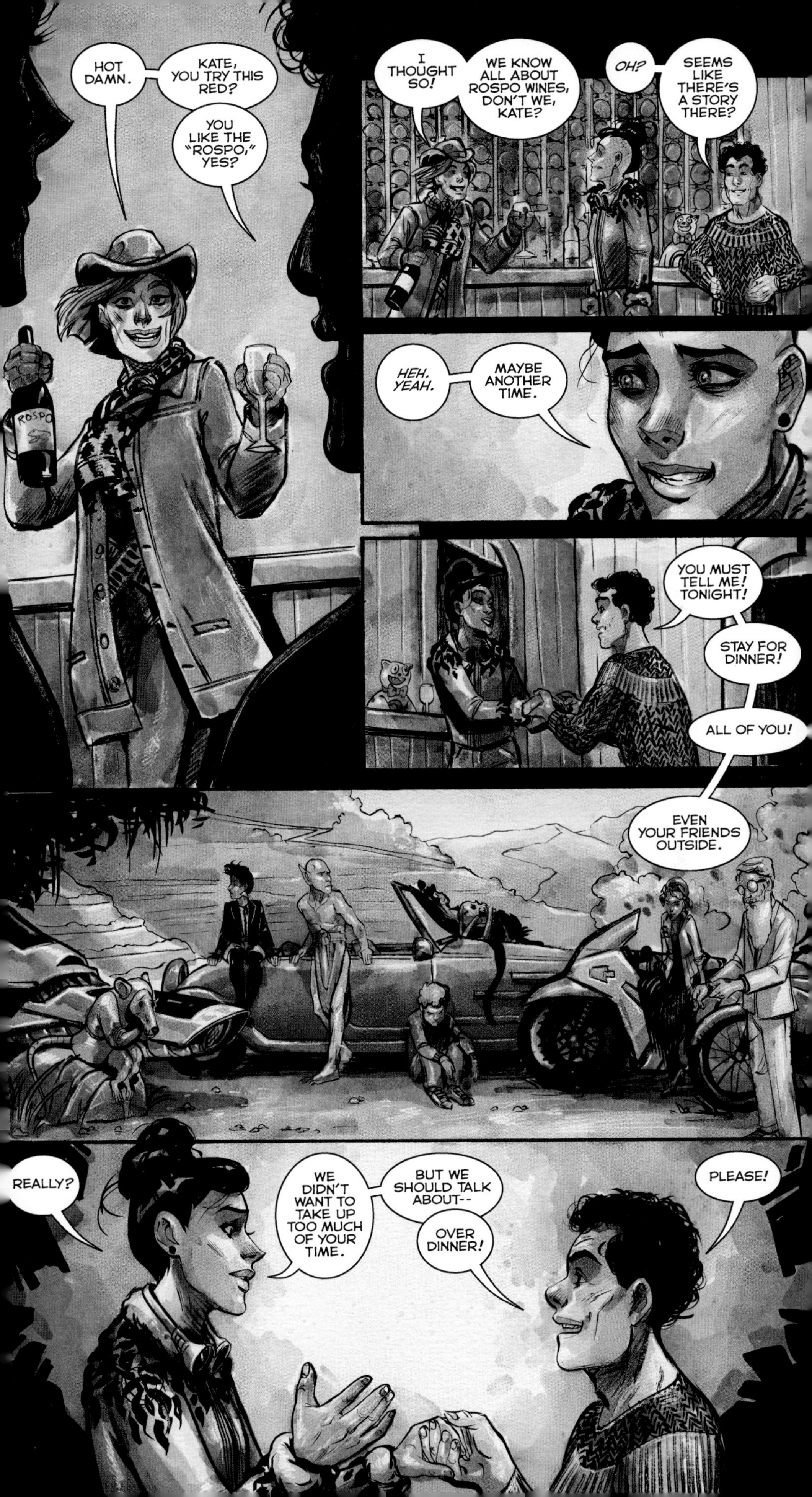

HOT DAMN.
KATE, YOU TRY THIS RED?
YOU LIKE THE "ROSPO," YES?
ROSPO
I THOUGHT SO!
WE KNOW ALL ABOUT ROSPO WINES, DON'T WE, KATE?
OH?
SEEMS LIKE THERE'S A STORY THERE?
HEH. YEAH.
MAYBE ANOTHER TIME.
YOU MUST TELL ME! TONIGHT!
STAY FOR DINNER!
ALL OF YOU!
EVEN YOUR FRIENDS OUTSIDE.
REALLY?
WE DIDN'T WANT TO TAKE UP TOO MUCH OF YOUR TIME.
BUT WE SHOULD TALK ABOUT--
OVER DINNER!
PLEASE!

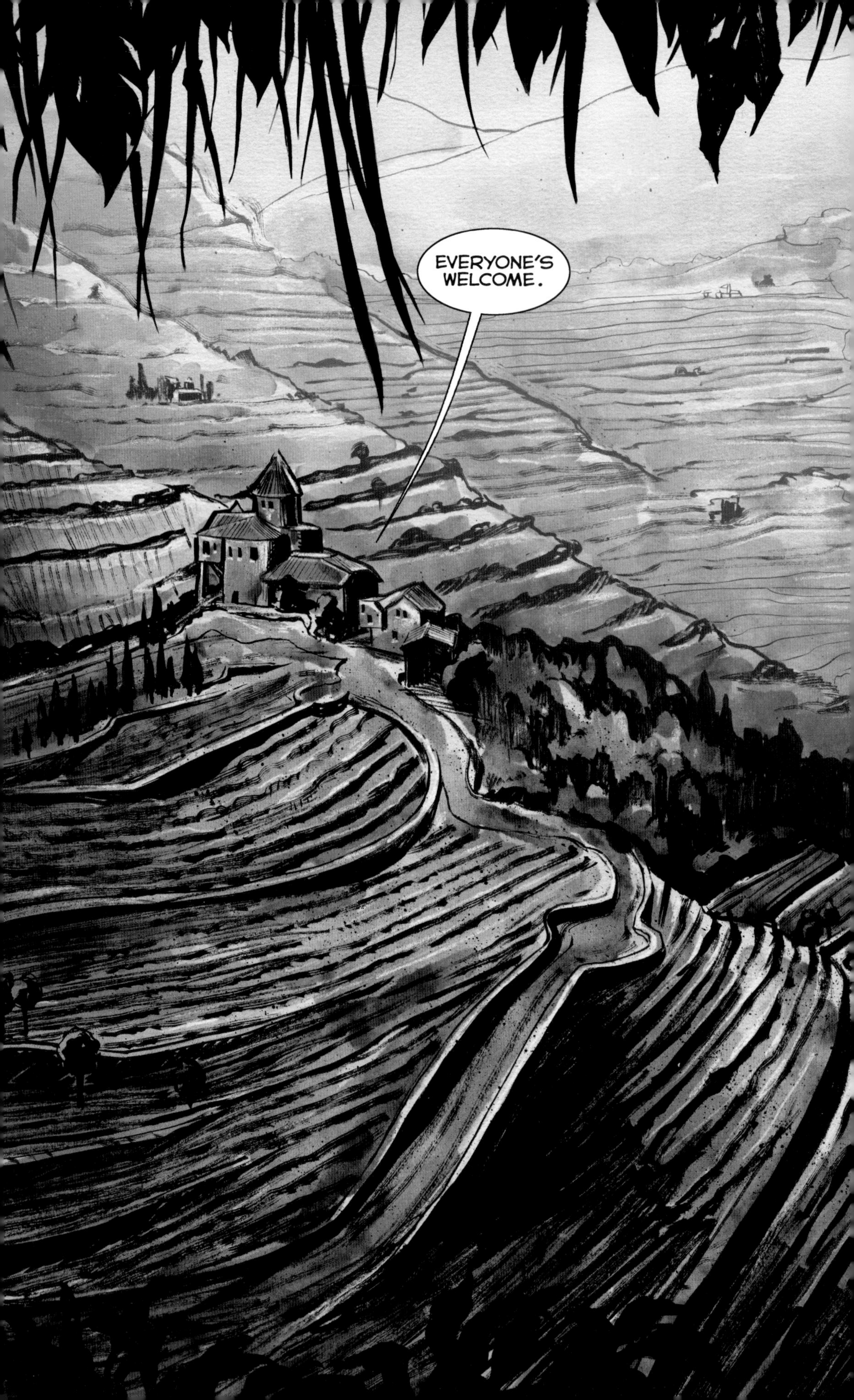
EVERYONE'S WELCOME.

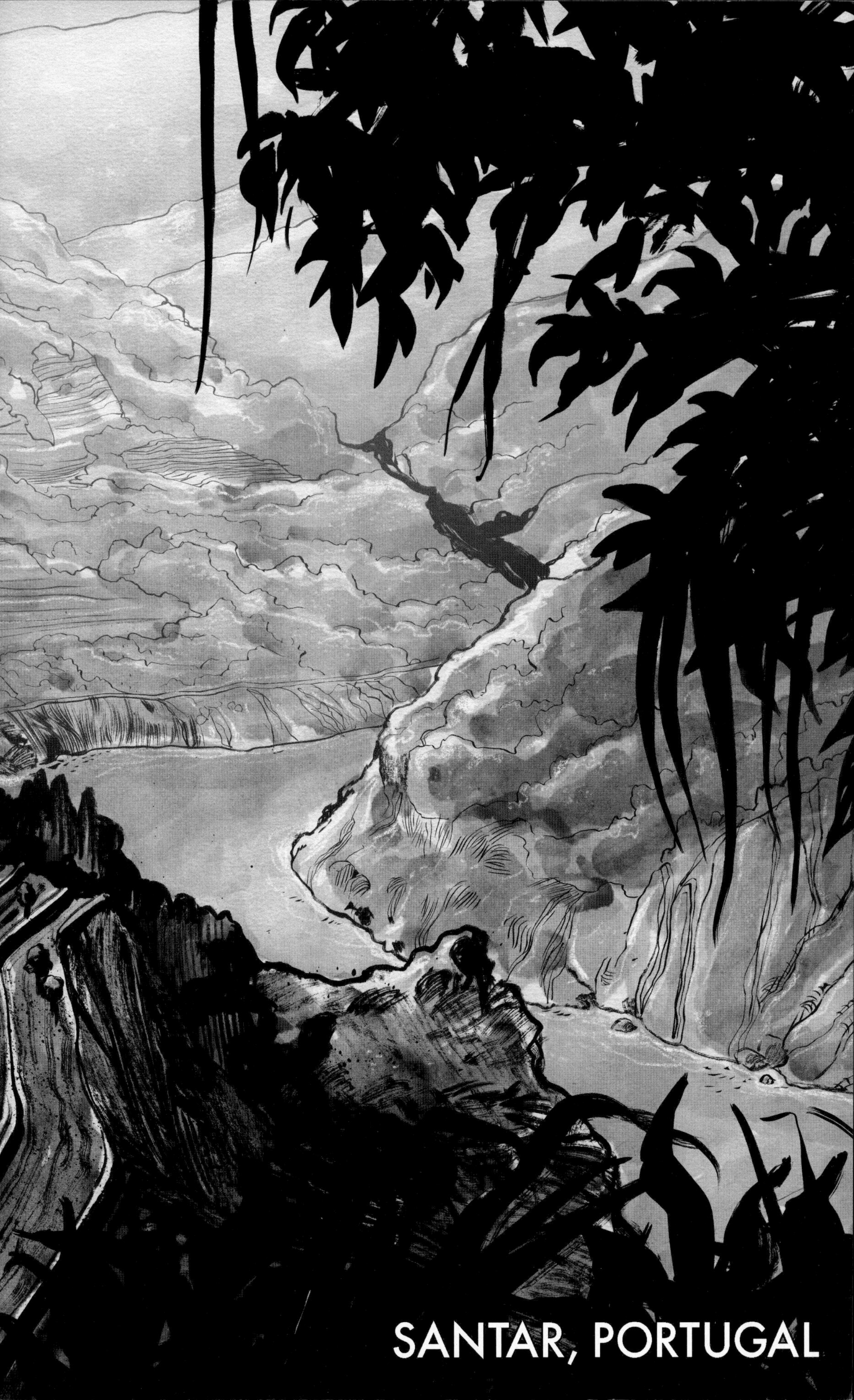
SANTAR, PORTUGAL

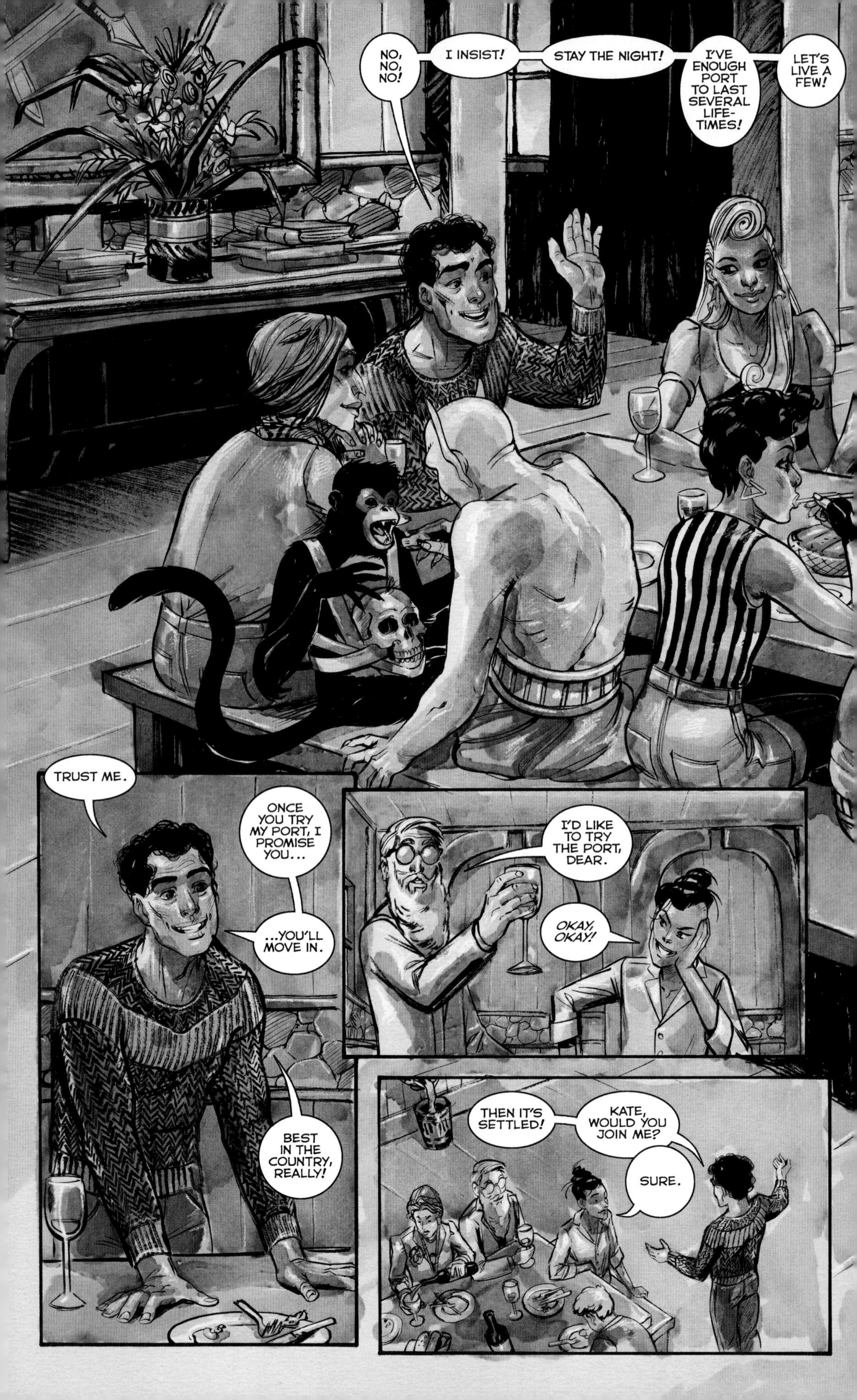
NO, NO, NO!
I INSIST!
STAY THE NIGHT!
I'VE ENOUGH PORT TO LAST SEVERAL LIFE-TIMES!
LET'S LIVE A FEW!
TRUST ME.
ONCE YOU TRY MY PORT, I PROMISE YOU...
...YOU'LL MOVE IN.
BEST IN THE COUNTRY, REALLY!
I'D LIKE TO TRY THE PORT, DEAR.
OKAY, OKAY!
THEN IT'S SETTLED!
KATE, WOULD YOU JOIN ME?
SURE.

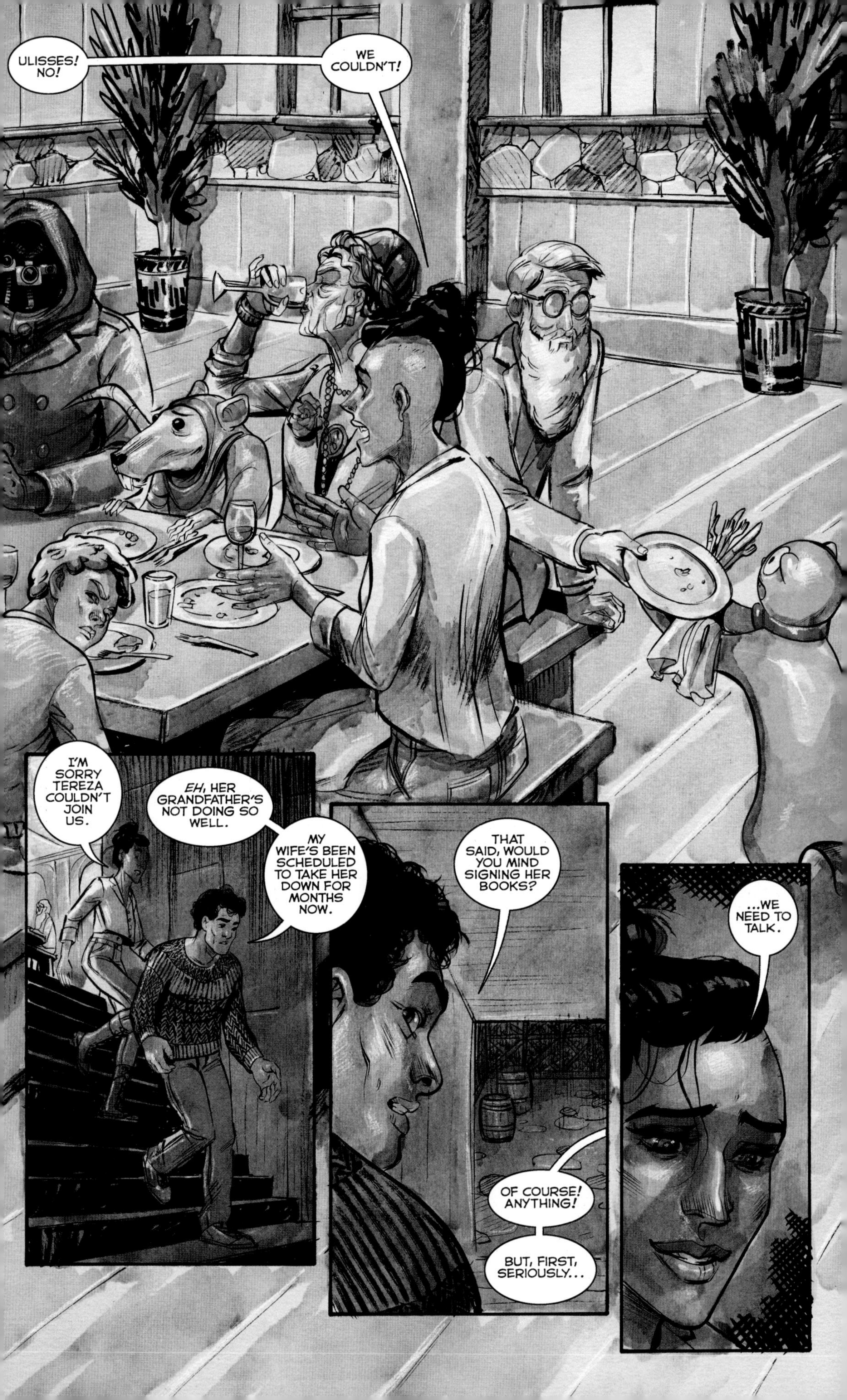
ULISSES! NO!
WE COULDN'T!
I'M SORRY TEREZA COULDN'T JOIN US.
EH, HER GRANDFATHER'S NOT DOING SO WELL.
MY WIFE'S BEEN SCHEDULED TO TAKE HER DOWN FOR MONTHS NOW.
THAT SAID, WOULD YOU MIND SIGNING HER BOOKS?
OF COURSE! ANYTHING!
BUT, FIRST, SERIOUSLY...
...WE NEED TO TALK.

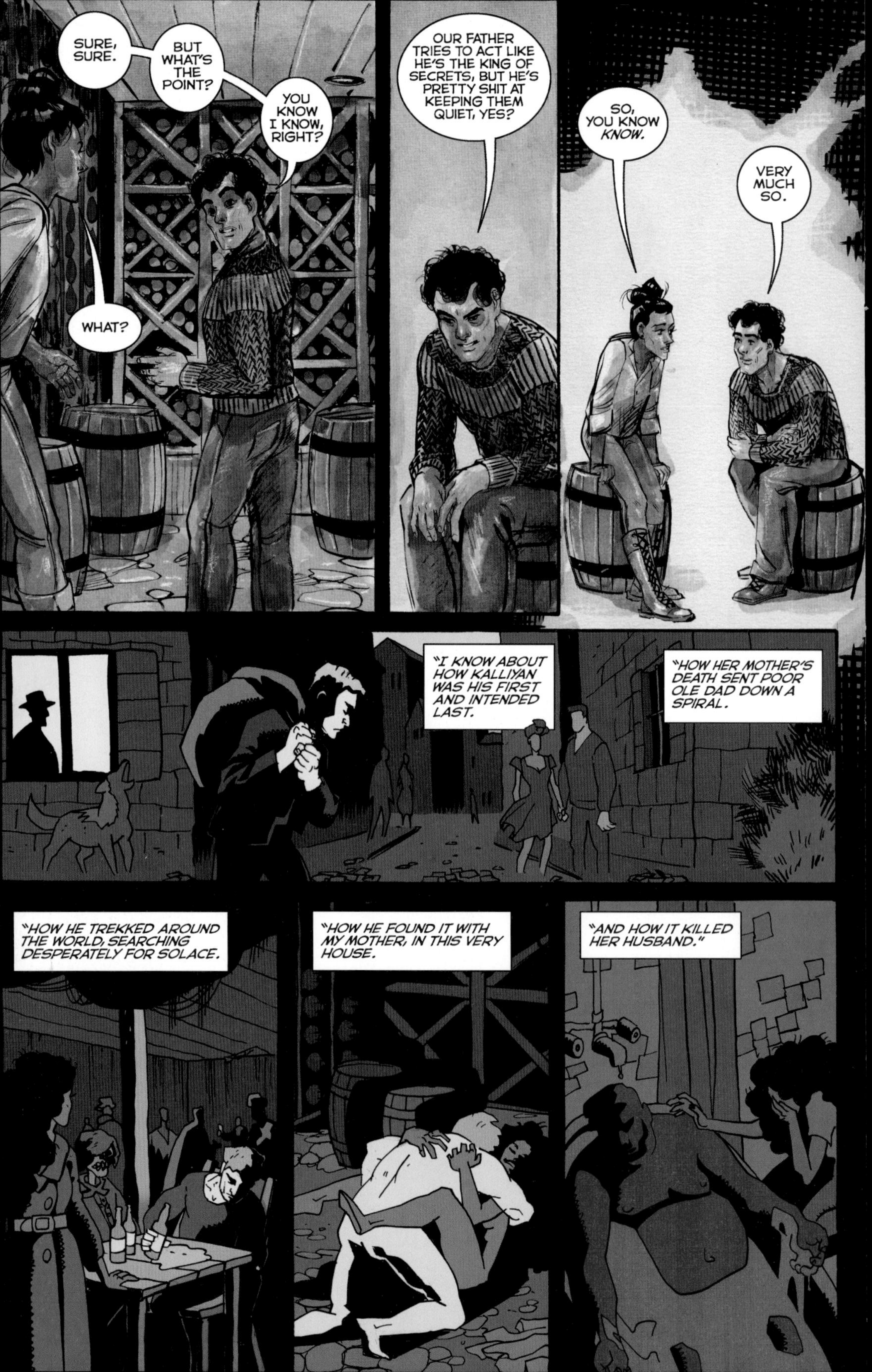
SURE, SURE.
BUT WHAT'S THE POINT?
YOU KNOW I KNOW, RIGHT?
WHAT?
OUR FATHER TRIES TO ACT LIKE HE'S THE KING OF SECRETS, BUT HE'S PRETTY SHIT AT KEEPING THEM QUIET, YES?
SO, YOU KNOW *KNOW.*
VERY MUCH SO.
"I KNOW ABOUT HOW KALLIYAN WAS HIS FIRST AND INTENDED LAST.
"HOW HER MOTHER'S DEATH SENT POOR OLE DAD DOWN A SPIRAL.
"HOW HE TREKKED AROUND THE WORLD, SEARCHING DESPERATELY FOR SOLACE.
"HOW HE FOUND IT WITH MY MOTHER, IN THIS VERY HOUSE.
"AND HOW IT KILLED HER HUSBAND."

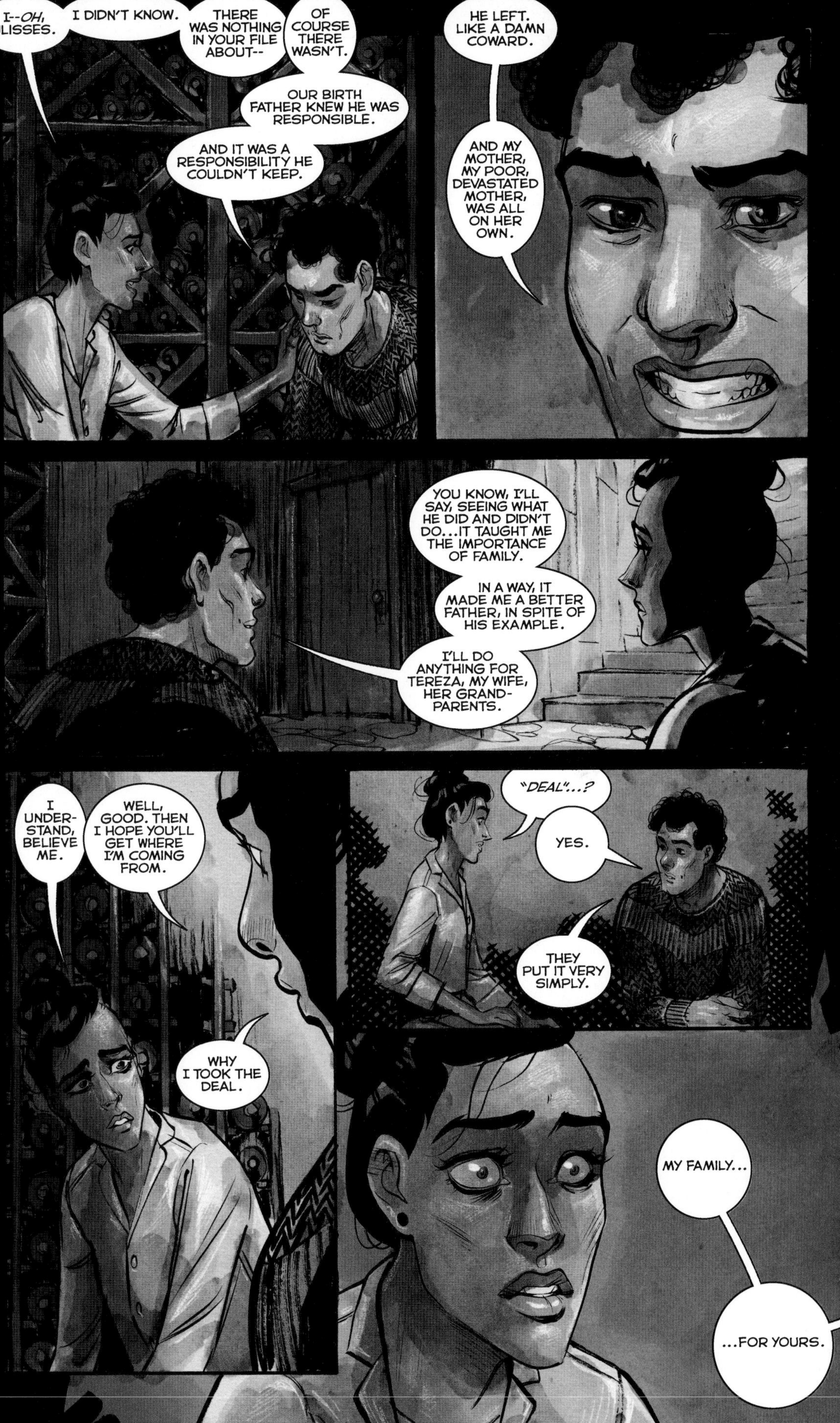

I--*OH*, ULISSES.
I DIDN'T KNOW.
THERE WAS NOTHING IN YOUR FILE ABOUT--
OF COURSE THERE WASN'T.
OUR BIRTH FATHER KNEW HE WAS RESPONSIBLE.
AND IT WAS A RESPONSIBILITY HE COULDN'T KEEP.
HE LEFT. LIKE A DAMN COWARD.
AND MY MOTHER, MY POOR, DEVASTATED MOTHER, WAS ALL ON HER OWN.
YOU KNOW, I'LL SAY, SEEING WHAT HE DID AND DIDN'T DO...IT TAUGHT ME THE IMPORTANCE OF FAMILY.
IN A WAY, IT MADE ME A BETTER FATHER, IN SPITE OF HIS EXAMPLE.
I'LL DO ANYTHING FOR TEREZA, MY WIFE, HER GRAND-PARENTS.
I UNDER-STAND, BELIEVE ME.
WELL, GOOD. THEN I HOPE YOU'LL GET WHERE I'M COMING FROM.
WHY I TOOK THE DEAL.
"*DEAL*"...?
YES.
THEY PUT IT VERY SIMPLY.
MY FAMILY...
...FOR YOURS.

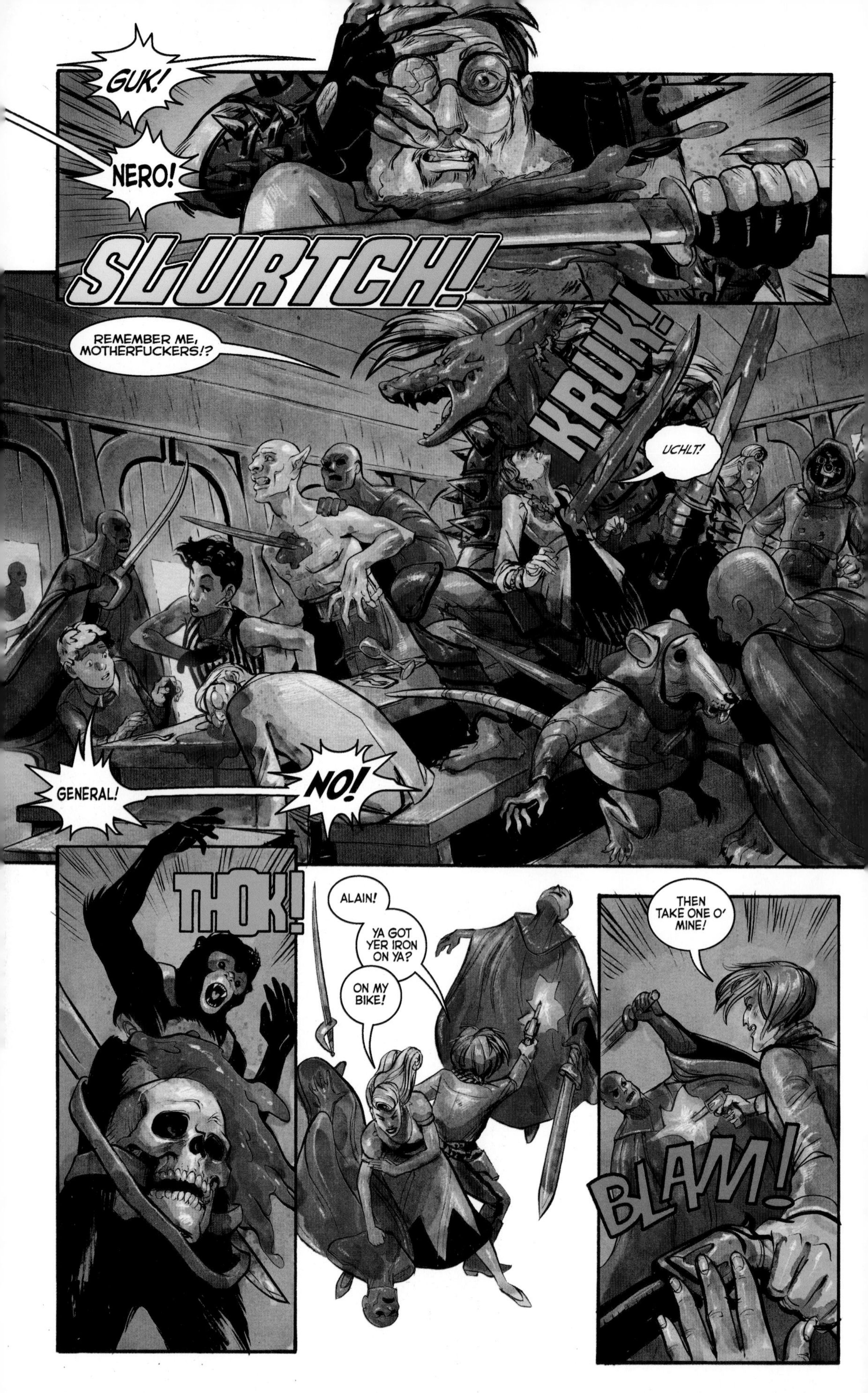
GUK!
NERO!
SLURTCH!
REMEMBER ME, MOTHERFUCKERS!?
KRUK!
UCHLT!
GENERAL!
NO!
THOK!
ALAIN!
YA GOT YER IRON ON YA?
ON MY BIKE!
THEN TAKE ONE O' MINE!
BLAM!

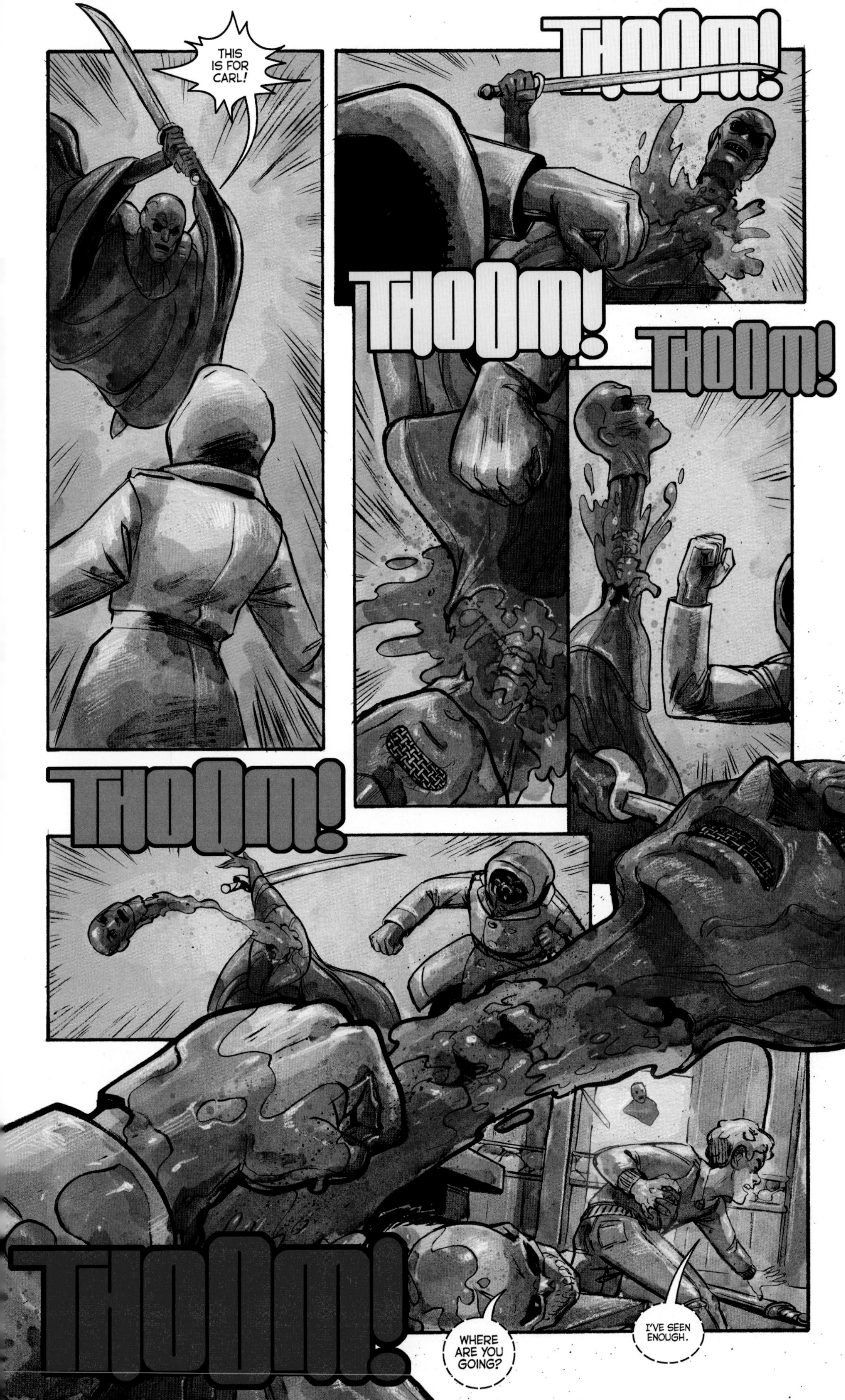
THIS IS FOR CARL!
THOOM!
THOOM!
THOOM!
THOOM!
THOOM!
WHERE ARE YOU GOING?
I'VE SEEN ENOUGH.

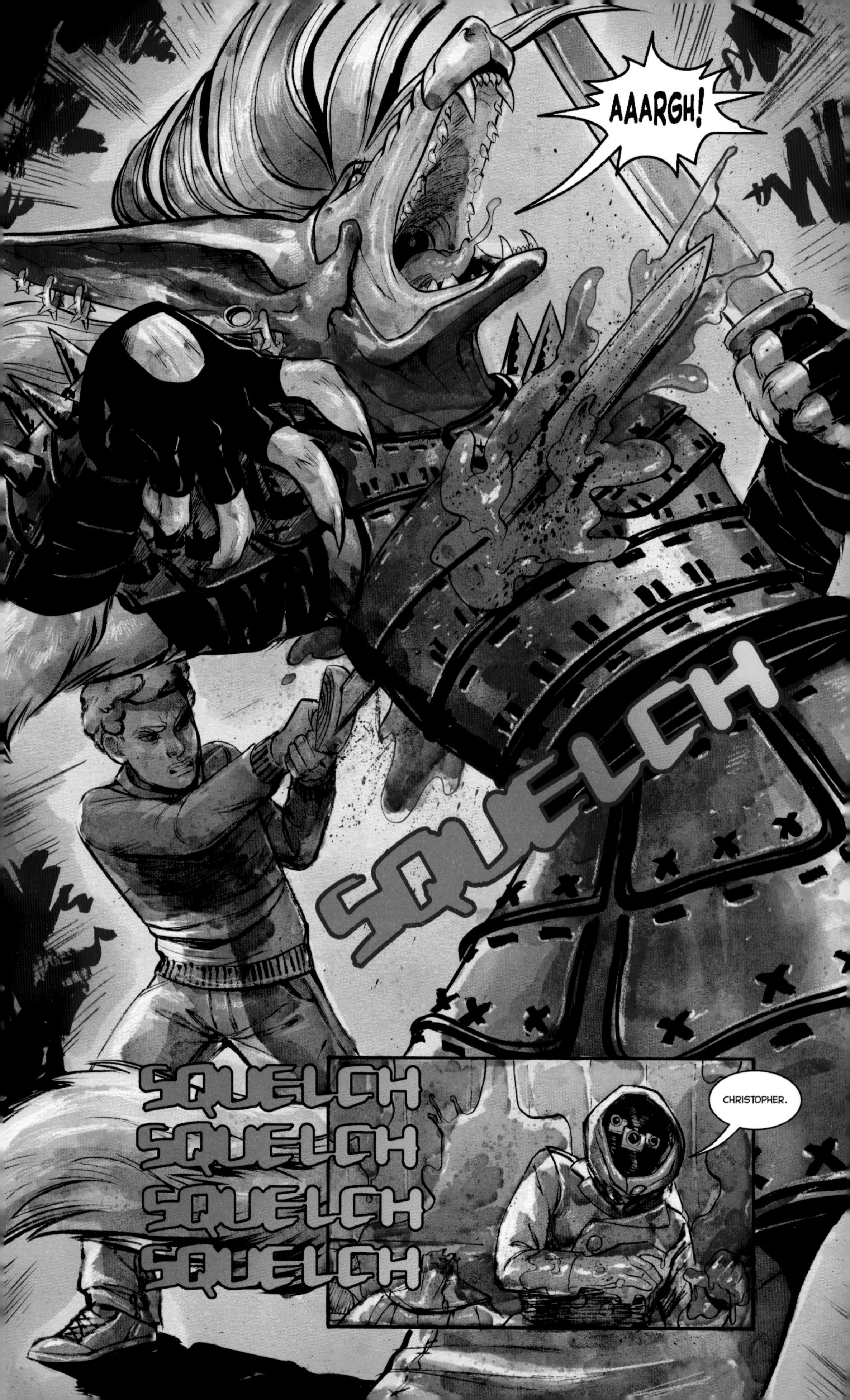
AAARGH!
SQUELCH
SQUELCH
SQUELCH
SQUELCH
SQUELCH
CHRISTOPHER.

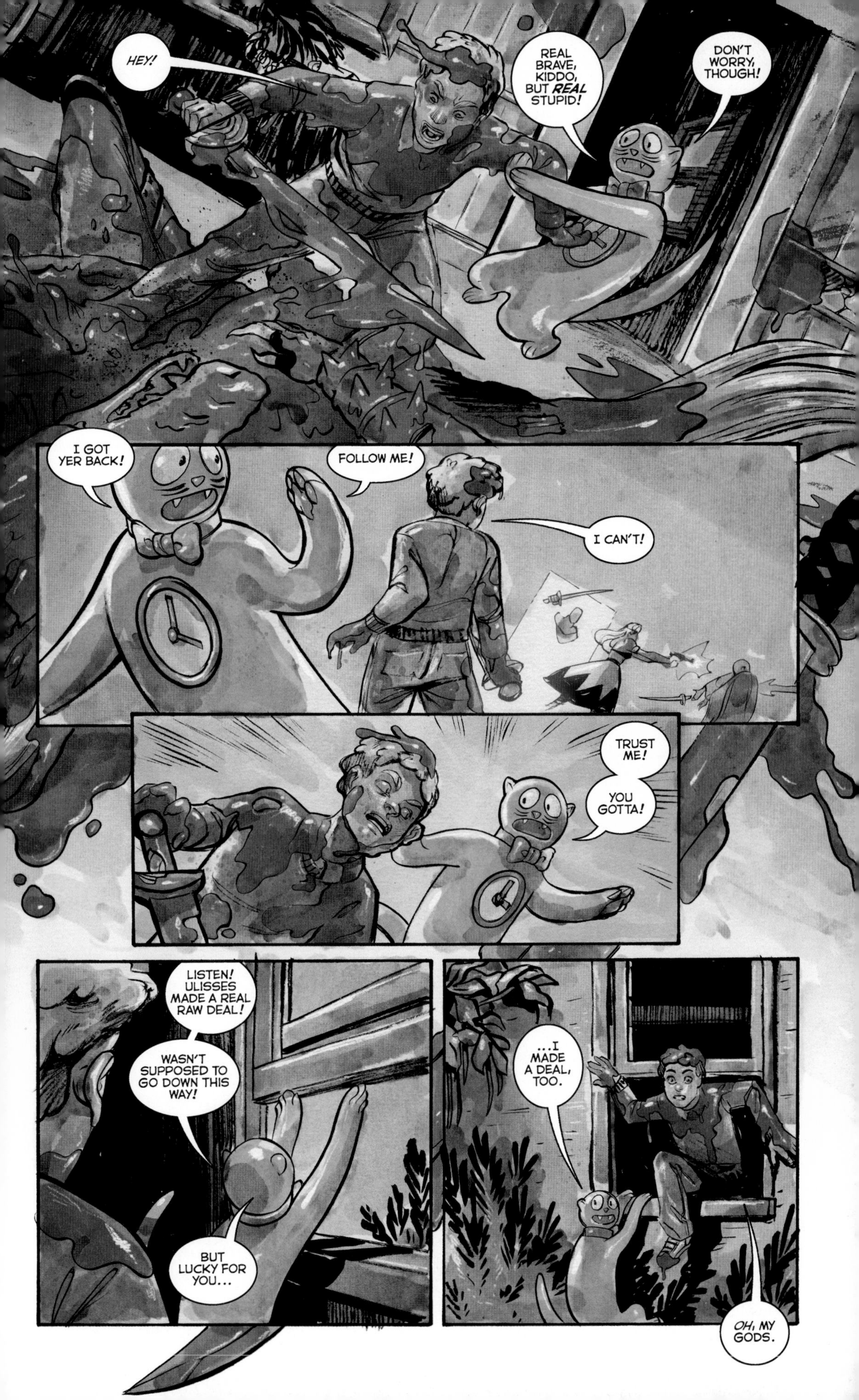
HEY!
REAL BRAVE, KIDDO, BUT REAL STUPID!
DON'T WORRY, THOUGH!
I GOT YER BACK!
FOLLOW ME!
I CAN'T!
TRUST ME!
YOU GOTTA!
LISTEN! ULISSES MADE A REAL RAW DEAL!
WASN'T SUPPOSED TO GO DOWN THIS WAY!
BUT LUCKY FOR YOU...
...I MADE A DEAL, TOO.
OH, MY GODS.

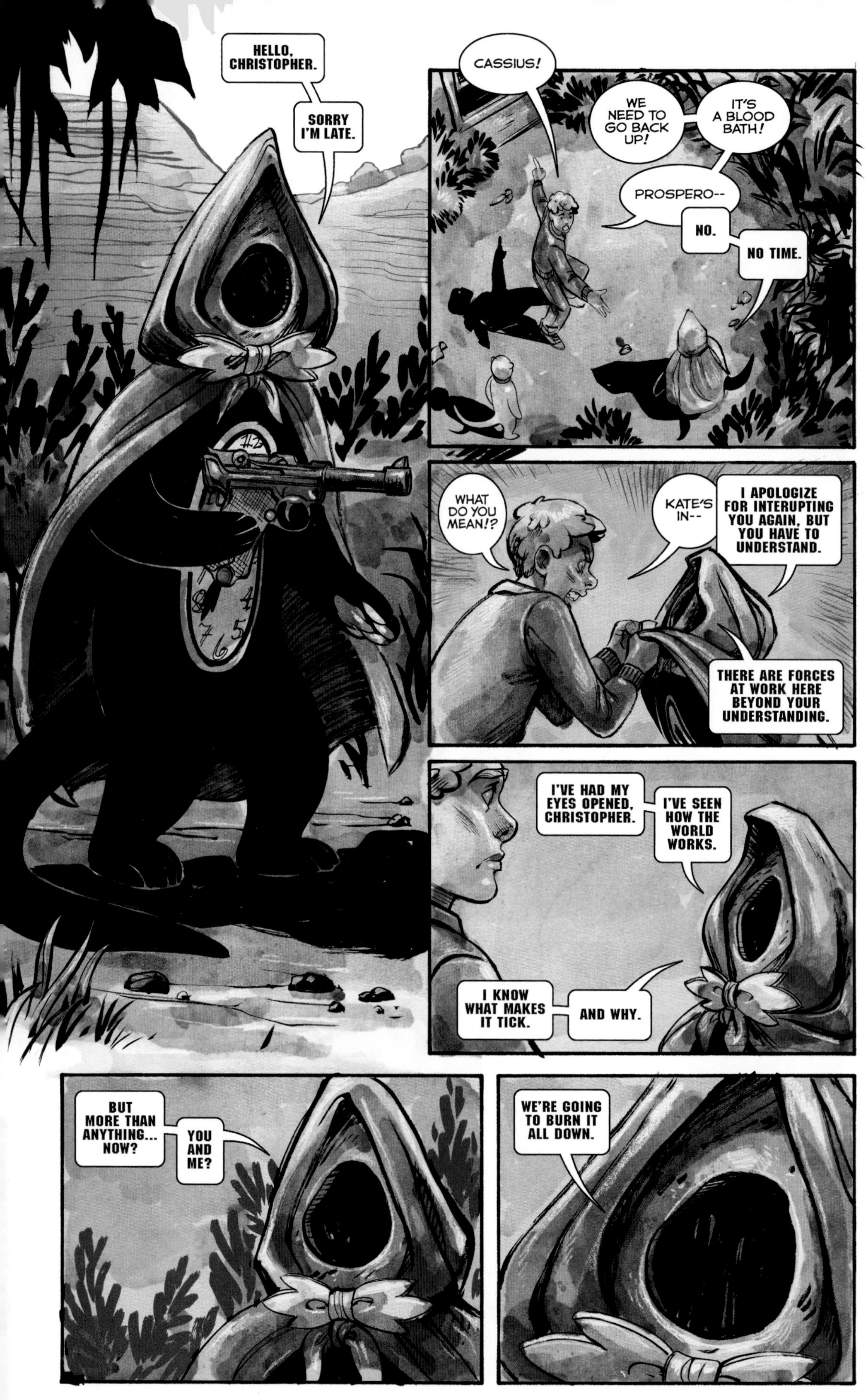
HELLO, CHRISTOPHER.
SORRY I'M LATE.
CASSIUS!
WE NEED TO GO BACK UP!
IT'S A BLOOD BATH!
PROSPERO--
NO.
NO TIME.
WHAT DO YOU MEAN!?
KATE'S IN--
I APOLOGIZE FOR INTERUPTING YOU AGAIN, BUT YOU HAVE TO UNDERSTAND.
THERE ARE FORCES AT WORK HERE BEYOND YOUR UNDERSTANDING.
I'VE HAD MY EYES OPENED, CHRISTOPHER.
I'VE SEEN HOW THE WORLD WORKS.
I KNOW WHAT MAKES IT TICK.
AND WHY.
BUT MORE THAN ANYTHING... NOW?
YOU AND ME?
WE'RE GOING TO BURN IT ALL DOWN.

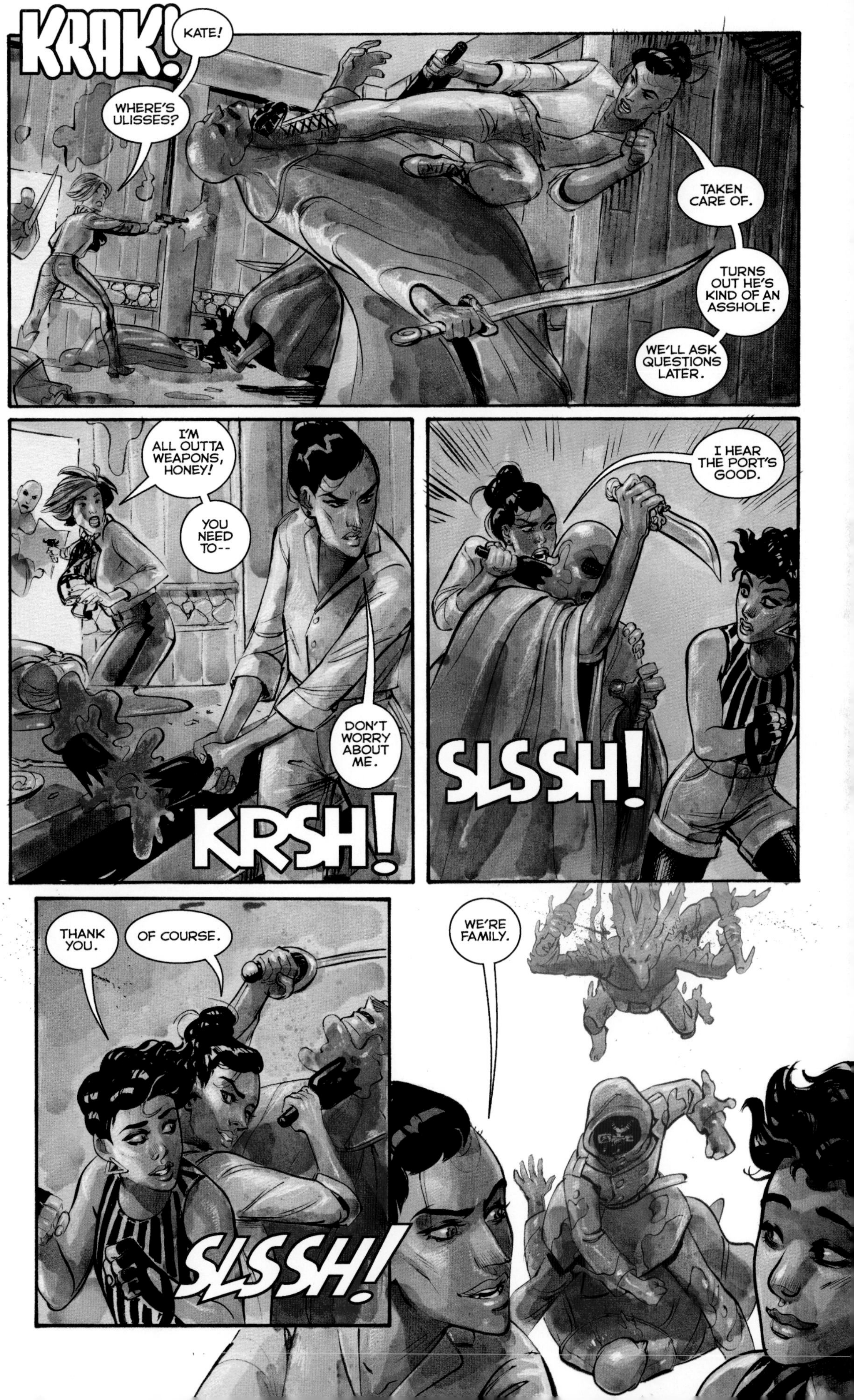
KRAK!
KATE!
WHERE'S ULISSES?
TAKEN CARE OF.
TURNS OUT HE'S KIND OF AN ASSHOLE.
WE'LL ASK QUESTIONS LATER.
I'M ALL OUTTA WEAPONS, HONEY!
YOU NEED TO--
DON'T WORRY ABOUT ME.
KRSH!
I HEAR THE PORT'S GOOD.
SLSSH!
THANK YOU.
OF COURSE.
SLSSH!
WE'RE FAMILY.

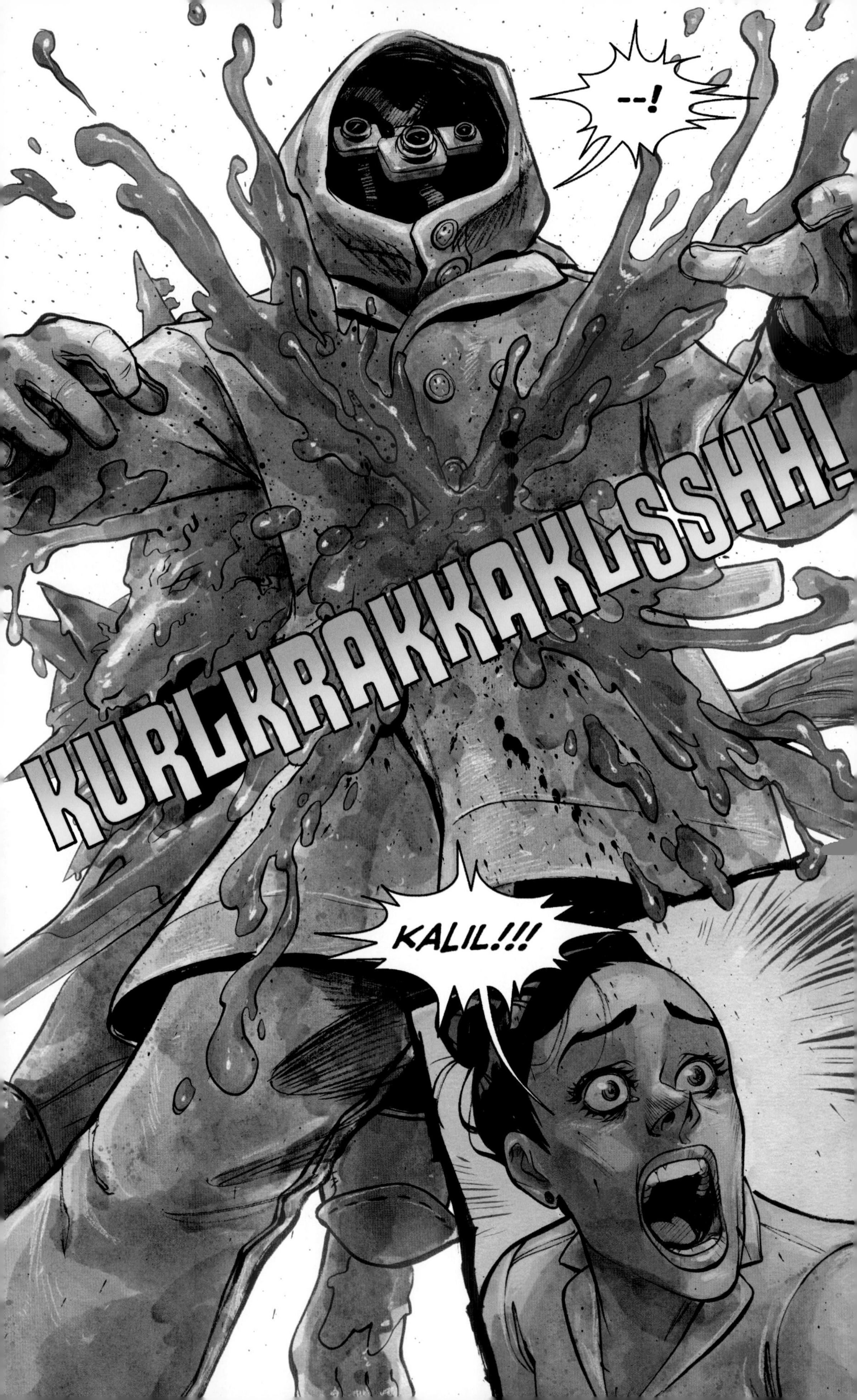
--!
KURLKRAKKAKLSSHH!
KALIL!!!

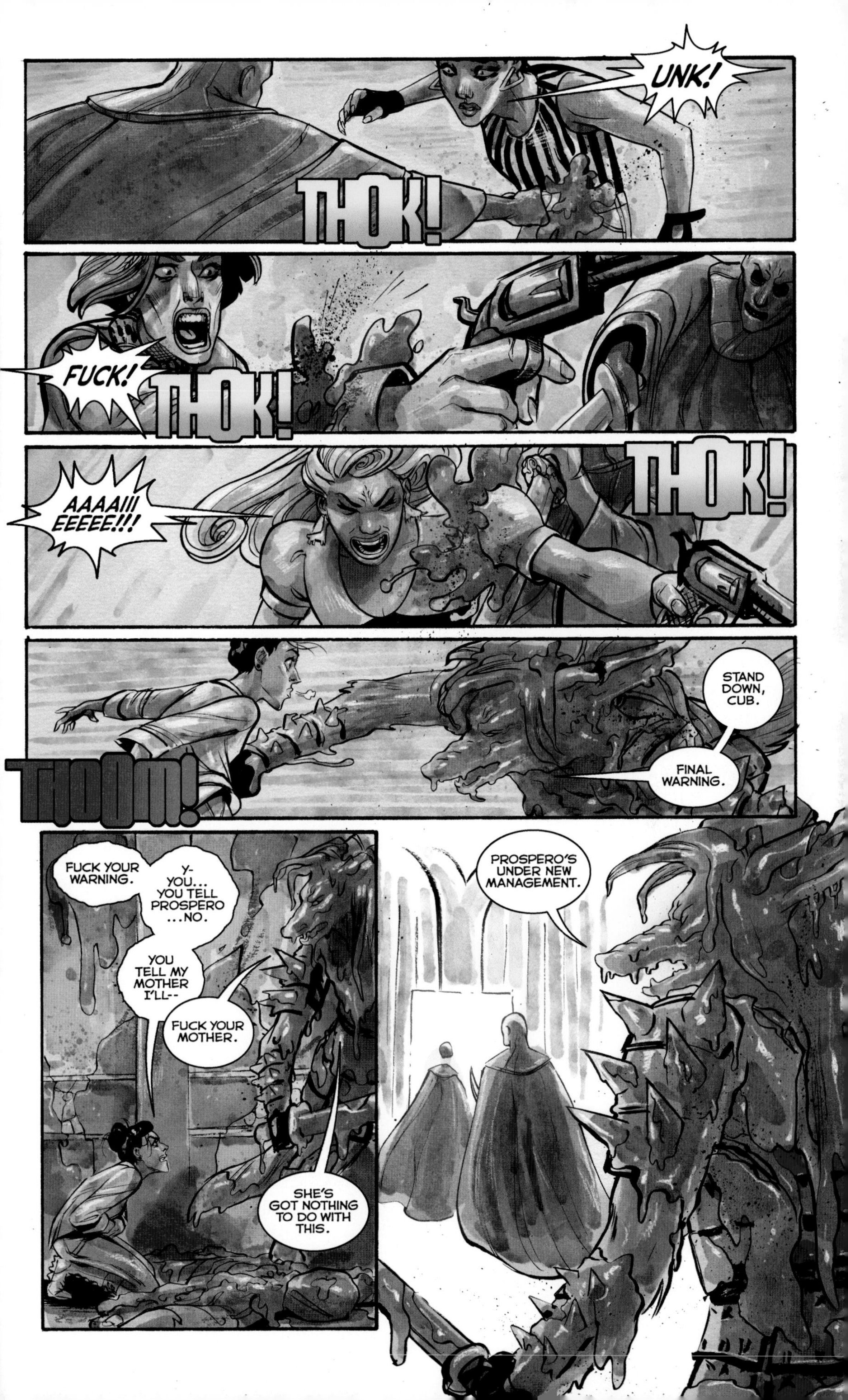
UNK!
THOK!
FUCK!
THOK!
AAAA!!!
EEEEE!!!
THOK!
STAND DOWN, CUB.
FINAL WARNING.
THOOM!
FUCK YOUR WARNING.
Y- YOU... YOU TELL PROSPERO ...NO.
YOU TELL MY MOTHER I'LL--
FUCK YOUR MOTHER.
SHE'S GOT NOTHING TO DO WITH THIS.
PROSPERO'S UNDER NEW MANAGEMENT.

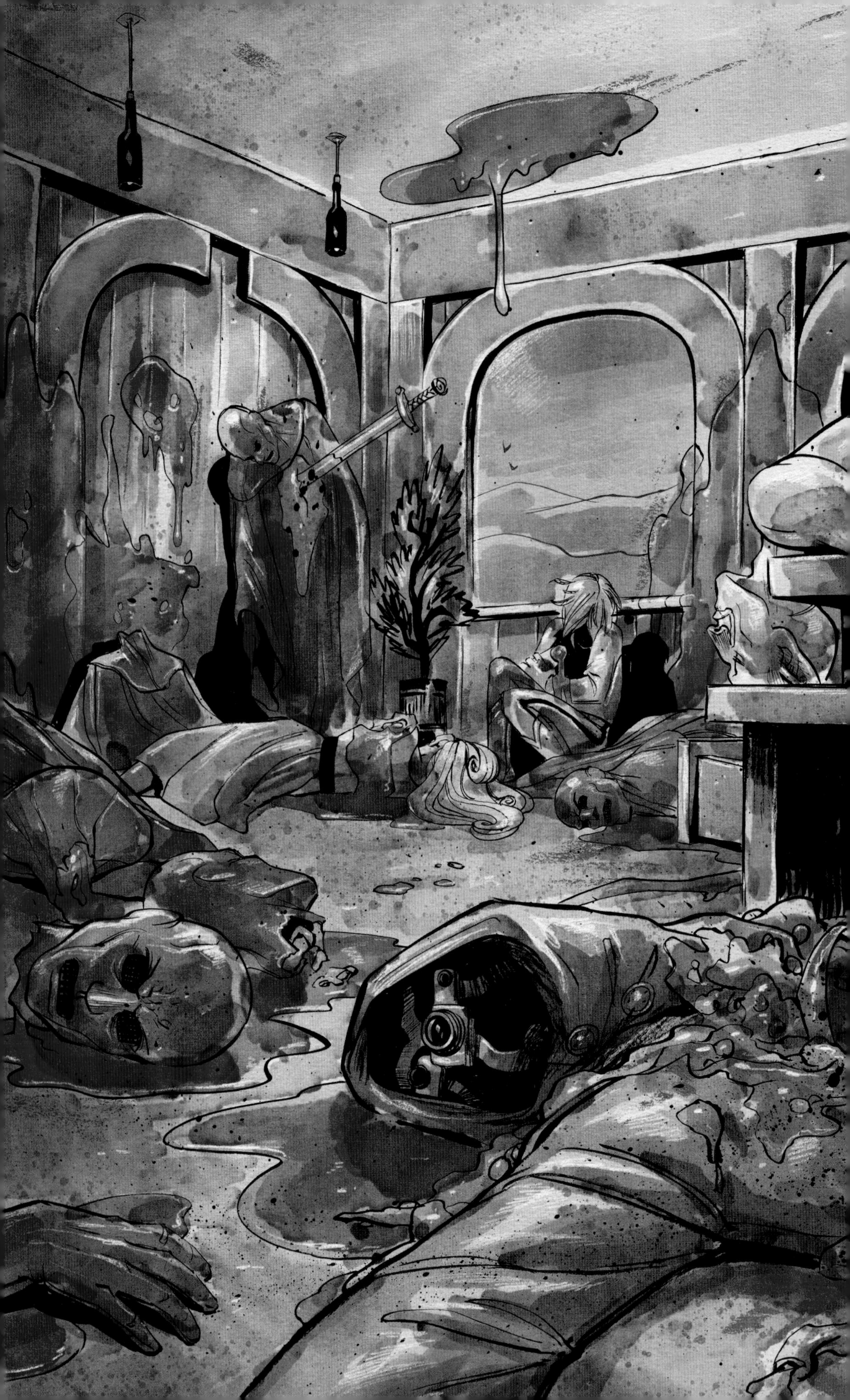

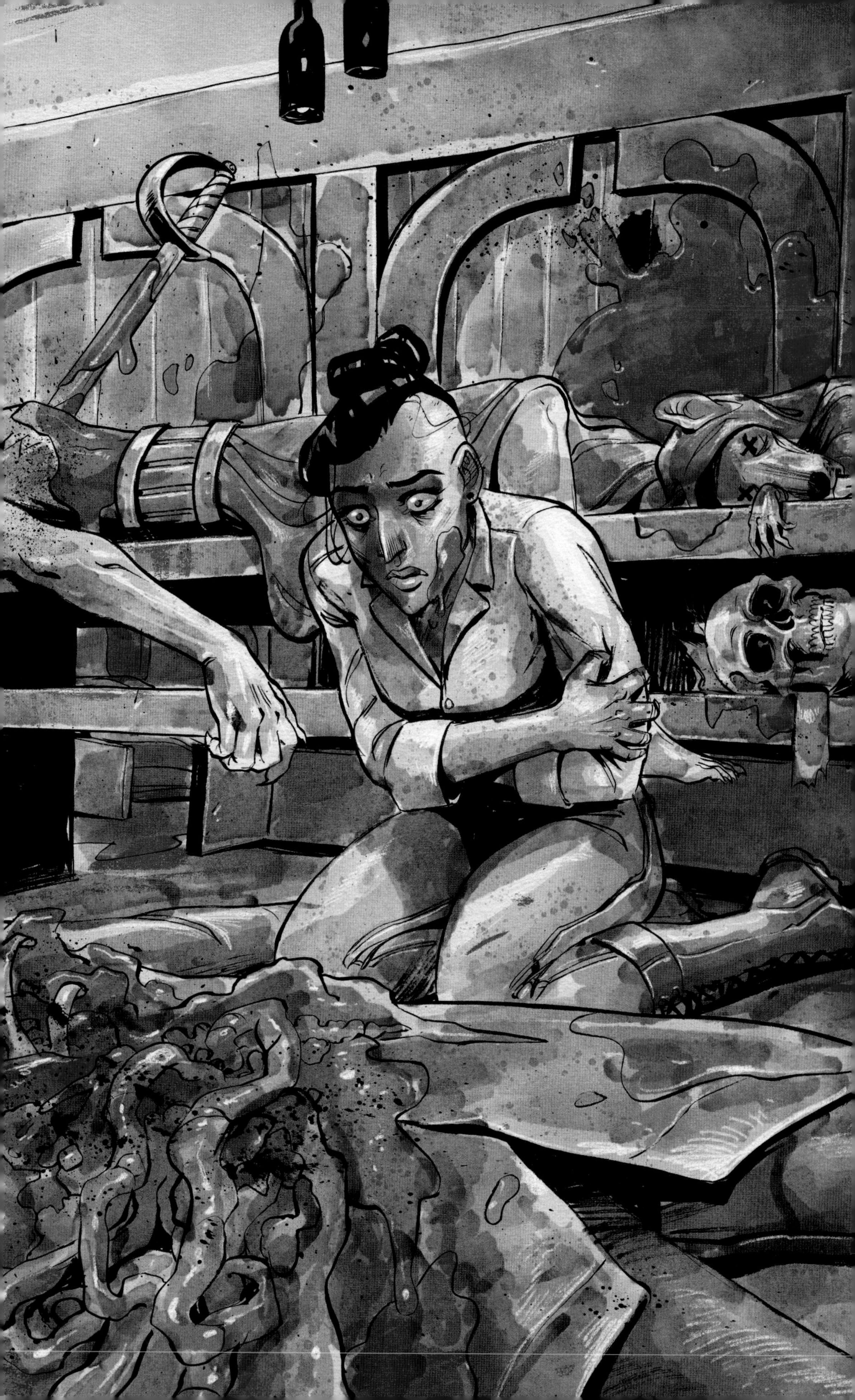

ACT TWO

END

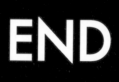

EPILOGUE

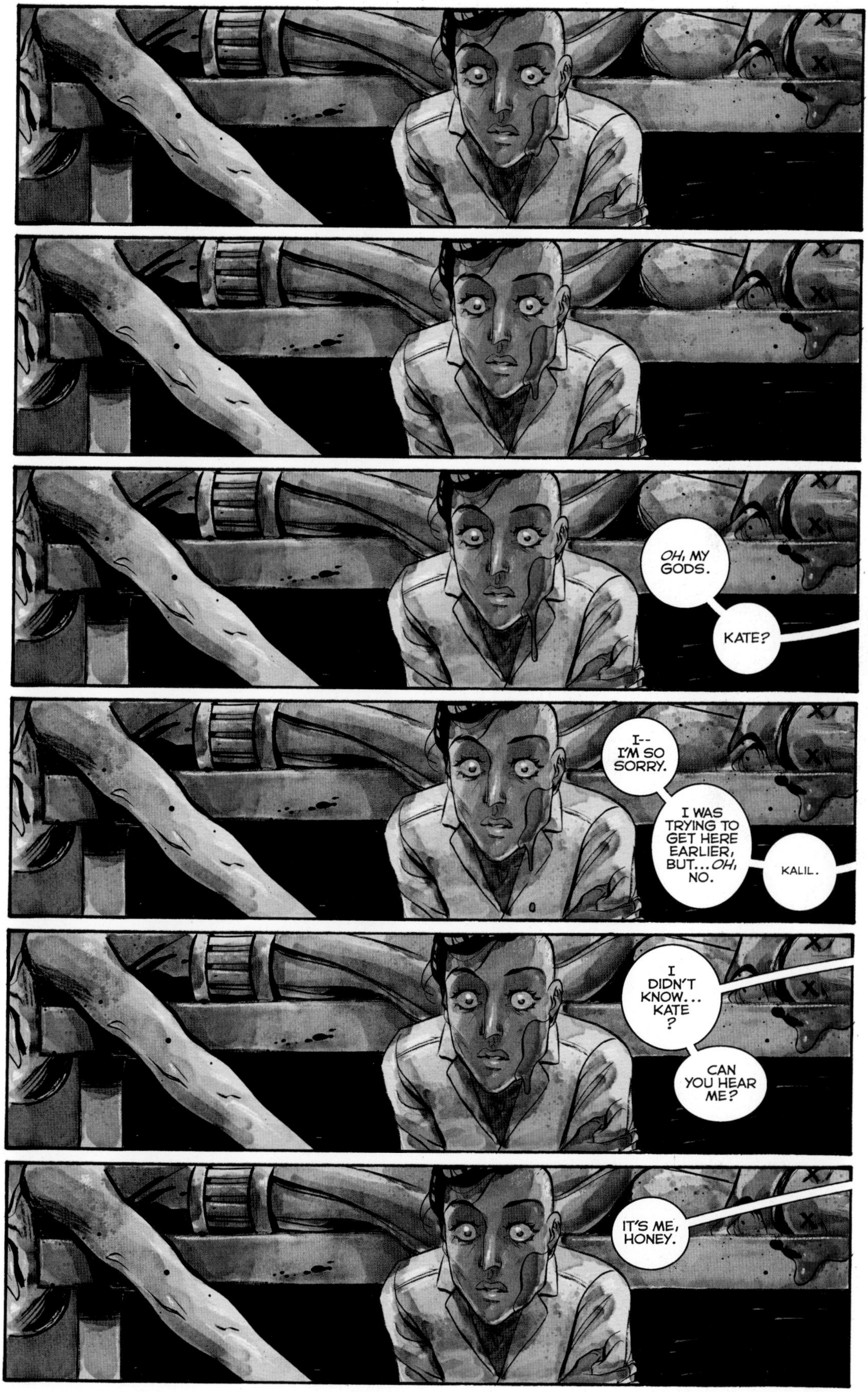
OH, MY GODS.
KATE?
I-- I'M SO SORRY.
I WAS TRYING TO GET HERE EARLIER, BUT... OH, NO.
KALIL.
I DIDN'T KNOW... KATE?
CAN YOU HEAR ME?
IT'S ME, HONEY.

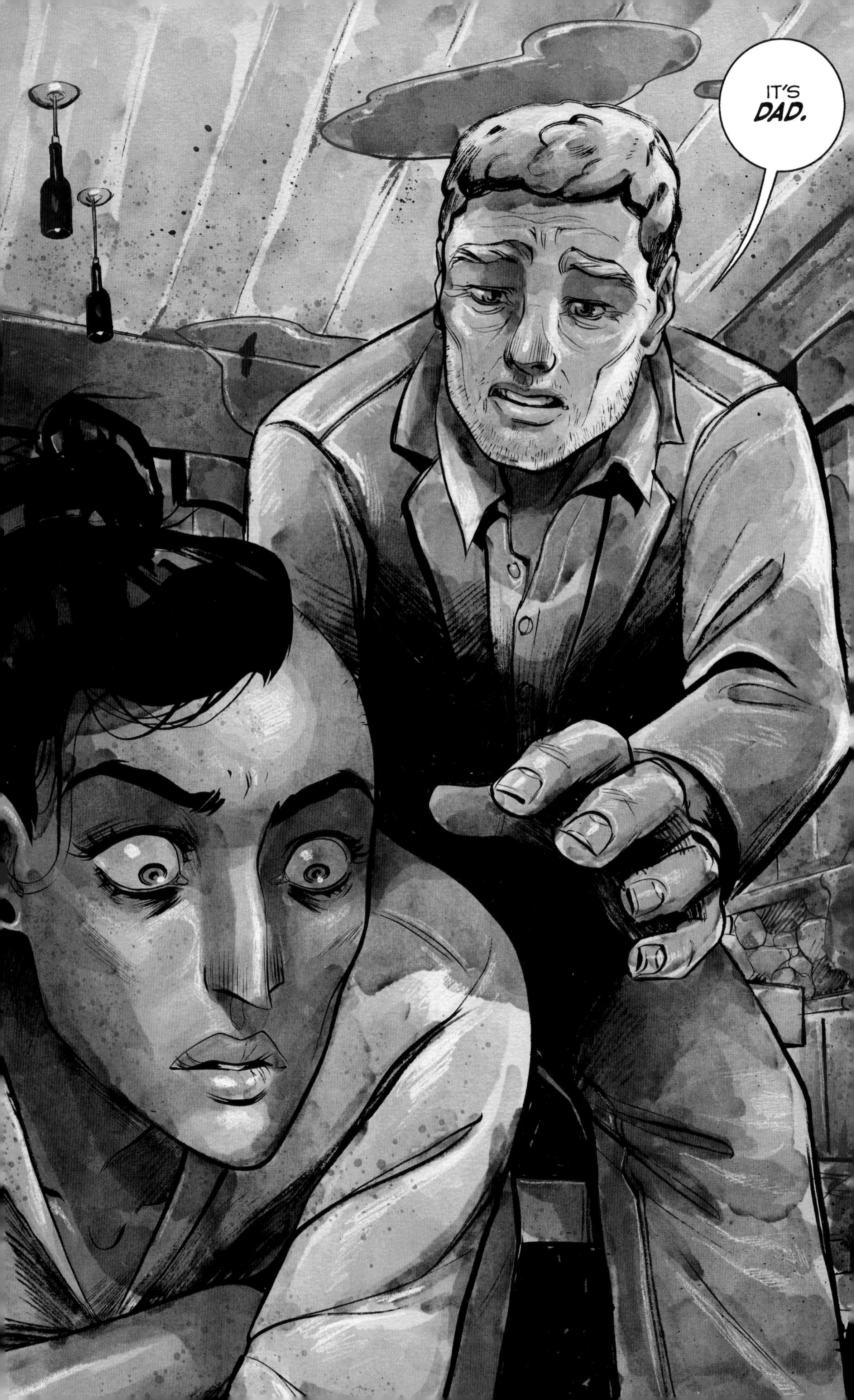
IT'S DAD.

CREATOR COMMENTARY

Leila: Finally an issue with romance! That's what I thought when Joe told me about the premise for #18. We had talked about Kate's orientation early on in the book, and ever since then I'd been dying to delve into it.

Joe: Finally an issue with romance! That's what I thought when I told Leila about the premise for #18. We had talked about Kate's orientation early on in the book, and ever since then I'd been dying to delve into it.

Leila: Regarding this issue, I'm most proud of the heartfelt closure scene between Kate and Huckleberry, which transitions into the next stage of their friendship.

Joe: One of the odder storytelling things we've done in structure is barely reveal anything about Kate when you first get to know her — it's like life, you don't know the most intimate details of someone until much later on. I liked you not discovering who she's been with until much later in the series, which is counter to how most serial fiction is structured.

Leila: I also loved drawing the party scene, which is where we introduce the bottle of Rospo wine that comes into play in #22.

Joe: One of my absolute favorite things to do in comics is plant tiny seeds which pay off later. There's stuff in #1 which doesn't pay off until #23, and some which won't pay off until the final issue.

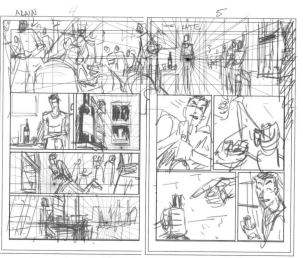

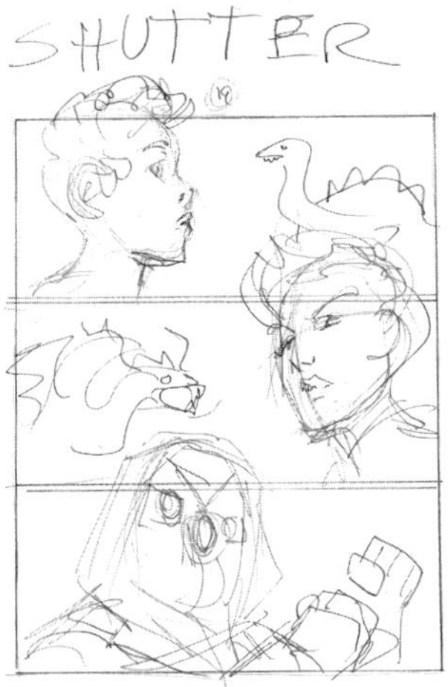
SHUTTER

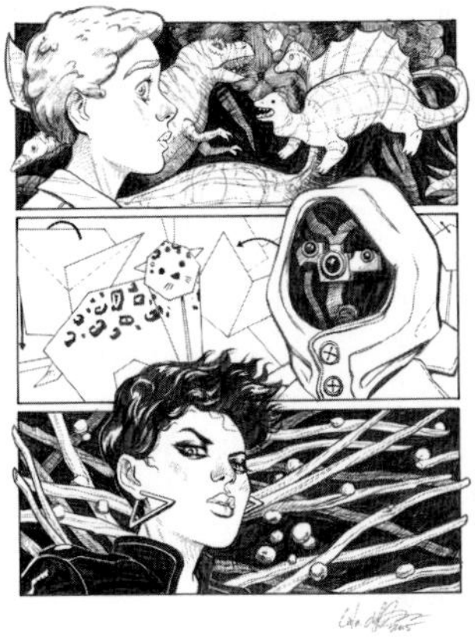

Leila: One of my favorite covers. I love a good panel break, and made me psyched for drawing the backstories of Chris Jr., The Leopard, and Kalliyan, all of who I was very curious about.

Joe: This issue was such a pain in the ass. I came up with one of the most difficult story structures to pull off during a pretty emotionally wracking period of my life, so this issue took about five hundred years to write. I keep wanting to do a writer's commentary, but I'm still too traumatized. Seems like folks liked it.

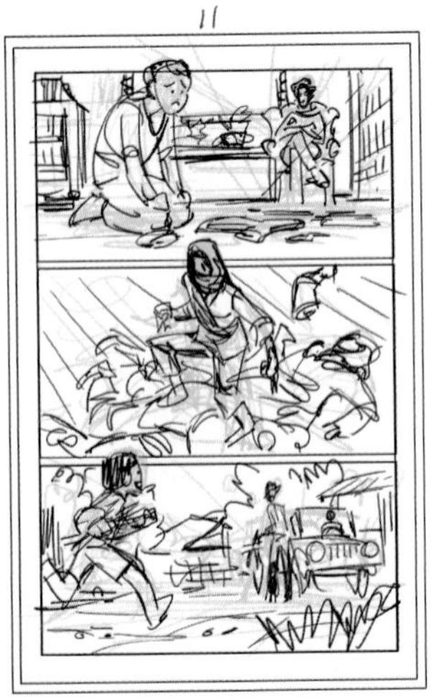
11

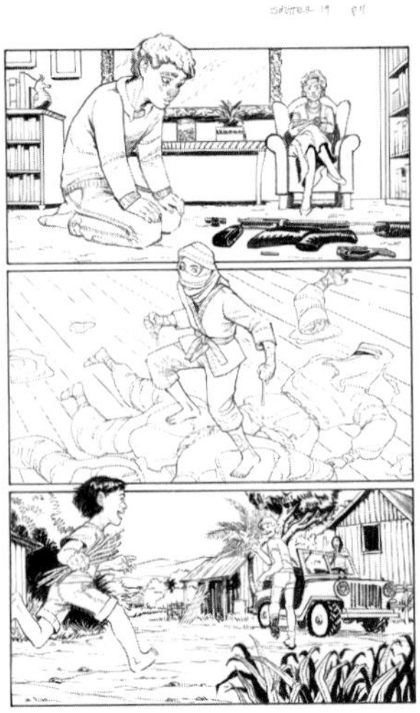

Leila: Again, making the characters pop out of their panels. This is an important page visually since we're focusing more on them instead of Chris Sr.'s side (well, except for Kalliyan's bit).

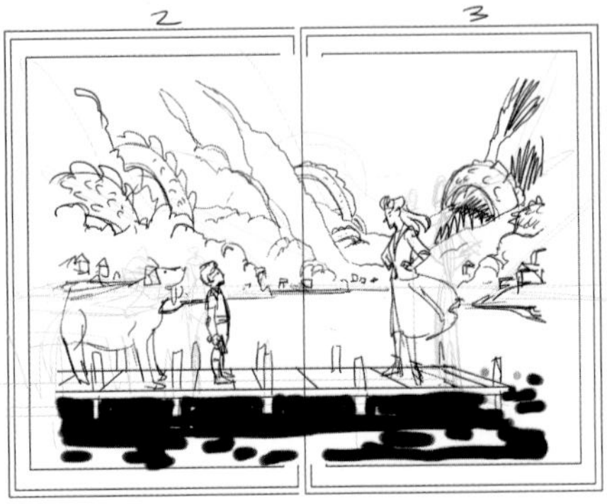
2
3

Leila: The ligne claire issue! Much to my surprise, drawing this way didn't go any faster than if I drew my own style. I thought because there were no line weights to worry about, it would be quick, but it wasn't. Over the course of this series, I've found that it's hard to copy other artists' styles. It doesn't come second nature like it does with my own art. But in the end, I love how it turned out, especially with Owen's colors, and I would like to work this way some day in the future.

Joe: I would like to see you work this way some day in the future.

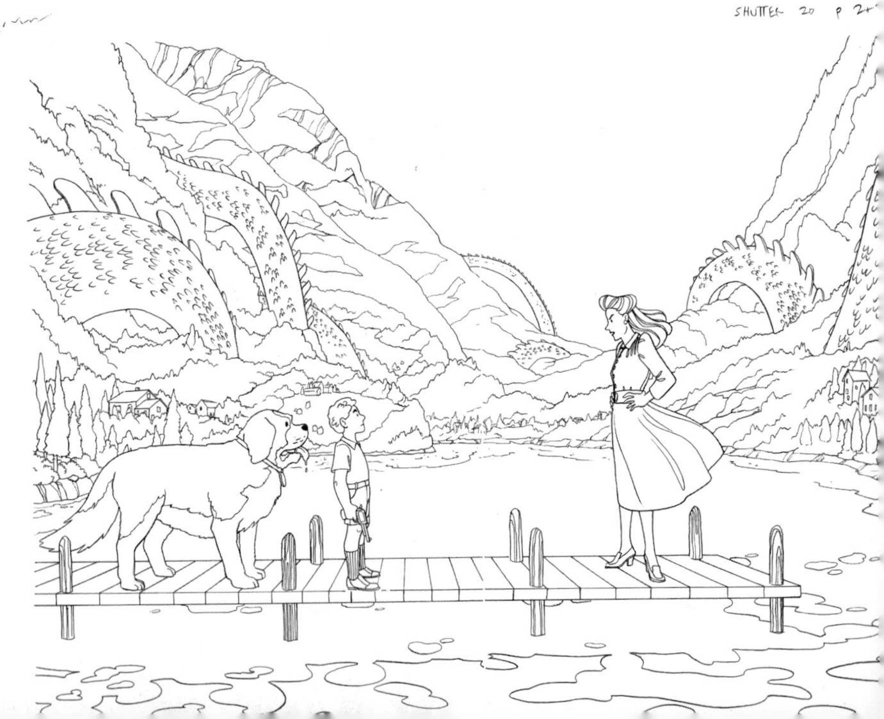
SHUTTER 20

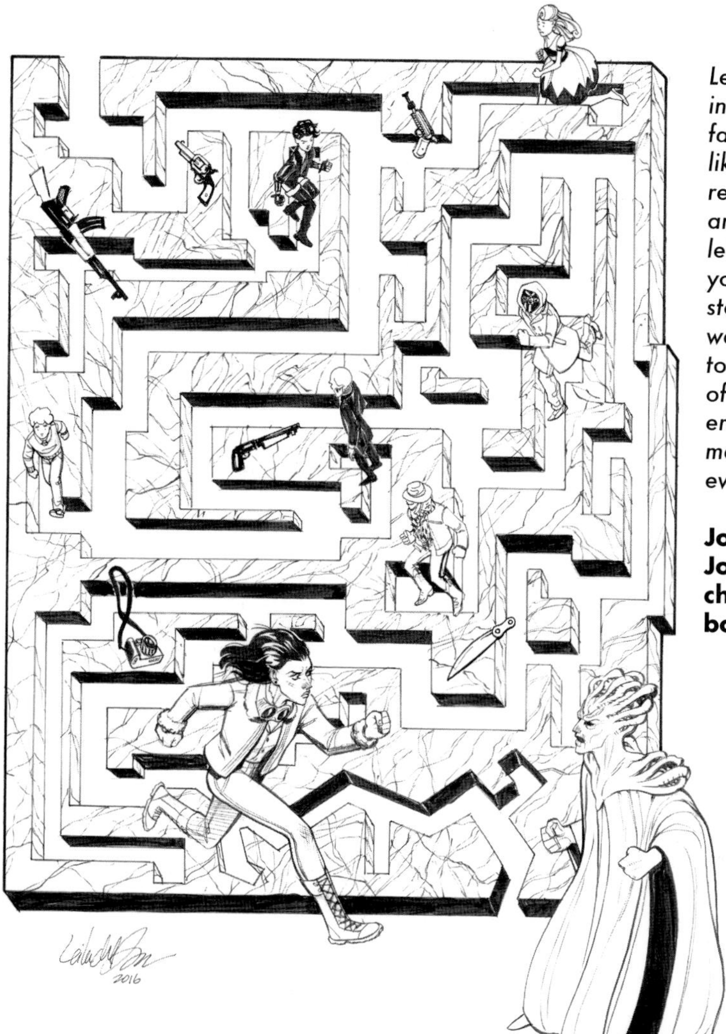

Leila: *Joe's pitch for the cover to #21 involved chess and our protagonists facing off with our antagonists. I didn't like the chessboard idea since I'd already seen it in Alice in Wonderland and didn't want people to draw parallels. Joe was like, well what the hell do you have as a better idea, so I brainstormed and came up with a maze. I wanted the challenge of learning how to make one and I also liked the idea of readers solving a maze on the cover. It turned out to be a super easy maze to solve, but it took for gol'darn ever to make!*

Joe: G'damn Lewis Carroll and John Tenniel gotta snipe my sweet chess ideas. I love chess. Everybody, play some chess today.

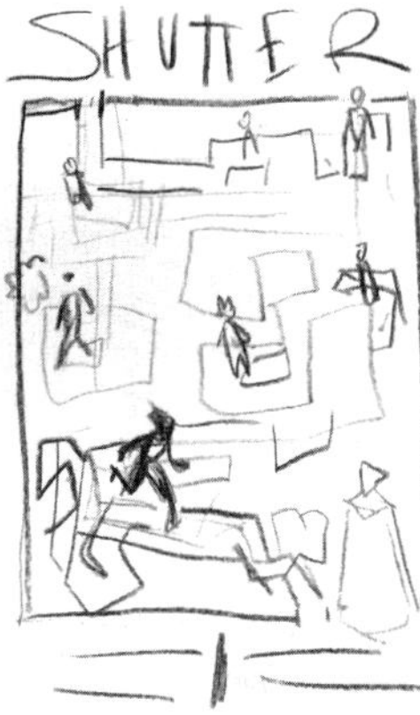
SHUTTER

Leila: *In #22 I was all about ink silhouettes and textures.*

Joe: Same.

Leila: *And then, of course, the carnage happened and slick blood became the texture on everything.*

Joe: R.I.P.

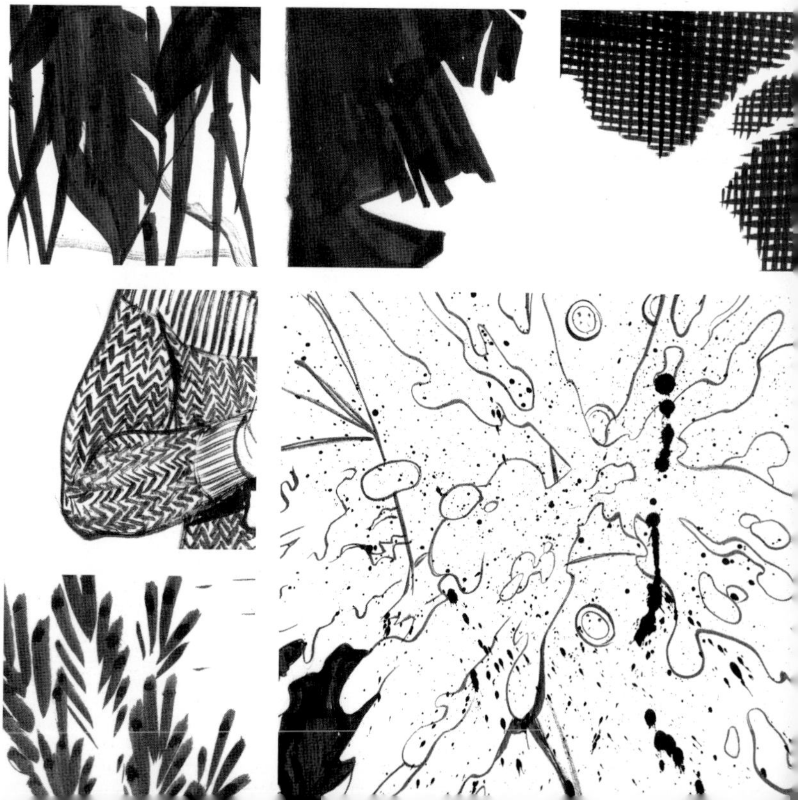

JOE KEATINGE - WRITER

LEILA DEL DUCA - ARTIST

OWEN GIENI - COLORIST

JOHN WORKMAN - LETTERER

COVER DESIGN BY LEILA DEL DUCA
AND ADDISON DUKE

CHAPTER BREAKS DESIGNED BY
TIM LEONG AND ADDISON DUKE

IMAGE COMICS, INC.
® Robert Kirkman - chief operating officer
Erik Larsen - chief financial officer
Todd McFarlane - president
Marc Silvestri - chief executive officer
Jim Valentino - vice-president
www.imagecomics.com

Eric Stephenson - publisher
Corey Murphy - director of sales
Jeff Boison - director of publishing planning & book trade sales
Jeremy Sullivan - director of digital sales
Kat Salazar - director of pr & marketing
Branwyn Bigglestone - senior accounts manager
Sarah Mello - accounts manager
Drew Gill - art director

Jonathan Chan - production manager
Meredith Wallace - print manager
Briah Skelly - publicist
Sasha Head - sales & marketing production designer
Randy Okamura - digital production designer
David Brothers - branding manager
Olivia Ngai - content manager

Addison Duke - production artist
Vincent Kukua - production artist
Tricia Ramos - production artist
Jeff Stang - direct market sales representative
Emilio Bautista - digital sales associate
Chloe Ramos-Peterson - library market sales
representative